Last Place

Louisa Scarr studied Psychology at the University of Southampton and has lived in and around the city ever since. She works as a freelance copywriter and editor, and when she's not writing, she can be found pounding the streets in running shoes or swimming in muddy lakes.

LOUISA SCARR

LAST PLACE YOU LOOK

First published in the United Kingdom in 2021 by

Canelo
31 Helen Road
Oxford OX2 0DF
United Kingdom

A CIP catalogue record for this book is available from the British Library.

Print ISBN 978 1 80032 346 9
Ebook ISBN 978 1 80032 345 2

Look for more great books at www.canelo.co

Printed and bound in Great Britain by Clays Ltd, Elcograf S.p.A.

For Dan and Charlie

Prologue

In his dreams, he's always back there, standing by the side of the road. His wet clothes stick to his skin; the cold seeps through to his core, rain running down his face, but he doesn't notice.

The car is at an angle, two tyres off the tarmac, the passenger door open. And it's on fire. He can smell the petrol, feel the heat of the flames on his skin, resilient, determined, arching up furiously to the darkened sky despite the downpour. There is no one else around. He knows he needs to leave, now, but he is rigid, frozen to the spot.

His body is shaking violently; the adrenaline is fading and the pain is creeping in – across his chest, down his left arm hanging useless at his side.

He takes a step backwards, his shoes sinking into the mud. Smoke stings his eyes. The figure in the driver's seat moves, but he makes no effort to try and help them. He's just watching.

Watching them burn.

Part 1

1

Friday

The house looks suburban. Dull even, Robin thinks, as he pulls up outside. Carefully tended hedges, a square of green lawn, a cheerful flower bed scattered with red and pink blooms. It looks so boringly normal that he wonders if he has the right place and checks the details again.

Fifty-six Wellington Crescent, he reads. Criminal damage, possible GBH. He looks at the house. Sure enough the front window is smashed, the glass broken into a tight spiderweb, a hole in the middle. A detective, let alone a detective sergeant, wouldn't normally be called out to a deployment like this but it's been a busy night, the PCs on Response and Patrol all out in town, breaking up early fights. He notes the cars parked outside: two in the driveway, another one blocking them in. An expensive Range Rover, an old Renault Clio with L plates and a Ford Fiesta. It's anyone's guess who – or what – he's going to find inside.

He gets out of his own battered Volvo, then smooths down his clothes. Shirt crumpled from a long day at the station, and a trace of five o'clock shadow on his chin. He's hungry, not had a chance to grab anything since lunch, and wonders how long this is going to take. Quick statement, a few photographs, then stop at the Indian on the way home? He's already thinking of chicken karai and onion bhajis as he walks past the cars and rings the doorbell. As he does so he notices a pineapple sitting on the doorstep, and squints at it, confused, until the door is answered by an older woman in a turquoise Chinese-style silk robe and fluffy slippers. He holds up his warrant card.

'Mrs Franklin? DS Robin Butler, I'm here about the window.'

She stares at him. 'I was expecting a woman,' she says at last. 'They said they were sending a woman.' She frowns and waits, as if expecting him to change gender in front of her eyes.

'Sorry,' Robin replies. 'I could get them to send someone else—' he starts, but she opens the door wide.

'It's fine. Let's get this over and done with.'

The house is dim, lights on low, candles flickering in corners. It's unnaturally hot and Robin takes his jacket off, draping it over his arm.

'Most people have already left,' Mrs Franklin says as she shows him into the living room. 'Nobody wanted to stick around once we called the police. Emma's through here.'

'And you were hosting a...' He pauses, not sure how to describe what this particular gathering might have been. He spots a bowl in the middle of a table, full of condoms in square foil wrappers, and can't help but stare at the large blue vibrator in full view on the mantelpiece. It's a stark contrast to the framed school photographs on the wall. 'Party?' he finishes.

'Just a few friends having drinks,' she says, but Robin can guess. She sees him looking. 'It's all legal, all consensual,' she snaps.

He nods and turns his attention to the woman sitting on the sofa. She's also wearing a dressing gown, but an old off-white towelling one, her legs and feet bare, head down, holding a tea towel against her forehead. It's stained red.

He sits next to her, a respectful distance away.

'Emma?' She looks up. Her face is caked in dried blood where it's poured from the cut on her forehead. 'You were the one hit with the rock?' he asks gently.

'Yeah, I was...' She points to another sofa next to the window. 'Lying there,' she says, looking away from him again.

'Can I see?'

She takes the tea towel away from her head, and instantly the cut starts bleeding again. Robin frowns in sympathy.

'The paramedics are on their way. You're going to need that looked at. You feel okay to answer a few questions now?'

'Sure.'

Mrs Franklin hovers close by. Her anger when Robin arrived has dissipated, and now she watches over them, her hand fluttering round her face.

'Did you hear anything before the rock came through the window?' Robin asks. 'Footsteps, shouting?'

'No, nothing,' Emma replies. 'Just smashing glass. The music was loud though, so I'm not sure I would have noticed.'

'And did anyone else see?'

'No. We were all... busy.'

'And your... partner? Was he...' Robin changes tack and opts for a gender-neutral term. 'Were they okay?'

'He was fine. He's gone now.'

'Okay,' is all he can think to say in response. 'Do you mind if I take a few photos?' he asks Mrs Franklin. 'To record the scene?'

She nods, somewhat reluctantly, then leaves as the doorbell rings again. Robin slowly goes round taking photos on his phone. Half-full drinks, abandoned on the table, lipstick marks on the rims. An array of what Robin can only describe as sex aids – tubes of lube, interestingly shaped cones, plastic beads. Robin can't help but wonder about hygiene – are they shared or individual? – then pushes the thought out of his mind. The paramedic arrives in his recognisable green, and immediately attends to Emma, bag by his side. Like Robin, he doesn't bat an eyelid. He must have seen it all.

Robin puts plastic gloves on, collected in preparedness from the stash in the boot of his car, then picks a condom out of the bowl on the table. They seem custom-made, *Select Events* written on the front in gold lettering.

7

'You can keep it if you like,' Mrs Franklin says, appearing behind him. He quickly drops it back in the bowl.

'And the rock?' he asks her.

'More like a brick,' she says, pointing to a large lump of red concrete sitting on the mantelpiece next to something large, metallic and rocket ship-shaped that makes Robin clench internally. 'Sorry,' she finishes. 'I realise now we shouldn't have picked it up.'

'It's fine. Where was it?'

She points to a corner of the room and Robin goes across, bending down. A scattering of brick dust marks where it fell, plus, just poking out from behind a table leg, a piece of folded-up paper and a broken elastic band.

Robin picks the note up with two gloved fingers, opening it out.

It's a sheet of lined A4, two holes down the left-hand side, as if taken from a notepad. *SLUT*, it says in blue pen, large capitals across the middle. Robin snaps a few photos then takes a plastic evidence bag out of his pocket and puts the note inside. He records the information on the label in biro, then does the same with the rock.

'Any idea who might have written this?' Robin says, turning and showing the message to Mrs Franklin. Her hand immediately flies to her mouth. Her face goes pale.

She shakes her head quickly. 'How— how dare he,' she stutters.

'Mrs Franklin,' Robin says slowly. 'What do you know?'

She looks at him for a moment, her eyes wide, then gestures towards the door. Robin follows her out and down a hallway. As they walk, Robin notices more photographs on the wall. Family shots: Mrs Franklin, an older man and a small boy, growing taller as the photographs progress through time.

They reach a kitchen. It's brightly lit, with uneaten food lying on platters. Glasses are laid out, bottles of spirits and wine next to them.

'Mrs Franklin?' Robin tries again. 'What exactly do you do here?'

She pulls out a chair, and slumps into it. 'I'm sure you can guess,' she sighs, reaching for the closest bottle of wine and pouring herself a large serving.

Robin sits down slowly. 'You're a swingers' club?'

'Yes. Although I'm not sure we will be again, after tonight. A rock through the window puts people off.'

'I'm sure.' Robin waits as she takes a long swig from her glass. 'Who wrote the note, Mrs Franklin?'

She looks at him, eyes pleading. 'Can you just forget you came here tonight?'

'I'm not sure—'

'Please?'

Robin taps his fingers on the table, thinking. 'How old's your son?'

She looks up quickly, then back to stare at her wine glass. 'Fifteen,' she says quietly, turning it round slowly in her hand. 'I didn't think he knew.'

'Where is he tonight?'

'Supposed to be with his grandparents. Obviously, we don't have him around when we run the parties.'

'Obviously,' Robin repeats, trying hard to keep the sarcasm out of his voice. 'Listen, I'm in no hurry to arrest a fifteen-year-old for criminal damage or GBH—'

'GBH?' she squeaks.

'He hit a woman with a brick. He could have caused serious harm.'

She looks down again miserably.

'So how about I take the note, get it processed, and then conveniently forget to follow up on the results?'

Mrs Franklin stares at him. 'You can do that?'

'Between you and I, yes. But if he does anything dodgy again, if we find anything, his fingerprints and DNA will pop

9

up and he'll be done for all of it. Perhaps you could tell him that.'

She nods, miserably. 'I will.'

'And maybe put the parties on hold for the time being, eh?' Robin adds. 'At least until your son's at university. And we'll need you and Emma to come down to the station and give a full statement when you have time. But as I said, if you forget, then maybe my caseload will be too high for me to have time to chase you up.'

Mrs Franklin breathes a long sigh. 'Emma will appreciate that, too. Her husband... Well, let's just say he's not into the scene.'

Robin stands, taking the evidence with him. As he passes, he glances back into the living room where the paramedic is finishing up. He opens the front door, turning to Mrs Franklin.

'Call me if you change your mind, though?' Robin says. 'Sometimes teenagers need the shit scaring out of them.'

'He's a good kid, DS Butler.'

'I'm sure.'

'And if you ever fancy a night out,' she adds, 'we're always looking for extra men, especially attractive ones like yourself.'

Robin feels his face go red. 'Thanks,' he murmurs, after a pause. 'But I'm not sure the job allows for it.'

He walks away, back to his car. The first responder vehicle is parked behind, blocking him in, and he waits outside for the paramedic.

He looks back at the house. The door is still open, and but for the broken window he'd never have guessed what was happening there on an innocent Friday night. He watches as the paramedic appears, closing the door behind him and joining him in the road.

'Orgies, huh?' he says as he stands next to Robin. He throws his bag in the back of the ambulance car. 'Didn't fancy asking for a freebie?' he laughs.

'Maybe another night, diary's full for now,' Robin replies drily. 'That woman okay?'

'Superficial head lac. They bleed like buggery though, make one hell of a mess. Told her to make sure someone watches her tonight in case of concussion.' The paramedic gets into the front seat. 'Think she was glad to get rid of me. Pity. I wouldn't have minded giving her a try.'

'Mate…' Robin starts, about to chastise the guy, but the door slams and the paramedic pulls out into the night. He wonders about the son, growing up in a house where sex parties are the norm. Would it make you more accepting of sex, or more of a prude? The latter, it seems.

Robin gets back into his car, wondering if he's done the right thing by letting the kid get away with it. But he knows that a criminal record on someone so young never does any good, and he's always open for second chances. He's had so many himself, after all.

He sighs, then picks up his phone and calls the direct dial into the control room.

'You got anything else for me?' he asks them.

The woman on the other end laughs. 'Anyone would think you've not got a home to go to, Butler,' she comments. 'You're off the clock. Go and have some fun.'

Robin thinks about his quiet house. Nothing but a television remote waiting for him, and the promised Indian takeaway.

Fun isn't how he'd describe it. But he starts the engine, and heads home.

She's never sure whether she feels seedy, guilty or excited when she makes her excuses and bunks off work early, driving home pre-rush hour and putting her key in the door with a burst of anticipation.

She kicks her shoes off in the hallway, then sends a text: *I'm home x*. She goes into the bathroom, has a shower, messy ponytail bundled up out of the way on the top of her head. After, she checks her hair in the steamed-up mirror, smoothing stray strands into place. She applies a quick brush of make-up and puts on jeans and a T-shirt over her best bra and knickers. Underwear she's bought especially for him.

A quick spritz of perfume, a frantic tidy of the house, and she settles on the sofa to wait.

She hopes he won't be long. Their relationship is made up of stolen fragments, a few hours here and there, pieced in between work and home life. His home life, not hers. She puts the TV on. An episode of *Tipping Point* plays out. Such a ridiculous concept, but she watches it anyway. Anything to distract her from scrolling absent-mindedly on her phone.

It's never certain when he'll arrive. Sometimes he gets caught up at work. Sometimes it's because of *her*. But today the knock is only a little late, and she switches off the television, walking quickly to the hallway, her stomach a jumble of nerves as she opens the door.

He looks contrite, mumbles an apology. But she can't help a smile; she'll forgive him anything, he knows that. He holds out a small parcel, neatly wrapped in silver paper with a sparkly ribbon.

'For me?' she jokes as he presents it with a small bow. She knows what it is, and unwraps it as he takes his shoes off, hanging his coat up next to hers.

Three tiny bottles: shampoo, conditioner and a moisturiser. Hotel freebies, from his visit away this week. He always saves them – remembering a comment from their first sneaked dirty weekend in a hotel – and she likes knowing he's thinking of her. He makes the effort to wrap them lavishly, like they're a proper present.

'Molton Brown,' she says approvingly, taking the lid off one and sampling the fragrance. 'Posh hotel?'

'It was.' He smiles. 'Wish you could have come up and stayed.'

She would have liked that too, but work had been frantic, trying to wrap things up before starting with a new sergeant next week. But she doesn't reply, just takes his hand and leads him up the stairs.

In her bedroom, she pulls him towards her then kisses him hard. He kicks the door shut with his foot and they stagger together into the room, his jacket, then tie, and her T-shirt, falling at their feet.

With him being away, it's been over a week since she saw him. She wants him, inhales him, as they fall together on the bed, his weight on top of her. He kisses her neck, her chest, her breasts, him awkwardly fumbling to remove her bra with one hand.

It's over quickly. The first one never takes long; too keen to have each other. After, they lie on the bed, her head resting on his chest, and he tells her about his week. It's not that interesting, if truth be told, but she likes the mundane nature of it, as if this is their normal lives.

As he talks, he runs his hand through her hair, wrapping a strand of it round his finger. She's proud of her hair. Unlike other women her age – unlike *her* – she still wears it very long, and doesn't have the need for expensive dyes to eliminate the grey. And she knows they look good together, his sandy-blond hair matching her own.

She's noticed over this past year that age is starting to catch up with him. Lines have become more pronounced at the corners of his eyes, wrinkles on his forehead. But it suits him. It gives him an air of authority where his boyish good looks previously couldn't.

'You've lost weight again,' she says, running her hand down his chest where she can feel his ribs. 'Are you looking after yourself?'

'I had a bit of food poisoning,' he mumbles. 'Dodgy stomach.'

Her fingers stop at a green-yellow smudge on his side. 'And what's this?' she asks.

'Hit by a squash ball,' he replies. 'And besides,' he continues, back to her original comment, 'wouldn't you rather this, than the beer gut that so many of my friends have?'

'I wouldn't care,' she says, looking up at him, conscious of the soppy grin on her face. 'Whatever you look like.'

He leans down and kisses her, smiling. 'You would. When I got man boobs and a double chin.'

'Never,' she laughs.

His phone beeps from his jacket on the floor, interrupting the moment. He ignores it, but she can sense him wanting to check.

'When do you need to get back?' she asks quietly.

He sighs, closing his eyes for a moment. 'Soon,' he says. 'We have plans for tonight.'

We. She wants to ask, but she won't.

'That's fine,' she says, feigning nonchalance. 'I'm off out tonight, too.'

'Really?' He seems surprised, and that annoys her. Yes, I have a life, she thinks. 'Where to?'

'Oh, just out with friends.'

'Who?'

She lists a few names, mainly men. That gets his attention, as she knows it will, even though she feels pathetic for playing these silly games.

'Any of them single?' he asks.

'Yes,' she says, but doesn't add any more.

It has the desired effect. He shuffles down in the bed until they're face to face, their noses touching. He kisses her, slower and softer than before.

'We still have time,' he says, his mouth pressed against hers, his voice husky and deep. 'For a bit more.'

—

After, he showers quickly and gets dressed in the same clothes. She wonders if his wife ever suspects when he returns home smelling sweet and fresh, even after a long day in the office. But she doesn't care. It won't matter soon.

She watches as he bundles up his tie and puts it in his pocket. She's lying on the bed, still naked under the duvet, and he comes and sits next to her, finishing dressing and doing up his belt.

'I'll call you,' he says. 'Once it's done.'

She nods. 'When are you going to tell her?'

'Saturday or Sunday. I don't know.' He looks away, out of the window to the grey sky beyond. She wonders if he's reconsidering. 'I need to pick a good moment.'

'Are you worried about how she'll take it? Come at you with a meat cleaver? Put cyanide in your Weetabix?' Freya's trying to lighten the mood, but it falls flat: he only looks back at her, a dark, thoughtful expression flashing across his features. Then he smiles quickly, seemingly pulling himself together.

'I'll see you soon,' he says. He leans forward and kisses her, one last peck to the lips.

He walks to the door, then turns back. 'I love you,' he adds as he opens it, as if it's a casual afterthought.

'I love you too,' she says, but the door is already closing.

She hears her front door open and shut, then falls back on the pillow with a groan. She doesn't allow herself to get her hopes up. They've been here before: the declarations of love, the promise he'll leave his wife. He will this time, he always says, he will.

But then something comes up. It's usually because of her. Because she's unwell, or emotional. Freya was joking before, but her comment must have been too close to home. She remembers the look on his face; he's scared of what she might do.

She used to wonder about this faceless woman and google her, learning all she could through Facebook and LinkedIn and Twitter. This wife: too delicate to be alone, but yet could go out with friends, hold down a busy job, go on holidays, post photos after 5k runs and sponsored walks for charity.

And after a while, she stopped asking. For these few short hours, these stolen moments, he is hers, and that keeps her going. Until the next time she can see him. She knows it's pitiful. She knows she should think more of herself, and find a man who will commit wholeheartedly, not just profess love, then screw her in her lonely bedroom before going back to his wife.

But this time, something's different. He seems more serious, more distracted. She believes him. To her detriment, she knows.

Next to her, her phone beeps. One of her friends, confirming time and a place. It's a shitty club, one she hates, but it's better than sitting at home.

He will do it this time, she tells herself. He will.

She just needs to wait for his call.

3

'Try the navy.'

Amy sits on the bed and watches as her husband pulls the tie from his neck and reaches for the one she suggests. He flips the collar up and wraps it round, knots it expertly, then turns for her approval.

'Much better,' she says, and tilts her face up for a kiss.

He bends down and pecks her lightly on the lips.

'We need to hurry up, or we'll be late,' Jonathan says.

'Everyone's always late. This is Kal, remember?'

'True.' He sits next to her on the bed, then slumps backwards. 'Oh god, and all his awful workmates are going to be there. All posh and braying.'

'Have a few drinks and you'll be fine.' Amy stands up and checks her reflection in the mirror, feeling the jitters rise in her stomach again. She presses a finger tentatively against the red and blue bruise blooming on her forehead.

'You sure you're okay?' Jonathan asks.

She glances back at her husband, lying on the bed, watching her.

'It's fine.' She takes a long breath in. 'What do you want to drink? I'll fetch one to get you started.'

'You sure?' Jonathan sits up, his forehead furrowed. She's complained about his drinking in the past; it's no wonder he's surprised.

She shrugs, pretending it doesn't bother her. 'I can put up with your drunken slurring for one night. What do you want?'

'We got any orange?' he asks. Amy nods. 'An Old Fashioned then.'

She walks out of the bedroom, down the stairs and into the kitchen. It's spotless – draining board clear, surfaces empty and wiped down – just as she likes it. She sees a plate on the side and a few toast crumbs left by Jonathan, and suppresses a ripple of irritation.

Amy remembers her appointment earlier that day. Following the nurse into the consulting room. Holding out her arm as she was prodded and poked, a sharp sting as the needle was pushed into her skin. She had watched fascinated as the dark red blood saturated each one, filling four vials.

The whole process had taken less than five minutes; very transactional, much like her husband's.

Jonathan had his appointment too, that morning, his sample to give, although in a different way. He'd flashed her a cheeky grin, a question, answered by her with a scowl. She had been reluctant to help out and wondered why. It had felt strange somehow; there was no romance here, no love or passion or understanding. Just wanking into a pot, and a hasty rush to get to the hospital in the allotted time for the test. She had heard him upstairs: the rhythmical sound of skin against skin, and had gone further away to block it out. She should have made an effort to turn it into something they could do together, to make it fun, but nothing about this feels like enjoyment. Just wave after familiar wave of resentment and anger.

In the kitchen, she gets a short, squat tumbler out of the pristine glass cabinet, holds it up to the light, then wipes a smudge off the side with a tea towel. She adds sugar and a generous dash of bitters, mixing them together. Ice next, then a large measure of Jameson, just how Jonathan likes it. No water.

She gets an orange from the fruit bowl and a knife out of the block. The knife is heavy and reassuring in her hand and she weighs it up for a second. How long would it take, she wonders, for him to bleed out on their bedroom floor? She could take him by surprise, press it to his neck and pull. Watch the look of astonishment on his face as the blood flowed. She's heard thirty seconds, if you cut the jugular. Would that be long enough for her?

But instead she presses the tip into the thick rind of the orange. It resists at first, then digs in and she cuts off the end, then a thick slice, chopping it in two and placing it in the glass.

Suddenly she stops, her breath catching. She rests both hands on the work surface, her head lowered, paralysed by the enormity of what she might be told as a result of the tests. Maybe they'd know why, after three years of trying, she is still not pregnant, when around her all her friends produced bumps and babies seemingly at will. She thinks about the smiles she's forced onto her face, all the tiny dresses and sleep-suits she's bought as gifts, while part of her withers inside.

Every month she cries, silently in the bathroom, sticking on another pad, inserting another tampon. Every month Jonathan tries to be sympathetic, but he doesn't understand. Not really. He doesn't get the yearning. The desperation to feel a tiny person squirming inside.

But she can't think about that now; she has bigger things to focus on tonight.

She picks the glass up and carries it to the bedroom, the ice cubes rattling.

'Here,' she says. He's standing in front of the mirror, fiddling with the front of his hair, and he turns and takes it from her.

'Sure you're okay driving?' he asks, then takes a sip. 'Mmm, perfect, thank you.'

'Yeah, not in the right frame of mind for drinking,' she replies. She's lying. She's just in the mood for sitting back and downing glass after glass of a cool white, but tonight is not the time. She needs to be alert; she needs everything to go right.

She notices him looking at her over the rim of the glass. He has a look in his eye, one she's seen before but ignored. Slight hesitancy. Worry. He looks away.

'What have we got on this weekend?' he asks. His tone seems light, but she detects an air of forced casualness.

'Nothing, why?'

He pauses. 'No reason.'

She leans up and kisses him, pressing her body against his. He feels unwieldy at first, reluctant, then eases. She tastes the whiskey, the cool of the ice cubes on his tongue.

She feels an urge to do more with him, but the sadness hits her and she pulls away. 'Drink up, before the ice cubes melt and it gets too watered-down. You know how much you hate that,' she adds, then walks downstairs to antibac the kitchen again.

–

It's getting late, Amy realises as she pushes the door open to the pub. The party is in full flow, music blaring, conversation loud, some people already drunk enough to dance. Kal has gone all out for his fortieth, renting the whole place. Balloons in silver and red pull to the ceiling on their strings; a large banner on the back wall shouts *Happy Birthday Kal* in huge letters. She wonders who put all this together – not his girlfriend, that's for sure: a dainty twenty-something-year-old, the latest in Kal's long line of pretty but useless women. She spots her now, giggling with a group by the bar, all in tiny skintight dresses, leaving nothing to the imagination.

She looks around the room and sees Kal, who turns and waves. She heads over.

Kal was the best man at their wedding, Jonathan's friend since university. Tall, dark, with a physique honed from early mornings at CrossFit and protein shakes, she's always liked him. Fancied him a bit too much, if the truth be known.

He's drunk, she can tell. His hand slightly forceful at her waist, his eyes unfocused as he goes in to peck her on the cheek. They misjudge the distance and she kisses a corner of his mouth, thinking inappropriate thoughts as she gets a waft of his expensive aftershave.

'Jonny about?' he shouts over the noise.

She flutters a hand dismissively. 'I was parking the car. He's gone already, off socialising. You know Jonathan.'

'Social butterfly,' Kal agrees. 'Bar's free, help yourself to whatever you like. Probably a few bottles of champagne still making the rounds if you're quick.' He leans in closer, and she can feel his stubble on her cheek. 'Listen, Amy. About the other week…' His voice trails off, and he looks at her.

'It's forgotten.'

'It's just…' His eyes dart around the bar; she knows he's looking for Jonathan. 'Jonny and I. We go back a long way.'

She shakes her head. 'We both have a lot to lose, Kal. Forget about it. Seriously.'

Kal takes a step back. Then the grin returns. 'You see my latest photos?' he asks. He takes his phone out of his pocket, scrolls with a thumb, then thrusts it in her face. She looks at the bright picture – a small, chunky toddler, caramel skin and dark eyes, smiling on some sort of trike.

'He's gorgeous, Kal,' she replies. She feels the familiar ripple of jealousy, a burn in the pit of her stomach. How come Kal has everything? His kid was an accident, result of a one-night stand, and yet he's a father while she remains childless. She feels the urge for a drink resurface.

'Champagne, did you say?' she adds, and Kal points towards the barman on the other side of the room, circulating, a large bottle in his hand.

'Go grab him quick, Amy. Have fun.'

And just like that, she's dismissed. She feels the tension return to her neck and shoulders. The car keys weigh heavy in her hand, but she needs a drink. Something to take the edge off.

Something to help her forget.

4

The car park is already swarming with blue and yellow by the time Robin arrives. He flashes his ID through his open car window and is let past the cordon, then parks up behind the huge purple-signed building.

The uniform in reception recognises him and directs him towards the lift.

'303,' he says.

Robin nods a thank you, and heads up.

He doesn't need the signs when he gets to the right floor. He can hear the buzz of the crime scene as soon as the lift doors open, and walks down the beige corridor towards the noise. Carpet worn in the centre, scuff marks on the wall. The hotel's old, in desperate need of a refresh. People crowd the corridor – nosy onlookers, PCs starting to make enquiries, the paramedic packing up his things, having already pronounced life extinct.

Robin pushes past them all. A uniform greets him at the hotel room doorway with a grimace.

'You were first on the scene?' Robin asks as he puts on gloves and shoe covers. The PC nods. 'Everything left as you saw it?'

'Except we cut the guy down.'

'You moved the body?' Robin replies, exasperated. 'Is it all on BWV?'

The PC taps the body-worn camera on his chest, then looks apologetic. 'Paramedic needed to examine him properly.'

'And you think it's a cat two, G 28?'

But Robin doesn't wait for an answer, and steps inside.

It's slightly cold, the aircon turned up high, but apart from that there's nothing strange about the room. The bed looks untouched – the duvet tightly tucked in at the edges of the mattress, the purple throw draped over the bottom. Clean, white pillows, terrible artwork on the walls. One black coat hangs on the rail and Robin picks it up, looking in the pockets.

He finds a black leather wallet and an iPhone, opens the wallet and pulls out the driver's licence.

'Jonathan Miller,' he reads to no one in particular. 'Date of birth nineteenth of May.' He reads the year then stops, looking to the ceiling, doing the maths. 'Thirty-nine.' He reads the address aloud. 'Ashcroft Drive, Winchester.'

Robin turns to the PC still behind him. 'He lives just down the road. What was he doing here?'

The PC doesn't answer, just points to the body lying on the floor, partially hidden by the bed.

Robin takes a step forward, seeing it in full for the first time. 'Ah, shit,' he mutters.

'You going to be the one to tell next of kin?' the PC asks.

Robin sighs. 'I guess so, yes. Find out who it is, will you?'

He walks forward and crouches next to the body. The cause of death is clear: a brown leather belt looped round his neck, now loose and gaping. An angry red mark cuts into the flesh, showing the clear pull upward.

Robin scans the wall and furniture around them. 'Where did he tie it?'

'Round the door hook.'

Robin glances back to the main door. The small silver hook doesn't seem sturdy enough to take the weight. 'And we think he was here overnight?'

'Initial enquiries say so, yes. Cleaner assumed the room was vacated, even though he hadn't checked out. Let herself in just past midday and found the body.'

Robin stands up. He notices a magazine lying open on the desk, and goes over to it. A double-page spread of a naked woman confronts him, her legs apart, mouth gaping.

'It was open to this?' he directs to the PC behind him, who nods. Robin flicks to the next page, another woman, red lipstick, pubic hair completely absent. Standard porn, he thinks.

'Preserve the scene for now,' he says to the PC. He hands him the phone and wallet. 'Put these into evidence. And that.' He points to the porn magazine. 'And I want that video as soon as possible. Where am I going?'

'Eight Ashcroft Drive,' the PC confirms. 'Wife. Amy Miller.' Robin thanks him, then dials a number.

'West?' he barks. 'We've got a death to report. Meet me at next of kin. I'll text you the address.'

–

The house is big and grand and recently built, on a new estate at the edge of town. As he drives past the identical cul-de-sacs Robin notices a half-finished child's playground. He indicates as he approaches number eight.

There's a car parked by the side of the road. One of those pastel-blue trendy Fiat 500s – old style made new. He pulls up behind it and his DC gets out.

'Apparently they're going to put a Co-op in when it's all done,' Freya comments, pointing to the muddy field in front of the house, where they clearly haven't finished building.

Robin grunts in response. He's known DC Freya West for a few years in CID, but it's only this week that she's been assigned to him.

'You can't work by yourself for ever,' his DCI, Neal Baker, had said, with forced cheer. 'You'll enjoy the company.'

Robin wasn't so sure. He knows her from around the station: she's keen, seems intelligent, but sometimes her enthusiasm grates – a constant chatter about whatever enters her head at that specific time. He just wants to get the job done. He doesn't need to know about town planning and the placement of local conveniences.

He looks towards the house. There's a car in the driveway and a light on in one of the top bedrooms, even though it's barely two p.m.

'You're leading, right?' Freya asks, and Robin nods. He's rehearsing the words in his head, a speech he's used too many times. Back in uniform, he was told: always have a hat. Always, always have a hat. And today, in plain clothes, he does up the buttons on his suit jacket, straightens his tie.

He's not sure how he's going to broach the question that every next of kin asks: *how did he die?*

'Who's the deceased?' Freya asks as Robin rings the bell.

But he doesn't have time to answer. The door is opened by a pretty woman, wearing jeans and a white T-shirt, with a short, blunt blonde bob. She's slim to the point of skinny, her cheekbones jutting out from her pale face. He notices a large bruise on her forehead, a few days old, he guesses, mottled purple and green.

'Amy Miller?' Robin asks and she nods. 'I am DS Robin Butler, this is DC West. Can we come in?'

Amy moves out of the way and lets them through. Her body language is wary, as most are when the police arrive courteous and polite. They know, deep down, what's going to happen.

'It's about your husband, Jonathan. Would you like to sit?'

Next to him, Robin notices Freya stiffen, no doubt preparing herself for the news they have to deliver.

'What's happened? He's at work,' the wife says, indicating the sofa opposite her. He sits down; the sofa's large and soft and Robin finds himself sinking too far in. 'Do you want anything to drink?' she asks. 'Tea, coffee?'

'No. Thank you—'

'What's he done? Has he been arrested?'

Robin struggles against the soft sofa and sits up straight on the edge. He looks Amy Miller right in the eye. 'We're sorry to tell you this, but your husband was found dead this morning.'

'Dead? What do you mean?' Amy looks from Robin, to Freya, back again. He's used to a range of reactions when people find out their loved one has died: disbelief, rage, confusion. Some just melt before you, hit the floor. Amy Miller seems to be in denial. 'It's not him.' She reaches for her phone. 'I'll call him, you'll see. Whoever you've found, it's not Jonathan.'

'We have his wallet and driver's licence. We believe it's your husband. I'm sorry, Mrs Miller,' Robin adds again.

Next to him, Freya utters a quiet 'excuse me' and gets up from the sofa. He glances back at her as she leaves the room, hurrying towards the door. He frowns. This can't be her first visit to notify next of kin, Robin thinks. Please don't say his new DC can't hack it. He'd assumed she'd be made of sterner stuff.

But he hasn't got time to worry about West.

'What happened?' Amy Miller's asking again, nervously fiddling with her phone. 'Was it a car accident? It's probably a car accident. He's always driven too fast, I'm always telling him to slow down.'

'No, no, it wasn't a car accident. He was found at the Premier Inn on the other side of town. Do you know why he might have been there?'

'The Premier Inn?' Robin is used to next of kin repeating his words back to him as they struggle to make sense of the news. 'Why was he at the Premier Inn?'

'Has he ever gone there before?'

'No, not that I know of. Why would he go there?' And then she asks the question Robin's dreading. 'How did he die?'

Robin remembers the body. Grey, limp. Naked. The belt loose round his neck.

'We believe he asphyxiated.' He clears his throat. 'He was found hanging in his room.'

'He killed himself?' The wife's face is a mask of horror, eyes wide, skin white. 'Why would he do such a thing? Did you find a note?'

'No, we…' Robin takes another breath. 'I'm sorry to have to ask you this, but have you heard of auto-erotic asphyxiation, Mrs Miller?'

'Auto what?' the wife asks, in little more than a squeak.

'It's when the victim, usually a man, limits oxygen flow in order to gain greater sexual pleasure.'

'Greater…' Her voice trails off, and she starts to cry. Robin reaches for a tissue box on the side and hands it to her.

The wife dabs at her eyes. 'Was he alone?' she asks.

'We don't know at this stage. We're still investigating his death. Do you know if he was seeing anyone else?' he asks quietly.

She shakes her head, a quick movement, over and over.

Robin waits for a moment, watching Amy Miller cry. Poor woman, he thinks. It's a lot to take in. First the news that your husband's dead, then that he died in such a way. Alone in an anonymous purple-tinged hotel room, cheap leather belt round your neck, wanking in order to— In order to what? he wonders. Have a slightly better orgasm? Was that worth the price he had to pay?

'Do you know if your husband had tried anything like this before?'

'No, that's not something I'd want to get involved in, absolutely not,' she replies, still staring at the floor.

Not the question I asked, he thinks, but he lets it go.

'And when did you see him last?'

'Yesterday morning. He was working from home Monday, and then had a meeting at one of the other offices today so drove up last night. He works at Synaptics, in town.' She twists the rings on her left hand and the diamond catches the light. It's big and bulky, worth a bit, Robin guesses, not that he has any experience in these things. 'At least, I thought that's where he was.'

'So he has a car with him?'

'Yes, a black Mazda.'

She recites the number plate, then starts crying again. Robin knows he's not going to get much more out of her today.

'Can I call someone for you?' he asks.

She shakes her head.

'Are you sure? You shouldn't be alone.'

'I'll call my sister after you've gone,' she replies, and Robin gets up to leave.

'Can I see him?' she says, looking up at him through her tears. Her voice is wet with snot.

'Yes, of course.' Robin digs in his pocket and hands Amy a card. 'Please call me and we'll arrange for you to come in. You'll need to formally identify the body.'

The wife wipes her eyes with a corner of the tissue then scrunches it up in a small ball in the middle of her palm. She stands up, waiting next to him. He gets the feeling she wants him to leave, and he doesn't blame her.

'We'll need to ask you some more questions later,' Robin adds. He walks to the front door, the wife trailing behind him. 'Before you go, do you know the unlock code for his phone? It would help us a lot at this stage. To get a picture of what he was doing before he died.'

She nods and he hands her his notebook. She scribbles six digits inside. 'We'll be in touch, Mrs Miller,' Robin finishes. 'I'm sorry for your loss.'

He walks outside, the front door closing behind him. Freya is standing next to her car, her back to him, looking down at her phone.

'Did you see her face?' Robin directs to her as he approaches. 'A bit of a domestic, do you think?'

Freya glances back when she hears Robin's voice and he sees she's been crying.

He frowns at her. 'You okay?' he asks, confused.

She nods, the movement quick and sudden. 'The victim,' she asks. 'What did he look like?'

He shows her a photo on his phone, a picture taken of Jonathan Miller's driving licence. She looks at it for a second, then screws her eyes tightly shut.

'Did you know him?' Robin asks.

She nods again.

'Were you close? Should you be on this case, Freya?'

She opens her eyes, then takes a long breath in, her vision fixed in the middle distance. Then she turns to him. 'No, not close. I'm fine. Just a shock, that's all.'

Robin looks at her, unsure whether to believe her. But when she meets his gaze, she seems genuine. 'Meet me back at the station,' he says at last.

Freya leaves, Robin waiting as her car goes out of sight. He turns back to the house. Amy Miller is watching him through the living room window. She raises a slow hand, then disappears, pulling the curtains shut behind her.

Poor woman, Robin thinks. He hopes she's got someone to call, to help her through. It'll get worse before it gets better.

He remembers that feeling. The initial incomprehension, the shock. Then the darkness that follows. The darkness that doesn't fade.

The darkness he still knows now.

5

Freya drives until she is out of sight of her sergeant's car, then pulls down a side road and stops. She feels dizzy, her breathing is sharp and shallow, but there is nothing she can do to slow it down. The panic is thick.

She holds her phone in her hand, gripping it tightly. She pulls up his contact details, but she can't call him, she can't take the risk. But the photo – it was him. *Him*. Oh god. And that was her – Jon's wife.

She's never met her before, and on social media she looks different. She's lost weight, her face narrower and her hair shorter, but now she recognises the pinched smile and the sharp nose. And Freya had never been to his house, she hadn't known where he'd lived. It had been where *she* was; there hadn't been any need.

Freya remembers the weekend. Waiting. Sitting around, willing him to call. And now he's dead.

Dead.

But how? She's struggling to get her head around what she heard her new boss tell Amy. She'd stood outside the room, her head whirring, as Butler's low tones gave the awful news. Auto-erotic asphyxiation? It's too bizarre for her to take in. Jonathan – her Jon – died in an accident in some strange sex game? That isn't him. It couldn't be. Jon, a man who would only do it with the lights on if she forced him, trying some kinky strangulation experiment? She just can't believe it.

But he's dead.

The thought makes her body crumple. A heavy weight takes over. Her head drops, her legs feel weak. And she puts her hands on the steering wheel and cries.

–

After fifteen, maybe twenty minutes, her phone starts to buzz next to her. She stares at the screen: *Butler*. She knows he must be back at the station by now, wondering where she is.

She looks out of her windscreen into the street beyond. A few people walk, hands thrust in pockets. The season has just edged into autumn, the air is colder, sky grey, colours muted. It feels apropos to her life now: he has gone. A hole has been left where he once was.

She knows she needs to go back and tell Butler what's going on. He'll find out soon enough. She'll be excused from the case, moved to work on something else and the investigation will carry on without her.

She faced her new assignment with trepidation. Robin Butler is known by her colleagues for being brash, grumpy, rude. But a solid detective.

'You'll learn a lot from him,' DCI Baker said. 'Just try not to piss him off on your first day.'

'How might I do that?' she asked her colleagues.

They laughed. 'Breathing,' they replied.

She pulls down the mirror in the sun visor and tidies herself up as best she can. But she looks like she's been crying: face puffy, eyes red. There's not much she can do, except lick her finger and rub off the mascara under her eyes. Then she drives to the police station.

When she gets there, Butler's sitting at his desk, staring at the screen, twisting to and fro on his chair. His middle finger taps repeatedly on the desk like he has a slight excess of energy, the momentum at the beginning of a case making him restless.

He sees her arrive and a frown forms. He has almost permanent ridges on his forehead, an expression so overused it's worn creases across his face.

'West,' he begins without greeting. 'The PC has sent over the CCTV from the Premier Inn. Need you to look at it, and try and track down traffic cams or ANPR.' He talks fast, his gaze back on his monitor.

'Sarge?'

'Hmm? And I wouldn't mind following up on that potential DV. Maybe he liked his sex a bit experimental, a bit rough. Would fit with the way he was found.'

Freya reels. Domestic violence? Surely not. Not Jon. Butler fires instructions at her. Follow up with forensics from the hotel. Get a warrant for his medical records. Maybe speak to his friends, family, cover off all lines of enquiry and see if he was suicidal.

'You think he might have done this deliberately?' Freya stutters.

'I don't know, maybe.' Butler's head is down; he's looking at the phone in his hand, typing numbers through the see-through plastic evidence bag. 'Ah, here we go. Wife was right. We're in.'

Freya sits down next to him and looks over his shoulder as he navigates the screen. She knows she needs to say something. Now. In mere seconds her superior officer is going to discover her name, her messages. He's going to know she was having an affair with the victim. But her lips are dry; she can't seem to open her mouth.

The office is noisy. Rows of desks and computers, detectives talking, shouting to each other across the room. She makes a small sound, trying to attract his attention but he doesn't notice, too focused on the phone.

She watches as he clicks on WhatsApp, selecting the first message. She recognises the text, sent by her on Monday morning. *Are you okay?* she wrote, desperate to hear from him after a silent weekend. *Call me. Xx*

Butler scrolls back; other messages appear on the screen. Freya knows there will be nothing there about their get-together on Friday – they'd made those arrangements in person the week before. But the messages are revealing of their affair: some of them loving, others slightly dirty. Not much though, Freya knows. Gentle suggestions, nothing too lewd. Jon wouldn't have liked that. *But*— her brain screams, *look how he died!*

'So he was seeing someone on the side,' Butler observes. 'No name.' He shows her the screen, and it's a row of digits. Jon hadn't entered the number in his contacts, he'd been that wary. 'Let's try it.'

Butler picks up the desk phone and looks from one to the other, carefully punching in the numbers. Freya knows where that phone is now. On silent. In her bag. A second mobile, given to her by Jon when they started seeing each other. 'My own private line,' he'd joked. Then more seriously, 'Keep the voicemail anonymous. Never leave your name. I can't have Amy finding out who you are.'

She watches as Butler listens. She knows it'll be ringing, then cutting to voicemail. He puts the phone down, his face disappointed.

'No message?' she asks.

'The answerphone was generic, no clue who this belongs to,' he replies.

He sits back in his chair, thinking. Freya stays mute. Tell him, the voice in her head says. Tell him.

'Accidental death?' he mutters, half to himself. 'Do you think? If we have nothing that indicates suicide and nobody was there with him, then what else could it be?'

Freya knows what he's saying, but something about this feels very wrong. The Jon she knew wasn't this guy. This man, dead in a hotel room, a leather belt round his neck. 'We need to be sure,' she manages to say.

Her boss looks at her. 'How well did you know him, West?' he asks.

This is it. Tell him. Excuse herself from the case, leave him to it. But what if this isn't an accidental death? What if it's something more sinister? Freya knows this weekend he was going to leave his wife. His wife, who had threatened him in the past, who Freya knows he was wary of. Freya joked about it on Friday night, and the thought of this haunts her. What if she *did* kill him?

Freya knows the mere idea is ridiculous, but she also knows that only she has this insight. What if Butler isn't as good a detective as people say he is? What if he just lets it go, does a half-arsed investigation, puts it down to an accident and leaves it at that?

And her new sergeant has no way of knowing the identity of the mystery woman in Jonathan Miller's life.

'Hardly at all,' she replies. She turns away from Butler, feeling her body grow hot. 'I'll get on to forensics,' she says. 'Get them moving.'

'Great, you do that,' he replies.

Just like that, the lies are in place. And Freya knows there is no return.

6

Robin replaces the phone in its evidence bag on the desk, looking at it thoughtfully. He briefly wonders if the unknown messenger might be a man, maybe someone still keeping their sexuality a secret, but no. The style of the writing, some of the things they discuss. It does seem to be a woman.

And he really wants to speak to her. Find out if this sort of thing, this sexual experimentation, was normal for Jonathan Miller. But it'll have to wait for now. Follow it from the beginning, he tells himself.

He clicks on his email, finds the one he's looking for and loads it up. It's a message from the manager of the Premier Inn: CCTV file from the car park attached, list of guests and times and rooms to follow. Plus the electronic log of the room key. The ins and outs from that night. He starts with that.

Room key issued Monday 17:05. Room 303 accessed 17:12. Then nothing again until Tuesday at just past midday, when he knows the maid went inside. What a thing to find. Another unwitting victim of this man's death.

He loads up the CCTV footage. This is all they have. There are no cameras in the lobby, nothing in the endless corridors. And this footage is grainy. He presses the forward button until Monday at half four. It's black and white, hard to see what's going on, and he squints as a few cars drive in and out of the square of concrete.

And then he spots it. Jonathan Miller's black Mazda 3. It glides in slowly, stopping on the right-hand side. He looks over at Freya. She has her head down, seemingly staring at her keyboard.

'West?' he says. She doesn't reply. 'Freya?'

She looks up quickly. 'Hmm?'

'Miller's Mazda is in the Premier Inn car park, can you get it impounded?'

'Sure, yep,' she replies, and he frowns. What is it with her? he wonders. Is she normally like this?

He presses play again, and watches as a door opens and a figure gets out. It's dark, it's hard to see their face, but Robin guesses from their broad shoulders, their clothes – a black hooded jacket and jeans – that it's a man. It's the same rain jacket Robin remembers seeing in the hotel room, some expensive North Face thing. The man walks quickly towards the reception of the Premier Inn and is gone.

So he walked through, used the self-service machine to check in, then up in the lift to the hotel room. And from there – nothing. The night manager didn't see him, the people in room 304 next door heard nothing, and the other side, 302, was newly vacant.

And then the maid started screaming Tuesday lunchtime.

Robin sits back and loads the footage taken from the body-worn camera of the PC arriving first at the scene. It's jerky, but Robin can clearly make out what happened as Jonathan Miller's body was found.

A hand on the wooden door. A push, a hard push, for the PC to get into the room. Robin can see the force needed, and knows what the obstacle was behind the door. He sees the camera move as the PC turns, showing the paramedic just behind him.

And there it is. A naked body hanging from the back of the door, leather pulled taut, legs crumpled up underneath. The belt is looped around the coat hook on the back of the door, buckle threaded through the belt, then looped round his neck, pulling upward by the side of his face. It digs in hard to his neck, leaving a ridge. His feet are still on the floor – he wasn't a tall man, and the coat hook not high, but the weight of his body was obviously enough to kill him. Head slightly to one side, mouth open, swollen tongue protruding.

What a way to go, Robin thinks. Hardly dignified. He picks up his empty mug and walks to the kitchen, thinking. What was going through Jonathan Miller's mind that day? Had he done it before? And why go there? A sodding Premier Inn, of all places?

While the kettle boils, he spoons instant coffee into his mug, then picks it up, looking at the yellow pigtailed character on the side. Little Miss Sunshine, it says, a present from last Christmas' Secret Santa. He took it in good grace, the sarcasm clear, mentally trying to work out with a forced smile which one of his dickhead colleagues had given it to him. But strangely, he's found himself using it every day since, hoping the optimism might permeate through.

The kettle clicks off and he pours the water in. He goes to the fridge and tentatively sniffs the semi-skimmed, then swears. 'Black again then,' he mumbles with a scowl, then looks at Little Miss Sunshine. Not working today, are you, love? he thinks. He carries his mug back to his desk.

Had Miller planned to stay at the Premier Inn overnight? He'd lied to his wife, saying he was away with work, so maybe he'd reckoned on having a little fun, then inviting his mistress over after. Robin picks up the mobile phone again, scans the call log and the messages, but there's nothing for that day.

Perhaps this was as simple as an accidental death. Robin looks at the files littering his desk, at the other investigations ongoing when he got the call to come out to this one. Homeless guy, found dead in the street (probably natural causes, waiting for post-mortem). A series of seemingly random break-ins in empty houses across the city, resulting in potential burglary and criminal damage. Plus numerous others.

And now Jonathan Miller. Experimenting with a new sexual practice in a hotel room, and royally buggering it up.

Poor guy, he thinks again. And his poor wife.

His phone buzzes and he looks at the text. *Drink? Tonight?* From Steph Harper. Not a bad proposition, although whenever she gets in touch he's never sure what her intentions are. Still, he thinks, as he replies sorting out a time and place, as long as she doesn't want to choke him with a belt, he's happy.

–

Robin first met Dr Steph Harper, forensic pathologist, at a crime scene four years ago. It was hardly the start of a brilliant friendship. The guy in pieces in front of them had blown his head off with a shotgun. There was no brain left, let alone a pulse, and Steph was annoyed at being called out at two a.m.

'You don't need me to determine cause of death,' she snapped from behind the white crime scene mask. She pulled the plastic gloves off and stalked back to her car.

Robin didn't see her again for another year, but she remembered him, smiling a greeting as they both turned up at a suspicious death. A man, knife wound, gut split open in the street. She was nicer that time, meeting with him after and patiently answering all his questions. Then she invited him out for a drink.

Sometimes she had a boyfriend, sometimes she didn't. It didn't seem to matter. Sometimes they went back to her place, sometimes they didn't do anything at all, merely parting with a chaste kiss in the doorway. Robin didn't really care. She was fun to be around, and she understood a cop's black humour.

And tonight he is grateful for the company. He doesn't want to go home, the sight of Jonathan Miller's naked corpse dwelling on his mind.

He is at the bar, ordering their next drinks. Pint of ale for him, G and T for her. He idly looks at the menu; the food's good here, they should order something. He puts the menu under his arm and carries it back to the table, drink in each hand.

The pub's nice, a regular haunt for them both. Low, squashy, dark brown leather sofas. Battered oak tables. Large mirrors, in rusted metal frames. Smart, but not so smart he feels awkward turning up messy straight from work.

Steph's been telling him about the post-mortem she carried out that day, a drug overdose in one of the local parks. Sixteen-year-old kid, such a waste.

'And I heard about your guy,' she finishes. 'My colleague had the wife in at six to identify the body.'

'Amy Miller?' Steph nods. 'How did she behave?' Robin flags down a passing waiter and orders a sharing plate for them both. Mezze, or some other pretentious name for a bit of houmous and some flatbread, but he can't stomach proper food after the previous two pints of beer.

'He said, much as you'd expect. Pale, crying, nothing out of the ordinary. Did she know what he was into?'

'Interviewing her tomorrow. But I'm guessing not from what she said today.'

He looks at Steph in the low lighting. Even after all this time, he doesn't know much about her. He guesses she's younger than him: she's in better shape by far. He knows she runs triathlons: muscular shoulders, flat stomach, low fat percentage. Unlike him, he thinks, feeling the pints sloshing in his belly.

'Poor woman,' Steph comments, repeating Robin's own thoughts. 'Imagine arranging a funeral for a husband who died trying to get his rocks off in that way. What makes a man do that?' She stares at him pointedly over her G and T.

'Don't look at me!' he protests. 'I'll tell you now, if you ever find me dead in that way, make sure you investigate properly. It'll be murder for sure.'

'You don't fancy it then?' She takes a sip from her drink, her eyes amused.

'What? Wrapping a belt round my neck and sitting naked on a scratchy hotel carpet, wanking off to some shitty porn?'

'That's how you found him?'

'Yeah, limp dick and all.'

Robin stops as the waiter brings the food out to the table.

'Limp dick?' Steph repeats, and the waiter flashes them a look before he leaves. Robin pulls off a piece of bread and dips it in the houmous. He puts it in his mouth, watching her. She seems deep in thought. 'You sure it's an accidental death?' she adds.

He frowns. 'Why?'

'Just that… normally in these cases there's still some sign of an erection.'

'Even on the deceased?'

'Yeah.' She pauses, looks at him. 'Body still around?'

'On ice. You want to take a look?'

'I'll have a word with the coroner. Get it transferred to me tomorrow.'

Robin chews thoughtfully. 'Don't take too long on it,' he says, through a full mouth. 'I mean, there's nothing suspicious there.'

But he doubts himself. He wonders whether he should have called a pathologist to the scene rather than just the ambulance service attending as is usual procedure with sudden deaths. Maybe he should have upgraded it to a category one, but it didn't seem dodgy. It didn't look like any offence had been committed.

His own words echo in his head – *make sure you investigate properly*.

They go back to her place. They have perfunctory sex: more like scratching an itch than high-level eroticism. But Robin can't bear to think about doing anything adventurous, not after poor old dead Miller, and Steph propositioned him with the words, 'Fancy a quickie, then?' so she couldn't have been expecting anything earth-shattering either.

She goes into the bathroom after, still naked, making no effort to cover herself up, and Robin wonders why neither of them has made the move to get together properly. He likes her, she seems to like him, so why not?

But as she comes back to the bed, he stays quiet.

'You staying?' she asks, pulling the duvet across her.

'Do you mind? I can't be arsed to get a cab this time of night.'

She leans over and kisses him on the cheek. 'Just don't snore, Butler.'

She's the closest thing to a relationship he's had in years. He's had girlfriends in the past, before, but something stops him from getting too close. He sighs, then rolls over in the bed, listening to Steph's steady breathing next to him, knowing he's far away from sleep. It's not a fucking mystery, he thinks. Any two-bob shrink could get to the bottom of his intimacy problems within minutes. He should make an effort to sort himself out.

But in a way, he likes it. He nurses the ball of misery in his body like a lurking teratoma, reluctant to get it removed. It's a part of him now, fully formed. Something, he knows, that's staying for good.

7

Somehow, Freya gets through the day. Butler stays busy, barking instructions at her every now and again. Normally a brusque style like her sergeant's would get to her, but today his lack of care is welcomed. Any proper attention he put her way and she'd crumple – game over.

Once she gets home, she sheds her clothes quickly, as if trying to discard the day, pulling a T-shirt over her head. She shuts the curtains, climbs into bed. She feels tired, so very tired, but her body can't relax, like it knows something is missing. That he is missing.

She gets up, walks quickly down the stairs in the cold to the kitchen. She plucks a bottle of wine from the fridge, not caring which one, quickly opens the screw top and grabs a wine glass from the cupboard. She carries it back to her bed, then pours a full glass, taking frantic gulp after gulp, not even tasting it.

She remembers that last time she saw him, in this very bed. Her mind tries to recall everything they spoke about, every word, every nuance, hoping to remember something that will make what happened make sense. But it doesn't.

He said he was going to leave his wife. But clearly he'd made no move towards that – Amy Miller knew nothing. Jon said he loved Freya, but he'd died trying something he'd never even come close to hinting he enjoyed.

Freya finishes the glass, pours another. She remembers when they first met. Summer, over a year ago. A mutual friend's barbecue. He was there alone, so was she, and they started talking, instantly hitting it off. She liked the way he laughed: soft, self-deprecating. His complete lack of arrogance was refreshing, and she was gutted when she realised he was married, with the ring to prove it. Yet, there he was a week later, bumping into her in Waitrose.

'It must be fate,' he said. 'Do you fancy a coffee?'

Yes, she did. And she fancied him. And apart from that first offer, she was the one to pursue their relationship. He backed away, more times than she could count. *I can't, we can't, my wife...* Even before anything had happened.

Then, one day, it did.

They met up to go for a walk. Still pretending things were innocent. Cold winter air, a deserted forest, a gravel track meandering through. We're just mates, she'd say to her friends. Until his face was close, his hand holding hers as he helped her over a stile, and she leaned forward for that final few inches and kissed him.

The connection was instant. But even then they waited before having sex. The first time, they were at her house. Dinner cooked at home – they couldn't go out, too much risk – dessert finished. He was chivalrous, constantly asking is this okay, can we do this? She was desperate for him; he could have done anything, she wouldn't have minded, but he was more reserved. Usually in a bed, preferably at hers. Curtains closed, eyes shut. Maybe in the shower. Blow jobs were okay, finger up the arse definitely not. He liked her underwear lacy but classic black or white. Orgasms were quiet, stifled groans in the dark. But she was happy. Always happy.

Freya hasn't seen the crime scene photos or the video of the BWV from the PC who found him. Maybe if she saw them she would start to believe what has happened, but for now everything seems too surreal.

She gropes for her phone, picking it up in the dark and scrolling to Twitter. She searches for his username then loads his tweets. Jon wasn't prolific, only posting occasionally. She took some solace from knowing what he was doing when she wasn't with him, even if it was information shared with the whole of the internet.

One from Friday night – a close-up, Jon's grinning face next to a dark-skinned guy. She knows this is Kal, his best friend, and reads the text below.

Happy 40th mate!! So happy to celebrate with you. #gettingold #oldman #bestmates

She stares at Jon's bright blue eyes, willing him to materialise out of the photograph. *How can you be gone?* she thinks. *You were just here.* She wonders if anyone has told Kal yet, and knows they'll need to interview him.

She keeps scrolling, but the remaining photo is dull. A shot of some trees, a path through the woods. *Walk with Amy* is the only caption, followed by a tree emoji. She stares at it, desperate to know what happened that weekend.

They'd had a plan. Jon was going to talk to Amy, tell her he was leaving, and then call her. She'd imagined him arriving at hers, suitcase in hand, and they'd have spent the rest of the weekend together. Talking, laughing, shagging. So much time to play with. The whole of their lives from that point on, together.

So what happened? *What happened??* the voice in her head screams. With frustration she throws her phone to the floor, hearing it thump onto the carpet next to her discarded wine glass and the empty bottle. She pushes her face hard into the pillow as the sadness overwhelms her. She doesn't try to stop it now; the wine has unlocked something and she howls until her voice is hoarse.

Then she curls up, her legs tucked tight into her stomach. The room lurches slightly from the alcohol, her stomach empty, her body a shell. And at last, she falls asleep.

8

Wednesday

Amy Miller seems thinner than he remembers, shrunken in on herself since learning of her husband's death. She cradles a large takeaway Costa coffee; Robin can smell the tempting aroma, desperate for one himself.

But her hair is brushed and styled, her smart black trousers and shirt expensive-looking and clean. She arrived on time, which is more than he can say for West. Freya texted an excuse this morning claiming she'd been throwing up all night. Something she ate, sleeping it off, hopefully in later.

Robin could do with a nap himself. Steph prodded him awake much too early this morning, already dressed in her running gear. She told him to let himself out, she was going for a long one. Ten miles, she said, and he squinted at her in the morning half-light, vibrant and already bouncing on the balls of her feet. He rolled over in bed, feeling tired and old.

But she texted as he arrived at the station and confirmed that the coroner had given their plans the okay. She'd been in contact with the undertakers, making arrangements for Jonathan Miller to be transferred to her mortuary.

While they sit in the family room in the police station, he explains this to the wife.

'I thought you said he wouldn't need a post-mortem,' she asks him.

'Sometimes the coroner asks for one if the cause of death is uncertain,' he replies, and she looks confused.

'But you said it was an accident,' she says.

He gives her his best reassuring smile. 'We just need to be sure.'

They've moved on to easier ground, and Amy Miller is now telling him about the weekend before. Her speech is quiet and hesitant, her eyes downcast.

'We were at a party Friday night, Kal's fortieth,' she says.

'Kal?'

'Khalid Riaz, Jonathan's best friend.' Robin writes down the name as she spells it out. 'Works for Sterling and Blake, a hedge fund in London. Saturday we didn't do much, just went for a walk in the morning, takeaway Saturday night.'

'Sunday?'

'I went for a run, Jonathan went to the tip.' She makes an apologetic face. 'Sorry, our lives aren't that interesting.'

'When was the last time you saw him?'

'Monday morning. I left about eight for work.'

'What did Jonathan do?' Robin realises the past tense of his question, but there's no avoiding the stark reality.

'He was a procurement manager. Negotiating contracts, finding suppliers, stuff like that.'

No obvious motives for murder, Robin thinks. Except maybe accepting bribes for contracts? Backhanders in brown envelopes? She looks like she's going to cry again, so Robin asks another question quickly to distract her. 'And where were you on Monday and Tuesday?'

'At work. I'm on days this week: I'm a sous chef at the Hotel Continental in town. And I went out with my sister on Monday night. Since Jonathan was working. Or so I thought.'

'And you were off work this weekend?'

'Yes, I get one in four. Lucky really, given that...'

The tears come swiftly now, and Robin hands her another tissue. She wipes her eyes, delicately dabbing to avoid transferring mascara underneath.

'Have you managed to find out what he was doing at that hotel?' She sniffs.

'We believe it was— Well, what it looked like. Mrs Miller, I'm sorry, but I have to ask. Were you aware of Jonathan doing anything like this in the past?'

She shakes her head, a quick motion. 'No, no, not at all.'

'And your sex life? It was... er...'

Amy's face goes red and she looks down at her hands. 'Pretty normal,' she replies.

'Mrs Miller? Please? Anything you say will be strictly between us, and it would be helpful to get a complete view of your husband.'

'Well, he... we...' She stutters for a moment. 'He liked it when I talked dirty.'

Robin does his best not to show his disappointment. 'Saying what?' he asks as sensitively as he can.

'You know, fuck me harder, that kind of stuff.'

Robin leans back in his chair. It was hardly *Fifty Shades of Grey*, nothing that would explain why he'd been found as he had.

'And your face?' he asks, pointing to the bruise on her forehead. It's faded to no more than a yellow and green smudge, but still visible under her foundation.

'This? Oh!' Amy Miller looks surprised. 'I walked into an open cupboard door. You know, silly accident. You don't think—' She stops. 'Jonathan didn't do this!' she exclaims. 'Jonathan was the nicest, the gentlest, the most loving...'

Her voice trails off and she starts sobbing, harder this time. Robin sits forward awkwardly, offering her the tissue box again, but she doesn't take one. Instead, her eyes stay cast downward, her hands covering her mouth. 'I always tried to make him happy, do things the way he wanted,' she mumbles. 'I know I wasn't the best wife.'

They end the interview. Robin waits as Amy writes down names – her sister from Monday night, the other people at the party on Friday, the name of the takeaway they used on Saturday – and they walk together towards the door. But before she goes, as much as he doesn't like to ask, Robin needs to know.

'Mrs Miller, did your husband stay away a lot?'

She stands in the doorway, grasping the handle of her handbag tightly. 'A bit. With work.'

'Weekends?'

'No, why would he?' she asks. Then her face changes. Her eyes open wide and her mouth wobbles. She knows why; Robin started to ask her the day before. 'Who was she?' she asks, voice quivering with barely contained emotion.

'We don't know, Mrs Miller. Do you have any ideas?'

'No. No, I don't. He never… There was no…' Her hands flap weakly and she starts to wail, 'How could he? How could he do this to me?' She looks up at Robin, red-rimmed eyes watery. 'I didn't know. But they all say that, don't they, the wives? You must think me so stupid.'

'I don't think that at all, Mrs Miller. I'm sorry.'

They've reached the reception now, and she turns and walks away from him. Head down, she pushes out of the double doors, back into the grey autumn day.

He so hadn't wanted to be the one to confirm the affair. But her reaction spoke volumes. The uncontrolled emotion. A sudden burst of disbelief. So she hadn't known, Robin thinks, watching her go. One less motive to consider.

9

Freya wakes early with a banging headache and a churning in her stomach that she puts down to part hangover, part nerves. She can't face breakfast, but forces herself to eat a slice of toast, the pieces feeling like sawdust in her mouth.

She's already texted Butler, his curt reply lessening her guilty feelings for lying about her absence. But hangover aside, she knows she has something more important to do today.

She showers, puts on jeans and a jumper, then gets in her car. She drives the twenty minutes down the road, to the house she only visited yesterday for the first time.

In her darker moments, when Jon wasn't returning her texts, or when she knew he was spending time with Amy, she'd imagine them together. She'd had a picture in her head of what their house looked like, and she'd torture herself imagining Jon with her, doing the everyday things that she yearned to do.

And she'd imagined herself walking up to their front door, ringing the bell, then confronting Amy.

I'm Freya, she'd say. *And I love your husband.*

But she never had. And now he's dead.

Today, she sits and waits. She's insignificant, ignored. She's parked around the corner in the next street: far enough away that she won't be noticed by the wife, but close enough so she can still see the house. She knows the white Audi parked in the driveway is Amy's, and she also knows that Mrs Miller has an appointment at the police station at ten. An interview that Robin will have to do alone, because she is here. Watching, waiting.

She looks at the space next to the Audi on the driveway, imagining Jon's black Mazda sitting there. She knows where that car is now – impounded in the police garage, waiting to be examined by the forensics team.

She realises, her body growing hot, that they might find evidence of her. Of them.

Nine months ago, the two of them met in a deserted car park. Christmas, and they'd barely been able to catch a minute together. Jonathan had said Amy was more clingy than usual, not going out, not leaving his side. And this was the best they managed – a hasty excuse by him to go to the supermarket. No time to get to hers or to a hotel.

She hurried out of her car, ducking in the freezing rain and throwing herself into the passenger seat of his Mazda. The inside of the car was warm and muggy, suffocating air blowing out of the vents, steaming up the windows. But this wasn't the slightest bit *Titanic* movie-perfect. It was awkward, clumsy – his seat rolled backwards, her straddling him, knees painful against the door and the centre console. But they laughed, and kissed, and—

Shit.

This is a ridiculous idea, sticking with the investigation. She is risking the job she loves, everything she's spent so long working for. But this is important. That tryst in the car was the most adventurous they'd ever been. Something badly wrong happened in that hotel room, she knows it.

She'll come clean, she will. Once they've found out what happened. Once she's ensured first-hand that Butler's thoughts aren't taken off course. He's already mentioned other cases they both need to look at. All it will take is an upweighting of one of those, and Jonathan's death will be pushed to the side.

Freya feels tears threatening again, but pushes them away as the front door opens. There she is. Amy Miller is dressed in smart black jeans and a shirt, a posh coat over the top. Her hair is shining and blow-dried, and even from this distance Freya can tell her make-up is immaculate. She doesn't look like a woman torn apart by grief.

Freya watches as Amy clicks her car open, climbs inside then drives off. She waits a few minutes, biding her time in case Amy comes back, then gets out and hurries across the road towards the house. Freya glances around quickly. She knows where Jon keeps the spare key, a chance remark from her a month ago where burglars had got into a house using the key found in a fake rock. Piss-taking followed when Jon revealed he did exactly the same thing.

She hopes he didn't take heed of her warnings, and sure enough, she picks the key out of the plastic rock in the flower bed. She puts it in the door, and she's in.

She closes the door with a click, then stands, breathing hard, her back against the wall. She has shoe covers and plastic gloves in her hand, and now puts them on, not wanting to leave a trace of her having been there that day.

What is she doing? she asks herself. The house seems tidy, with a faint smell of detergent in the air. Has Amy been cleaning? she wonders. Cleaning what? Who cleans when they've just been told their husband is dead?

Freya's more than mindful she hasn't got long, but she can't resist looking around. She barely registered it the previous day. This is the house of her imagination, Jon and Amy's marital home, and she takes in the details as she walks. The kitchen – worktops bare, washing-up tidied away. The lounge – cushions plumped since Freya and Robin were there, coasters stacked in a neat pile on the coffee table. It's show-home perfect – impersonal, fastidiously neat. Her own house is nothing like this, especially since she found out about Jon's death. She left it in a state: the empty wine glass on its side on the bedroom carpet, clothes scattered, washing-up piled in the sink. She didn't have the energy to do anything about it, and wonders again how Amy, the grieving wife, can keep her house looking so spotless.

A bookshelf runs the length of the main room, and Freya traces her fingers along the spines, wondering which are his and which are Amy's. She remembers a comment once, that Amy doesn't read much, scorn in his voice. The paperbacks turn into non-fiction. Economics textbooks from Jon's university days, a few travel books, and then some strange ones. *Your Day-by-Day Pregnancy. A Midwife's Guide to Your Newborn.* Is Amy pregnant? The idea shocks Freya.

Jon hadn't mentioned still sleeping with his wife. And Freya had never asked. But they were a married couple in their late thirties; it was more than likely children would be on the agenda. They'd always used protection, but he wouldn't have used condoms with his wife, would he?

For the first time Freya wonders about other women. She'd always assumed she was the only one, but if Jon cheated on his wife once, what would have stopped him from doing it before? Or even at the same time?

What else had he been lying about?

She suddenly feels hot, a surge of nausea rolling up from her stomach. Saliva fills her mouth and she runs towards a closed door in the hallway, guessing correctly at the location of the downstairs toilet. The door bangs against the wall. She falls to her knees, throwing up the toast from this morning's crappy breakfast. She stays there for a moment, vomit abating to a painful dry retch, then sits back, wiping her eyes, her nose, her mouth, with a piece of toilet roll.

Was Jon telling the truth when he said he was planning on leaving his wife? Was their affair just that? Something fun, to pass the time, while he carried on with his marriage? Trying to conceive, hoping to have a baby?

She blows her nose, then flushes the chain, washing away the foul reek of her vomit. Whatever the truth, she needs to get on with it. Get what she's come here for.

Freya goes back into the living room, walking through and opening the door at the far end. And the moment she steps inside, it stops her in her tracks.

This room is different from the rest of the house. His office. It reminds her so much of him it physically hurts. More mess, more dust. There was always something dishevelled about Jon. His slightly curly hair had too much bounce to sit straight. His clothes were always coming untucked, a stray button undone. She'd never minded. They were holes she could poke her fingers into, touch the warm skin that lay underneath.

And this office – this is him. She starts her search, opening drawers, checking shelves. In his desk there's notepads, Post-it notes, pens, spare phone chargers. She flicks through a few of the notebooks, in case he's hidden a stray photo, but there's nothing. A pair of his reading glasses, old ones she remembers him replacing early on in their relationship, lies on a shelf.

The smell of his aftershave, his jacket hanging behind the door, books on the desk he told her about. Just him. And she misses him, so much.

She can't believe that all their shared moments were a lie. Not Jon. Not her Jon. He loved her. He was going to leave his wife for her. She knows that's true, from her very core. Perhaps the baby books were from earlier in the marriage. Perhaps they were given to them by well-meaning friends, and forever ignored.

But she can't think about that now.

Freya moves along. She knows what she's looking for, anything that might give her away. Early in their relationship she would email him photographs. Of her, with next to nothing on. He'd laugh, red, embarrassed spots appearing on his cheeks, saying he'd have to get rid of them. But once, he confessed to deleting the emails but saving the photos on his laptop. Password-protected, hidden in a folder and safe from Amy. But not from the clever brains of the police's digital department. If they got their hands on them, that would be it: they'd know and she'd be off the case. Probably fired. Not to mention the shame of her colleagues seeing photos of her with her tits out.

She finds it in the next drawer – his laptop. She lifts it out and places it on the desk, opening the screen. It pops into life, asking for a password. She has no idea, but she closes the lid again, putting it under her arm.

Then she hears it. The sound of a car pulling up outside the house. She swears under her breath, her heart beating hard. There's no way she can get out of this room without being seen, and she looks around for a solution. Her eyes alight on the window – large, big enough for her to climb through, and facing out to the garden behind the house.

She pushes it open fully, and climbs awkwardly onto the windowsill. She knows she's disturbing dust, leaving behind evidence of having been there, but the gloves and shoe covers are still on. They'll never know who. She leaps out of the window into a flower bed, pushing the window closed, and hurries round to the front of the house. Through a gap in the gate, she watches Amy stand at the front door, her key in her hand. Freya remembers the spare key, still in her pocket, but there's nothing she can do about that now.

She hears the front door close, waits a few seconds, then scuttles quickly through the gate, out into the street and back to her car.

Breathing quickly, the stolen laptop clutched tightly to her chest.

10

Amy Miller gone, Robin spends the rest of the morning raking through the contents of Jonathan Miller's phone. Call logs, text messages, everywhere he went across his last few days.

As much as people claim invasion of privacy, Robin knows social media and the geotagging on mobile devices is invaluable on a case like this. Phones, especially lovely iPhones like Miller's, record the user's every move. Where they've been, where they were when they posted on Twitter or took a photograph. What time they sent a text, made a call or logged onto WhatsApp. And with the passcode provided by Amy Miller, they can see everything.

Plus the techies have come through with the information from the car telematics. Jonathan Miller's Mazda is new enough to have a satnav and engine management system, so they can tell where it has been, and exactly what time the car was started or turned off. Every single change of electronics, from the seat position to the boot opening and closing, was recorded. Combined with the phone, it is vital data.

Freya has finally made it into the office. She looks distinctly green, and Robin makes a silent pledge to keep a good arm's distance away, but he needs her here. There's work to be done.

Between the two of them they plot Miller's movements onto a whiteboard. Freya reads from the car telematics and adds them to the iPhone details they have: Friday night, and King's Wine Bar in town for Khalid Riaz's fortieth. Home, via a brief stop on Jewry Street. Waitrose on Saturday. Then a walk along the River Itchen. Phone call to Domino's Pizza at 19:15 Saturday night.

To the municipal tip on Sunday morning. Working from home Monday, then the hotel, where he, and his phone, stayed until Robin picked it up and entered it into evidence on Tuesday.

Freya prints out the photos from Twitter and sticks them on the board. There is nothing here that raises a red flag. The satnav in the car matches the geotagging on the phone. Even a few searches on Google seem to correspond: late Sunday night he types in *what is erotic asphyxiation?* And follows it up with a few videos on YouTube. Then: *what do you need for auto-erotic asphyxiation?*

'Bloody quick learning curve,' Robin remarks to Freya.

'Hmm?' she replies, her back to him, staring at the board. She's still distracted, hardly listening to him.

'West?' he says, and she turns. 'Should you be here?'

'Yes, yes, sorry, Sarge. I'm fine,' she blusters, then adds a few actions to their list. *Follow up with Domino's Pizza, chase forensics on car, interview neighbours to check movements.*

She puts the marker pen down, then grabs the bottle of water on her desk, taking a desperate swig. Robin eyes her warily. Hangover? he wonders. But it's something he's done on more than one occasion, and he lets it go.

He's seen her around the station many times before. Chatting, laughing with other DCs, swinging that mane of blonde hair around. Since she's been working for him, she's been silent. Sullen even. Is that his effect on people, Robin thinks, even after one day?

'So, what?' he says, trying to get Freya's attention again. 'Miller googles erotic asphyxiation on the Sunday night, then decides to try it on the Monday? Wouldn't you want to give it a bit more thought before you choked yourself in a hotel room?'

Freya cringes at his words. 'Perhaps somebody mentioned it at the party on Friday night,' she suggests.

'That would be quite a topic of conversation,' Robin replies. 'Although who knows what these banker types talk about after a few glasses of champagne.' He remembers the list of guests provided by Amy Miller and passes it across to Freya without looking at it. 'Follow up on these guys. And the sister for the alibi from Monday night.'

He adds another note on the board: *Interview Khalid Riaz.*

'We'll go tomorrow,' he says, drawing her attention to the last action. 'Give him a call, set something up, will you?'

Freya nods, slumping back on her chair and picking up the phone. Robin stares at her. Her normally glossy hair seems lank and unwashed, her face drawn. He knows he looks like crap at the best of times, but she's winning the award today.

'Freya,' he whispers, getting her attention as she talks on the phone. He holds up his mug, silently asking her if she wants coffee. Making an effort. She smiles, her face tight, and holds her hand in a thumbs up.

It's the first smile he's seen from her all day, but he'll take it.

11

Amy's hands are still shaking an hour later. She gets back from the police station, shuts the front door behind her, then stands in her hallway, breathing heavily. She's home. She can relax now.

She walks through to the kitchen and puts the kettle on. She takes a teabag from the cupboard, camomile and lemon, carefully putting it in a mug, the tag hanging over the left-hand side, handle on the right. As the kettle boils she mentally runs through the conversation with the detective.

She doesn't like him. He shows little understanding for her, his generic sympathetic words ringing insincere in her ears. She guesses him about the same age as Jonathan was, maybe slightly older, but unlike Jonathan he has marked frown lines between his eyebrows, mouth always turned down. She felt him watching her, judging, with those unnerving brown-green eyes.

She picks up her mobile and clicks on the top number in her recent calls. She listens to it ring three, four times, then it's answered, the woman's voice slow and tired.

'It's early, Amy,' her sister says. Amy's unsurprised by her sister's coldness; their relationship has never been easy. But Amy has nobody else to speak to – their mother is dead, she has no friends. And whose fault is that? Amy can almost hear her sister comment.

'I've just got back from my police interview,' Amy replies. 'They think it was me.'

A sigh at the other end of the phone. Amy hears the rustling of bedcovers, knows her sister has probably just woken up, even though it's nearly lunchtime.

'Why would they think that?' she asks patiently.

'The questions he asked, the look on his face.' Amy pours the boiled water into her mug then carries it to sit at the kitchen table. 'They're going to be in contact with you to check we were out for dinner Monday night.'

'Fine.' More rustling. 'The restaurant will confirm too, Amy. They say he died on Monday, right?'

'Yes.'

'Well, then. You have nothing to worry about.' A pause. 'How are you doing?'

'I'm...' Amy feels her throat narrow and takes a deep breath in. 'I'm fine. Considering. Can you come over tonight?'

'I can't, I'm sorry. I'm working at the club. Tomorrow?'

Amy agrees and hangs up.

She wraps her hands round the mug, taking solace from its heat. She thinks about phoning Kal, but knows he won't take the call, and wonders when the police might be speaking to him. What will he say, about her and Jonathan? Did he know about the affair?

She listens to the silent house – there is nothing except the slow tick from the clock on the wall, the hum from the refrigerator. Is this how it's going to be now? Time, stretching out, with nothing to occupy her? Work have signed her off for a fortnight, and Amy knows there are probably things she should be doing. People to notify about Jonathan's death, paperwork to fill in. A funeral to arrange. But she assumes it won't be for a while, now that they're going to do a post-mortem.

Just procedure, the detective said. And the thought of it makes her hands shake again.

Her phone rings in front of her, making her jump. She's jolted the mug, and a splash of tea has hit the tabletop, leaving a yellow puddle. *No Caller ID*. The police again? But she answers the phone.

'Mrs Miller? This is the doctor's surgery. We wanted to call you as soon as possible. Your results are back.'

It's a woman, kind voice, talking slowly. 'Results?' Amy asks.

'Yes, from your blood tests? The fertility results?'

'Oh! Yes.' How could that have escaped her mind? The police interview must have rattled her more than she'd thought.

'It's good news, Mrs Miller. Your progesterone levels came back within expected limits, confirming an ovulatory cycle. So there's nothing here that would indicate anything other than normal fertility at this stage.'

'And my husband's results? Jonathan Miller.'

'Oh, er...' There's a pause and tapping on a keyboard. 'Nothing back yet for Mr Miller, I'm afraid. We'll call as soon as something comes through. And then it might be worth us booking an ultrasound, check your ovarian reserve. Explore other reasons why you might be having trouble conceiving.'

Amy thanks the woman, then hangs up.

Normal. The relief floods through her. And even though Jonathan's results aren't back yet, she knows what they'll say. It was him. His fault. She takes a celebratory sip of her cooling tea, a smile on her face.

She was right.

12

It's late by the time Robin makes it home, doing a messy parallel park in the road outside his house, key in the door, shoes carelessly discarded into the cupboard under the stairs. His first port of call is the fridge. He picks up a bottle of beer, opens it, then downs it almost in one, standing there with the fridge door open. He leaves the empty bottle on the side then takes out another and carries it up the stairs to his bedroom to get changed.

Something still feels wrong about this case, but he can't put his finger on what. Yes, everything is lining up as it should. Nothing contradicts the wife's story. The hotel have confirmed she was at work all day on the Monday; Freya was going to follow up with the sister, calling in to interview her on her way home, and check the restaurant they apparently went to. They've even spoken to the Domino's delivery guy from the Saturday night – one large pizza, half and half (Mighty Meaty on one side, Chicken Feast on the other), and a side of garlic bread. All delivered Saturday night at 7:54.

He takes his shirt off, pulling it over his head still done up, and throws it towards the washing basket. It misses, falling in an untidy heap on the floor, and he leaves it there, with a lone sock from yesterday's attempt.

His phone starts to ring, and he looks at it. *Liam*, it says on the screen, and he silences it then puts it back down on the bed where it continues to buzz angrily. Eventually it stops, and he waits, slowly undoing the belt on his trousers, until it beeps again, showing a new voicemail.

'Sod off,' he mutters at it. 'Take the fucking hint.'

He's paused, glaring at the phone, and now looks at the belt in his hand. It's a normal black leather belt – a buckle at one end, holes at the other. The same type he knows Jonathan Miller used that night. He pulls it out of his trousers and holds it, looking at the buckle, then at his own closed bedroom door.

He takes a few tentative steps towards the door. It has a hook on the back, the same as the one in the hotel. What was going through Jonathan Miller's head that day?

He picks up his beer again and finishes it, then replaces the empty bottle on the side. He feels a pleasant buzz from the alcohol, two bottles drunk in quick succession on an empty stomach. He looks at the belt again.

Slowly, he threads one end through, holding the buckle in his left hand, the loose end in his right. He looks at it, thinking. Did Miller have the buckle at the back or the front of his neck? His mind goes to that awful crime scene, the belt tight under his chin. The back.

He lifts the belt and puts it over his head. The leather is hard and uncomfortable as he pulls the buckle tight. He feels slightly foolish, slightly silly. How did Miller feel on that Monday evening? Was he excited, nervous? Turned on?

Robin's cold, his shirt off, in his empty bedroom. Miller was completely naked, not something Robin's about to do, still in his trousers and socks, but it makes him wonder. The hotel room was cold, the aircon on high. If anything, wouldn't Jonathan Miller have turned it down?

Belt still round his neck, loose end in his hand, Robin looks back at the door hook. How did Miller get it to stay up? Did he do a knot first, secure it in place, then put the noose over his neck? Or the noose first, then over the door hook?

He decides on the former, and takes the belt off his neck, tying a single knot in the end. Because of the stiff leather it holds fast, and he walks over to the door and puts it over the hook. He pulls, first tentatively, and then with more of his weight. The leather creaks, but it doesn't move.

Then, without thinking, he slips the noose over his head.

There's not much room to move, but slowly he places his bare back against the cold door and lowers himself into a squat, then a crouch. The leather feels tight; already he can feel the pressure on his throat. It's uncomfortable, but not painful. He can still breathe easily.

Until his feet slip.

The force is sudden, cutting off all his air. He scrabbles frantically with his fingers at the belt, his legs kicking out, trying to get purchase on the carpeted floor. He feels his nails claw at the noose, tight, too tight, vision starting to blur, trying to get his feet back under him, push himself up.

And then, as quickly as it started, he finds himself prostrate on the ground. He pulls at the belt and manages to get his fingers under the leather, tugging it away from his neck. He takes big gasps of oxygen, then coughs uncontrollably, his throat aching, lying on his back on the carpet. He looks up through watering eyes at the door. The hook has snapped off; a piece of sheared metal lies by his side.

He sits up slowly, heart beating hard, and takes the now loose belt from his neck, throwing it on the floor. He runs his fingers under his jaw. It's sore and rough, and he can feel a slight raised ridge where the belt must have cut in.

Fuck. What a fucking idiot. A better-engineered hook, and that would have been it. A fate like Miller's.

He pulls himself up on wobbling legs, then sits on the edge of the bed, breathing heavily. He looks down at the belt, the knot still in the end, and remembers Jonathan Miller. A bit more luck, and the guy would have been fine. Embarrassed maybe, as Robin is, but okay. And now look at him. Dead in a mortuary, ready to go under Steph Harper's knife.

Robin stands up and puts a T-shirt on, then changes into a pair of tracksuit bottoms. He grabs the discarded shirt and stray sock, putting them in the laundry basket, followed by the trousers, then picks up the fated belt to put it in the wardrobe.

But something stops him. He holds the buckle in his hand again – in his left hand. He remembers when he put it over his head, it ended up on that side, just behind his left ear and facing towards the right. But Jonathan Miller's?

He races downstairs and picks up his bag and the file, the crime scene photos inside. He pulls them out and looks through them, until he finds what he's looking for. Even allowing for the camera angle, the buckle faces the other way, towards the left-hand side.

Assuming Jonathan Miller was right-handed, as most people are, same as him. And assuming Miller had gone with the same action, holding it in his left hand, pushing the end through the buckle, putting the noose over his head. Assuming all of this, the buckle would have been on the left, facing towards the right.

How might this have happened? He turns the belt round in his hand. It's awkward, it feels unnatural. Why would Miller have reversed the belt?

But then the thought makes Robin stop still, standing in his hallway. He catches a glimpse of himself in the mirror, face pale, red bruise already visible, rising painfully on his neck. What if someone had been in front of him and had put the belt over his head?

The answer is suddenly clear: the buckle would have been reversed, if someone else had been there.

13

Thursday

Freya meets him at the train station. Robin notes she's looking better this morning – hair washed, eyes brighter – although still unmistakably tired. She greets him with a puzzled, 'What happened to your neck?'

'Don't ask,' he mutters, trying to pull the collar of his coat higher. He knows how bad it looks – he woke with an angry red and blue welt under his chin, and there's little he can do to hide it.

She stares at it, curiously. 'Did you try—' she starts, but he cuts her off.

'I said don't bloody ask,' he growls. 'Now go and get some coffee.'

He watches as she goes off to the café, hair swishing down her back. He's annoyed at having to trek all the way into London to see this Kal. Apparently too busy to come to the police station. Robin was damned if he was going to let this guy off scot-free, so off they go.

Freya returns with the coffees, just as the train rushes into the platform. They fight the commuters to two cramped seats, Freya next to the window, Robin sticking his legs out into the aisle. She gives her coffee to Robin to hold and rests her bag on her lap.

'So, Khalid Riaz,' she starts, pulling the case file out of her bag, as the train rattles out of the station. 'Hedge fund manager, has worked at Sterling and Blake for twelve years, Goldman

65

Sachs before that. Graduated 2001, same year as Jonathan Miller. They both studied economics.'

'Okay,' Robin says, passing her coffee back and looking over her shoulder at her scribbled notes. They're pushed close together, and he gets a waft of her perfume, something delicate and floral. He puts his coffee up to his nose and takes a sip through the plastic lid, trying to block out the feeling the scent induces in him. What is it about women? he thinks. They always smell so bloody nice.

'Best man at Miller's wedding. All over social media, see?' Freya holds her phone up in front of his face. He takes it, scrolling through the many photos this man posts: people, darkened clubs, women laughing.

'Quite a social life,' he replies, handing it back.

'Exactly. What do you think he'll be like?'

'Arrogant prick, probably.'

'Does he have a girlfriend, do you think?' Freya adds.

'Probably has many,' Robin comments. 'Men like him.'

'Like what?'

'You know. Attractive, money. Women love it.'

'Do they?' Freya gives him an amused look. 'You know a lot about women, do you, Sarge?'

'Only my limited experience.'

'Limited? I'd have thought you got a lot of interest,' Freya says. 'All that brooding and scowling.'

Robin rolls his eyes at her, reluctantly enjoying her teasing. It's clear that being away from the formality of the police station is doing their working relationship the world of good. After the tension of the last few days, Freya seems to have relaxed.

'I don't brood,' he replies, only too conscious of the frown on his face. Freya chuckles quietly.

He looks around the carriage. No one seems to be paying them much attention, but you can never be sure. 'We shouldn't be discussing this here.'

'Oh, okay, yes.' Freya's voice lowers to a loud whisper. 'Do you want to see my list of questions?'

'Go on then.'

She pulls out a piece of A4 paper and passes it to him. Neat lines typed and printed out. As he reads it, she pulls a Tube map out of her pocket.

'Jubilee line to Canary Wharf,' she says.

'These are good,' he confirms, handing the questions back. They are, and Robin feels guilty — he hasn't even thought about it. He's more of a wing-it-on-the-day sort of man. 'How did the interview go with the sister last night?'

'Yeah, as Amy Miller said. They met about seven thirty, Côte Brasserie on the High Street. Drinks and three courses, left at ten. I'm waiting for the restaurant to confirm, but seems tight. And I went to see the Millers' neighbours this morning.'

'You've been busy,' Robin says, impressed.

'Not that they were much use.' Freya refers back to her notes. 'Left-hand side, number six, were away. They do the same every week and are never around Thursday to Monday. Right side, number ten, is vacant. Rented. Last people left two months ago. No houses built opposite, yet.'

'So nobody saw anything?'

'No.'

'Hmm.' Robin closes his eyes and leans his head back against the seat. The thought about the backwards belt still echoes in his head, but he's tired and the movement of the train is lulling him into a stupor. Next to him, Freya seems to have taken the hint and is quiet. He feels her leg resting against his, knows he's probably taking up more than his allotted space on their seats, but he's warm and sleepy and can't be bothered to move.

He wakes with a jolt as the train gets into Waterloo. He glances at Freya; she's staring at him with an amused smile.

'Was I snoring?' he asks, wiping his mouth with the back of his hand.

'Only mildly,' she says, swinging her bag over her shoulder as they get off the train, setting off at a brisk pace down the platform to the Tube.

It's a simple journey and they arrive in plenty of time. Robin looks up at the shiny glass building.

'So this is the private sector then?' he observes.

'You've never fancied it?' Freya asks.

'What would I do?' Robin points to the security guy in black, outside the main entrance. 'I'd be that guy. Hardly going to be one of the bankers, am I?'

Freya pauses, watching a man leave in a smartly tailored pinstriped suit. She looks back at Robin. He didn't even iron his shirt this morning.

'I guess not,' she says, quietly.

They approach the building and show the security guy their warrant cards. He lets them inside and they walk up to the massive reception desk, where a woman smiles broadly.

'We're here to see Khalid Riaz,' Robin says, showing his badge again. 'He's expecting us.'

She prints out ID, points towards the bank of lifts. 'Twenty-first floor,' she says. 'I'll call up.'

The lifts are see-through and open, and Robin watches as Freya presses her nose to the glass as they ascend, looking out across the vista of London. It's impressive, he can't deny that, but he's happier standing against the back wall. He resists the urge to hug the floor, choosing to close his eyes instead, trying to pretend he's not miles up in the air.

The doors open silently; another woman is waiting for them. She doesn't check who they are, obvious in contrast to the corporate suits and grey shift dresses, and hurries them along the corridor.

'Kal has a meeting in half an hour, so he can't talk to you for long.'

Robin pauses at the door. 'It'll take as long as we need,' he replies sharply.

Khalid Riaz is exactly as he expected. He smiles a broad grin at them both, white teeth against dark skin, neat black hair and a perfect suit. His silver tiepin is probably worth more than everything Robin is wearing. He holds out his hand and Robin shakes it: firm, but not the bone-cracking style that Robin's experienced in the past from men like the one in front of him.

'Call me Kal,' he says, flashing a charming smile at Freya. Robin notices she simpers slightly, head tilted flirtatiously to the side, before catching his look and stopping herself. Kal gestures to the two seats in front and they sit down, Kal going back to his own chair behind the desk.

'Incredible view,' Freya remarks.

London is particularly beautiful that day. The sun casts a glow on the buildings around them, making the glass dazzle like diamonds, the sky a perfect blue.

'Good, huh?' Kal says, and even Robin has to admit it's stunning. 'The people I had to fuck to get this office,' he laughs. Robin stares at him, and he looks slightly chagrined. 'Sorry,' he mumbles. 'Anyway, how can I help you? You said on the phone it was about Jonathan's death. I thought that was sorted?'

'Sorted, how?' Robin asks.

'Well, you know.' Kal's caught off guard. 'You know what happened.'

'We're exploring all possibilities.' Robin pauses. He likes the silence and he can tell it unnerves Kal. 'When was the last time you saw Mr Miller?'

'At my party, Friday night. It was my fortieth.'

'And this was the party at King's Wine Bar in Winchester?'

'Yes. I rented out the whole place.'

'What time did Jonathan arrive?'

Kal frowns, looks skyward. 'Not sure. Late. It was in full swing by the time they got there – Jonny and Amy.'

'So…?'

'About nine-ish?'

'And what did you talk about?'

69

'Talk about?'

Robin knows what he's doing, repeating the questions, deliberately stalling for time to think. 'Yes, at the party,' he repeats slowly, as if talking to an annoying child. 'What did you and Jonathan and Amy talk about that night? Anything? Just general topics will be fine.'

'Oh, you know, the usual.' Robin allows another silence. 'Look, I can't remember, okay? I was out of it.' Kal leans back in his expensive office chair with a creak of leather. 'It was my birthday. I'd been partying since lunchtime. By nine I couldn't remember my own name, let alone what conversations I had with people.'

'You were drunk.'

'And the rest.'

Robin knows what he doesn't want to say. A party boy like Kal, he would have had more than alcohol flowing in his veins. Coke, most likely, probably a few other illicit substances. Nothing he'd be in any hurry to discuss with a police officer.

'But look.' Kal sits forward and picks up his phone. 'Jonny sent me this on Saturday.' He scrolls, then passes Robin his handset.

Robin looks at the image. It's the photo from Twitter, with the dark background, and Jonathan Miller, his arm round Kal, their faces close to the screen.

'We've seen it. He took this Friday night?'

'Yes, so it proves he was there.'

'I'll need to seize your phone.'

'No!' Kal reacts like Robin's going to chop off his hand. Robin smiles; it's not necessary, just wanted to mess with the guy.

'Fine, then email me the photo, please.'

Kal nods, relieved, and Robin hands him his card with his details. He watches as Kal does the transaction.

'How would you describe Jonathan?' Robin asks.

Kal looks up from his phone. 'He was a good guy. Loyal. Reliable.' Kal smiles sadly. 'Makes him sound dull, but he wasn't.

He was the best, the sort of bloke you'd want to have your back, you know?'

'And how well do you know Amy Miller?' Freya asks.

'Amy?'

Robin glances across to Freya. 'Yes, Jonathan's wife?'

'Er, you know. Fairly well,' he replies. But he picks up his phone, puts it down again, his fingers tapping.

'Has it ever been just the two of you?'

'The two of us?'

Robin sighs and leans forward, resting his hands on the desk. 'Listen, Kal,' he says. 'This is all friendly now. But unless you're going to cut the crap and be honest with us, we might have to request your presence down at the station. And your employers might not be so understanding about a recorded interview with lawyers present.'

'Fine, fine.' Kal holds his hands up defensively. 'Yes, okay. There was something between Amy and I. Once. A few weeks ago. She and Jonny had had an argument, she came to my house. We got plastered. Snorted a bit of coke.'

'What were they arguing about?' Freya asks. 'Jonny and Amy?'

'She said it was to do with money. Their credit card bill had arrived and Jonny hadn't been too impressed. I could well believe it. Jonny was always careful in that regard.'

Robin takes over again. 'And you slept together?' he asks.

'No. Yes. Kind of.'

'Which is it?' Robin snaps.

'Yes. Strictly speaking. But I… you know. Pulled out. Before the deal was complete. I couldn't do it.'

'Shag your best friend's wife?'

'No. She left. And I didn't see her again until the party Friday night.'

'And what were your movements on Monday and Tuesday?' Robin asks.

'Work. Here. And Lisa came over Monday night. My girl-friend,' he adds with a charming smile back at Freya. Robin wonders if Lisa knows about the unconsummated shag with Amy Miller. He guesses not.

'Do you know who Jonathan was having an affair with?' Robin asks instead.

Kal recoils in surprise. 'What? Jonny? I don't believe it.'

'We have evidence that he was seeing someone else.'

'Not Jonny,' Kal scoffs.

'You're saying you have no idea who that was.'

'Not a clue.' Kal leans forward slightly over the desk. 'Is it true? What they're saying?' He looks from Robin to Freya, then back again. 'That Jonny was, you know.'

'Was what?'

Kal glances at Freya again, as if wanting to avoid damaging her delicate sensibilities. 'Doing that hanging thing, with the wanking?' he finishes, lowering his voice.

'Auto-erotic asphyxiation?' Freya says, matter-of-fact, and Kal nods, his face colouring.

'We're still investigating,' Robin replies. 'Had you known him do anything like that in the past?'

'Jonny? No. Not at all. Same with this affair you say he was having. He just wasn't that sort of guy. The opposite, in fact. We arranged his stag do in Amsterdam, and we were all, you know...'

Robin did know. 'Prostitutes?'

'Yeah. But Jonny wouldn't even go and watch. We bought him a blow job and everything, but he refused.'

'How unreasonable,' Robin says sarcastically. 'Just before he was going to get married and everything.'

Kal gives him a look. 'Yeah, alright, it was hardly gentle-manly. But we were in our twenties, we were having fun. Although...' He pauses, thinking. 'About four months ago, Amy asked me if I knew of any escort agencies. The dodgy kind. Said she was arranging a surprise for his birthday, but wouldn't tell me what.'

'And you gave her the name of one?'

'Yeah. You want it, too?'

Robin gives him a disparaging look. 'What do you think?'

—

They leave Kal in peace and his PA walks them to the lifts.

'What a prince of a man,' Freya grumbles as the doors swish closed behind them. 'And was it just me, or does he pluck his eyebrows?'

Robin snorts, grudgingly enjoying Freya's company. 'They did look suspiciously precise for a man.' They walk out of the building then head towards the Tube. 'So Jonathan and Amy were definitely there Friday night,' he continues. 'Although it might be worth speaking to a few of the other guests, get confirmation.'

'What do you make of this stuff with the escort agency?' Freya asks. 'What do you think his wife was up to?'

'I don't know,' Robin replies. 'But one thing's for sure: Amy Miller isn't as she seems.'

14

Butler falls asleep again the moment they leave Waterloo. Luckily this time he slumps up against the window, rather than on Freya's shoulder as he did on the way there. She'd sat, frozen, his body pressed against hers, unaccustomed to a strange man being so close.

He is an odd bloke. She can look at him more closely now he's unconscious, the red mark clear on his neck. It's obvious what he's been doing, although exactly how far he got she neither knows nor wants to spend too long thinking about. He's not bad-looking, short dark hair, growing grey at the temples. Standard cut, slightly longer on top, due a trim. A man who dresses in greys and blues and blacks – colours that can't clash, clothes neutral in style. Maybe that's his charm – the complete lack of self-interest.

She looks at his eyelashes, flickering against his cheek. Too long, wasted on a man. Nice eyes that slope down slightly at the corners, giving him a kindly air, despite his brash manner.

He has a rare smile that slips from his face almost as quickly as it arrives, as if his brain can't sustain the happiness to hold it there. Never verbose, he talks in clipped tones, often mistaken by her colleagues for rudeness. She's never heard him discuss his weekend, or ask about someone else's. But despite this, she finds herself liking him. He's clever, his mind always two steps ahead of hers, challenging, directing, asking her opinion. And unlike other sergeants she's had in the force, it seems he's not afraid to let her take the lead when it counts.

Like today. He's already said he wants her to be on point for the interview with the escort agency. They don't like the police, he said on the walk back to Waterloo, so a gentler touch might help. Yours, he added with a small smile, acknowledging his own failings.

Watching Butler in slumber, she feels her own eyes starting to close. She didn't sleep well last night, crying for hours, then tossing and turning through dreams about Jon. Dreams where he's alive, with her, feeling so real she can almost reach out to touch him.

She woke drained, but full of determination. As ridiculous as she knows it sounds, she feels like he was speaking to her, spurring her on to find out what happened on that Monday night. And the more she hears about Amy Miller, the more she doesn't like her.

So she had cheated on Jon. And with his best mate, of all people. The injustice of this burns. If he'd known what she had done, then maybe he'd have left her sooner. They could have been together, and maybe he'd be alive. Maybe. Maybe. There's so much she's desperate to have done differently, to still have Jon here. It creates an almost constant ache that makes her feel sick inside.

The Jon that Kal described, the man turning down hookers, the man you want by your side, that was her Jon. She knows she's doing the right thing, keeping this quiet from her boss. There is more information out there. She wants to know what happened, and being here, on the case, is the best way of finding out.

–

Freya may have a woman's touch, but ten minutes into the conversation with the escort agency and things aren't going well.

Butler insisted on driving, and they left her car at the train station. Freya wondered whether it was good old-fashioned sexism, or the fact that he didn't want to be seen in a girly blue Fiat 500, as she opened the passenger door to his dirty Volvo. It was a car more suited to a family of four, discarded sweet wrappers and fizzy drink cans left strewn in the footwell. She brushed crumbs off the seat as she got in; he put on some music, then turned it down – some sort of late-nineties rock.

The agency is run by a woman who introduces herself as Frankie Rosa. She's older, maybe fifty or so, with a matronly air. Big shelf-like bosoms, rounded cheeks, no trace of make-up. And not taking any shit from them.

They arrived at the registered business address, a detached house in a neighbourhood where disused fridges are left out the front and dogs bark noisily from the back. She opened her door, but isn't letting them inside.

'We run a respectable business,' she snaps to Freya, arms crossed, blocking the doorway. 'What are you suggesting?'

Freya holds her hands up in front of her, defensively. 'We're not interested in arresting you—'

'What for?'

'—we just need to know about Amy and Jonathan Miller.'

'I've told you already, any information about our clients is strictly confidential.'

'Jonathan Miller is dead. Can you just confirm he was a client?'

'I will not, and now I must ask you to leave.'

Freya feels Butler touch her lightly on the arm, indicating it's time to beat a hasty retreat. They're clearly not getting anywhere today.

Back in the car, Freya looks to her boss, flustered.

'What now, Sarge?' she asks. 'Get a warrant?'

'For what?' he replies. Freya looks back to the house and sees Frankie watching them out of the window, greying net curtains pushed aside. 'We have no grounds, no evidence. And storming in there all guns blazing is hardly going to get a result. If Amy Miller did hire an escort, we need to know who, then speak to her about it.'

'So how do we do that?' Freya asks, but Butler just frowns, back to tapping his fingers on the steering wheel, deep in thought.

The curtain flips back, and Frankie has gone. Another dead end, Freya thinks as she feels her phone buzz in her pocket. She pulls it out and answers it.

'DC West?' the voice says at the other end. 'PC Wallis. I was told you're investigating the Jonathan Miller death?'

'Yes?' Freya says, taking the phone away from her ear and putting it on speaker. Butler cranes forward, interested.

'Sorry I didn't call before, I only just joined the dots,' the PC continues. 'Just that we spoke to the wife Friday night. Amy Miller? Was parked on double yellows outside a chippy.'

'Where are you?' Butler asks, starting the engine. 'We'll come to you.'

—

They meet in the middle, Butler pulling up behind the yellow and blue panda in one of the car parks in town. PC Wallis gets out, introducing himself quickly with a handshake to them both, then leans back, resting his ample behind on the bonnet of his patrol car.

'North end of Jewry Street, near the steakhouse,' he says, in answer to Butler's question of where he saw Amy Miller. 'She was blocking the road, so we pulled up alongside and asked her to move.'

Freya wraps her arms round herself, bouncing to try to defeat the effects of the cold. In her eagerness she left her coat in the car, but she doesn't want to get it now and risk missing the conversation.

'She was driving?'

'Yeah. But when she spoke she sounded like she'd had a drink or two, so we did a breathalyser.'

'And it was below the legal limit?'

The PC nods. 'Nought point two. Well below. She said she'd had a glass of champagne at a party.'

'Was she alone?'

'Nah, her husband was there. In the chippy. She pointed at him through the window. She seemed nervous though, keen for us to be gone.'

'She didn't want her husband to see you?'

'Not at all, no. I'll get the BWV for you, you can see for yourself.' His radio crackles on his shoulder and he bends his head to listen. 'Got to go, Sarge. Shout if you need anything else.'

Butler thanks Wallis, and he and Freya get back into the car.

'Do you think she was scared of him? The husband?' Butler asks.

Freya knows there is no truth in it but can see where his chain of thought is going. 'You're still thinking DV?' she asks. Domestic violence might make sense. But there was just no way.

'Would tie up with the bruise on her forehead. And a reason to kill him,' he replies, fingers drumming on the steering wheel. 'What about Kal, the best mate? In love with Amy Miller? Wants to get the husband out of the way?'

Freya frowns. 'He didn't seem much like a jealous lover to me. So much into Amy Miller that he can't even... you know... complete the transaction,' she finishes, resorting to a euphemism.

Butler nods. 'And, of course, we have nothing to show he was murdered.' He turns to face her. 'What *do* we have? What are we still waiting for?'

'We have the CCTV, social media, the mobile phone data and the telematics from the car,' Freya says, counting them off on her fingers. 'Khalid Riaz confirms he was at the party, and Amy Miller's alibi has been confirmed for Monday.'

'So just the post-mortem,' Butler says. Freya watches as he takes his phone out of his pocket and sends a quick text. 'I'll chase up Steph.'

Steph? Freya thinks. Interesting her boss and the pathologist are on first-name terms. But a sinking feeling is growing in her stomach: there's nothing to show Jon's death isn't precisely what it seems.

'And then what?' Freya asks, quietly. 'Assuming Dr Harper doesn't find anything odd.'

Butler shrugs. 'Then we type it all up, and move on,' he says. 'No matter what our guts are telling us.'

Freya turns away from him as he starts the car, putting it into gear. She feels hot tears behind her eyes and blinks them away in frustration. She's letting Jon down.

But Butler's right, there's nothing, she tells herself as they drive back to the police station. Nothing.

15

Given the situation he managed to get himself into the night before, Robin's in no rush to go home at the end of the day. He takes a small detour, back to the house where Frankie lives. Something in him wonders whether it's not just the administrative hub of the escort agency, but where actual transactions take place. Illegal transactions.

He parks a good distance away and kills the engine. Before leaving the police station he picked up a sandwich, a can of Coke and a Twix from the vending machine, and now sits in the darkened driver's seat and opens the wrapping. The bread is slightly stale, the ham curled around the edges, but it'll do – it's more than he's eaten all day.

The road seems quiet. He recognises Frankie's Ford Fiesta parked outside, identified through the check on the Police National Computer. Lights are on in the house but there's none of the activity he'd expect to see. Brothels have people – men – coming and going at all hours, but the road is silent until a single car pulls up in the drive. A woman gets out – tall, long dark hair, pretty, wearing a short, smart cocktail dress and high heels. She goes into the house without knocking; Robin makes a note of the number plate and calls it in.

Control report back immediately: car is registered to an Olivia Cross, resident of Winnall, Winchester. So not this address, despite how much she seems at home.

'Anything more about her?' Robin asks.

'IC1, thirty-eight, single. Caution for soliciting in 2018, but nothing else,' comes the reply. So he's on the right track, Robin thinks.

Then the front door opens again and Frankie herself comes barrelling out. She's moving at speed towards him, wearing a tight pink tracksuit. His hand immediately goes to the ignition key and he starts the engine as she bashes on his car door.

'Fuck off!' she screams, her spit showering his driver's side window. 'This is harassment.'

'Okay, okay, I'm going,' he shouts, and quickly drives away.

–

He leaves his car at home, and heads into town. It's Thursday night, and the pavements are busy as he walks towards King's Wine Bar.

It's a nice place – small and homely, pretty art deco-style stained glass at the tops of the windows, with a chalkboard of cocktails and a decent line of local ales on tap. He finds a seat at the bar and orders a pint of Ringwood Forty Niner, happily taking a long gulp the moment it's presented to him. As he pays, he asks about the party and the barman goes to get the manager.

The manager's a young guy, with long hair tied back in a man bun and an impressive thick bushy beard.

'Yeah, course,' he says, when Robin asks if he was working. 'Wanted to personally make sure it all went down okay.'

'And did it?'

'A good night was had by all,' he says, smiling. 'Especially me. The bar tab was huge. These London guys can drink, I'll tell you that.'

'Do you remember seeing this man?' Robin asks, showing him a photo of Miller.

The manager shakes his head. 'No, sorry. But it was heaving that night and we were rushed off our feet. Didn't stop for a minute.'

'CCTV?' Robin points to the camera above his head.

'Sorry, not from Friday. We rotate the tapes every three days. You should have come here sooner.'

Robin curses under his breath. 'Can you check the receipts, see if our guy paid for anything?'

The manager looks apologetic. 'Nobody paid for anything, that night.'

'Nothing?'

'Nope. The entire tab was picked up by the guy whose birthday it was. Kal something?'

'Fucking hell,' Robin says, then internally chastises himself. He is there asking questions as a police officer, after all.

But the manager doesn't seem to mind his language, and laughs loudly. 'Alright for some, eh?'

He leaves, but not before pouring Robin a fresh pint. Robin downs the final swig of the last one, then moves on to the full glass.

The bar is starting to fill up properly now: people coming for a quick drink after finishing at restaurants, friends meeting friends, the barman chatting away happily to a few. A DJ has taken up residence on the far side of the room, playing music that Robin hasn't heard before: a combination of jazz and something more modern. Robin's enjoying the ambience, then becomes aware of someone sitting down on the bar stool next to him. He turns.

The woman orders a glass of sparkling mineral water, then looks at him.

'You want a drink?' she asks.

He recognises her. Olivia Cross, from Frankie's house. She's in the same smart dress, but her hair is tied up high now, a few tendrils loose around her face.

You don't look like a tom, Robin thinks, then wonders if he's spoken out loud.

'No, thank you,' he says.

He turns back to his pint, but she doesn't leave. He can feel her looking at him.

'You were at Frankie's,' she says. 'You're that cop.'

'Guilty as charged,' he replies. Then, despite knowing the answer, he asks, 'And you are…?'

'Liv.' She holds out a slim hand and he shakes it. It's cold where she's been holding her glass. 'I work for Frankie.'

'Robin Butler,' he replies. 'Is this coincidence, or did you follow me?'

She laughs. 'You're not stupid, are you? Even after a few pints.'

He doesn't reply. She's flirting with him. Officially he's off duty, but still, this isn't great.

'You're not Frankie's favourite person, Robin. I'd stay away for a while if I were you. She was about to report you.'

'Thanks for the tip.'

'What did you want, anyway?'

'A man called Jonathan Miller used the escort's services. We wanted to know why.'

She nods, thinking, taking a sip from her glass, her lipstick leaving a mark on the rim. She rubs at it with her finger.

'Off the record, right?' she says quietly.

'I'm not a journalist.'

'Well, don't arrest me if I tell you what you need to know.'

'Deal.'

'He was my client. Or rather, his wife was. She paid me. I went out to see them both. At their house.'

'And this was?'

'A few months ago. Maybe May?'

'What service did you provide?'

'You're not going to arrest me, right?'

'I'm off duty.'

'They wanted a threesome.'

Robin raises his eyebrows. 'Him and his wife?'

'Yeah. She said it was his birthday present, except… well. He didn't seem that keen.'

Robin finishes his pint, then raises his hand to the barman. 'You want one?' he asks her and she shakes her head. 'What do you mean, not keen?' he asks, once he's been served.

'He was reluctant at first. I thought he was just shy, but he stayed away. His wife was into it, though – came over, started kissing me, took my clothes off.'

'Where was he?'

'He watched. Then she got a few drinks down him and he seemed to relax. Gave him a blow job. Then he did his wife from behind while she kissed me.'

She looks over quickly, wondering whether she's given too much detail.

'So, he didn't...'

'Fuck me? No. Still asked for the full amount, though. No refunds.'

'And the wife paid?' Robin gets his phone out and shows Liv a photo of Amy Miller. 'That her?'

Liv squints at it. 'Yeah, that's her. Real Stepford Wife sort. Controlling.'

'Interesting,' Robin says. To his surprise he notices another pint has gone while they've been talking. 'Assume you won't come down to the station and give us a statement?'

'You're kidding, right?' Liv replies. 'Now buy me a drink. And let's talk about something else.'

He does as she asks. And he finds himself enjoying their conversation. Despite their professions being seemingly at odds with each other, they talk, as Robin moves from pints to whisky.

They go outside for a smoke, Robin sharing Liv's cigarette. They pass it to and fro, huddling together in the cold autumn air.

And then the alcohol takes over and – nothing.

–

He wakes with an acidic taste in his mouth and a skull-splitting thump in his head. He opens his eyes. He's at home, in his bed, in his boxers, the duvet askew. He looks around the room, wincing. And then he sees it – a black lacy bra, draped over the back of the chair, a navy dress next to it.

'Oh...' Robin groans. Nothing else comes out. He couldn't have, could he? Surely not. He lies back on the pillow, praying for the pain in his head to subside and some sort of memory to come back. He can remember the bar. He can remember them talking. Him drinking. Far, far too much. Then... nothing.

'Oh, shit,' he mutters again.

He can't have slept with a prostitute. Detective sergeants simply can't go around shagging toms. It's an investigation from Professional Standards, a warning at best. How could this have happened?

He hears footsteps on the stairs, then the bedroom door opens and she walks in. Liv's wearing one of his T-shirts, her legs bare, her hair loose around her face. She has a cup of tea in her hand.

'You're awake,' she says, and sits at the end of the bed, sipping at her mug. She smells of cigarettes, and it makes his stomach turn, although he acknowledges he can't smell too good either if the taste in his mouth is anything to go by.

'I'm sorry,' he starts.

'What for?' She gives him a small smile.

'That... I don't know,' he moans. 'Did we...'

'Shag? No.'

'Oh, thank god,' he sighs. Then realises what he's said. 'Not that... You're not... you're very good-looking... it's just...'

She's obviously enjoying his discomfort. 'No offence taken. You were so drunk the taxi wouldn't take you unless I came along. And then I stayed the night. Just slept here, next to you. Same bed. I was worried about you puking again and choking on your own vomit.'

'Again?' He runs his tongue round his teeth. They're furry and sour. 'I'm so sorry,' he repeats.

'It's fine, really. It made for a nice change. Did you know you have a Dorset accent when you're drunk? You sound like a farmer.' She goes around to the head of the bed and sits next to him, resting against the pillows.

'It's Devon. Where I grew up.'

She reaches across him and passes him the glass of water on his bedside table. 'Drink something.'

He leans up awkwardly and takes a sip. The water is insanely refreshing and he takes another gulp.

'Did I try and sleep with you?' Robin asks.

'No, not at all. You kept calling me Georgia.'

'My sister,' Robin says quietly.

'That explains it.'

Robin thinks about the many times his sister helped him home after a night out. Put him to bed, like Liv did last night. She's been on his mind more recently, after Liam's missed call. Now spilling out into his subconscious when pissed.

'I was thinking about what you said, about how Jonathan died,' Liv says.

'Oh, no. I shouldn't have told you that. That's confidential. Please...' he begs.

'My lips are sealed. I promise. But I've had some experience with auto-erotic asphyxiation.'

Robin looks over at her.

'Not me,' she continues. 'But men who want me to do it to them. I tried it with one client. It scared me.' She shakes her head, looking thoughtfully into her tea. 'Never again.'

'What happened?'

'He went blue, passed out. We must have pulled too tight, I don't know. I had to do mouth-to-mouth. He came round, begged me not to call 999.'

'Lucky guy.'

'For me too. Can you imagine? Do you think the wife was doing it to him, to Jonathan? Maybe it went wrong and she panicked.'

'She has an alibi.'

'Ah.' Liv shakes her head again, her hair falling prettily over her shoulders. In another life, maybe, Robin thinks, they might have had a future. 'He didn't strike me as that type, though,' she adds.

Robin sits up more in the bed. The water is helping, hydrating his poor addled brain.

'The men that want it. It's not their first rodeo, you know?' Liv looks at him, and he nods. 'They try a few things first. BDSM, role play, pain. This is their next big thing. You know what I'm saying?'

Robin remembers their conversation from the night before. 'You don't go from being a reluctant participant in a threesome to full-on erotic asphyxiation a few months later.'

'Right.' She looks at the clock, then swears. 'Call me a cab? I'm so late.'

She jumps up from the bed, pulling Robin's T-shirt off and putting her dress back on. Robin does as he's asked, the cab company confirming arrival in ten minutes. As she gets dressed he sees a flash of her nearly naked – a tattoo, a Chinese dragon, curling round her lower back – and an insight to what could have been. She picks up her bra and puts it in her pocket.

He puts on the T-shirt she's just taken off and follows her down the stairs.

'And Frankie? You'll leave her alone now, won't you?' she asks, turning round at the front door, reaching down and putting her heels on. 'She's one of the good ones. Always lets you know what you're in for. No surprises.'

Robin nods. 'We'll back off. Thank you,' he adds again.

She opens the door, then leans back and gives him a slow kiss on his cheek. 'Look after yourself, DS Butler,' she says. Then she stops, and pauses for a second. 'It's a shame about Jonathan. I felt sorry for him,' she adds quietly. 'He seemed sweet.'

Robin watches her get into the cab, then closes the front door with a click.

A man dead from an experimental sex practice, when he'd refused a wife-sanctioned shag with a prostitute? None of this adds up. And it is certainly more than his hungover mind can compute this morning.

16

Friday

This is Steph Harper's domain, not his. And the smell of decomposing flesh and dead bodies is not sitting well with his hangover. He's already had a near-miss second dry-heave in the road outside the hospital as he clambered out of the taxi. However, he now dons the gloves and mask as requested, and walks up to her side.

Poor Jonathan Miller is on the slab. Naked when he died, naked for his post-mortem. Robin can see the cut running up the middle of his stomach and chest, culminating at his neck, then shooting off in the standard Y-incision on both sides. His eyes stare, open and unblinking, at the ceiling.

Freya's back at the station, working her way through his – now their – sorely neglected caseload. Robin's glad; he's hardly firing on all cylinders. And it doesn't pay for your DC to see you in such an obviously self-inflicted state.

Steph's still got the Dictaphone in her hand, and is talking quietly, making final notes. She switches it off as Robin approaches.

'Figured you didn't want to wait for the report,' she says.

'Rather not. What did you find?'

'Much as you'd expect from a strangulation. Numerous petechiae around and on the eyes. Pronounced ligature mark on the neck,' she says, pointing to the red lines and bumps circling his head. 'Mild pulmonary congestion, but no further abnormalities. No injury to neck tissues. No pericardial or pleural haemorrhage or petechiae.'

'Which means?' Robin asks.

'Carotid artery obstruction resulting in cerebral hypoxia. All things considered, it appears he asphyxiated.'

'Ah.' Robin feels a swell of disappointment, then wonders why. This isn't a bad thing. He knows how Miller was found, he knows what it showed. 'Wouldn't you expect more injury to the neck?' he asks. He's only too aware of the last remnants of the bruises under his own chin, now faded to a pale red mark, hopefully passing for a shaving rash or something else innocent.

'Not necessarily,' Steph replies. 'Because he was found incompletely suspended—' She glances at Robin. 'Not hanging off the ground,' she clarifies. 'There wouldn't be much pressure to the neck. And you're sure it's not a suicide?'

'No note, no previous depressive behaviour,' Robin replies. 'Why?'

'It's just…' Robin sees Steph frown behind her mask, then she gestures to her office at the rear of the main mortuary. He follows her in, as she pulls off the protective gear. 'You want tea?'

He nods, and she turns on the kettle propped up on a fridge behind them.

'I went through the crime scene photos you sent me,' she says, laying out two mugs and popping teabags in. 'And some things don't make sense.'

'Such as?'

'I did some reading up. Typical auto-erotic cases, especially men, would have other indicators. Cross-dressing, something wrapped round the genitals, such as an elastic band or a ribbon.' Robin winces. She continues, enjoying his discomfort. 'Foreign bodies in the rectum – vegetables, tampons, table legs—'

'Now you're taking the piss,' Robin interrupts.

'I'm not. I'm really not. The literature reports one case of a traffic cone.'

'Oh, bugger off,' Robin mutters.

'But there's none of that here.'

'There was porn in the room,' he says.

'Yes, but no penile engorgement or semen consistent with a recent ejaculation.'

'Perhaps he hadn't got going,' Robin suggests, and Steph shrugs. 'Tox results back?'

'Not yet. Although…' She goes back into the mortuary and returns with a lidded glass jar with a green-beige liquid inside. 'Stomach contents,' she says with a smile, swirling it round in front of him.

Robin's own insides twist in response. 'Which was?'

'We'll have to wait for full analysis to be sure, but my first guess when I opened him up was that he hadn't consumed much food close to time of death. And it definitely contains alcohol.' She goes to open the lid. 'Want to take a sniff?'

Robin retches slightly and Steph laughs at his distress. She carries it back to the mortuary. When she returns she bends down to the small fridge next to a filing cabinet and gets out the milk, adding it to the stewing tea, and Robin is very grateful for the separation of the two refrigerated units. Steph passes him the mug, then sits down at her desk.

'Any unexplained marks on his body?' Robin asks, desperate to change the subject.

'No defensive or offensive injuries to the hands or arms.' She thinks for a moment, taking a sip of her tea. 'I'm sorry, Rob. I don't know what to tell you. You didn't find any disturbance in the room?'

'Nothing.'

They sit in silence for a moment. Robin's seen her at work before, surrounded by corpses and the smell of disinfectant, and it's where he's always found her oddly more attractive. Something to do with her confidence: her assurance and knowledge where she's clearly the expert.

'You want to go out?' he says, and is surprised by himself.

She raises an eyebrow. 'With you?'

'Yes, with me.'

'Out out? Not just for drinks and a casual shag?'

He knows she's baiting him. 'Out out. For dinner.'

'Okay.' She smiles. 'When? Text me and book a restaurant.'

He finishes his tea, and they walk together to the exit to the mortuary.

'What would compel a guy to do something like that?' he asks, almost to himself.

'The theory is the constriction of the neck heightens the sensation, making for a better orgasm.' She watches him as she says it, clearly observing his response. 'Or perhaps it's the thrill – more arousing because of the danger and the risk.'

'Hmm,' is all he can think to say as he pauses in the doorway.

'You want to try it when we go out?' she says, mocking him.

'Fuck off.'

'I might be able to pick up a traffic cone?'

'Seriously, fuck off.'

She laughs and he appreciates knowing someone who can tolerate this level of humour. 'So, nothing else weird from the PM?' he asks, mentally closing the case.

'Nope. Although…' Steph stops for a moment, thinking. 'Come and look.'

They go back into the main room, putting fresh gloves on and standing next to the body. 'Help me roll him.'

Robin goes over to the other side of the cadaver and leans over, putting his hand on the dead man's skin. It feels cold and slightly squishy, not unlike uncooked chicken. He pulls and they tilt him onto his side.

'See here, and here.' She points to the white patches on his bum. 'Post-mortem hypostasis, where blood pools after death. The pale areas are where the greatest pressure was applied.'

'So why here?' Robin asks, indicating the one on his upper back.

Steph frowns, and they return him face up, stepping back and snapping their gloves off again. 'That one I wasn't sure about. I assumed it was where he was leaning against the door.'

'But?' Robin stops. This is it; this is the sign he's been looking for. 'What if he was killed elsewhere?' he says, quietly.

'But you have the CCTV...'

'But what if?' Robin says. He feels a swell of excitement growing in his chest. 'How would you interpret your findings then?'

'I'd say the hypostasis was more consistent with a body which lay on its back after death...' Steph's thinking out loud. 'And...'

'What?'

'The time of death. It doesn't make sense.'

'What do you mean?'

'The PC that found him reported his body being cold and floppy. But if Jonathan Miller died the night before, as you're assuming, then he would have retained some rigor mortis. The body would still be stiff, even a little bit, until about thirty-six hours after.'

'Can't you run tests now?' Robin pauses in the doorway. 'This could be really important, Steph.'

'It's too late. The further away from time of death, the less accurate it all becomes. If we'd acted sooner it would have been possible, but not now. He's been dead for four days, and refrigerated for a lot of that time. There's no way I can tell for certain.' She sees Robin's determined expression and rolls her eyes in resignation. 'Fine. I'll have another look. But the cause of death is still the same, Rob. He asphyxiated. No doubt about it.'

'Just...' Robin's already backing away from her, starting to walk fast down the corridor. 'Don't file that report just yet.'

'I'm being pressured by the coroner,' Steph calls. 'What am I supposed to say?'

Robin turns back. 'Recommend an open verdict for the moment.' Steph shakes her head, disbelieving. 'Please?'

'Fine,' she shouts after him, but Robin's already running.

Back to the police station. Back to review the evidence.

17

'Butler, have you nothing better to do?'

Robin waits in front of his DCI, the file clutched in his sweaty hand. Freya's sitting next to him, up to speed on what Robin and Steph discussed in the mortuary.

'Guv, there's just too much about this that doesn't add up,' Robin begins.

DCI Neal Baker stares at him across the desk. 'You have a crime scene with no signs of foul play. Eyewitnesses saw the dead man up until he entered the hotel, something you also have captured on CCTV.' He rubs his salt-and-pepper goatee in exasperation. 'Data from multiple sources back this up, plus one of our own PCs saw the guy in a fish and chip shop. When *exactly* do you think he was murdered?'

'The pathologist says the normal signs of auto-erotic asphyxiation are missing, he had no previous predilection for this sort of stuff, the post-mortem hypostasis is dodgy so the body might have been moved, Steph can't be sure on time of death, and—'

'And who are you saying killed him? The wife? The wife with an alibi?'

'Maybe. The best friend isn't telling us everything.' Robin's acutely aware of how daft this is starting to sound. 'I just have—'

'A feeling, yes.' Baker taps his fingers on the desk. He looks to Freya. 'And what do you think, West?'

Robin told her not to come, he didn't want her to get caught up in this mission of his, but she insisted. He watches as a blush of red creeps up from the neck of her shirt.

'I agree with DS Butler, guv,' she says. 'Something doesn't feel right.'

Baker rolls his eyes. Robin's got a lot of respect for his DCI. An ex-boxer, Baker's once large muscular chest has given way to flab, but otherwise he's an intimidating figure. A strong black man, he's worked his way through the ranks, pushing aside every bit of institutionalised racism he encountered and proving himself through hard graft. He's an experienced cop, but he's more than that to Robin – he's a trusted friend. But today he's his boss. And a grumpy one at that.

He runs his hand over his shiny bald head. 'Fine,' he says at last, in his strong London accent. 'Look a bit closer. But do it on top of your normal caseload; I don't want your other investigations to suffer as a result of this ridiculous quest.'

Robin and Freya both stand up quickly, about to leave before their boss changes his mind.

'And you have zero budget, you hear me?' Baker shouts after them. 'Zero!'

'You should have stayed out of it, Freya,' Robin whispers as they walk quickly down the corridor. 'You didn't need to bugger up your reputation on this, too.'

'It's fine,' she replies quietly. 'It's important.' She stops in the corridor, and he pauses in response. Her face is solemn; it's clear how seriously she's taking this case. 'But Sarge,' she says. 'How are we going to find anything? Baker's right, we have nothing. It's the perfect murder.'

'The perfect murder?' he repeats.

'Yeah. Where no one has any idea who did it or why. Where they leave no clues, no exhibits, no lines of investigation. Where nobody even suspects it *is* a murder.'

But she doesn't wait for Robin's response. She smiles, her expression pinched. 'I'll get back on it,' she says, and hurries off, leaving him standing in the corridor.

Robin stares at her departing back. After the jubilation of Baker's agreement, Freya's words have shaken him. Because Robin knows all about perfect murders.

He knows only too well.

Part 2

18

Sunday

Robin wakes in the night with a jolt. His body is cold and clammy; the sheets are soaked with his sweat. But he can still smell it. He can taste it, the image from the dream so clear in his mind.

He lies in the darkness, waiting for his heart rate to return to normal. He forces himself to take a juddering deep breath in, slowly, then lets it out. He knows why this is happening. It's soon. The one date he tries to forget.

He gets out of bed, feeling the cold air on his damp skin. He knows he needs to wake up fully, get the image of the dream out of his head or he'll never get back to sleep. The digital clock next to his bed reads 2:36. He can't start the day at this time. He needs some rest.

He misses her.

But she's gone. Everything's gone.

He thinks of Liam. Does he feel like this? Does he struggle to get to sleep at night, wake in the black, body tensed up in knots? Liam's alone, just as Robin is, and he thinks again about calling him, extending a branch of reconciliation. He would love to see Liam, but still, something stops him.

He thinks about the days before. Before the accident, even before the kids. A carefree world where he and Liam and Georgia would spend Saturday night at the pub. Drinking pints, playing darts, chatting, laughing. Just whiling away the hours, assuming this would be something that would always happen.

Little did they know.

He pulls a jumper over his head then walks down to the kitchen and flicks the light on. He stands for a moment, blinking, in the middle of the tiled floor, feeling his bare feet get cold. He sees the mess left from his day of doing nothing: the sink piled with dirty dishes, crumbs, puddles of coffee, discarded spoons, pizza boxes, just left on the side. The floor feels gritty under his feet. He can't remember the last time he cleaned this place, or took any pride in his surroundings.

He listens to the noises of his world. The hum of the fridge, an occasional car going past in the road. The rain falling on the pavement outside. He knows that if he goes into the living room, everything there will be as he left it: the cushions discarded, an array of dirty mugs abandoned.

Saturday night, Sunday morning, and he stands in his boxer shorts, grubby sweatshirt, his hands by his side, his head bowed. He doesn't know why he came down here now. He just feels the empty hole in his chest.

Nothing changes. Nobody cares.

He feels so incredibly alone.

19

Monday

Freya faces Butler outside the interview room. Amy Miller is inside. They're recording this one: the paperwork is signed and the video ready to go.

Her boss stares down at her.

'Ready?' he asks.

'Sure you want me to lead?' Freya replies. Her voice wavers slightly. She wants to do this, but she's aware of how much is riding on this interview. They have one shot. As soon as her suspicions are raised, Amy Miller will ask for a lawyer and it'll be *no comment* from then on.

'She won't suspect you. Blonde hair, blue eyes, you're the picture of innocence.' He smiles, brief and flickering, then opens the door, holding it for her to go inside.

Amy looks up as they enter and sit down opposite. Her face is slightly confused, gaze shifting anxiously between Freya and her sergeant, waiting for someone to speak. She's wearing an expensive-looking cream silk shirt, lace bra just visible underneath. Her diamond ring shines in the overhead light as she fidgets with the delicate silver pendant around her neck.

'Thank you for coming in, Mrs Miller,' Freya begins.

'Amy, please.'

'Amy.' Freya forces a smile, willing it to seem natural. She hates this woman, and her anger sears like heartburn in her chest. 'I know this may seem strange,' she continues, 'but we wanted to talk again. Confirm a few details before we wrap up our investigation.'

'What do you need to know? I thought I gave you everything last time I was here.' Freya watches as Amy glances to Robin, but her boss keeps his expression neutral.

'Would it be possible for you to give us access to search the house?' Freya asks, nerves flickering in her chest. She knows they don't have enough for a warrant at this stage, and they are desperate to see what they can find.

'The house?' Amy's face twitches. 'Why? Jonathan was found in that hotel, wasn't he?'

'Yes, but we have some concerns around how he died. We'll be quick and respectful, we promise. We're just worried it might be suicide, and having a look around the house might help to rule that out.' Freya leans forward, as if sharing a secret with Amy. 'We know how awkward a verdict of suicide can get. With life insurance, and such.'

Amy's brow furrows. 'Life insurance, of course.'

'Any excuse, and those bastards won't pay out. So, you see, the sooner we can sort it, the better. For all concerned.'

'Yes, of course.'

Butler slickly pushes the required paperwork towards Mrs Miller, followed up with a biro. Amy reads it for a second, then signs an elegant swirl at the bottom. He pulls it swiftly back into the file.

Amy Miller turns her large doe eyes to Butler. 'Do you know when we might be able to bury him?' she asks. 'When will you...'

'Release the body?' Freya finishes for her. 'We don't know yet, unfortunately, Mrs Miller. As soon as we can.'

'I might arrange a memorial instead then,' Amy says quietly, almost to herself. She looks up at Freya. 'People are asking when they can pay their respects.'

'Of course, I understand,' Freya replies. But she doesn't. Why can't you just wait, you devious cow? she thinks. Why are you so keen to have closure?

But instead, Freya says, 'And tell us again about your weekend. What was Jonathan like? How was he acting?'

Freya listens as Amy Miller goes back over her movements across Jonathan's last days. She knows these by heart by now, and nothing differs. Freya asks for more names from Khalid Riaz's birthday party: Amy writes them down. Aware of the lack of food in Jonathan's stomach when he died, they ask about his Saturday-night pizza: apparently he ate it all. Freya asks again about Amy's whereabouts on the Monday and Tuesday, when Jonathan was dying in the Premier Inn, and Amy's note-perfect. Again.

'Had Jonathan ever mentioned trying something new? Sexually?' Freya asks. She and Butler have already agreed not to mention the threesome, her sergeant filling her in on his conversation with the escort the other night, but they want to see how far Amy Miller will go. How much she'll lie.

And, sure enough, Amy shakes her head. 'Never, no.'

'No sex toys, vibrators, that sort of thing?'

'No. Not at all.' The wife pauses. 'Do you think someone else might have been there? In the hotel room?'

'We don't know much at this stage,' Freya replies, dodging the question. 'But we will leave no stone unturned, we promise.'

And with that last sentence, Freya was one hundred per cent sincere. No stone unturned, you nasty bitch, she thinks, the smile still plastered on her face.

–

They let Amy Miller go.

'I honestly didn't expect her to say yes,' Freya says as the two of them watch her walk across the car park and climb into her white Audi. 'What docs that mean?'

Butler turns. 'Either she's got nothing to hide and we're wrong about her. Or she's arrogant enough to believe we won't find anything.'

'She might have disposed of it already,' Freya suggests, following her boss back into the station. 'And do we like the life insurance angle for a motive?'

'Let's try and get a warrant,' Robin begins, pausing as they hear someone shout from reception.

'Rob!'

They both turn, and Freya notices her skipper's expression change at the sight of the man walking towards them. His eyes narrow, his shoulders immediately tense.

'What are you doing here?' he snaps.

The man's tall and slim, short grey hair, dressed in a smart suit and tie.

'You won't return my calls, Rob, and I need to speak to you. You're never home. What do you expect me to do?'

Butler pulls the man to the side of the police reception, but Freya can still hear their conversation.

'You could get the hint and leave me alone, Liam.'

'It's this week.'

'I know it's this week,' Butler almost shouts. Then he catches himself and growls, more quietly, 'So what? You going to throw a party?'

The man recoils, hurt clear on his face. 'I was going to visit her grave, Robin. *Their* graves. And I wanted to know if you would join me. But it's clear how you feel.' The man turns, his shoulders hunched. 'I'll leave you alone from now on, Robin. Don't worry.'

He walks out of the reception, the double doors slamming behind him. The room is quiet, conversation stilled to an awkward hush.

Butler turns and walks quickly past Freya without a word. If Freya didn't know better about her immovable boss, she would think from the look on his face that he was about to cry.

20

When Freya gets back to the incident room, Butler is nowhere to be seen. She wonders about the visitor, who he was talking about. She's heard the whispers, some tragedy in his past. Apparently he was nicer before. Sorry you're stuck with him, her colleagues said.

But she's glad of the space after the interview with Amy Miller. It was difficult, to be so close to the woman and not spit in her face. Not shout: *what did you do to him? How did you kill him?*

Because she knows it was her.

The weekend was a struggle. Endless hours with nothing to do. Friends called, but Freya shut herself away. None of them know of her relationship with Jon.

When they interviewed Kal, Freya wasn't worried – Kal doesn't know about the affair. Nobody does. Jon had been insistent – he didn't want Amy finding out or, more specifically, knowing it was her. He'd been so adamant and she hadn't asked more, just gone along with what he'd said, not wanting to fess up anyway to the shame of her affair with a married man. She'd always felt reticent with her friends; most of them were married, and she'd known they'd disapprove. So none of them now would understand why she was such a wreck. None knew just how much in love she'd been.

But she spoke to her mum, bawling down the phone with snotty tears, until her mum threatened to drive up from Salisbury at that precise moment. 'No, I'm fine, don't come,' she said, sniffing loudly, not wanting her mother to suffocate her with her fuss. 'I'm fine. I just miss him, that's all.'

That's all. Master of the understatement.

Sleep still comes in bursts; she spends her waking hours crying in the dark, scrolling through the same photos and messages from him on her phone. She tried to get into his laptop, but she doesn't know the password – the door into his hidden world she's desperate to see, as if it holds the secret to his state of mind in those last few days.

Eventually she gave up and came into the office. She spent hours diligently working on Butler's backed-up caseload, typing up reports, filing away evidence.

There'd been another break-in on the Friday night to add to their investigation. Not that they had the capacity to actually do anything on it. That was the fourth now. This time the damage had stretched to graffiti: messy daubs across the previously spot-less living room walls. She ensured the initial house-to-house had been done by the PCs in the area, linking the statements to the correct file on the Record Management System. There was no useful intel, but at least the paperwork was up to date, any evidence logged and sent to the lab.

Butler was impressed Monday morning. He won't be so keen on you when he finds out what you're hiding, she told herself. That you were in love with the victim. That it's you he's looking for when he goes through the call logs on the mobile phone. The telematics from the car show Jon's trip to her house on Friday afternoon, but Butler has no idea where she lives, and they haven't focused on much before the party. Now she's buried the records in her drawer, telling Butler there's nothing of note. Another lie. Another crime, perverting the course of justice, to add to the potential charge of burglary that she's already committed. She's heard the voicemail from Robin on the secret mobile: a calm message asking the mysterious woman to call in to the station, to make herself known.

But it's too late. She's in deep now; she needs to follow it to the end.

She turns in her seat and looks up at the whiteboard where Jon's timeline is neatly written. He'd mentioned the party Friday night. She remembers he wasn't looking forward to it, although looking at the photo of him and Kal stuck up on the board, it looks like he was perfectly happy. Had he been lying to her? Another dishonesty to keep her close? To keep her happy while he fucked her?

She clenches her teeth, pushing away the misery threatening to turn into tears in the middle of the office. She looks at the photo, searching for the honesty behind his blue eyes. And then she frowns. She looks closer, squinting at the image, then turns and pulls it up on her computer screen, zooming it in to a point on the base of his neck, just next to the collar of his shirt.

She's aware of Butler coming back into the office, sitting beside her at his computer.

'Sarge?' she says, without looking away from the screen.

'Hmm?' He scoots up next to her on his chair.

'Here.' She sits back, chancing a look at him. He seems calmer now, the anger from earlier gone from his face. She points to the spot on the screen. 'See that mole?'

'Yeah? And?'

'He'd had that removed,' she blurts out. She remembers it clearly. Six months ago. The worry about possible skin cancer, the relief when the results were negative.

'How do you know that?' Butler asks. She feels him looking at her, her face growing hot.

'I…' Shit. Think, Freya, think. 'I noticed on the crime scene photos.'

He moves away to his own computer, clicking. She knows what he's doing but she doesn't dare turn around. She hasn't seen the shots from the hotel. She doesn't want to remember Jon like that, but there's no avoiding it now.

'Bloody hell, you're right,' Butler says from behind her.

She turns. But luckily he's done the same as her, blown up the photo so only pale skin is visible. And sure enough, there's a narrow silver line, where the mole should have been.

Slowly, Butler shakes his head, then pulls the photo of Jonathan and Kal down from the board. 'So this…' he starts.

'It's an old photo,' she finishes for him. 'That tweet is a lie.'

'And if that's a lie,' Butler continues, 'what else is?'

21

Robin mentally thanks Tripadvisor for the restaurant recommendation, as he and Steph walk across to their table. So far, he hasn't screwed anything up. He ironed a shirt, put on a suit, nice shoes, tried a tie and discarded it. He was on time to pick Steph up; he even remembered to open the car door for her, a gesture she raised an eyebrow at.

Steph had been busy over the weekend, so they'd agreed on Monday night. And as the time for their date approached, Robin found himself getting nervous. This felt right, a tiny step towards letting someone else into his life. And although he and Steph had done things in the past, if they were going to turn it into something more, he knew he needed to invest some proper energy.

The waiter holds the chair out for Steph and she sits. Robin notices she's made an effort too – her hair is shiny and down round her shoulders, and she is wearing a dress, rather than her standard after-work uniform of jeans and a top. She looks nice, and he tells her so.

'Just nice?' she says, teasing him.

'Better than nice. Beautiful.' This stuff doesn't come easy to Robin, and he finds himself stuttering over the words. He stares at the menu in his hands – thick white card, small black printed lettering. Like the rest of the restaurant, it's simple, clean and elegant. The lighting is low, the music gentle and muted. The waiters move effortlessly around, their voices no more than a low murmur.

They order. He can't resist the steak; she has something vegetarian. He asks about her day and she tells him about a post-mortem completed on a body fished out of a river. Neither baulks at such a disgusting conversation while they eat, and Robin thinks, this can't be normal.

The conversation turns to Jonathan Miller. It is inevitable, a shared interest, and work being the only thing going on in Robin's life.

'And Baker's letting you use uniforms for the search?'

Robin nods through a mouthful of steak. It was a hard sell for Baker to allocate more resources. But he accepted that leaving his DS and a DC to do a full recon of a house alone was going to take for ever. 'First thing tomorrow,' Robin replies.

'I can't believe she agreed to it. I wouldn't let police anywhere near my house without a warrant.'

'But you're part of this world. She's not suspicious.'

Steph points a fork at him. 'Are you sure she's not completely innocent?'

'I don't know, Steph. I don't. If she did do it, I have no idea how. She has an alibi for him arriving at the hotel. She was miles away when he died.'

'So maybe she didn't do anything?' Steph repeats. 'Someone else was complicit?'

'But who?' Robin shakes his head. 'The best friend's alibi checks out, and we still haven't found the mistress. Did you get any further with narrowing down the time of death?'

Steph looks apologetic. 'No, and I don't think we're going to.' She starts to explain in the face of Robin's grumpy expression: 'We use a lot of factors to estimate TOD – changes in muscle tone, stage of rigor mortis, level of decomp—' she counts them off on her fingers '—and these can all be utterly unreliable. Body temp is the only one that's vaguely useful, and that's still subject to problems such as clothing and temperature of the room.'

Robin remembers the chill in the hotel room that day. 'So what did you conclude for Jonathan Miller?'

'Nothing that tied up. Minimal decomp, but low liver temp. So the honest answer is, I don't know.' She pauses, putting her knife and fork together on the plate. 'Maybe tracking down this mistress is your best bet after all.'

'Easy for you to say,' Robin replies with a smile. 'Freya's been through everything with a fine-tooth comb. There's nothing. I'm beginning to think she doesn't exist.'

Steph shrugs. 'I'm just saying,' she replies, as the waiter clears their plates. 'Take all your assumptions away. Look at it from a different angle. And who knows what you might find.'

She reaches across the table and takes his hands. Hers are soft and warm; her eyes shine in the candlelight. 'Now, are we bothering with dessert, or shall we go somewhere else for a nightcap?'

—

Robin pays the bill. They get into his car. He starts the engine, his intention to drive to hers, but she stops him.

'Let's go to your place,' she says.

'My house?'

'Yes, your house. Unless you have a canal boat or hunting lodge I don't know about.'

They've never gone to his place before. Hers is nicer and, truth is, Robin likes it that way. He knows that the moment Steph steps in the door she'll be creating a view of him that might not be favourable. Sure enough, as they walk into the hallway, he can see her taking in the tired decoration, the dated patterned wallpaper he's never got round to replacing, the miscellaneous crap strewn about — spare screws in cereal bowls, receipts discarded on the side. It's not that he's actively untidy, more that he hasn't had the energy to sort it. After work, it's all he can do to slump on the sofa and make himself food. And nobody ever comes here anyway.

For the first time he's seeing it through someone else's eyes, and it's not pretty.

'Coffee?' he asks, and puts the kettle on, more as a way to distract than because he wants it. But then he feels her arms round his waist, and he turns to face her.

'No, thank you,' she says, and she leans up to kiss him.

He's never done this sober. But it's an experience he's welcoming. They stay in the kitchen for a while, just kissing, her hands finding their way under his shirt, a soft caress up his back. But he wants to get into that dress. Taking it off standing next to his grubby cooker seems wrong, so he stops, and leads her slowly up to his bedroom.

There are clothes on his bed – the discarded tie, his dirty shirt from work – and he pushes them onto the floor. He mentally calculates the last time he washed his sheets – after the unmentionable night with Liv – and deems it acceptable.

He kisses her again, stronger this time, and she's not hanging around, undoing enough buttons on his shirt so he can pull it over his head. He finds the cursed hidden zip at the side of her dress, and tugs it down.

This is new. A bra and knickers he hasn't seen before – he would have remembered *these*. But they don't last long, and nor do his trousers and boxers. They fall together on the bed, him on top of her, and for the first time their connection feels like it could be something more permanent. Something he'll want to do more often.

–

After, they lie on their backs on the bed, and Robin pulls the duvet across to keep them warm.

'Can I have that drink now?' she asks, running her fingers down his chest.

'Whisky or beer?'

'Whisky.'

He gets up to fetch it, feeling very naked, her eyes on him as he puts on a pair of boxers, then goes to the kitchen. When he comes back, she's pulled on his shirt, legs still bare, and is standing looking at the narrow bookcase in the corner of his bedroom.

He hands her the tumbler and stands next to her. She has a book in her hand, an old hardback of *Charlotte's Web*.

'What's the story behind this?' she asks, putting it back on the shelf.

He looks at the line of books. A few Famous Fives, a battered copy of Roald Dahl's *The Twits* and *George's Marvellous Medicine*.

'They were my sister's.'

'Were?'

'She's dead.'

He reaches down and picks up a photo frame. It's an old one, but his favourite. In it, Georgia is laughing with the twins balanced one on each knee – a chaotic shot, nobody's facing forward, nobody looking where they should be, but one that Robin's always thought summed them up the best. Full of love, and chaos, and laughter.

He holds it out to her, and she takes it.

'James and Alex,' he says, pointing to the boys in turn. 'They were two when they died. Georgia was thirty-eight.'

He can't bear to look at it any more, and goes back to sit on the bed. Steph slowly puts the frame back on the bookcase and joins him, pulling the duvet up to cover them.

'How did they die?' she asks quietly.

He looks at the ice cubes in his glass, and swirls the brown liquid. 'Car accident. A guy in an SUV ploughed into the side of them while they were stopped at traffic lights. Killed Georgia and James instantly. Alex was on the other side of the car, and he held on for two days in hospital before he died too.' Steph rests her head on his chest but he can't look at her. 'The guy was drunk. Three times over the legal limit.'

'I'm so sorry.'

Robin shrugs. There is no other response.

'What happened to the driver?'

'He got a concussion and a broken arm. The judge sentenced him to three years in prison, disqualified from driving for one, post-release.'

Steph takes a quick breath in. 'Why so short?'

'He pleaded guilty to a lesser charge of causing death by careless driving. CPS didn't push for more. The judge's remarks at sentencing were vague, although we believe he was sympathetic because the guy sought treatment for alcoholism afterwards. Both me and Liam – their father – spoke at the hearing about Georgia and the boys. But it didn't make any difference.'

Robin feels a flash of guilt for the way he treated Liam at the police station this morning. He knows he needs to apologise, phone, go round, something, but so many words have been said over the past year, the weight of them seems insurmountable.

'So, he's out of prison? The guy?' Steph asks.

Robin takes a long sip from his glass. The whisky is bitter on his tongue. Saying it all out loud hasn't helped. If anything, he feels worse. 'Can we not talk about it? I'm sorry, it's just...' He takes the last gulp from the glass, but continues to hang on to it, willing the ache in his chest to subside.

Steph leans up and kisses him lightly. 'It's fine. I understand,' she says.

–

Later, when they've turned off the light and Steph is sleeping beside him, Robin thinks of that man, the alcoholic.

It was Neal Baker that told him, at the time a detective inspector. He appeared next to him in the incident room, his face serious, then pulled Robin away to an empty interview room. Robin couldn't take it in at first. This beast of a man, standing in front of him, tears in his own eyes, telling Robin that his family was dead. He remembers Liam sobbing in the corridor of the hospital. Later, the two of them sat next to Alex's bed, his tiny body covered in bandages and wires, evidence of the heroic efforts to keep him alive that ultimately failed.

Weeks later, once Robin had returned to work, he read the incident report. The man, pissed out of his mind, drove into Georgia and the twins. And then he'd reversed and driven away, leaving them dying, alone, in the road.

He could have saved them. He could have called 999 and the emergency services would have arrived five minutes, ten minutes sooner.

But he hadn't. He'd driven away, and they'd died.

That man deserved everything that had come to him. And in that, Robin has no doubt.

22

Tuesday

Freya watches Amy Miller glare at them from behind her rain-spattered windscreen. Fuck off, bitch, she thinks, then pulls the collar up on her coat, ducking back inside the Millers' house. She wishes she would just leave. Why does she have to wait there? Staring at them?

They arrived at the prearranged time that morning. Freya had driven to Butler's house first thing, wanting to arrive at the Millers' in the one car so as not to look heavy-handed, and she found him reluctant to let her inside.

'But I need to pee!' she'd begged, that first cup of tea of the day having made itself known, and he'd grudgingly moved aside as she came face to face with the reason for his hesitation.

Steph had been finishing up a mug of tea in the doorway and Freya had stopped, mouth open.

'DC West,' Steph had said calmly, putting the empty mug on the side and picking up her coat.

'Dr Harper,' Freya had replied, her cheeks colouring, then dashing inside the bathroom. As she'd sat and peed, she'd thought about her boss. Dark horse, that Robin Butler, having a thing with the pathologist. It was strange to think about him being close with anyone.

By the time she'd finished, Dr Harper had gone and Butler was waiting impatiently for her in the open doorway.

'Can we go now?' he'd growled, and she'd not dared to ask him any more.

Now, Freya hears Amy Miller's Audi start up and drive away. Four of them stand in the Millers' hallway – her and Butler, and the two borrowed PCs, gloves and shoe covers already on. They both seem young, cocky in their new uniforms. One, tall and thin, a sprinkling of acne across his chin, introduced himself first as Mayhew. The other – PC Graves – is shorter, baby-faced, with a large grin.

They have Scientific Services on speed dial, evidence bags at the ready.

'What are we looking for, Sarge?' Mayhew asks Butler. Graves is hovering behind him, uncertain.

Butler's already told them about the nature of Jonathan Miller's death. 'Sex toys, porn, anything similar. Things that look out of the ordinary. Anything weird. You both start downstairs, I'll tackle the garage.'

Butler turns and leaves the three of them, and Freya waits as the two PCs grumble then go into the living room.

She hears the taller one comment as they go: 'Butler's weird, does that count?'

Graves gives a snort of laughter. 'You heard the story about him?'

Freya can't see them now, but she lingers, out of sight. Part of her knows she should go, but the other part is curious to find out more about her enigmatic boss.

'No, what?' She imagines the pair looking around nervously, heads together.

'Crawley joined the force same time as him. Said he was an alright guy then. Bit quiet, but alright. You know, few beers on a weekend, good bloke. But then a few years ago...' Their voices lower further and Freya has to strain to hear them. 'His sister and her kids died in this messed-up car accident, and after that he just went mental.'

She remembers the case, five years ago. It was discussed in whispers and glances in the incident room, a joint investigation between the CID and the SCIU, the Serious Collision Investigation Unit.

The PCs continue. 'What?' Mayhew asks. 'Like Hulk mental?'

'No, you wanker. Like shut down. Didn't talk any more. Heard he spent a few weeks in the Priory, and then when he came out he wasn't the same. Apparently his parents were already dead and the sister tipped him over the edge.' Freya hears a small chuckle coming from the PCs, and clenches her jaw in anger. 'You notice he won't let anyone drive him anywhere, always has to take his shitty Volvo?' Another snort of laughter. 'That's why.'

Freya grits her teeth. She wants to go in there, tell them off for being so insensitive, but she has no authority over them: she's the same rank, despite her detective status. But another part of her, a shameful part, doesn't want to defend him. To be associated with her sergeant's gossip.

She quickly walks away and up the stairs to the bedroom, their words echoing in her ears. If it's true, it explains a lot. Butler's air of sadness, his reluctance to talk. She saw his house this morning. It was hardly the residence of someone functioning normally: mess, dirt, everywhere. She spotted the unpaid bills on the side, the carpet that can't have seen a hoover in months.

She stands in the doorway to the master bedroom. In direct contrast to her boss's house, this room is pristine. The bed has multiple throw pillows draped artistically across the covers, the duvet pulled tight. Like the rest of the house, it's clean. Unnaturally so. She's beginning to agree with Baker. They're not going to find anything here.

She starts her search, going over the bedside tables, looking in drawers. It's strange, going through her lover's belongings in this way. She recognises jumpers he wore, shirts and T-shirts. One particular rugby shirt pulls her attention. It's a faded blue one; she remembers it from their first walk in the woods and now takes it out of the wardrobe, pushing it against her face.

And it's him.

The smell of him, the feel of the rough cotton, remembering the warmth of his chest when he wore it, and she starts to cry. It's too much; she shouldn't be here. She shouldn't be doing this.

She hears footsteps on the stairs and hastily puts the rugby shirt back, turning away from the door and drying her eyes with a corner of her cardigan.

'You find anything?' Butler's voice from the doorway.

She crouches down, her back still towards him, and busies herself in a drawer. 'Nope,' she replies. She pushes Jon's socks and boxers aside: nothing untoward underneath.

'No porn?'

'Not even a vibrator or a pair of handcuffs.'

She hears him sigh, and risks turning to face him. He's opened the wardrobe next to her, riffling through Amy Miller's clothes.

'She's probably removed anything already,' he mutters. 'We shouldn't have given her warning.'

'But what was the alternative?' Freya asks. 'We have no grounds for a warrant, no reason to arrest her. Anything in the garage?'

'Bagged up a few items. Duct tape, rope, things that might have been used to strangle Miller.'

'You think?'

He shrugs. 'Not really. A stab in the dark. Plus all their rubbish.'

Freya wrinkles her nose. 'Nice.'

'I know.' Butler turns and smiles at her. She feels a swell of affection for her boss, and a flash of embarrassment for not telling off those sodding PCs. He's obviously been through a lot and yet, here he is, trying his hardest to work out what happened to Jonathan. 'It gives us an interesting insight into this woman, though.'

'What do you mean?' Freya moves on to the chest of drawers, opening the first. It contains what looks to be exercise gear: tiny Lycra tops, folded neatly, rows of pink and purple and baby blue.

'I've been in loads of people's houses after a loved one has died – you too, I expect.' Freya nods. He continues, 'And few look like this.'

Yours doesn't, Freya thinks.

'This level of organisation and cleanliness – Amy Miller is meticulous, detailed. She likes things just so. If she has killed Miller, she's not a woman to leave evidence behind.' Butler shuts the wardrobe and stands frowning in the middle of the room. 'Plus, she agreed to this. She knows we won't find anything.'

'Nowhere you could store a dead body?' Freya asks.

'A chest freezer in the garage,' Butler replies. 'Come and see.'

Freya follows her sergeant down the stairs and through the house to the door leading to the garage. As they pass the living room, Freya looks in on the PCs who are still searching, now quiet, gossip time obviously over.

The garage is as methodically organised as the house. Large white boxes, labelled with their contents. *Tools*, *Spare Bulbs*, *Painting*. A posh-looking racing bike is propped up against one side, the freezer on the other.

Butler opens it with his gloved hand. Freya looks in, a waft of cold air hitting her in the face. It's full to the brim. Vegetables organised in white mesh baskets. Meals frozen in plastic boxes, descriptions written on the side in black pen. *Chilli. Spag bol. Casserole.*

Freya feels the disappointment. There's nothing interesting here.

'Sarge?' There's a call from the door and Butler and Freya both turn.

PC Graves stands, waiting for them.

'We have something,' he says.

23

The coffee shop is loud and busy, but Amy barely notices. She sits alone, empty mugs in front of her, hands shaking, although now she doesn't know whether it's because of nerves or the caffeine. She should have stayed. She should have made sure they didn't break anything, trampling through her house in their dirty shoes, although she knows they had little blue booties on their feet. That's worse somehow. Treating her house like a crime scene. Like she's done something wrong.

Of course, she knows it's going to be fine. Elimination purposes, they said, and that's what will happen. They'll find nothing, and they'll leave her alone. Still, she can't help but worry. People go to jail all the time. Innocent people.

She picks up her phone and calls a number. It rings, then goes to voicemail. She hangs up and tries again. This time he answers.

'I told you not to call me.' His voice is sharp.

'Kal, I need you. Please.'

There's a long pause. She imagines his face, those handsome dark eyes.

'Amy, please.' His voice is softer this time. 'I need some space. Jonny's death is…' He pauses again. 'It's too soon.'

He hangs up.

Amy picks up the cold coffee mug. The dregs inside are black and disgusting, and she stares at them, then lifts a hand to order another. She thinks about Kal. She knew he would need time. Jonathan was his best friend. But she mustn't let him slip away, not after all she has done.

Amy's proud of what she's achieved. She had a bad start in life, but she pulled herself out of the dirt-filled, shit-stinking council flat, leaving her mother and everything she associated with her behind. Amy knew that the things her mother had done to her were due to her own pathetic shortcomings. The beatings, the cupboard under the stairs, the cold baths. She'd avoided the worst of it, her sister receiving the brunt of her mother's abuse – and a better option for the punters. Skinny, tiny Amy had been no erotic fantasy, even for men as depraved as these.

Her mother was weak. Unable to get control over the alcoholism that eventually left her dead and rotting on the kitchen floor. She was not like that. Her, Amy Miller. She had the beautiful house, the respectable job. But it hadn't come easy. She'd had to make sacrifices to get what she wanted, and this was the hardest of them all.

She picks up her phone again, and pulls up a different number.

'The police are at my house,' Amy says when her sister answers.

'The police, why?' the voice replies.

'They think I had something to do with Jonathan's death.'

'But that's ridiculous. How did they get a warrant to search?'

'They didn't. I gave them permission.'

'You... Amy! Why did you give them permission?'

'I thought it would make me look guilty if I didn't!' Amy shouts. She feels people looking at her, and forces herself to stay calm. 'I need you to help me,' Amy adds, more quietly. 'I need you to find out what they know.' A pause. 'You can do that, can't you?'

A sigh at the end of the phone, and Amy knows she's won.

'Fine. Just this once. But Amy?'

'Yes?'

'Hire a bloody lawyer.'

Amy puts the phone back on the table, just as her next coffee arrives. She smiles up at the waitress.

'I said extra hot. This is barely warm.' The waitress scowls, and goes to take it away. 'And a chocolate croissant?' Amy calls at her back. 'Please.'

It's going to be okay, she tells herself. It's going to be okay.

24

Robin and Freya stare at the small black box in the PC's gloved hand.

'And where did you find this?' Robin asks.

The PC – Graves or Groves, Robin thinks his name is – points to the bookshelf. 'In there.'

It's clever, Robin has to admit. On the shelf among the boring hardback economics books was one that blended perfectly with the rest. But the middle of the book had been hollowed out, pages cut carefully with a knife, to conceal something inside.

'How did you even find this?'

The PC smiles. 'A trip down memory lane. I have this book myself but haven't picked it up in years. I studied finance at uni.'

'You did?' the other PC says.

'Don't be so surprised,' he retaliates to his colleague. 'Just because I found it, not you.'

As the coppers verbally swipe at each other, Robin considers the book in one hand, the black box in the other. It's a camera, a surveillance unit, with a tiny lens on the end of a thin cable, linking to a main box concealed in the body of the book. A small hole has been drilled in the spine, and now Robin holds it up to the light, looking through it. Robin's seen similar units on Amazon, but never one in use.

'And the video will be in there?' Freya asks, pointing at it.

'No, it would transmit the video to a laptop, via Wi-Fi,' Robin replies.

'Jonathan's laptop?'

'Maybe.'

There's no way Amy knew about this, Robin thinks. Unless she set it up to video *them*? He looks at the space where the book was, then at the room. Assuming the lens is wide enough, it would probably capture most of the lounge.

'Have you found any more?' Robin asks.

The PCs stop squabbling and shake their heads. 'We called you as soon as we found this one.'

The four of them start to look again, checking each book on the shelf thoroughly. There's nothing else there, but when they move into Jonathan's study, they find one more.

'We need his laptop,' Robin says, and they start up again.

But it's not there. A charger cable lies under his desk, still plugged into the mains, but no computer. Robin swears under his breath.

'Keep looking,' he says. 'We need those video files.'

–

Hours later, Robin sits in front of his television, empty Chinese takeaway boxes and bottles of beer in front of him, and thinks about the cameras. They left the Miller house pretty much empty-handed. The two cameras, bagged and tagged, now passed to forensics. No laptop. No spare phones, no porn, no dodgy sex toys that would indicate that either Jonathan or Amy had a predilection for such things. They took photos, the house at every angle. They took samples from the drains, from the large chest freezer, from the bath – Robin hoping for something that might show blood or drugs. Anything to indicate foul play. They even took the contents of their bins, ready for someone to filter through.

They couldn't find any trace of a document relating to life insurance policies on Miller, and Freya confirmed that the warrant to specifically request it had been denied.

'Baker wouldn't even put it through to a magistrate,' she relayed to Robin. '"No evidence Amy Miller's responsible, where's your reasonable grounds?"' she said in a passable imitation of Baker's London accent. "'It's no more than a fishing expedition. You can't just apply for warrants in the hope you find something".'

Chicken and egg, Robin thought angrily. Can't find the evidence without the warrant, and can't get the warrant without evidence.

Robin hates doing things this way. It's all wrong. You don't warn a suspect, then search a house to look for something to tell you what direction to take a murder investigation in. You do a search once you know what you're looking for. To back up a theory, to find evidence to convict. You don't wander round a house fruitlessly. Desperately.

And – as much as Robin hates to admit it – perhaps there is nothing to find. So someone had planted cameras. Assuming it was Jonathan Miller, it showed he didn't trust his wife. That isn't a crime. And without finding the video it produced, they have nothing.

Perhaps Jonathan's death really was an accident.

The doorbell rings, and Robin looks up in surprise. He looks at the clock: eleven p.m. Who comes round unannounced at this time of night?

He pulls himself up from the sofa and goes into the hallway, turning on lights as he goes. He opens the door, and Liv Cross is standing there.

She's dressed casually tonight. Tight blue jeans, brown knee-high boots and a light pink jumper, a coat over the top. She looks natural, pretty. And off duty.

'What are you doing here?' he asks gruffly. He inwardly curses himself for being so rude.

She looks embarrassed. 'I…' she starts. 'I was passing, and I saw your light was on. I wanted to check you were okay.'

'Come in.' Robin holds the door open and she walks past him. Her hair is free, curly, over her shoulders. 'Do you want a drink?' he asks.

He shows her through to the kitchen and she takes her coat off, draping it over the back of a chair.

'Wine? Beer? Whisky?'

She smiles. 'I'm driving.'

'Tea, coffee? Water?' he says apologetically. 'I have ice.'

'Water. Sure.'

He gets a glass and fills it from the tap, then pops a few ice cubes in from the freezer. He grabs himself a beer, then gestures through to the living room. But as he follows her, he tells himself a stern *no*. You dodged it last time, he thinks. Don't even think about sleeping with her.

'You working tonight?' he asks, more to make conversation than anything else, but then realises what he's said and regrets his words.

But she laughs. 'Yes, but not for Frankie. Some of my work is legal, you know. I also dance at For Your Eyes Only. You know, the one in town?'

'I know of it,' Robin replies.

She laughs again, and he thinks how pretty she is. 'I get that not many of your friends are strippers.'

Is that what we are? he wonders. Friends? But he doesn't say anything, just takes a swig from his bottle of beer.

'I was asking around for you,' she continues. 'About your strangulation guy.' She takes a sip from the glass, then places it on the floor next to the sofa. She undoes the zip down the side of her boots, pulling them off, then curling her feet up under her, making herself comfortable. 'I thought he might have tried things before. Made use of some of Frankie's other services.'

'And?' Robin asks, curious.

'Nothing. Nobody's heard of him. One girl did mention a guy into that sort of thing, likes to be choked while she stands on his testicles.' Robin flinches. 'But he was into dog leads and butt plugs. That's not your guy, is it?'

'Doesn't sound like him, no,' Robin replies. It just reinforces what Steph was saying – that auto-erotic asphyxiation is usually accompanied by other similar tastes. He takes another swig of beer.

'And you've never tried it?' Liv asks.

Robin inhales a little too sharply and beer goes down the wrong way. Liv laughs as he coughs. 'I'll take that as a no,' she says. 'Why not?'

'Why not?' he repeats, once he's got his breath back.

'Yeah.' She smiles across the sofa. 'You might like it.'

He shakes his head. 'I'll give that one a miss, thanks.' He goes to drink again, then realises his bottle is empty.

Liv gets up from the sofa. 'I'll get you another,' she says. 'Can I use your bathroom?'

He watches her go. This is odd, he thinks, her turning up out of the blue. He'd never have said they were friends. Apart from that one night last week, they've had no contact. And a prostitute being friends with a cop is certainly not a common occurrence. Confidential informant, maybe, but never friends.

But he's in no hurry to kick her out. Her company is nice, welcome in the echoing silence of his life.

He hears the fridge open, then the hiss as she takes the top off the bottle. She comes back into the room and sits down, this time slightly closer. She hands him the beer and as she does so he finds himself looking down her top, catching a glimpse of a lacy cream bra.

He forces his eyes away. You're acting like a little schoolboy, he tells himself.

'Anyway, you were saying,' she says.

'I was?'

'What are you into?' Her eyes are dark as she meets his gaze. He looks away again quickly.

'What am I into?' he repeats, caught off guard.

'All men like something,' she says, quietly. 'What about you?'

He frowns. He can't be talking about this. He feels a stirring in his groin and fidgets. Any more conversation and this is going to get very uncomfortable, very fast.

But she shows no signs of dropping the topic. 'That's assuming you like women, of course.'

'Yes, I like women.' He takes a large mouthful of beer.

'But what else?' She leans forward towards him. 'What's your fantasy? Threesomes, role play? Maybe you like it rough, handcuffs, a little slap here and there. You are a cop...'

He shakes his head. She's on all fours now, coming towards him on the sofa.

'Maybe a little domination,' she whispers. She takes the beer out of his hand, then pushes it against his mouth. 'Drink it,' she says, sternly.

She holds it up, and he does as he's told. Swallows once, twice. She's almost on top of him now, her face close to his, near enough to kiss him. She puts the bottle back to his lips. He takes a gulp, the last dregs gone, and she discards it on the floor where it lies on its side on the carpet.

She straddles him, her hands either side of his head, nails running through his hair. He wants to kiss her, but he can't. *He can't.* But then he realises it's not horny he's feeling now, it's something else.

His head feels muddled. He's tired, his eyes half closing. He forces them open, but he can't focus. He wonders how much he's had to drink. It wasn't a lot, surely. Not enough to feel like this. Not enough to—

And the last thing he sees before he passes out is her face. Her eyes, watching him. Closely.

25

Wednesday

Robin wakes on the sofa. He pulls himself to a sitting position, stretching out his protesting neck and back. Light filters in from behind the curtains. It must be morning, but he has no idea of the time. His head is pounding, his mouth dry.

He squints at the empty beer bottles on the floor, one on its side. He didn't drink that much, did he? He remembers Liv coming round, and glances about for any sign of her. But the house is silent, her coat gone from the back of the chair.

He's fully dressed, and for that he's relieved. So nothing happened, but what on earth... He searches his mind for any recollection of last night, but everything seems muddled and dark.

His phone rings and he searches around for it. He eventually pulls it out from the side of the sofa cushion and answers the call.

'Sarge? Where are you?'

'Home.' Robin squints at the time: 9:56. Shit.

'You just woken up?'

'Yeah. I...' He doesn't know what to say. This doesn't feel like a hangover, a level of confusion and memory loss that seems new. Yet... He struggles to articulate how he feels. He stands up, his phone still against his ear, listening as Freya chatters away. Apparently the cameras have been dusted for prints and compared to Jonathan Miller's. It's a match.

'Any other prints?' he asks, standing in his kitchen. He opens the recycling bin and looks inside. Two bottles, plus the two in the living room. Four wouldn't be enough for this level of hangover, surely? Fuck, he needs to stop drinking.

'All clear,' Freya replies. 'So it was Jonathan who planted the cameras.'

'Give me half an hour,' Robin says, then hangs up.

He continues to wander through his house. He remembers answering the door to Liv, but not a lot after that. He walks into the hallway, then stops. He stares at his bag, hanging where it always is, on the banister at the bottom of the stairs. But unlike normal, the top is zipped up.

Slowly, a feeling of dread building in his stomach, he opens it and looks inside. His wallet is there. He pulls it out; the cash is gone, but all the cards are in their usual place. He digs again. And there's his warrant card, still attached to its lanyard.

He breathes out a slow sigh of relief. Then looks again, and he realises that he has a problem. His investigator's notebook, the formal police record of all lines of enquiry and decisions on a case. The one for Jonathan Miller.

It's gone.

26

'What the hell is this?' Amy asks, holding up the flimsy purple notebook. 'I thought you were going to get something useful?'

They're sitting in Amy's kitchen, mugs of freshly brewed coffee in front of them.

'What did you expect?' Liv snaps. 'He's hardly going to let me log in to his secret police files, or whatever he uses.'

Amy sighs, and flicks through the pages. The man has the handwriting of a lobotomised spider, small scribbled black letters running into each other, most of it incoherent.

'It's going to take me ages to read this.'

'Well, next time get it yourself. He's going to know it was me; there's no way I'm going back.'

'I didn't tell you to drug the guy. I thought you'd just get him pissed.'

'Yeah, well, it was going to take too long.'

Amy leans back on the sofa. She sees Liv's face, scowling and angry. She knows she shouldn't be so harsh. 'I'm sorry, Livia. I'm sorry.' Liv's face softens a little. 'I'm just scared, that's all.'

Liv leans forward and gives her a hug. 'They know Jonathan's death had nothing to do with you. They're just fishing.'

Amy nods. She's been telling herself that. What could they possibly know? But they have already worked out more than she anticipated.

Kal told them about the escort agency, stupid prick. And they found Olivia. Now all they need to do is make the connection between Olivia and Amy, and questions will be asked. But Liv is right; it's going to be okay.

She looks at the notebook again. She flicks to the last page; she can just make out the writing. *Camera? Links to??*

Camera, what camera? She frowns. She flicks back again. A list of names, people from Kal's party. Jonathan's social media accounts. Something she can't make out about a buckle on a belt.

This is useless, she thinks, frustrated, feeling tears prickle behind her eyes. She knows Liv is watching her, her eyes sympathetic, and allows a few drops to leak out.

'Hey, hey,' Liv says softly. She leans forward and takes Amy's hand. 'You'll get through this, you'll be okay.'

Amy nods, but makes no effort to wipe away the tears. 'You won't leave me, will you?'

'Hey, Amy, I'm your sister. Of course I won't.' Liv gets up and fetches the tissue box, placing it in front of her.

'It's just, I'm so sorry about what happened between us. So sorry about pushing you away.'

Liv smiles, her expression soft. 'I'm back now, it's fine. And I'll do whatever you need. You know that. Do you need help to arrange the memorial? What can I do?'

Amy pulls a tissue out of the box and dabs at her eyes, suppressing a small smile. Jonathan's death has its upsides, she thinks. All previous ills forgiven, just like that.

'No, no, it's fine, that's all in hand. But you'll be there on Thursday? Please.'

'Of course.' Liv nods. Then Amy sees her pause. 'There was one other thing, Ames.'

'What?'

Her sister thinks for a moment, then goes to her bag and takes out her purse.

'I couldn't help but nick his cash, and this was caught up in the back of his wallet.' She takes out a small piece of paper and smooths it out on the table.

Amy leans forward to look at it.

It's a newspaper clipping, worn where it's been folded, edges ripped. It looks old, and well thumbed.

'Just some ancient investigation,' Amy comments, seeing the date. 'Why might he have this?'

Liv taps a long red-painted nail on the image. 'I was going to bin it, but then I recognised the guy in the photo. I knew him.'

'Who?' Amy reads the name below the black and white picture. 'Trevor Stevens?'

'Yeah. From AA. Back when I first started going. I heard he'd died. Some accident or something a few years ago.'

'Yeah. And?'

Liv's face is grim. She taps again on the photo. 'Read it.'

Amy stares at her, puzzled, then picks up the clipping, squinting at the old worn text. 'Says here he died in an accident – driving when pissed. So what?'

'I remember thinking at the time it didn't seem right. He wasn't drinking.'

'He was an alcoholic, alcoholics drink.' Amy can't resist the dig at Olivia, still unconvinced by her sobriety. She's so not interested in this. And all this talk of alcohol is making her thirsty. She glances at the clock – just past ten, that'll do – then gets up, takes a glass out of the cabinet and a bottle of gin from the cupboard. 'You want one?' she asks, deliberately.

But Liv's not listening.

'He'd been sober for over a year. And Trevor was one of the good ones. You know, the ones that took it seriously. I remember thinking, if he was drunk, there'd be no hope for the rest of us.'

Amy pours a large measure of gin, then a smaller one of tonic. She carries the glass back to the table, looking over Liv's shoulder.

'Says here they found the bits of a bottle of JD in the car.'

'But that's not right either.' Liv looks up at Amy. 'Alcoholics have a drink of choice. They stick to the same ones.'

Amy waves the G&T in Liv's face. 'So you wouldn't want this, then?'

'Fuck off, Amy. I just mean, ones we prefer. Trev was a vodka guy, maybe white wine if he was desperate. He wouldn't have gone for a bottle of JD.'

'People change,' Amy comments as she sits down. 'But why does this matter to me?'

Liv points, and Amy starts reading it out loud.

'Trevor Stevens had been released from prison one year before the accident,' she reads. 'After killing local mother Georgia Riley and her two-year-old twin boys in a hit-and-run while intoxicated.' She looks at Liv. 'Not a nice guy then.'

Liv gestures to the newspaper article again. 'Keep reading.'

Amy rolls her eyes. 'Georgia Riley is survived by her husband Liam and her brother... oh shit.' Amy looks at Liv, then back to the paper. 'And her brother Robin Butler.'

Liv raises her eyebrows at Amy. Amy feels a smile creep across her face.

'What does this mean?' Amy asks, but she knows already.

Liv shrugs wearily. 'If you want your favourite detective distracted away from his investigation into your husband's death,' she says, 'then I know how we can do it.'

27

By the time Robin gets to the station, it's gone eleven. As usual, the incident room is a hive of activity, and Robin manages to make it in without anyone noticing. But not so Freya. She's by his side the moment he sits down at his desk, handing him a coffee.

'You were right about the camera,' she says, without greeting. 'Digital confirmed it transmits to a remote location – probably a laptop or a phone. And there's nothing on his phone,' she adds before he can ask.

'No sign of the laptop?'

'None,' she replies, but he notices a slight hesitation.

'What?'

'Nothing,' she says.

He knows what she's thinking: that he's hungover, yet again. But he's not. He knows he's not. This doesn't feel like a normal hangover. This… absence, in his head.

He reaches into his bag and pulls out two beer bottles, sealed separately in clear evidence bags. He passes them to Freya.

'Send these to the lab. Get them to test the contents for drugs. Roofies, sedatives, anything.'

She looks at the labels. But she doesn't ask.

'What case shall I say they're for?'

'Put them against the Miller investigation,' he mutters, then turns away. He presses the coffee against his lips, the mere smell making him feel better. 'And thank you for the coffee,' he adds grudgingly.

She disappears and Robin tries to enjoy the peace and quiet. He wants to put the events of last night out of his head. Liv turns up, and he ends up blacked out, again. He wonders about that first night in the bar with her, but he remembers the sheer amount he'd put away. That had been alcohol, no doubt, but this time he knows he didn't drink that much. And she's stolen his notebook. But why? He keeps on coming back to that. What could the notebook possibly hold of interest to her?

The continuous bustle is starting to make his head worse, so he picks up his laptop and heads back home, leaving a brief Post-it for Freya. The drive is short but he can barely concentrate, and he feels an almost palpable relief when he gets inside his house.

He clears the mess off the kitchen table, then reconsiders and spends half an hour loading the dishwasher and doing the washing-up. The effect when it's done is cheering, and Robin makes a mental note to take better care of himself from now on. Maybe give the drinking a break for a few weeks, too.

He sets up his laptop on the table and gets to work. A few reports wait in his inbox, work completed since yesterday. There's not much of interest, but he spends the next few hours catching up on his neglected cases: reports that need writing, paperwork that needs logging. The homeless guy's post-mortem has been completed – unfortunate, but natural causes. He ties off any loose ends on the system, closing the case. It's mindless and repetitive, stuff he's done hundreds of times before.

His email pings, and he looks at it. Evidence logged, he reads, then a list of items taken from the Miller house the day before. *Three bags of recycling, three bags of general rubbish.* He notices nobody's offering to go through it, and he doesn't blame them.

Then another file. The body-worn video from PC Wallis, taken the night of Khalid Riaz's party. He clicks on it, then scrolls through to find the images of Amy and Jonathan at the chippy. Eventually, there it is.

Body-worn video is always so jumpy it's vomit-inducing, and this is no exception. But he can clearly make out Amy Miller's Audi, then her sitting in the front seat as the cop car pulls up alongside. An exchange of words, and he can see why the policemen decided to breathalyse her. Her eyes flicker from them to the fish and chip shop, and when she goes to get out of the car, she staggers slightly, then ends up leaning on the car door. But the result was clear: she wasn't even close to the legal limit.

But she's nervous, that much is obvious. The camera shifts as the police officer turns, looking towards the chippy. Sure enough, there's a figure standing next to the counter, but the video moves again and the image blurs. Was that Jonathan Miller? Robin rewinds the tape, and squints again. In that fraction of a second it's impossible to tell.

His phone buzzes, a text message from Steph.

Can you meet me? it reads. *4:30pm? Costa?*

He glances at the time. He could, he thinks, but he was late to work this morning as it is.

Can we do tonight? he replies.

I need to talk to you, Steph comes back straight away. *It's important.*

What's so urgent? Robin wonders. Then he feels a flash of guilt. Perhaps she knows about Liv's visit last night. But how? And nothing happened, he tells himself.

Robin replies, agreeing to meet her, then picks up his coat. He'll find out soon enough.

–

When he arrives at the coffee shop, Steph's face is serious. He can't have screwed this up so soon, he thinks. Even by his standards, that's impressive.

She stands up when she sees him, kissing him on the cheek. She's come from work, dressed in simple black trousers and a blue top. She's bought him a coffee already, a large mug waiting in front of her.

'You okay?' Robin asks.

She looks pale, nervous. She nods. 'Rob, listen. Something happened this afternoon that I need to tell you about.'

He's confused. 'Okay.'

'But if I tell you, I could lose my job.'

'So don't tell me.' He reaches over and takes her hand. It's hot and clammy. 'Steph,' he says. 'It's fine. I know how these things work.'

'Robin, they're thinking about reopening the inquest into Trevor Stevens' death.'

She blurts it out, a rush of words, and they throw him back in his seat, her hand dropping from his. 'What do you mean?'

'The coroner spoke to me this morning. He wants me to go through the original PM and pathology reports, review them in the light of new information.'

Robin feels his body grow cold. 'What new information?' he asks slowly.

Steph leans closer to him. 'Apparently there was an anonymous message. Someone emailed him this morning, questioning some of the findings from the original inquest.'

'What findings?'

'I don't know, he wouldn't say. But he wants to know if there's anything in it, before he formally reopens the investigation.'

Robin can feel the blood rushing to his head. He feels dizzy, confused.

'I know I shouldn't have told you, but it's your sister, Rob,' Steph continues. 'I didn't want you to find out another way and realise that I'd been involved.' She reaches over and takes his hand. 'Given everything between us.'

'Uh-huh,' he manages. The words feel thick in his mouth. He clears his throat. 'Thanks, Steph.'

He stands up, the chair making a sudden squeak against the low murmurs in the coffee shop. Steph reaches out to him, but he steps quickly away. 'I need to go back to work. I'll call you,' he adds hastily, then rushes out.

He hurries quickly down the street, back to his car. Breathing heavily, too heavily, his heart beating fast, his hands starting to shake. His legs feel weak and he stops, his back against a wall, head down, his hands supporting him on his knees.

He can't go back there. To the trial, the sentencing, the parole hearing. Every day, people talking about how his sister and the twins died. Constant reminders, of their pain, their last terrifying moments.

Trevor Stevens is dead. Good riddance. At the time, he thought, so that's it. The line in the sand. He got what he deserved, and Robin could move on with his life.

But it's back. And Robin has never been more terrified.

28

Freya walks the strange beer bottles down to the lab herself. As she goes, she looks at them through the clear plastic. Two normal glass bottles of Beck's, a small amount of beer still sloshing in the bottom, some on the sides of the plastic bag. What on earth is going on with Butler?

He looks worse than normal. His skin has a grey pallor, more than a few days' worth of stubble on his chin. His shirt is crumpled, his hair barely combed. Something's on his mind.

And as she walks back to her desk, he's gone.

'Have you seen Butler?' she asks the DC sitting next to her.

Her colleague points to a yellow Post-it note left on her desk. *WFH*, it says, in his small scrappy handwriting.

Alright for some, she thinks.

Freya logs on, but before she does anything she sees an email from the DCI's secretary. A meeting invite, for this afternoon – in an hour's time. And in the subject heading: Strictly Confidential. *Please do not notify DS Butler where you're going.*

Odd, she thinks. But it's more than odd. It's downright worrying. And the main thought that runs through her head is: they know. They know about her and Jonathan.

When they found the hidden camera at the Millers', Freya's first thought went to the unauthorised, very illegal visit to the house. That would have been captured on camera. But once the techies confirmed the feed went out remotely, probably to the very laptop she had concealed at her own home, she was reassured. But perhaps it went somewhere else.

She doesn't have to wait long to find out. An hour later, she stands outside the DCI's office. She's barely been here throughout her career, and now twice in a week. Keep your mouth shut, she remembers Butler saying last time, and she bears this in mind as Baker's secretary ushers her in.

'DC West,' Baker says, once she's sitting in front of his desk. She nods. 'I hear good things about you, and not just from Robin.'

'Thank you, guv,' she says, surprised her new boss has said anything complimentary in the small time that they've been working together. 'Butler's happy with my work?'

'Well, he hasn't complained,' Baker replies. 'And that's just as good where Robin's concerned. I need you to do me a favour,' he continues swiftly. He rests his hands, palms down, on the file in front of him. 'But it needs to be between you and I, West. No one else.'

'Of course, guv.'

He hands her the file; she looks at him quizzically. She opens it.

'This is the man that killed Butler's sister,' she says quietly. She glances up at Baker, and he nods.

'I need you to look into it for me.'

'But... but...' she begins.

'The coroner wants us to do some digging, on the quiet.'

'But this was an RTA.'

'That's what we believed, yes.'

'What we believed?'

Baker sighs. 'We need to be sure. It would be embarrassing if the coroner has to reverse his decision, so he doesn't want to reopen the inquest unless we find good reason.'

'But...' Freya pulls herself together at last. 'I can't do this. I report to DS Butler.'

'You've only worked for him for the past week or so, and he can do without you for a few days. Everyone else is stretched to capacity, West. You're the only one vaguely free.'

'But what about the Jonathan Miller case?'

'That can keep.' Baker slumps back on his chair; his face is grim. 'Listen, Freya, you know I don't hold much stock in this murder theory of yours, but if anyone can find something, Butler can.'

'But you don't want me to tell him about this?'

'Not yet, no. He has…' Baker pauses. 'He's been through a lot, and nobody followed the Stevens inquest more closely than Robin. Let's just say I don't want to open old wounds for no reason.' Baker leans across the table again, and Freya feels herself wilt slightly in his stare. 'Will that be a problem?'

'No, guv, absolutely not.'

Her DCI clasps his hands together with satisfaction. 'Good. I'll tell Butler that you've been reassigned for a week, some boring admin project that he won't question. Report to me, and only me. And you can speak to Dr Harper.'

'Steph's on it?'

'She's reviewing the medical findings. Between the two of you, I have faith you'll find anything we missed. If it's there.'

He nods and turns away. Freya takes that as her cue to leave.

She stands out in the corridor and looks at the file in her hands. She feels a slight thrill of excitement. This is hers, and hers alone. Her own little investigation, and a perfect chance to prove herself. It's going to be fun.

If only she didn't have to lie to her boss. If only she didn't feel so damn disloyal.

29

Robin walks away from the coffee shop in a daze. Someone knows something. But what? What could they possibly know?

He drives home, as thoughts rush through his head. He parks badly, almost hitting the cars either side. With shaking fingers, he opens the door to his house, locking it behind him. He walks quickly up to his bedroom, closing the curtains, then, fully clothed, he bundles himself into his bed.

When he wakes, it's dark. His house is silent. He feels hot, fully dressed under his duvet and kicks it off, lying there for a moment in the black. He has no idea what time it is. He's left his phone downstairs; he feels weary, too tired to pull his head up.

He's felt like this before. A week after Georgia and the twins died, he remembers the overwhelming feeling of nothing. Not despair, not depression, just a blank where feelings should have been. He had no energy to eat, to get up, to answer his phone. In the end, Neal Baker came to his door. His boss, the big man himself, broke in and found him, skinny, weak, lying in his filthy house. Baker made calls, efficient and decisive, and checked Robin into the Priory.

Robin emerged a month later, prescriptions for different drugs clutched in his hand. Better, but still grieving, and Baker allowed him back to work under his watch, where Robin had stayed. But he knew Baker still kept a close eye on him, ready to shift him to administrative duties or sign him off sick if required.

And he didn't want that. He wanted to stay on the job. It was the only thing that kept him going through the trial and the sentencing of Trevor Stevens. Kept him moving, kept him distracted. Until now. It's back, and thrust into his face.

Robin knows he can't let it happen again. He pulls himself up to a sit, then switches the light on. He feels sweaty, and stands up, undressing as he walks, letting his clothes fall to the floor as he goes to the shower.

He stays there, hot jets washing over his face, pulling him back into reality, until the water turns cold. Then he gets dressed: an old Iron Maiden T-shirt, tracksuit bottoms, socks, hoodie. He feels okay. Awake. Ready.

He goes into the hallway, then opens the door to his spare bedroom.

The shard of light expands as the door opens wider, illuminating a cross section of the floor. A perfect triangle, showing first the dark grey carpet, then the bed in the centre. He switches the light on.

To the casual observer, it's no more than a boring spare room. Large double bed, made up with pale blue sheets and a duvet. Curtains on the window. Shelves on the far side, empty. But then you might start to see the small details. The two pictures on the wall are cartoon paintings of dinosaurs. The corners of the bookshelf are protected with see-through bumpers, the plug sockets are shielded with white plastic covers.

Robin doesn't go into this room any more, but he needs to today.

He walks in, then reaches under the bed and pulls out a large, flat box. He sits down on the duvet, places it next to him and takes the lid off. Slowly, bit by bit, he takes the contents out.

This is where he put it all. The memories he couldn't bear to look at. Photos of him and Georgia, aged eight and ten, grinning, ribs showing through pigeon chests, standing next to a sandcastle on the beach. Older, teenagers, New Year, drunk. Him, smart in an usher's suit, next to Georgia, looking so, so beautiful at her and Liam's wedding. Then, him with the twins.

Oh, that day. He had the call from Liam – a garbled message while he was at work. 'They're here,' the voice said. 'The twins, they're here.'

He phoned back, spoke to his sister. Alex and James, she told him. Tiny, early: four pounds ten, and four pounds five. In the neonatal ICU, but they're fine, she said, her voice heavy with emotion. They'll be fine.

When at last he was allowed to hold them, he looked down at their tiny faces and felt nothing but pure love. One resting each side, they were small enough that their entire bodies ran down his forearms. They smelt of milk, and the hand sanitiser he had to coat himself with. They moved slightly in their tight swaddles.

'They're beautiful,' he said to Georgia, his voice husky with barely contained tears. And, by god, he meant it.

He watched them grow. They were his family. His parents dead, they were his *only* family – Georgia, Liam and the twins. Georgia and Liam had at first tolerated his presence and then, when they learnt he could be trusted, they were grateful, letting him babysit. Two babies are a handful, and none more than these two. Insanely inquisitive, they'd stick their fingers up his nose, grab hold of his ears, cackle when he blew raspberries on their tiny chubby stomachs. Then, when they were bigger, he'd take them to the park. Herding cats, running around after a football, their little podgy legs pounding furiously across the grass. Georgia would sometimes join them, watching from afar, laughing, then racing across for reassuring kisses when one of them inevitably fell over.

Converting this room, his spare room, was Georgia's idea.

'What else are you using it for?' she said. 'Then they can come and stay with you.' She looked at him with a knowing smile. 'We're going to need all the help we can get when the baby comes.'

And she held out the scan photo. A tiny black and white blurry image, and he knew what it was.

'Only one this time,' she said as he hugged her. 'Thank goodness.'

She was six months pregnant when she died.

He feels the pain throb in his stomach. A feeling he's done so well to block out, putting their photos in this box, never looking at them, never thinking about them. But what good has that done him? They come back, in his dreams, and he wakes, his face wet with the tears he doesn't allow himself to cry during the daytime. He blocks out that emotion, but with it, he ignores any other feeling. Of happiness, of joy, of love. For the fear that he'll experience it again.

Because these kids, these perfect, beautiful boys, gave him a small, sneaking look into a future he hadn't considered. The idea that he could be a father. That one day he would meet someone and have kids of his own. And that, actually, this was something he wanted, that he'd be good at.

He doesn't think that now.

He picks up another photo from the box. This time, one of him and Liam. He didn't just lose a sister and his nephews that day. He lost a brother, too.

Liam is nothing like him. Older, a sensible, office-based man, at first Robin kept his distance. Georgia would force nights out on them, making Robin take him to the pub. 'My favourite boys,' she'd say. Then, whispered: 'I know you'll like him. One day.'

They had nothing in common – but her. And of course, Georgia was right. Robin did get to like Liam. Love him, even.

Liam wears his heart on his sleeve. He liked to envelop Georgia in huge hugs, literally sweep her off her feet. Robin knows he himself has been described as a cold fish. But he liked Liam's embraces, not that he'd ever have admitted it.

But Robin and Liam don't talk now. Not since... well. Robin puts the photo down swiftly, then replaces the others in the box. But before he puts the lid back on, he reaches inside again, and pulls out two small purple elephants, placing them on the bed next to him.

Robin bought them when the twins were born and they lay in those tiny incubators, keeping watch when they were so little. And as they grew, the elephants were always clutched in their hands, their ears sucked into their mouths until Georgia could bear it no longer and they went in the wash.

Liam gave Robin the elephants at their funeral. 'You should have these,' he said. 'They were their favourites.'

'No, keep them,' Robin replied, pushing them away.

But Liam insisted. 'They used to say "Rob-Rob give us".' His voice cracked as he said it. 'They loved them because they reminded them of you.'

Robin hesitates, then picks up the elephants, holding one in each hand. Their colours have faded, washed into obscurity, their fur worn. And slowly Robin lifts them to his nose.

He can still remember their smell. That warm, biscuity, malty aroma, as they put their little faces next to his, their pudgy hands on his cheeks.

And oh *fuck*, how he misses them all.

The emotion hits him like an avalanche. Everything he's ignored for so long, everything he's pushed away since their deaths. He can't breathe. He can't see.

He rests his forehead against the cool duvet; his arms go up over his face as he collapses on the bed. He lets out a howl – a cry of pain, of pure anguish that comes from deep within his chest.

And, the two elephants clutched in his hands, he curls into a ball and sobs.

30

Thursday

Appropriately enough, the day is cold and grey. A layer of drizzle hangs in the air; it settles on Robin's hair, creeps under his coat. He pulls the collar up higher, and frowns.

He awoke early. His eyes puffy, his emotions raw. A low strain of light was drifting in through the gap in the curtains and for a moment he lay in bed, looking at the triangle of asphalt sky. Georgia wouldn't have wanted this for him. This half of a life. This mess that had become his daily existence.

He got out of bed and walked into the bathroom, opening the cabinet door and taking out a half-used box of Fluoxetine. He pushed two pills out of the packet and downed them with some water. He hadn't taken them for the best part of a year, but after last night, today seemed the right time to start again.

He had a shower, got dressed in the only clean clothes left, and came here.

He could have done without being at a funeral today. Although, strictly speaking, this isn't one – Jonathan Miller's body still being firmly ensconced at the mortuary. It was a strange decision on Amy Miller's part, holding a memorial prior to the body being released. He wonders what that says about her – guilty or not?

He and Freya stand at the back of the graveyard, watching the mourners arrive. A dreary procession in greys and black, they shuffle slowly into the church. Robin can hear quiet organ music from inside.

A large black BMW pulls up, and Khalid Riaz gets out. Everything about him screams money – from his black wool coat to his crisply creased trousers and shiny leather shoes. He is the opposite of Robin, conscious of the creases in his shirt, the parts of his collar where the seams are starting to wear out.

Freya has put on a better show. She has on a smart black jacket, a neat shift dress underneath. Black tights, high black heels. She looks nice, he has to admit, her long blonde hair loose down her back. She hasn't said much since they arrived, her face fixed in a stern expression.

Kal walks past them, then double-takes before nodding and moving on without further acknowledgement.

'I hear you're leaving me,' Robin whispers to Freya.

She turns, her mouth open. 'Baker called,' Robin continues. 'Some admin assignment he wants you to work on?'

'Yeah, sorry,' she mumbles. 'It shouldn't be for long.'

Robin protested down the phone that morning, but Baker was insistent. 'A few days,' his DCI said. 'You'll cope.'

It was going to be tight, Robin knew, but what could he say? Directive from on high, Freya was only obeying orders. But even though it's only been just over a week, strangely Robin feels slightly bereft at the thought of her not being around. Like someone else has abandoned him.

'There's the sister,' Freya says, changing the subject and nodding towards the back of a woman in a flowing grey dress, tall and elegant. Robin's breath catches in his throat.

'Whose sister?' he croaks.

'Amy's. Olivia Cross, her name is.' Freya stares at him. 'Her alibi for Monday night.'

Shit. It all makes sense now. Liv is Amy's sister. How could he be so stupid? Robin thinks, a bad feeling growing in his stomach. How could he have allowed a suspect's sister to get so close to him? To come to his house, steal confidential case files out of his bag. Of all the mistakes to make, this is a fucking bad one.

Liv walks down the path towards them but doesn't stop, just acknowledges Robin with a small smile.

Freya catches it and turns quickly towards him.

'You know her?'

'She's the tom I was telling you about. The one from the bar? Works for Frankie?'

'Oh!' Freya stares at Liv as she goes into the church. They follow. 'I didn't realise.' Then she clicks. '*You* didn't realise.'

'No,' Robin says, and leaves it at that.

He remembers their funeral. Georgia and the twins. Two tiny coffins, next to their mother's at the front of the church. The cruel irony haunted him: that the twins, who had been together their entire lives – in the womb, in the same cot, holding hands – were separated when dead. But everything about that day was wrong. Friends Georgia hadn't seen in years, ones he knew she didn't even like, dabbing at their eyes. Liam, grey and crying next to him, Robin unable to muster the emotional reserve to comfort his brother-in-law. And life continuing, when his whole world had ended.

But then Robin notices people turning, the low, murmured conversation coming to an end, dragging him back to the death at hand. Robin looks behind him: a long procession of people in black is filing into the church.

Amy Miller has arrived.

31

Freya's just about holding it together. She's not thinking about Jonathan. She can't. If she associates the man she loved with the people in this church, with the things they're about to say, she'll lose it.

And if she starts crying, she won't be able to stop. And then Butler will know.

She watches as Amy Miller walks down the aisle. She's dressed completely in black – pencil skirt and a loose silk blouse, tucked in at her tiny waist. People reach out and comfort her, and she smiles gracefully. Her heels make sharp clip-clop noises on the stone church floor. Her make-up is minimal, her hair tied back in a small ponytail at the nape of her neck. The perfect epitome of a grieving widow.

An older couple walks next to Amy, arm in arm, their faces ashen. With a flash of pain, Freya recognises Jonathan in their features. His father is an older version, the same eyes, the same curly hair, his now thinning and grey. Her throat tightens as she thinks about what Jon would have looked like as he grew older. Not now, she tells herself, clenching her hands into fists and looking up at the roof of the church. Don't cry now.

A hush falls across the crowd. The vicar walks up to the front and talks about God, then reads a passage from the Bible. Jon wouldn't have given a shit about this, Freya thinks. He was apathetic about religion, agnostic at best. He wouldn't want to be remembered in this church.

Freya feels a curious detachment from the proceedings. She knew Jon better than many of the people here, yet she's right at the back, and nobody has the faintest idea who she is.

Kal stands up, walking to the front and clearing his throat. He starts to talk, slowly at first, telling a story about their university days. How they met, a drunken brawl, Jonathan trying to break up the fight and getting punched in the process, nearly arrested by the police. Kal calls him Jonny, almost too casual for the persona that Freya knew. People laugh at the story, but it's restrained. A noise made because they think they should, rather than an expression of real humour. What story would Freya tell, given the opportunity? What would she say?

Maybe she'd tell them about the time he broke into her house. A crash from the living room, in the middle of the night, her hand hovering over her phone. And then a recognisable voice: 'Oh, shit.'

She went downstairs and switched the light on, to find Jon blinking in the middle of the room.

'I broke your lamp,' he said apologetically, looking at the pieces in his hand. 'Your window was open,' he added, as if that was a valid excuse.

He looked so comical, so completely unthreatening and unlike any burglar she'd ever seen, that she couldn't help but laugh.

'I nearly called the police,' she replied. 'Why aren't you at the conference?'

'You are the police! And we finished a day early. I couldn't wait to see you. I…'

'What? You stupid man!'

'I love you.' He looked at the floor as he said it, bashful. 'I just wanted to tell you that.'

She was so caught off guard, standing in front of him in her pyjamas, that all she could do was utter, 'And you couldn't have rung the doorbell?'

She would tell everyone here, this congregation who don't know her, how she loved him, more than anybody else. How she eventually told him she loved him too, that night, and how she bunked off work the next day and they spent a blissful twenty-four hours doing nothing more than enjoy each other's company. Because that was the pleasure of being with him: she felt no pressure to put on airs, to try and be interesting or fun, or some other version of herself that she'd been with other men. He liked nothing more than to sit, her legs rested on his on the sofa, and read a book, him absent-mindedly wrapping her hair round his fingers.

She smiled more with him, laughed more. She loved the creases round his eyes, the curls in his hair when it dried after a shower. Even the way he bit his nails when he was thinking.

But she can't say any of that, because she doesn't exist.

To take her mind off Jonathan, she starts looking around the church at the other mourners. Most of them are Jonathan's age, she assumes from school, or university or his job. Some are older, maybe relatives. She knows he was an only child, but maybe some are cousins. It's a good turnout, and she's pleased. Jon was loved, and not only by her.

A different air falls across the church. Everyone is silent; nobody moves as Amy gets up and stands at the front. She doesn't have anything in her hands, unlike the other speakers. No crumpled piece of paper, no soggy tissue. She stands straight and tall.

'She's so strong,' Freya hears the woman in front whisper to her friend.

The friend nods. 'So beautiful.'

Freya looks forward at Amy Miller. And she is. Beautiful. Even she has to admit it. She has a fragile, china doll quality – slender arms, slim waist, high cheekbones.

She takes a deep breath in, then starts to talk.

'I met Jonathan at a nightclub. I didn't like him at first.' She looks out to the church, and smiles. People laugh. 'He knocked into me, spilling my drink. He apologised, offered to buy me another. I was about to say no, but then his friend came over, and I fancied his friend.'

Heads turn, looking at Kal. Kal smiles, shrugging.

'But Jonathan soon won me over. He wasn't like the other guys – he did what he said he was going to do. He was solid, reliable. He was my rock.'

She looks downward, suppressing a tear, then takes a shuddering breath and continues.

'I don't know what I'll do without him.' She looks out to her audience, a single solitary tear rolling down her cheek. She brushes it away with long, delicate fingers. 'As you all know, Jonathan and I weren't blessed with children. He would have made a wonderful father—' murmurs of assent from the room '—but it wasn't meant to be.' She looks skyward. 'God obviously had other plans for us. For him. But now, I just can't understand what that plan could be.

'Except I know what Jonathan would say.' She smiles, beaming. 'Be happy, Amy. Go on, live a happy life. And never forget me.'

She looks at the huge photo, displayed at the front of the church. 'I'll never forget you, Jonathan.'

Amy finishes, then steps down from the podium. Freya suppresses an urge to slow clap.

There are more murmurs from the room. 'That was wonderful,' the friend whispers in front of Freya.

Butler leans close to her. 'Laying it on a bit thick, don't you think?' he whispers into her ear.

Freya frowns. She knows what Jon would say, and it wasn't the pious, trite words coming from Amy's mouth.

Catch the bitch, he'd tell her. *Catch the bitch that killed me.*

32

Amy feels eyes on her as she walks out of the church, Jonathan's mother on her arm. His parents have aged markedly since she last saw them, the effects of their only son's death clear on their faces. She feels a pang of sympathy, but it quickly fades as she basks in the attention. It's all gone as she planned. The flowers, the hymns, the speeches: all perfect.

After, they eat crustless salmon sandwiches and soft, delicate pastries. She murmurs words of thanks to the people who come and talk to her, sharing their stories, saying how much Jonathan will be missed, how wonderfully she did today. But she doesn't need their affirmation; she knows how brilliant she was.

The detectives have gone. They leave without a word, and she feels a certain impermeability. They can't touch her at his memorial. They can't ask their ridiculous questions, not today. But she felt their stares, their judgement.

She walks into the kitchen to instruct the staff to pass round more bottles of wine, and stands there, watching the mourners through the door.

For a while Amy suspected Jonathan had been having an affair. But he'd been careful, never leaving his phone unattended, always shoved in his back pocket, always locked. But it would beep, and he'd smile. She'd ask why and he'd say it was Kal, but she knew. The response for the detectives when they told her was no more than an act. Perfectly executed. She knew there had been another woman.

And what better time to work out who it was than at his memorial.

She knows she will be here. Amy posted the time and date on social media. She even put a notice in the paper, wanting to ensure everybody attended. She looks at the women in the room, feeling anger beginning to grow, tensing in the bottom of her stomach. But nobody stands out.

None of these people looks sufficiently upset to have been in love with Jonathan. Maybe she was wrong. Maybe he had been faithful to her. She glances back into the room where mourners are starting to move away and Amy hates them all. Who are all these people, these friends? Where have they been for the past ten years? Not in Jonathan's life, she knows that.

'Babe?' Liv comes out into the kitchen. 'You okay?'

Amy forces a smile. 'Fine.'

'I noticed the cops were here. Did they say anything to you?'

'No.' Amy glares at her. 'Your plan obviously hasn't worked,' she growls bitterly. 'The only thing I could see while I was up there was that detective's ugly face staring at me.'

'I can think of worse people to stare at you,' Liv says. 'He's not bad-looking.' She's trying to make Amy smile, but it's a wasted effort.

'Not every guy is there for you to screw and make some extra cash, Olivia,' she snaps back.

Liv recoils. 'People are starting to go, they want to say goodbye,' Liv says quickly, then leaves Amy alone.

Amy stares after her, then looks out into the room. She pushes down the bile, the feeling of hatred towards the people eating her sandwiches, drinking her wine. Gawkers, that's all they are. No better than the people who rubberneck at the scene of a road accident. They're just here for the misery, to make themselves feel better.

But she pulls a smile back on her face and goes out. Soon, this will be over. The detectives will realise there's nothing to find. The body will be released, and they'll be able to bury Jonathan properly.

And she'll move on. To her new life. To the next part of her plan.

33

Robin and Freya part ways outside the church, Freya saying she's going to start on this new assignment from home. He wonders briefly what Baker's got her working on, and watches her walk back to her car, her head bowed, shoulders slumped. She seemed more downcast than usual today, and he remembers her comments at the beginning of the case. Freya knew Jonathan Miller, didn't she? And he realises he never asked how.

He gets in his own car, but he doesn't drive towards the police station. Jonathan Miller can wait. There is somewhere else he needs to be.

–

Robin hasn't been back here for over a year. In that time the trees have grown, the paths have been tidied and a smart oak board has been erected at the entrance to the woodland.

West Downs Natural Burial Ground, it says, in large carved letters.

He zips up the front of his coat, then walks down the path. He knows where he's going.

Twenty years ago, this area was no more than a large field. Small saplings had been planted at regular intervals and he remembers standing there, dew seeping into his trainers.

'Are you sure this is the place?' he said to his sister.

Georgia nodded. 'I remember Dad mentioning it. He said it was a good idea. Of course, he didn't meant it for himself, but...' Her face crumpled and Robin leaned over, putting his arm tightly round her shoulders, pulling her close.

Their mum was already dead. He doesn't remember much of her – a woman with long straight brown hair and a broad smile. He struggles to distinguish the images of her in his head: genuine memories or ones taken from the many photos their father had shown them. Robin had been eight when she'd died. Ovarian cancer, and the aggressive kind.

And from then on it had been the three of them. His sister, only ten, forced to grow up fast, cooking and looking after him while their dad was at work. He'd done his part, working in menial jobs to pay his way through sixth form and university. Until a gasping call late at night from Georgia told him their father was dead. Heart attack. Nothing anyone could have done.

And they buried him there. Ashes in an easily decomposable cardboard box, a small wooden plaque noting his spot.

Robin stands here now. The oak marker has aged with time, dirty and worn, and Robin bends down, running his fingers over the carved lettering. *Gordon Butler. Died August 2000.*

And Georgia was right, of course. The woodland has grown into a beautiful spot. Even in the grey drizzle, the leaves provide a dappled canopy of greens and browns. It's peaceful, only the gentle rustling of the wind in the trees, and the flap of a disturbed pigeon. Robin has always had the intention to move his mother's ashes from the more formal graveyard in their hometown, but he's never got round to it. He makes the resolve anew in his head. They should all be together.

Robin hears footsteps and turns towards the sound. A tall man is walking towards him, head bowed, a small blue flowering plant in a pot in his hand.

'I hoped you'd be here,' Liam says when he's closer. Robin notices he doesn't reach out a hand or offer a hug as he would have done in the past. Robin doesn't blame him.

His brother-in-law walks past him to the next tree and places the pot plant at the bottom. He takes a trowel from his pocket, digs a small hole, then pulls the plant from its pot, placing it in the dirt. He pushes the mud back down hard with his hands.

Robin knows what words are written on the sign there. *Georgia Riley. James and Alex Riley. Died Sept 2015.* Five years ago today.

Liam stands up and dusts the mud from his hands. He looks across at Robin.

'You okay?' he asks.

'I'm alright,' Robin replies, although he knows what Liam is thinking. He looks like shit. And has for a while.

In contrast, his brother-in-law seems well. His narrow face is lined, but he has colour, a tan left behind from the summer. Robin remembers something about cycling, a hobby picked up after Georgia's death. A holiday to Majorca, photos on Facebook of Liam standing in Lycra at the top of a big hill.

'Work okay?' Liam asks.

'Hmm,' Robin replies, non-committally.

It's the most the two have spoken in a friendly tone for nearly two years.

'You look good,' Robin throws back. 'Single life treating you well.'

'Rob...' Liam starts. 'Not now. Not here.'

Robin shakes his head, his jaw clenched. It was a ridiculous comment, one he regretted the moment it left his mouth, designed to keep the wedge between them. He turns before he can say anything else and starts to walk away.

'Robin!' he hears Liam call to his back. 'Please.'

But he doesn't stop. Liam's right. Georgia's grave is not the place to start a new argument. And what would it solve? Robin doesn't begrudge Liam any sort of happiness; he knows how much Liam loved his sister and the boys, of that he's in no doubt. But the other... that's the bit Robin can't understand.

As Robin gets into his car his phone rings, and he answers it.

'Butler? It's Greg from the lab. The results from those beer bottles are back. West told me to call you.'

'Beer bottle?' For a moment, Robin can't make sense of what Greg's saying. Then he realises. The ones from his house, after his supposed hangover.

'Yeah. One of them was completely clear, but the second had traces of a benzodiazepine in the bottom, specifically flunitrazepam.'

Robin knows what that means. 'How much?'

'A small amount, but enough to render someone unconscious. Full report's in your inbox,' Greg finishes.

Robin ends the call. He sits for a moment, rain spitting on his windscreen, and he feels the fury growing inside, adding to the ball of anger already there from his exchange with Liam.

He places a call to Control.

'Yeah, home address for Olivia Cross,' he says, hand already on the ignition key. 'Age late thirties.'

He listens to the reply. 'That's the one,' he agrees. 'Brown hair, brown eyes.'

He makes a mental note of the address, and guns his car out of the car park.

34

Freya's glad Robin's distracted as they leave the church, refraining from asking her too many questions about her so-called admin assignment. She collected the CID case files from work this morning, a huge box in her boot.

She drives home quickly and unloads it, placing it on her kitchen table. She makes a sandwich, tuna and mayo, then sits eating it, reading the basics from the report Baker gave her the day before.

Trevor Stevens, fifty-four. Received a paltry sentence of three years in prison for causing death by careless driving, released after two. Twenty-four months in a minimum-security jail for the hit-and-run on Georgia Riley and two-year-old twins Alex and James. She remembers Robin testifying at the sentencing hearing, then arriving back to work two days later, red-eyed and silent. The sentencing notes talk about the accused's attempt at rehabilitation, Stevens' teary, apologetic appeal to the judge, the letters from his family and friends, talking about what a great bloke he was. Blokes are always great, Freya thinks, as she looks at his picture, until they get blind drunk at lunchtime and kill three innocent people.

Notes from his parole hearing talked about his commitment to AA. How he hadn't touched a drop since the accident. How he had a sponsor, daily meetings to attend, plus a recent commitment to God. How much of it was true, Freya didn't know, but barely a week after his licence had been reinstated (only disqualified for a year, what a joke) his car was found destroyed and burnt out at the edge of Cottingham Forest, a body inside. Analysis confirmed the body was Trevor Stevens, but that was all it could show. The flames had burnt him to a crisp.

Freya looks for the crime scene photos but they seem to be missing. Stored at the SCIU, she assumes. She looks up the name of the investigating officer – Sergeant Kevin Burton – then sends him a quick email asking to meet.

She reads on. No witnesses to the accident, car and body spotted at eleven p.m. by a dog walker. And a broken bottle in the passenger-side footwell.

That bottle was a distinctive shape – Jack Daniel's whiskey. So Trevor hadn't been so abstemious. And when he'd fallen off the wagon, he'd fallen hard, driving his car into a tree.

Freya sits back at her kitchen table. The whole box is laid out in front of her, the scribbled notebooks from the detectives, the typed witness statement from the dog walker. There's not much, but it all seems present and correct. So what?

She wonders if Steph has found anything additional, and calls her. She answers immediately.

'I heard you were the DC on the case,' Steph says. 'Have you told Robin?'

'Baker told me not to. Have you?'

A pause. Freya remembers Steph being at her boss's house that Tuesday morning. Then: 'No, of course not. Have you seen him?'

'At the Miller funeral today. Why?'

'I don't know, he just…' Another pause. 'He doesn't seem to be doing so well.'

'He always looks, you know, a mess,' Freya suggests.

'Yeah, but more than usual.' At the other end of the phone, Steph sighs. Freya can hear the hum of a car engine. 'Have you reviewed the case file yet?' Steph asks.

'Yeah, but…'

'Where are you?' Steph says. 'I'm coming to you.'

Freya hangs up and texts Steph her address. Ten minutes later she's standing on her porch.

Next to Steph, Freya always feels unhealthy and large. Steph screams fitness, from her all-year tan to the way she moves: lithe, with energy. Freya offers her a drink and she refuses, pulling out a bottle of water from her bag – reusable, of course – and an apple, which she takes a bite out of.

If Steph is seeing her sergeant romantically, it seems like a strange match to Freya. Butler doesn't drink anything that isn't either alcoholic or caffeinated. Most of his food comes from the vending machine or takeaway shops. Yet Freya knows that women find him attractive. That beaten, melancholy persona, mistaking him for a strong, silent type when in fact he's just miserable.

Steph sits down at the table, apple still in her hand, and takes a file out of her bag.

'The medical side of things,' Steph explains, passing it to Freya.

Freya opens the file and flicks through. She pulls out the post-mortem report. 'It's short.'

'That's not unusual.' Steph reaches over Freya and selects a photograph from the pages. She hands it to Freya, who can't help but gasp. It's clearly human, but the body's black, constricted, shrunken. Almost burnt beyond recognition.

'What was the cause of death?' Freya asks.

'Multiple injuries, consistent with given history of road traffic collision.'

'Had he been drinking?'

'Inconclusive.' Steph finishes her apple and stands up, throwing it into the bin from a distance, easily making the shot. 'Fire burnt everything up. I've got the tissue samples, though. I'll take another look. Our tests have got better since then, more sensitive. They might pick up something new, you never know.'

'You're not going to exhume the body?'

'No,' Steph scoffs, and Freya feels stupid for asking. 'Would be even less to find now, and digging up a body is hardly going to keep things below the radar for the coroner.'

'Do you know what this additional evidence is?' Freya asks. 'That caused the coroner to get us to investigate?'

'No, you?'

'No.'

Steph shrugs. 'So we'll just need to do what we're told. Take another look at what we have.'

Freya feels the pressure, looking at all the reports, all the mess. Steph, as if sensing her indecision, starts to stack the paperwork into piles.

'I don't even know where to start,' Freya mumbles, helplessly.

Steph looks at her. 'What does your training tell you to do?' she asks.

Freya pauses. But instead of that, she thinks about Butler. What would he say? They haven't worked together long, but she can imagine. 'Start from the beginning,' she says. 'Do the interviews again, look at the crime scene. Make my own mind up about what happened.'

'So do that.'

Freya nods, and picks up one of the witness statements from that day. She feels Steph's eyes on her.

'Freya, how well do you know Robin?' Steph asks.

Freya looks at her. Steph seems unsure; she's blushing slightly, her usual confidence evaporated.

'He's been my sergeant for just over a week.'

'I don't mean like that. I mean…'

'No, there's been nothing like that.' Freya dismisses it quickly. 'And I've never heard any rumours from around CID either.'

'Never? I mean, I wouldn't blame him if he had. He's single, attractive, all those late nights working,' Steph says, the words flying out of her mouth.

'No, never,' Freya repeats.

She knows what Steph is referring to. Even though it's not strictly speaking allowed, there's a lot that goes on between the police. The hours are unsociable, and nobody outside the force understands the pressures that detectives experience. It's only natural that people hook up. And Freya knows about the sheer number of marriages that crumble as a result.

But Butler? No. No one's ever talked about him in that way.

She looks back to Steph. 'You like him, don't you?' Freya says.

Steph laughs, slightly sharp. 'Stupid, aren't I?' She gathers her files back up, shoving them hastily into her bag.

'Not at all. I've seen you two together. He feels the same.'

'Yeah, but men like Robin Butler?' Steph shakes her head, sadly. 'By the time they realise, it's too late.'

35

Robin holds his finger tight to the doorbell of the mid-terrace house and waits. He can hear the bell inside, ringing over and over, then a voice shouts, 'All right, I'm coming, I'm coming.'

The door opens and Liv stands in front of him. She's got changed after the memorial and is now in jogging bottoms and a loose, light pink T-shirt, feet bare and arms crossed. She looks sleepy, as if he's woken her.

He forcefully pushes past her into the house, her face shocked at the sight of him in her hallway.

'You fucking drugged me,' he shouts. 'You roofied me.'

She glares at him, hands now on hips. 'Get out of my house.'

'I should arrest you.'

But she laughs. 'I'd like to see you try. Explain that one to your police buddies – how a prostitute managed to drug you while you were at home with her, late on a Tuesday night.'

He knows she's right. Shit. 'Give me my notebook back.'

She scowls, then walks past him into her kitchen and picks up the purple notebook from the table. 'Fine. Amy couldn't make sense of it anyway. I don't know why I bothered.'

Robin snatches it out of her hand. 'Your *sister* Amy, you mean.'

'You know about that.'

'Hard to miss, you standing next to her in the bloody church.' Then he realises. 'You had a threesome with your sister?' he says, his voice rising at the end with incredulity.

She sighs in frustration. 'I…' she starts. 'Oh, for fuck's sake.' She goes to the kettle and switches it on, taking a mug out of her cupboard. Her kitchen is small, but clean and bright. 'You want one?'

'No, thank you,' he says, sarcastically. 'Explain.'

'I hadn't seen Amy for about ten years,' she says. 'I didn't know where she lived, didn't even know she'd got married.'

'How come?'

'Our childhoods were less than perfect. As kids we were close, but then our lives took different paths.' She pours water into her mug and adds a herbal teabag, hanging the tag over the edge. 'She went down the manic-obsessive route, perfect little Amy. I... well. I preferred to self-medicate a different way. Drugs, alcohol—'

'Prostitution?' Robin adds, spitefully.

'Yes. Thank you for the reminder.' Liv carries her mug to the small dining table and sits down. Robin makes no attempt to join her, just watches from the doorway as she takes a cigarette from the packet on the table and lights it.

'We fell out. And then I turn up at her house six months ago.'

'And then what?' Robin snaps. 'Emotional reunion?'

Liv takes a long drag from her cigarette and blows out smoke. 'Not quite.' She screws up her face. 'Amy thought it was funny. Thought Jonathan would get a kick out of it, screwing both sisters.'

'He didn't?'

'No, his reaction was much like yours, complete disgust. She persuaded him to have a blow job, and then she told him after. He went mad, said she was sick. Kicked me out of the house.' She shrugs, takes another drag. 'Don't blame him.'

'But you kept in touch?'

'Yeah.' She sighs and stubs the finished cigarette out in the ashtray. 'She's the only family I have.'

'So why tell me all that about her in the pub that night?' Robin leans back against the wall, still wary. 'If you're so loyal?'

'I… I don't know. I was curious. About Jonathan's death. And I thought if you trusted me, if I told you what you wanted to know, then you might tell me something too.'

'And I bloody well did,' Robin sighs. His anger has dissipated with Liv's explanation. He believes her. 'So why did you steal the notebook?'

'Amy wanted to know what you had on her. She knows you think she killed him.'

'And did she?'

'Fuck, how would I know? I didn't lie, I was out with her that Monday night. And I meant what I said about Jonathan. He was a nice guy. From what I saw of him. Sweet. Normal.'

Robin suddenly feels knackered. This whole case, this whole situation. It's ridiculous. They have nothing to prove Amy Miller killed her husband. And he's got himself into a whole load of trouble as a result.

He slumps down at the table opposite her. 'Give me one of those,' he mutters, pointing to the pack of Marlboro Gold. She offers the box.

He hasn't smoked since university, but he needs the relief. The tobacco grates at the back of his throat, the nicotine making him feel dizzy, but he relishes the feeling. She watches him through the haze and takes a sip from her tea.

'I'm sorry for drugging you.' She smiles weakly. 'You looked sweet,' she adds. 'Asleep on your sofa.'

'Sorry for bashing your door down,' he offers in response. 'Did I wake you?'

'Trying to have a nap. Late one last night from Frankie. Had to go straight from there to the memorial.'

'You should give it up.' He puts the cigarette against his lips, takes another long drag in.

'I should. But it's good money. Most of the guys.' She waves her hand dismissively. 'They're harmless enough. Take the man last night. Late fifties, single. Just wanted someone to take to a work event.'

'Who did he say you were?' Robin asks, curious.

'Old family friend. But I'm sure they knew. Sad, really. I think he was just lonely.'

Aren't we all, Robin thinks with a sting as he stubs out the cigarette. 'So it was just the work event?'

'Nah, had to fuck him as well.' She laughs, bitterly. 'Paid extra for me to call him Daddy.' She takes another cigarette out of the packet and puts it in her mouth. 'And I wonder why I have such a warped view of men,' she mumbles as she clicks her lighter into flame.

36

He's gone. More subdued than when he arrived, but most likely never to return.

Liv sits in her kitchen, herbal tea in front of her, and miserably watches the rain pepper the window. Her body is weary. She aches, and shifts position to alleviate the pressure on the parts of her she knows shouldn't hurt.

This is no way to live her life, she thinks. She's proud of the things she's overcome – the alcohol, the drugs that previously dictated her life – but this? The men? Handing fifty per cent of her earnings to Frankie while she is the one being fucked and bruised and held down and fisted? She told Frankie last night she won't go out with that guy again.

'Next time,' Frankie said, pulling her dressing gown around herself and lighting a fag. 'We'll charge him double.'

As if money could make up for this feeling. This beaten-down, hollow shell of a body.

The stripping, that's fine. It's a job, like any other. Never routine or dull, and on the quiet nights she has fun with the girls. There are a few, of course, who do it to support their coke habit, but most are normal women, from all walks of life. Some supporting a family, others wanting to be dancers and this is the only way they know how. And she likes the hustle, the attitude. Thrusting her boobs into some guy's face, pretending she likes them to get tips. Private dances, two and a half minutes in her underwear, thirty seconds naked? She can do that, no problem.

But working for the escort agency, working for Frankie? Frankie is one of the good ones, that's true, but it's a low bar to start with.

She picks up her cigarettes and lights another. She takes a long breath in and blows the smoke out in a graceful plume, and her thoughts move to Robin Butler.

She's found she's been thinking about him more over the past few days. She regretted it the moment she stole that notebook, and now he's come round to her house, shouting and swearing. But he didn't arrest her. She meant what she said to him. She'd looked at him, asleep on his sofa, drugged into oblivion, at his long eyelashes, stubble across his jaw, and she'd slowly run a finger across his face. She'd traced the line of his cheekbone, then down his neck to his collar.

And then she'd kissed him. Gently, hardly more than a peck on the lips. And he hadn't stirred.

Normally she has an apathy towards men that mostly veers to hatred. But Robin seems different. That haunted frown. Words that seem on the edge of his lips, reluctant to say them out loud.

And what would she say to him? Hey, I'm a hooker and a stripper and I drugged you, but would you fancy going out one evening? It's bullshit, and she knows it.

She liked Jonathan, on that one occasion she met him, and was shocked when he died. It didn't seem right, what they said about the circumstances of his death, and she wanted to help Robin find out what had happened. But she felt torn, between the loyalties to her sister and the truth she'd told Robin.

Her phone rings next to her, and she looks at the screen, then mutes it and turns it over. It continues to vibrate, then stops. After a second, it starts again. She doesn't want to answer it. She's had enough of her sister's crap. Her life had hardly been perfect before she bumped into Amy again, but now it's a hundred times worse.

Liv's spent her whole life making excuses for Amy. Even as children, Liv would be the one getting into fights, defending her little sister for something she'd done or said. Liv could throw a punch, but Amy was manipulative and devious. Getting other kids into trouble from schemes that she herself had come up with. Amy liked the control, and if she wasn't in charge, then god help you.

And Liv knows why. Like her, their mother was an alcoholic. An unpredictable drunk, happy one moment, unconscious the next. Money was scarce. Food even more so. Liv had to grow up fast, keeping life normal for her baby sister, getting her dressed while mopping up vomit and smashed glass from their mother's latest bender. Keeping Amy away from the guys. *Those* guys. The men that decided they wanted the younger model. Who wanted to know why they had to pay fifty quid for the run-down, worn-out lush when they could have the sixteen-year-old virgin instead. And what did it matter? She had a bit of extra cash, and they left Amy alone.

So, as they got older, Liv turned to alcohol and coke, and Amy went the other way. Amy had been protected. And as a result she was free to build a life for herself with a nice career, in a big house, with a loving husband. Everything Liv had been denied.

And now? Liv lights a new cigarette from the butt of the old. Amy is something else entirely. And, if the truth be known, it scares the living daylights out of her.

37

Friday

Freya spends the night tossing and turning. At five a.m. she gets up and fetches the file again. She had a message from Butler that evening – *How's it going?* – but she didn't dare reply. Hiding all this from her boss, it feels more like a punishment. And in the dark cold early morning, she doubts herself.

She's never run an investigation alone. What if she makes a wrong turn, what if she misses something important? Previously, it was her and Butler. And before him, another DS or DI. She's had someone there, asking the right questions, telling her what to do.

But she's a good detective, she tells herself. Cover all your bases, follow the evidence. And she knows it's not all here. Her first stop, arranged via text the night before, is to the SCIU, to meet with the investigating officer from all those years ago.

–

Freya misses the road at first, turning round in the forecourt of the Volvo garage and heading back. And then she spots it.

Look for the hideous seventies building, she was told, *you can't miss it.* And, sure enough, there it is. He wasn't joking.

A low concrete roof, ugly grey curves and brown-tinted windows underneath. A hedge blocks the worst of it, but it's clear the local planning department were having an off day when that design was approved. She drives past it and parks in one of the bays marked *SCIU*. In the distance she can see the distinctive yellow fluorescent vans, and climbs out of her car, walking away from the seventies monstrosity towards an altogether more beautiful building.

The Serious Collision Investigation Unit is located in the manor house next door. Ivy climbs up one side of the curved bay window, a large pillared doorway in the middle. A man waits on the steps, dressed in the usual distinctive black uniform, and holds out his hand. His muscular arms are covered with two full sleeves of tattoos – skulls, roses, thorns – his head completely shaved. His nose is wonky from previous breaks and he has one cauliflower ear. But despite his intimidating appearance, his smile is wide. Freya warms to him instantly.

'Kevin Burton,' he says, towering above her. 'You must be DC West. Come inside.'

The hallway is large and grand but has clearly seen better days. The carpet is stained and threadbare, the paint chipped and peeling. A large metal shelving unit has been set up on one side, containing rows of identical black kitbags and fluorescent vests.

'Supposed to be here temporarily, that was two years ago,' he says. 'Want a cuppa?'

'Please.'

'How do you take it?'

Freya follows him down the low-ceilinged corridors, watching him duck to get through the doorways. Temporary green fire exit signs have been put up, at odds with the period features that Freya knows must have been part of the of the original decor. He makes them both tea, handing her one in a pale blue mug with *Keep Calm and Know Your Rights* written on the side. Some union thing, she assumes.

He leads her into the main office. Square functional desks and computers line one side, contrasting with the round bay window behind them. One of the sash windows is open, propped up with a box file, a cool breeze blowing through. Burton pulls out a chair and she sits down next to him.

'So, what do you want to know? It was the Stevens accident, right?'

'Yeah. November 2018.'

'Got it here.' He points to the pile of brown boxes by his side. 'Where do you want to start?'

'Tell me everything you know.'

Burton sits back in his seat, clearly relishing the distraction from his normal work. Because of his height, the computer is propped up on two reams of paper, his chair set to the highest setting. It makes Freya feel tiny: a primary school kid listening to her teacher. But she doesn't mind, she's there to learn.

'It's always the dog walkers,' Burton says, with a smile. 'Remote crime scene, guarantee it'll be those guys that find them.' He wiggles his mouse to wake up his computer, then clicks around, finding the right file.

A photograph is loaded and Freya cranes forward. A long, straight road, early dawn, trees on one side, tall hedge on the other. To the left, a car waits, half on, half off the road. Even from this view, taken from behind, Freya can see the effects of the fire.

'The guy saw the flames, called the fire brigade. They were the first on the scene. They called us.'

'No ambulance?' Freya sips her tea again and listens to the sergeant talk.

'No need.' Burton clicks the photograph forward and a different view appears on the screen. A side view, glass smashed, black body in the driver's seat. 'They knew he was dead. Melted onto the seat. Took the body recovery team an age to get him out.'

'And you did the investigation?'

'Yeah. Let me get the report up.'

More clicking and a document loads. Burton scrolls down through the text.

'So,' he begins. 'Debris field was wide, shit scattered all across the road.' A new photo, small reflective studs and yellow paint visible on the grey concrete next to the familiar yellow triangles marking the positions of the evidence. 'You can see from the markers the car swerved, seemingly out of nowhere, skid marks here—' a large finger prods the screen '—and here. But he must have been going at some speed. There was a huge amount of damage to the vehicle.'

Another photo, the bonnet of the car concertinaed around the trunk of the tree.

'And why did it catch fire?' Freya asks, finishing her tea and putting the mug back down, freeing up her hands to take notes.

'Mechanics had a look at it back at the compound. The force of the crash sheared the bonnet completely from the car, which dislodged the fuel injectors from the engine. Petrol sprayed on a hot engine, and boom.'

'So, unlucky?'

'Very. Especially for us. Fire destroys absolutely everything. Both airbags deployed, and we'd normally check them for mouth DNA, work out who'd been sat where, but there was nothing left.'

'Sorry.' Freya stops him. 'What do you mean, "who had been sat where"? Trevor Stevens was the only one in the car, wasn't he?'

'Well, yeah. That's what we concluded in the end. But, you know, I always wondered. See here—' Burton goes back to an earlier photo. 'The passenger door was found open. Of course,' he adds, seeing Freya about to speak. 'That could have happened in the crash, but the seat belt was odd, too.'

'What do you mean?'

Burton sits back in his seat and picks up his mug of what must now be cold tea. He takes a sip but doesn't seem to mind. 'So, seat belts, when they lock at speed, the mechanism gets super-hot, super-quickly. There are a lot of forces involved in an accident like this one – people thrown forward in their seats, a lot of pressure on the seat belt. And it deforms. See, like this one.'

He clicks around again and points at the screen. Freya can clearly see raised ridges and bumps on the black fabric.

'And the position of these bumps would indicate someone else was in that car.'

'But – what?' Freya asks. 'Is it possible to survive a crash like that? They must have been injured?'

'Absolutely,' Burton agrees. 'People in car accidents get thrown around like they're in a washing machine. Head injuries on the A pillar, leg injuries as the engine and dashboard push forward into the car. Whiplash, at least.'

'So where did they go?'

Burton shrugs. 'We had no other evidence to show anyone was there. But—' he adds, remembering some other information. 'The airbags definitely deployed, so whoever it was would have been blinded.'

Freya knows that when airbags explode out of the dashboard a fine white powder comes with them. It's designed to stop them catching fire, but has the added effect of temporarily blinding whoever's sitting there. It's not fun.

'Did you get anything from the engine control module?'

'Burnt out. Not even the engineers in Amsterdam could save it.'

'And there were no other witnesses?'

'Nope. We put appeal boards up at the scene, did a media release, but nobody came forward.'

Freya sits back in her chair, her pen lowered. 'So what did you conclude?'

Burton shakes his head. 'The only thing we could – accidental death from a road traffic accident. My guess? The guy was drunk, as the papers said.'

'Why do you say that?'

'The JD bottle in the footwell. You know about that, yeah?' Freya nods. 'And the fact that he comes flying off a totally straight road. Look at it.' He pulls the photo back on the screen. 'Not even a bump in the tarmac. The patterns on the road and the tyres are different depending on whether the car was under power when it crashed—'

He flicks through another few photos – black marks on the road, the remaining tread on the tyre. Burton continues, '—and this one never slowed. He's pissed, dozes off a bit, comes to, realises he's strayed into the middle of the road and overcompensates, losing control and charging into the tree.'

Freya nods, thinking it all through.

'Alcohol slows down reaction time and judgement. When you're pissed and driving that fast you can't multitask. Plus it was raining that night. Hard. If this guy lost control, it was a foregone conclusion.' Burton whacks the back of his hand against the palm of the other to illustrate his point. 'Straight into the tree.'

'And there was nothing wrong with the car?' Freya asks.

'Not that we could find. Speed on the dash sometimes indicates speed on collision but that was fried to hell. You want to take this lot?' Burton asks, pointing to the three boxes.

'Please.' Then something occurs to her. 'While I'm here, could you help me track down another case? A bit older?'

She passes him the case reference and Burton nods slowly. 'I didn't know this was up for review as well?'

'It's not, but it's…' Freya tails off. Why *is* she curious? 'Just a side project,' she finishes. 'Will it be easy to find?'

Burton laughs. 'Sure,' he says, but something about his tone makes her doubt. 'Follow me.'

He stands up and she walks after him out of the office, watching his practised movements, bending automatically as he goes through doorways. They arrive at the back of the house, and he opens a heavy wooden door.

He reaches round and flicks on the light. Freya gasps. Inside are rows and rows of brown cardboard file boxes, stacked up on each other, going back as far as the eye can see.

Burton chuckles. 'It's all yours.'

Freya spends the next three hours going through the boxes. This isn't what she's here for, she tells herself over and over, but for some reason she keeps going. And despite Burton's obvious amusement, there does seem to be some sort of order to the chaos, she reflects, eventually noticing a row of dates from 2015: February, March, then, at last, September.

And then she finds it. It's old, water-stained and crumpled from the effects of the three other boxes that have been piled on the top. Written on the end: *September 2015. Riley*.

The case files from Butler's sister's death.

38

His phone wakes him.

'Butler?'

Robin mumbles something incomprehensible into his handset.

'You know your CCTV?'

Robin sits up in bed, and rubs his hand over his hair. He's not awake, only dimly registering that someone's talking.

'CCTV?' he manages.

'Yeah. The one from the Premier Inn? Your hanging wanking guy. Butler? You there?'

'Yeah.' Robin's realised who's talking at last. It's Greg, from the digital lab. 'What about it?'

'I need to show you. Are you in?'

Robin squints at the clock. Shit. He's overslept again.

He hasn't had a proper night's sleep for as long as he can remember. During the day, he's shattered, desperate for half an hour of shut-eye, but the moment he gets into bed his brain refuses to switch off. He lies there, warm, comfortable, but awake, as the clock ticks round to two, three, sometimes four a.m. His mind will wander, on the edge of dreams. But then he'll hear a small cry, or a voice, maybe real, probably imaginary, and he'll be jolted awake again, his heart thudding in his chest. Finally, he'll drift off, but then he'll wake, barely hours later, blurry, exhausted and desperate to be left alone.

But Greg's not shutting up, still talking down the phone.

'I'm on my way,' Robin says.

An hour later, Robin's dressed in something vaguely clean and sitting at Greg's desk, takeaway coffees in hand. Robin's worked with Greg for years, and Greg's complete lack of care for social niceties means the two men have always got on. Robin's blunt manner matches the techie's, both understanding the need to get to the point fast, as well as the desire for a continuous supply of caffeine. Greg takes the matching coffee cup without acknowledgement and now presses it to his lips, while pointing at his screen with his other hand.

'What?' Robin asks.

Greg taps with his finger on the figure in the CCTV. It's the footage taken from outside the Premier Inn, on the evening that Jonathan Miller checked into the hotel.

'So your guy was about five-nine, five-ten, right?'

'Yeah, so?'

'This guy's not.'

'Pardon?' Robin asks. After his run-in with Liv, Robin drove home, stopping at the Co-op on the way for a frozen dinner and a six-pack of beer, asking for a packet of twenty Marlboro Golds as an afterthought when he got to the till. He spent the evening smoking and drinking, and as a consequence his brain is blurry, his throat scratchy and sore.

'This guy—' Greg taps again '—is too tall.'

Robin coughs, feeling the muck from the cigarettes rattling in his lungs, then takes another gulp of coffee. He isn't with it enough to understand Greg this morning.

'What do you mean, too tall?'

Greg talks him through some complicated process involving algebra and geometry and the height of the door of the car the guy is standing next to. Robin blinks.

'So how tall do you think this guy is?'

'Six-two, six-three?'

'You're kidding me.'

Greg stares at him through his glasses, stone-faced. 'Would I?'

'Shit.' Robin slumps back in the chair. He thinks about Jonathan Miller's Mazda – left at the Premier Inn, now impounded in the police garage. 'What about the forensics from the car? Anything back on that?'

'Wait a sec.'

Greg turns round and shouts to one of his colleagues. 'Sent to West,' Robin hears him reply.

Greg turns back, sees the look on Robin's face. 'I'll find it now,' he grumbles. 'Where is West, anyway?'

'On another case. Temporarily.'

'Pity. Still single?' Greg asks without turning from the screen.

Robin looks at Greg's unstylish haircut, his thick specs, the stained *Star Wars* T-shirt. Then he thinks about Freya. 'You don't have a chance, mate,' he replies, although he realises he doesn't actually know Freya's relationship status. He's never asked.

A glance from Greg. 'Well, nor do you. You smelt yourself this morning?' Robin does a surreptitious downward sniff. 'Just saying a shower wouldn't have gone amiss.'

He's not wrong, but before Robin has a chance to defend himself Greg's got the report on the screen.

'So. Samples taken from the driver's side show the presence of three separate DNA profiles. One belonging to Jonathan Miller, two unknown.'

'Two?'

'Yeah. Fingerprints the same – a load of Miller's, then a whole heap of partials we can't identify.'

'Anything else in the rest of the car?'

'Not anything helpful. Mud, dirt, crap in the boot. But no biologicals.'

So, no hair, no skin. No bits from a dead body, Robin thinks. 'And the belt?' he asks.

'Yep, yep, wait a sec.' More clicking from Greg. 'Not much on the top surface, shiny and smooth so less likely DNA would be transferred and retained.' Greg looks up. 'No fingerprints, either.' He focuses back on the screen. 'Under surface rougher and more porous, better transfer, and yep.' Robin looks up, interested. 'DNA from your victim.'

'No one else?' Robin says, disappointed.

'Nope. Oh, and here's the results from your porn,' Greg continues, his eyes not moving from the monitor.

'It's not *my* porn,' Robin mutters, but Greg's not listening.

'One DNA profile. And fingerprints, some of which match to Miller's.'

'Some?' Robin's interest is caught again.

'Yeah.' A pause while Greg reads from the screen. 'The DNA wasn't your victim's, but one handprint was. Oh, now this is odd,' Greg says, showing Robin the photo. 'A full handprint, across one page. And only that.'

Robin squints at the picture. Across the naked woman, Robin can see the telltale black mess of the fingerprinting dust, then a separate shot of the handprint once the dust had been removed. Four fingers, a thumb and a palm, laid out like someone had pressed their hand to the centre of the page.

'Have you compared the DNA on the porn to the trace in the car?'

'No, you want us to—'

'Yes. Please,' Robin adds as an afterthought. 'And the finger-prints, too. Call me as soon as you know.'

'Will do. What are you thinking?' Greg asks, curious.

'It's too precise.' Robin holds his hand out, fingers splayed, copying the handprint on the porn. 'Too perfect.'

'You think someone staged the crime scene?' Greg replies. 'What were they hiding?'

Robin stands up and throws his empty coffee cup in the bin. 'A murder,' he says, striding out of the lab without a goodbye.

39

Saturday

Freya wakes early, has a shower and leaves her house before breakfast. She's keen to get on the road. She knows where she's going.

She spent the rest of Friday in her living room, reading through the contents of the large brown boxes. There was a lot there – photographs, reports, Burton's scribbled handwriting in investigatory notebooks – and none of it contradicted what he'd told her that morning. They'd been thorough. The reports documented every aspect about the scene in minute detail – the camber of the road, the conditions, the torrential rain, the wind speed and direction. Maps showed the location, and a full GPS scan had been taken, recreating the entire scene in a computer program. She loaded up one of the CDs and flicked through hundreds of photographs of the crash.

But she knew nothing substituted seeing it all in real life. She pushed the paperwork aside and looked closely at the crime scene map. That would be her plan for tomorrow. She'd see for herself. Start the investigation from the beginning.

–

Now, air crisp with the beginning of autumn, she enters the postcode into her satnav and follows the instructions – down the motorway, then onto increasingly smaller roads. She picks up a coffee and an almond croissant on the way and eats it, dropping greasy fragments of pastry onto her lap as she drives.

She passes a small Texaco garage on the right, then drives for another mile until she spots it. Pulling into a dirt road further up, she takes one last gulp of coffee, then hastily sweeps the mess from her clothes as she gets out of the car.

It's a fast road, derestricted speed limit, windy and deserted. Grey tarmac, white lines down the centre. Trees on one side, tall hedge on the other, farmer's field beyond. She pulls her coat tighter around her, grabs a few of the crime scene photos, then walks down the grass verge towards the deadly tree.

There's nothing marking it out as the site of a fatal accident. From the crash investigator's report, she imagines Trevor Stevens driving down here that night, losing control, sliding and hitting the tree. The tree in question is a broad oak, untarnished, acorns littering the road below it, undergrowth grown up around it again. It's wide and sturdy. In the fight of vehicle versus tree there could only be one winner.

She looks down the road, and as it starts to drizzle, she walks back to her car and sits inside. She pulls the file out of her bag and reads the report again, looking at the photos accompanying it.

Sitting there, she takes in the scene in all its cold, hard reality. She holds the photo up, comparing it to the quiet roadside she looks at now. Fire engines took ten minutes to get there; by the time they arrived the flames had erupted into a fury. Freya agrees with their assessment of the speed; he must have been going at quite some lick. The tree is embedded almost completely in the front of the car, metal sandwiched round the blackened engine, the bonnet gone.

Freya wonders how much Trevor Stevens would have been cognisant of the accident. Whether he was conscious at all after the crash. Whether he knew what was about to happen. How he would die.

And then, for the first time Freya thinks, was the crash deliberate? Was Trevor Stevens trying to kill himself?

She doesn't remember seeing any statements from the family in the file boxes. She vaguely remembers there's a wife and a daughter, and makes a mental note to go back and check. And then she remembers the petrol station.

—

She starts the engine, and drives the mile or so back. She pulls into the forecourt. It's an old-style garage with a petrol station attached. Not one of the posh, corporate ones with a Jamie Oliver sandwich bar or Costa Coffee, but a display of chocolate running down the middle of the shop and a fridge at the back with cold drinks.

A bell announces her arrival, and she walks to the teenager behind the till.

'Fuel?' he asks, looking out to the forecourt.

'Detective Constable Freya West.' She holds up her ID and he glances at it, confused. 'I'm here about an incident that happened a few years ago. The accident about a mile away, down the A32?'

'I didn't work here then,' the kid says, and Freya curses silently. She should have called ahead. 'You'd have to speak to my grandad.'

'Your grandad?' Freya repeats, feeling a glimmer of hope.

'Yeah. He retired last year.'

'Could you call him?'

Freya expects the kid to pick up the phone, but instead he bellows 'GRANDAD!' at the top of his voice, making her jump. They wait for a second, then he does it again.

'WHAT?' a corresponding voice hollers back.

'Police want to speak to you!' The boy smiles innocently at Freya. 'Give him a moment. It takes him a while to haul his arse out of his chair.'

They wait in silence, and Freya eyes up the shelves. She fancies a Dairy Milk, maybe a can of Diet Coke to wash down her breakfast. She looks again, and she can't see any beer or wine.

'Do you sell alcohol?' she asks him.

'Not got a licence.'

'And your CCTV? How long do you keep it for?'

'A month,' the boy replies, and Freya's disappointed, although she expected as much. 'I remember that accident, though. The car that caught fire?' Freya nods. 'It was all anyone talked about round here. Some people say they heard the boom when the petrol tank blew.'

The side door opens, and an older man shuffles through. He has a stick in his hand, and a shock of grey hair sticking up at the back of his head. He smiles, and Freya can see the similarities between him and his grandson.

'She wants to know about the car accident,' the kid says.

'She?' The old man directs to the teenager. 'Go and get us a coffee,' he says and the boy goes without question. The man holds out his hand to Freya. 'Thomas Kinnaman, and you are?'

'DC Freya West,' she replies as she shakes his hand. His skin is dry and papery, but his grip firm. 'Do you remember that day?'

The old man invites Freya to the other side of the cash desk, and settles himself on a wooden chair. 'Not much happens round here, could hardly forget. The man came in, you know?'

'He did?' Freya's surprised; she doesn't remember reading it in the report.

'Yeah. Nice bloke. I thought you lot would visit, but you never did.'

'You didn't call them?' Freya asks. 'They were looking for witnesses.'

'I left a message, no one phoned back. Reporters caught on though, spoke to a few of them. I looked up the records. He bought a bottle of Coke and a Ginsters, plus a full tank. Paid for it on his credit card.'

'How did he seem?'

'Not drunk, if that's what you're asking.' The grandson comes back in with two mugs. He holds one out to Freya and she takes it. It looks weak and milky, but it's hot and caffeinated so Freya doesn't argue. The grandson settles back behind the till, staring at his phone.

'I read the reports in the paper, and I was surprised at the time,' the man continues. 'We had a quick chat about the rain, then off he went. And believe me, I've seen my fair share of guys that shouldn't be driving. Called the cops on a few. But he wasn't one of them.'

He takes a sip from his coffee. 'Ah, that's better,' he murmurs appreciatively. 'Did you ever track down the others?'

'Sorry?' Freya frowns.

'The other people that were here at the same time. A woman and a man, married couple, I think. And a squaddie, I heard them talking. Said he was in the army.'

'What did they look like?' she asks, trying to contain her enthusiasm.

'Woman was...' Kinnaman pauses, then shakes his head so furiously his jowls wobble. 'Nope, can't remember. We get so many folks through here. That was a long time ago.'

Freya frowns. A lead that's dead before it's even started.

'I can show you if you like?' Freya stares at him, and he points to the camera behind the desk. 'The CCTV? I kept the video. Assumed you lot would come back for it, but you never did.'

–

It's getting late by the time Freya makes it home. She puts her key in the lock and pushes it open, switching the lights on as she goes, excitedly clutching the evidence bag now containing the disc with the footage.

She quickly makes dinner, boiling up pasta and mixing in some sauce, then boots up her laptop, sitting down, bowl in front of her. She opens the CD tray and the disc loads slowly, the symbol whirring on the screen. Why didn't anyone follow up at the time? she wonders, waiting for it to load. Must have got missed, been one of those things.

The video starts automatically and she sees the garage shop, unchanged in the two years that have passed. The camera angle captures the middle aisle of sweets and chocolate, the fridges at the back, but the main door is out of shot, the quality crap and grainy. A few customers come in; Freya recognises the grey hair of Thomas Kinnaman, bobbing at the front of the video. She looks up the timings in her notes, then winds it forward. Then, there he is. Trevor Stevens, in black and white.

He walks to the front of the shop, sure and steady. Freya watches the wordless video as he smiles and speaks to the garage owner. She sees the couple Kinnaman mentioned before: the man comes to the front, waits behind Stevens to pay. The woman stays at the back, barely in shot. Because of the rain that night, everyone has their hoods up, their faces down. There's not much to go on.

Then the other man appears at the back. He faces the fridges, then turns slightly to the side to speak to Trevor Stevens as he leaves. Freya cranes forward, shovelling a forkful of pasta into her mouth, chewing slowly as she watches. But there's nothing to identify the guy. He's taller than Trevor Stevens, Freya can see that, but, like the others, his black hood is up and she can't see any of his face. Stevens smiles, gestures outside, then the two of them go out of shot.

That's it. Shit. Nothing.

She sits back in her chair, finishing the last few mouthfuls of her dinner. Dead end. She's already asked Kinnaman to track down the purchases made by the other potential eyewitnesses, and he gave her a doubtful look. 'Files could be anywhere,' he said, and Freya had a suspicion he wouldn't look far.

She stands up, clearing away her dirty plate into the dishwasher, then wonders what to do with the rest of her Saturday night. She knows her friends are out, a text earlier asking if she was going to join them, but she doesn't have the energy.

Most days she likes the peace and quiet. Space to do what she wants after a long day. To put her feet up and watch something mindless on TV. But today, more than ever, she misses Jon.

Communication between them was brief and sporadic. But she always knew he was there if she needed him. Sometimes it was just a quick message on WhatsApp. Sometimes she'd tweet, a cryptic message that only he'd understand, knowing he'd look and smile, and sometimes reply. And when they were together, they'd talk. About work, about everything. And now. Now there's nothing.

It's the silence she can't stand. She has an urge to call Butler, find out how he's getting on with the case, but he'll ask about what she's doing and she doesn't want to lie.

Instead, she pulls up Steph's number and presses the green button.

'Hello?'

'Steph, it's Freya.'

'Mmm-hmm,' Steph replies.

'You busy?'

'Yep, give me a moment.'

There's a rustling, and Freya hears Steph making excuses. Then footsteps.

'Okay, we can talk now.'

'You with Butler?'

'Yep.' Steph's responses are short and to the point. Freya assumes her boss can't be far away.

'Have you found anything new on the Stevens case?'

'Nope. I've reviewed the MRIs and X-rays taken at the time – nothing inconsistent with the findings.'

'Multiple injuries consistent with road traffic collision?'

'Yep.'

'What about blood alcohol?'

'Not tested the samples yet,' Steph whispers, 'although I'm not optimistic. Don't pin too many hopes on it. Did you go to the crash site?'

'Yeah.' Freya moves the photos about in front of her. 'Listen, Steph. Was there anything you found that would indicate suicide?'

'Suicide? No. Why?'

'Nothing on the road, nothing to cause an accident.'

'Perhaps a deer jumped out. Perhaps it all happened too fast. Consistent with lowered response times due to drinking.'

'Could you check his medical records, in case he was prescribed antidepressants or anything?'

'Sure.' Freya hears a male voice in the background. 'I have to go. I'll look later and text you.'

Freya hangs up. Hearing Butler's voice makes her miss her boss. That sounding board, someone to talk to about stuff like this. And she's envious of Steph. Not because she's with Butler, but because they have each other.

Her gaze shifts to the pile of brown boxes in the corner of the room, and the one from his sister's death that she hasn't yet looked at. He lost his parents, one by one, and then his sister and his nephews. She finds it hard to understand that level of loss, how he could have got over something like that. Perhaps he hasn't, the voice in her head says.

She stands up and goes over to the box, then crouches down and takes off the lid. It feels like an intrusion, looking into his life like this, but there's an itch of curiosity she wants to scratch.

It won't take long, she tells herself. Just a quick look.

40

Kal looks out into the darkness of the club, beer in hand, music deafening. The bass is so loud he can feel the vibrations in his chest. He watches his mates out there, dancing, flirting, drinking, but has no wish to join them.

Since Jonathan died, he's felt heavy. A weariness. A sadness ingrained in his bones that no amount of alcohol or powder or partying can fix. A woman standing at the bar catches his eye and smiles. Newly single, his latest girlfriend swiftly departing as his normal generous and fun nature gave way to grief, he manages a quick smile back and she walks towards him. She's leggy and young and dark, his type, but as she puts her hand on his arm and her mouth next to his ear, he finds himself shaking his head, no. She retreats with an angry frown, and he turns, walking down the stairs and out of the club without a word to his mates.

He walks quickly through the cold night air, flagging down a taxi, and arriving home earlier than he's ever considered in the past. It's barely eleven, and he still feels the last line of coke buzzing in his veins. There's no way he'll sleep now. He goes to the fridge, taking out a beer, then lies on the sofa, intending to while the hours away with a violent film, something nasty and over the top. Help him forget about Jonny.

Kal has an overwhelming urge to cry. While he and Jonny hadn't been close for years, it was more due to circumstances than want. He worked long hours in the City, commuting in from Winchester every day. Jonny had a simpler life, closer to home. Kal knew that Jonny couldn't match his drinking –

and drug-taking, if he was being honest – and the money Kal splashed around always made Jon nervous. Jonny had always been a cautious guy, ever since their time at university together. He was the one who made sure Kal got home when he was wasted. He stopped the fights; he called the taxis. He paid when a tip was forgotten.

Kal was ashamed to admit now that that side of Jon always made him a bit embarrassing in front of his City friends. Everyone there was more relaxed. But he'd always known that Jon was there for him. Jon – and Amy.

But she'd forced him to take sides. Amy had shown Kal a side of Jon that Kal hadn't liked. That he couldn't forgive.

Next to him, his phone buzzes, loud and distracting. He picks it up, expecting a torrent of abuse from his mates for leaving them, but it's Amy.

You in town? the message says.

He considers leaving it, but feels a flash of sympathy towards her. He replies: *Home.*

You okay?

No. He's surprised at his honesty. But if anyone can understand how he's feeling, it's her.

I'm coming over.

Don't, he types back, but there's no response.

Fifteen minutes later there's a knock on the door. He opens it, wearily.

'You shouldn't have come, Amy,' he says, then frowns. She's wearing a tight dress, breasts pushed up, high heels, more than her usual amount of make-up. 'You been out?' he adds as she walks into the house.

'What have you got to drink?' she asks.

'What do you want?'

'Vodka tonic. You got any blow?'

'No.'

'Pity.' She walks away from him, into the living room, and he makes her the drink. He carries it through, where she's sitting on the sofa, heels kicked off, legs crossed, showing a long expanse of toned thigh. She taps the sofa next to her with a smile.

He passes her the drink and sits down slowly. She's behaving strangely, even for Amy. Drunk, maybe, or on something else, it's hard to tell. She takes a sip from her glass, her eyes fixed on him.

'How can I help?' she asks, her voice almost a purr.

'I'm fine, Amy. I just... I can't stop thinking about him.' He stops. He can't even begin to articulate what happened to his best friend.

'I can take your mind off it.'

'I...' Kal goes to say something else, but she's pressing herself up against him, her body warm and eager.

He remembers the last time they were alone together. She turned up, out of the blue, crying, her face bloody and bruised. He comforted her, sat on this sofa, as she told him about her fight with Jonathan. How he'd done this to her.

And then they were kissing. He can't remember who made the first move, but there was no doubt that the rest of it was consensual. She was all over him, undoing his trousers, her mouth on his dick. He tried to stop her, but not really, because it felt so good, so fucking good, until he pulled her up, took her clothes off and screwed her, right there, on the sofa.

And after – *shit* – the guilt. What Jonathan had done to Amy was unforgivable, but screwing his best mate's wife was not the solution. And without a condom, either. He'd only realised at the last minute, and pulled out, coming violently across her bare stomach. He had one child in the mix already; he didn't want another. But it was okay, Amy told him by text. She wasn't pregnant, and she hadn't told Jonathan.

And now he's dead. Jonny will never know, but here she is again. And she's not hanging around. One hand is rubbing the crotch of his jeans, the other is up his shirt, and she's kissing him, hard. He pulls away. He can't do this.

She looks at him, her pupils wide and dilated.

'Amy, no,' he says, but her hand is still there, now trying to find its way into his trousers. He grabs her wrist. 'Stop it.'

She smiles. 'It's okay, I want this.'

'I don't.' She tries again with her other hand. 'Stop it,' Kal says again, standing up and moving away from her quickly. He feels sickened by what she's doing. 'Your husband's just died,' he says. 'My friend...'

Amy sits back on the sofa, her face dark. 'You didn't care much about your friend while he was alive, why do you give a shit now?'

'We shouldn't have done that then. It was wrong.'

'He was a bastard, Kal. A cheating, wife-beating bastard,' she shouts. 'He deserved to die.'

Kal shakes his head. He feels his throat tighten; a sudden sob comes up from his chest. 'You need to leave.'

'I'm not going. We need to do this.' She gets up from the sofa and stands next to him on her tiptoes, trying to kiss him again. 'I want you, Kal. I need you.'

But he places his hands on her shoulders and pushes her away. She backs off, stumbling slightly. 'Kal...'

'Go!' He shouts at her this time. 'You need help, Amy. This—' He points to her. 'This isn't normal. Get some fucking help.'

She glares at him, then picks up her shoes and angrily stalks out of his house. He hears the front door slam, but he stays standing in the middle of the room. His hands are shaking, and he raises them to his face, covering his mouth.

What have I done? he thinks. What the fuck have I done?

41

The weekends are the worst, Robin's always known that. Long drifts of time, punctuated by no more than the memories of what his life used to be like. Work fills the void for the main, and this Saturday has been no exception – hours have passed, Robin glued to his computer catching up on old case work, distracting him away from the lack of progress on Jonathan Miller.

There has been another break-in. Number five, report from the PC forwarded to Robin to follow up on. He looked at the photographs from the scene: scattered beer cans, glass shards from a smashed bottle of vodka, cigarettes stubbed out on the carpet. Much like the others. He read the witness statements: neighbours heard something the weekend before but hadn't bothered to call it in. Owners returned home from holiday to find the mess and their laptop and iPad missing. As before, the only things that had been taken were small and portable – easy to sell, hard to trace. New evidence had been gathered and forwarded to the lab; reports had come back from the one before – nothing. No DNA, no fingerprints. From here, all they could do was wait. With no further lines of enquiry, it would have to go on the back burner for now.

And now five p.m. has rolled around, and Robin's aware he's still in tracksuit bottoms and a T-shirt. Unwashed, unshaved, and mere hours away from going to see Steph for dinner.

Remembering Greg's words from the day before, he shaves, removing three days' worth of stubble, then has a long shower, cleaning his teeth and making some attempt to style his hair, despite its desperate need for a cut. He puts on jeans then irons his one remaining clean shirt.

And as he drives towards Steph's house, he finds himself humming along to the radio. It's the first time he's felt decent in days, the restorative power of the thought of a good meal, a bottle of wine and possibly a shag in his future.

He pulls up outside Steph's house and rings the bell. Considering the amount of times he's been here before, he's surprised to find himself nervous, a feeling that abates the moment she opens the door.

She's dressed in a denim shirt and black jeans, a pair of white wool slippers on her feet. She greets him with a kiss full on the mouth and encourages him in, squeezing past the bike in the hallway, the coats and technical running jackets hanging up alongside. He can smell something tempting cooking on the hob; soft music is playing in the background.

'Shall I open this?' she asks, holding the bottle of red that he's brought.

'Yep, do,' he replies, and she reaches up, getting a glass down from the shelf. 'You staying?' she asks.

'I hope so.'

And she smiles and pours him a generous serving, handing it to him, then picking up the tall glass in front of her. He can't tell what's in it, beyond ice and something clear, bubbling against the sides.

'How was your day?' she asks, and gestures for them to go through to the lounge. She sinks down on one of the sofas and he joins her. 'You still working on the Jonathan Miller case?'

'Yeah,' he sighs, and takes a sip of wine. 'Although I feel like I'm not getting very far. Just confusion, everywhere I look.' She looks interested, so he continues. 'I followed up with all the eyewitnesses from the party yesterday afternoon. All of them were wasted. Some remember Amy, but not Jonathan. Others say he was out in the smoking area – although,' he says, pointing his wine glass at Steph, 'he didn't smoke.'

'Anything on social media?' Steph asks.

'Again, some photos with Amy in the background, but nothing of Jonathan. And the photo of Kal and Jonathan that we now know was old.'

'So he might not have been there?'

'No. Although, as you and I both know, absence of something doesn't prove it didn't happen. Are his tox results back yet?'

'Should be next week, they're backed up at the lab.'

'Great. Thank you,' he adds with a smile, remembering he's supposed to be having fun, not interrogating Steph. 'Plus the person arriving at the hotel in Jonathan's car wasn't him, although we have no idea who it was.'

'So how did he get there?'

Robin shrugs. 'Not a clue. What about you?' Robin's desperate to ask, but tries his hardest to keep it casual. 'Have you found anything from the Stevens crash?'

Steph looks at him sympathetically. 'No. Nothing new.' A ting from the kitchen prevents Robin from asking anything further. 'Come through,' she says. 'Dinner's nearly ready. Just need to put the veg on.'

They get up and walk back into the kitchen. Steph turns and puts the kettle on. 'Lasagne,' she says. 'Is that okay?'

'Perfect.' Robin's stomach rumbles in response. He can't remember the last time he ate a home-cooked meal. He sits down at her kitchen table, laid up ready for dinner, feeling relaxed and comfortable. He's always liked Steph's house – minimal, her scientific mind never being one for clutter or fluff, but stylish. Photos on the wall from the places she's been; a corkboard is on the far side of the kitchen, medals from her numerous races and triathlons hanging from a hook below.

'You got any events planned?' he asks as she pours boiling water into the saucepan.

'Half Ironman at the end of the month, then that's it for the season,' she says. 'Water gets too cold in winter. You fancy joining me?'

The idea of swimming outdoors at any time of year seems insane to Robin. He can't remember the last time he went to the gym, or even broke into a run. But he knows she's joking.

'I'll give this one a miss, thanks,' he says. 'Maybe I'll stand and cheer on the sidelines instead, in a warm coat with a cup of coffee.'

'I'd like that,' she replies with a smile. 'You know, I often see families at these sorts of events. Some taking part, some supporting. I've always felt unbearably jealous of them all.'

She stops. He watches her carefully as she puts her glass on the side, then picks up a bottle of gin. It feels like a well-rehearsed comment. Not so much offered into the conversation, but forced there with a crowbar. He waits as she pours a large measure of the alcohol into her glass, following it up with tonic. He's not sure how to respond.

'Is it…' Steph starts, then pauses, taking a large swig of her drink. 'Is it something you've ever thought about?'

'Having a family?' he asks.

'Yes.' She looks at him at last. Her gaze is wide, almost pleading.

'I had a family.'

'One of your own,' she says quietly.

'I…' Robin stops. 'I haven't thought about it,' he lies. He knows there is a definite right and wrong answer here; this is a discussion that could go badly wrong.

'What? Never?' she asks.

He's already felt the previous good mood in the room evaporating, and now he stares down at his hands, feeling her close scrutiny.

'Do we have to talk about this now?' he tries, but she shakes her head, her shoulders rigid.

'I was going to bring it up later, but now is as good a time as any. I'm thirty-seven, Rob,' she continues. Her voice has lost its friendly edge, replaced by a dogged weariness he doesn't like at all. 'And I would like to have kids. I've wasted enough time.'

The saucepan's still furiously boiling away next to her, but she ignores it. 'You and I— When we first met, I enjoyed our little hook-ups, because that's all they were. But now...' She sighs. 'I like you, Robin—'

'I like you too—'

'No.' She shakes her head sadly. 'I really like you. More than you like me, I suspect, and that feeling's only going to get worse. I'd rather know now, before I get in too deep.' She walks across to the kitchen table and sits opposite him; he knows what she's going to ask. To get to the point she danced around earlier. 'Do you want to have children, Rob?'

'I...' he begins. He always thought he would. Being a part of Alex and James's short lives confirmed that to him. He knew then that he wanted kids of his own, little people to help form and grow and love. But the hard ball forming in the pit of his stomach as he thinks about it? That he can't deny.

The thought of a baby in his life terrifies him. The idea that he would love someone, like he loved those boys, then lose them again? It would be too much.

'I don't know,' he replies honestly. 'Probably not.'

He looks up now, and sees the emotion on her face.

She nods. 'Then you should leave.'

'Steph—'

'Please.' She's looking down to the floor, unable to meet his gaze. 'Just go.'

He pauses, about to protest, but there's something final in her tone. He stands up, then gently puts his hand on her shoulder. Without looking up, she puts her hand on his, squeezes, then takes it away again.

He picks up his coat. Desperately, he wants things to go back to the way they were before this conversation happened. But he knows that's not a possibility. He doesn't want to lose her. Not because of the sex, but because he suspects she's the closest thing to a friend that he has.

But he stays silent, then turns and walks out of her front door, pulling it closed with a gentle click behind him.

42

Fucking Kal. What an arsehole. Amy's furious – how dare he? How dare he say that she needs help?

She barely remembers the drive home, takes a diazepam the moment she gets in the door, then follows it up with a large glass of Chardonnay. Fuck them all, she thinks, pulling her ridiculous dress off in the kitchen and walking into the bedroom. She already feels the welcome fuzz descending. The warm blanket of delirium that only choice pharmaceuticals can provide.

She gets into bed and pulls her duvet over the top of her. Precariously holding her wine glass at an angle, she gets her phone out and sends a text.

Fuck you, she types, then presses send to Kal. Not exactly eloquent, she admits, through her addled brain. She giggles slightly. But to the point.

She sees a message has come in from her sister and opens it up.

That detective came to see me on Thurs, it says. *He knows I drugged him. He's angry.*

Amy replies: *So? Has he arrested you?*

She waits. Three small dots appear, then a ping. *No. If he does he'll get himself into trouble. But he's after you.*

Fucking detective. Arsehole, Amy thinks. She finishes her wine and sends a message back. *What am I supposed to do about that?*

Just don't do anything stupid. Got to go, working.

Amy throws her phone away from her with disgust. She slumps back on her pillow. Fucking slut sister, she thinks. She feels her eyes closing. What does she think I'm going to do?

Then her eyes snap open. She sits up again, grabbing her phone from where it's landed at the end of her bed. I'm a genius, she thinks, opening up a new email. And she starts to type.

43

Sunday

'Why do you ask? Why do you want to know?'

Freya knew this would be tricky. How to explain to Trevor Stevens' wife that they're looking into his death again. And on a Sunday morning, at that. Freya sits in the overheated living room, perched awkwardly on the edge of the sofa, the wife opposite her.

'We're doing a review of all deaths down that stretch of the A32,' Freya lies. 'With a view to reducing the speed limit. And thank you for meeting me at such short notice,' she continues, 'but with my busy case load this is the only time I'm free.'

Stevens' wife still looks confused, but nods slowly. She's a tiny woman, her face shrivelled where time and grief have removed anything that might make her attractive. She has a skein of bright green wool next to her and two knitting needles, which she fingers nervously.

'And Trevor was still attending AA meetings regularly,' Freya prompts again.

'Yes. Less than he was when he came out of prison, but still once or twice a week. And seeing his sponsor. Sure you don't want a cup of tea?'

'No, I'm fine, thank you.' She does, desperately, but doesn't feel she wants to disturb this woman any more than she should. 'Could I have the name of his sponsor?' Freya asks.

The wife looks at Freya as if she's stupid. 'I don't know his name. That's why they call it anonymous.'

'Right.' Another dead end. 'And how was Trevor feeling, around that time?'

'Feeling?'

'Depressed, happy, anything different to normal?'

The wife thinks for a moment, her lips puckering. 'The accident, the first one, you know, took its toll on Trev. He took it bad.' She picks up the knitting, as if to start again, then lowers it. 'He blamed himself for that family dying.'

And so he should have, Freya thinks, but doesn't say it. She spent the last evening going through the box related to the death of Robin's sister. The investigation was brief. Initial hit-and-run, followed by a confession from Stevens. The evidence was clear: even though five hours had passed between the crash and Stevens turning himself in, he was still over the legal limit. Stevens' massive Peugeot 3008 SUV had failed to stop at a red light and ploughed into the side of Georgia Riley's tiny Suzuki Alto. They hadn't stood a chance.

The photos were galling: the Suzuki pushed off the road, side caved in, barely recognisable as a car. Cones littered around; debris scattered across the tarmac.

In comparison, Stevens' SUV seemed untouched.

The wife continues: 'He thought it was an act of God that the judge only gave him three years in prison. He was desperate to make amends. He gave up drinking, joined AA, went to our local church. He sang in the choir. He had a lovely baritone.'

The wife beams at Freya and she forces a grin.

'He'd seen a lot, Trev, from his time in the army.' She picks up the knitting and pushes one needle next to the other then starts to work, her movements automatic. 'Twenty years, give or take. Iraq, Germany, Northern Ireland. We went all over the place. But nothing affected him like the death of that family. He even went to see them, to apologise, but they weren't having any of it.'

'He did?'

'Yeah.' The needles continue their clicking. 'Took a lot for him to do that. The husband had a long chat with him. And although Trev said they were far away from forgiveness, he felt better.'

'What about the brother?' Freya asks. 'Did he speak to him too?'

'Yeah.' The mouth puckers again. 'Robert something. He was one of yours, in the police, I remember that. Wouldn't even open the door. Told him to...' The wife clears her throat. 'Eff off,' she finishes quietly.

Sounds like Robin, Freya thinks. 'I'm sorry I have to ask this,' she begins. 'But do you think Trevor was trying to kill himself that night?'

'What? No!' The wife looks horrified. 'Trevor would never have done something like that. Not to me, not to Emily. His life was back on track. We were happy.'

Her fingers work the wool, and two fat teardrops roll down her cheek. Freya hands her a tissue.

'I'm sorry, but I wanted to be sure,' she says.

'He would never. Never,' the wife replies.

–

Freya thanks the woman and leaves, climbing back into her car. As she starts the engine of her tiny Fiat 500, she thinks about Georgia Riley's choice of vehicle. Would she have survived if she'd been driving something bigger? Something more solid? Suddenly, Robin and his massive old Volvo makes sense.

So the wife doesn't believe he was drinking. But then alcoholics can be secretive, everyone knows that. Still, it feels strange to Freya.

She gets home, makes a cup of tea, and goes back over the files from Trevor Stevens' death. She thinks about asking to meet Emily, the daughter, but she doesn't want to raise any more difficult questions. She's already called the Texaco garage and the kid confirmed they can't find the old transactions made by the other eyewitnesses, so that's a no go. The AA sponsor is closed off, too. So that's it. Although maybe Steph knows more by now.

Freya looks up at the time: 11:34. Respectable enough, even for a Sunday, and she picks up her phone and calls. As she listens to it ring, the thought flashes into her head that maybe Steph Harper is having a lazy lie-in with her boss, and her cheeks flush slightly in response. But before she goes to hang up, the phone's answered.

'Yes?' Steph sounds out of breath, but Freya is reassured by the sound of heavy footsteps and the rush of wind against the handset. Running, rather than shagging. 'You calling for the results, Freya?' Steph says, getting straight to the point.

Freya agrees. 'If that's okay, sorry to call on a—'

But Steph cuts her off. 'I'm three miles from your house. I'll take a detour. Give me half an hour.'

While Freya waits, she looks back through the files from the sister's death. Forensic reports, mechanical overview of the SUV (*no defects found contributory to collision*), pathology results from the basic post-mortem. She skims them all until something catches her eye.

A line, in the middle of the report about Georgia Riley's cause of death.

> ...*examination revealed a gravid uterus, containing a female foetus, estimated to be 21/40*...

Oh, Robin, Freya thinks. She was pregnant? As if it couldn't have been any worse.

Next to her, her mobile buzzes. But it's not her usual phone, it's the second one, the one she used for all calls to Jonathan. She was looking at it last night. Rereading the messages between them at two a.m. when she couldn't sleep, her mind too full of him. And now the battery is flat and she's charging it.

She picks it up and looks at it, recognising the number.

You don't give up, do you, she thinks, a fond smile for her boss. But it worries her. He's still trying to track down the mistress, and if he's calling the mobile, who knows what else he might be doing? It's only a matter of time before he finds her.

And there's the small matter of Jonathan's laptop. Stolen by her, potentially holding evidence from the hidden cameras that could show what happened that weekend. But hand it in now, and she's buggered. She's on there, too – in more ways than one. If only she knew his password, she thinks for the hundredth time.

Her doorbell rings and she hastily hides the mobile in a drawer. She opens the door and Steph stands in front of her, sweaty, decked out in skintight Lycra, trainers on her feet, water bottle in hand.

'I can't stay for long,' she says, getting her breath back and stepping into the hallway. 'Don't want to cool down too much.'

'You didn't have to come all the way over here,' Freya says.

But Steph shrugs. 'Makes a nice change. I was going to call you anyway.'

'You have the results from the tox screen? Was he drinking?'

'Don't know,' Steph replies, and Freya's disappointed. They walk through to the living room and, before Freya can stop her, Steph picks up one of the reports from the floor. 'You're looking into the Riley case, too?' Steph asks.

'Just wanted to know the background,' Freya says. 'Did you know Georgia Riley was pregnant?'

'Was she? No.' Steph's mouth turns down, her chin wobbles, and for a moment Freya thinks she might cry.

'Six months along. You okay?' she asks softly.

'Yeah, fine. Just me and Robin… we… split up.' She shrugs miserably. 'If we were together long enough to even call it that.'

'Oh, Steph, I'm sorry.' Freya goes to hug her, even despite her sweaty look, but Steph pulls away.

'It's fine, really, it's fine. I knew it would happen, it was inevitable. Anyway,' she says, pulling herself together. 'In response to your question, Trevor Stevens had no drugs prescribed, anti-depressants or otherwise. So nothing that supports your theory of a suicide. But I found something new about his death.'

'What?' Freya asks, her curiosity piqued.

'I went back over the pathology reports,' Steph continues, then takes a swig from her water bottle. 'I reviewed all the photographs from the post-mortem. There was considerable soot in the larynx, trachea and bronchi, and evidence of heat trauma to the mucosa.'

Freya stares at her, confused. 'What does that mean?' she asks.

'Trevor Stevens was still breathing after he hit the tree. The injuries from the crash didn't kill him.' Steph looks at Freya, her face grim. 'The fire did it. He was burnt alive.'

44

Robin sleeps late – a welcome change, waking up slowly, without the frantic beep of his alarm. After he left Steph, he spent the rest of the evening on his sofa, the takeaway pizza a poor substitute for the delicious-smelling lasagne he hadn't been able to sample.

He briefly debates calling her, but doesn't get further than that. There's no point. He hasn't miraculously changed his mind; he still knows that the idea of kids terrifies him.

He gets out of bed, walks down the stairs to his kitchen and stares into his empty fridge. He puts a coat on over his T-shirt and tracksuit bottoms, trainers on his feet and walks down to the Co-op, where he buys bacon and eggs and warm freshly baked bread. The air is cool, the sky grey, but it cheers him to be out of the house and actually getting some fresh air into his lungs. Maybe Steph isn't so off the mark with her constant exercise, he thinks. Maybe a run could do him some good.

But first things first.

Home, he cooks the bacon, fries an egg, and sandwiches it between huge slabs of crusty bread. Tomato ketchup drips onto the table as he eats it, washing it down with two mugs of coffee.

It reminds him of break-ups in his past. His first stop would always be his sister.

Georgia would cook the same. Her bacon was always crispy to the point of being burnt, her fried eggs always broken, but he never cared. She'd sit and listen to his tales of woe: he was always the dumped, never the one doing the dumping, driving his girlfriends to the point of desperation so that they had no choice but to split up with him. He was never cruel, just neglectful. Forgetting birthdays, working overtime, constantly late. Georgia would roll her eyes, say, 'Rob, you'll never fall in love if you don't *try*.' Then stand up and offer him another cup of coffee.

Later, Liam joined them for these post-mortems, enjoying the perk of his own bacon sarnie, while he half listened in contemplative silence.

'Perhaps they're just not right for you, Rob,' he'd say at last. 'When you're ready, you'll know.'

'And you knew, did you, love?' Georgia would say, dropping a kiss on her husband's cheek.

And he'd reply, 'From the moment I saw you,' looking up adoringly at his wife.

Sitting here, remembering the obvious love between his brother-in-law and his sister, makes Robin think again about the reason they don't speak any more.

It was a Sunday, like this one. Robin was alone, as usual, when he heard the knock on his door. He was about to answer it, when the man's voice shouted through.

'Please,' the voice said. 'I just want to talk,' and Robin knew who it was.

He'd had letters already, short calls on the phone. Trevor Stevens wanted to apologise for murdering his family. And he could go to hell.

Robin opened the door a crack, but not enough for the man to see through.

'Fuck off,' he shouted in return. 'I don't want to talk to you.'

'Please…'

'Fuck. Off,' Robin yelled, with so much intensity it made his throat ache, then slammed the door in his face.

He got straight on the phone to Liam. 'He came here,' he said, the force of his anger still reverberating in his body.

'And did you talk to him?'

'No.'

Liam paused. 'Maybe you should, Robin,' he replied.

Robin was speechless. 'You did? You spoke to that bastard?'

'Yes,' Liam said softly. 'He wanted to apologise, so I let him.'

'You've forgiven him? I can't... I can't believe you would do this to her. To the boys.'

'I haven't...' Liam started, but Robin hung up, hurling his phone across the room in disgust.

And that was it. The beginning of a series of arguments between them. Liam trying to explain his point of view, even sending a letter that Robin furiously screwed up into a ball and binned. He could never understand. Liam forgiving the man who'd killed his family? No. Just no.

Robin finishes his bacon sandwich and tidies up the mess in his kitchen. Then, with nothing else to do, and the thought of a Sunday run conveniently forgotten, he pulls out his laptop and files and gets to work.

The first thing he does is call that number again. The elusive mistress. It's been bothering Robin from the beginning, a woman who might know more about Jonathan and how he died. They traced the number back to a pay-as-you-go mobile bought from Carphone Warehouse over a year ago. But the records show it being bought and registered by Jonathan Miller himself, no way of knowing who he gave it to next.

The number rings, and Robin waits. He's tried it a few times over the last week, but each time it's been turned off. Robin's hopeful, but it rings out to the generic voicemail again.

He's not sure where else to look. Freya's been through the telematics for the car: no strange destinations. The laptop's still missing. He even went back to some of the names from Khalid Riaz's party, but no, they said, mistress? Not Jonathan, surely.

If it wasn't for the messages on Jonathan's mobile, he'd start to wonder if she even existed.

He looks at them again, now downloaded into an easy-to-navigate Excel document. Whoever she is, it's clear she liked him. And the feeling was reciprocated, declarations of love from both sides. Robin feels strange, reading someone's personal correspondence in this way, but needs must, and getting a picture of this other relationship in Jonathan's life is vital.

So where the hell is she? Why hasn't she come forward? Robin keeps on coming back to that. Jonathan's death was in the papers, along with his own name and the number of the incident room, so why hasn't she called?

He's still waiting on forensics. Tox screen pending at the lab. All other lines of enquiry exhausted for now, Robin sets his sights on this woman.

Whoever she is, Robin resolves, pouring himself another mug of coffee, he'll find her.

45

Freya and Steph stand at Freya's front door, Steph bouncing on the balls of her feet, readying herself to run home.

'What a way to go,' Steph says, zipping her top up tight under her chin. 'Trapped by your own car, smelling the petrol. Knowing your last moments will be in all-encompassing pain and terror.'

Freya winces in response to the vivid picture Steph presents.

'Why did they miss it before?' she asks.

Steph shrugs. 'Would have been a difficult decision, in terms of cause of death. His injuries from the crash were extensive. If the fire hadn't started, I don't think he would have lived long after.' She turns, jogging on the spot for a moment. 'The pathologist's call: he went one way, I'd go another. Doesn't make too much difference at the end of the day. The guy's still dead; nothing would have saved him.'

Freya watches Steph jog off down the road, then closes the door, simultaneously glad of her cosy central heating while feeling guilty for making no effort to do any exercise whatsoever. She hears her phone ring from the living room, and goes to answer it.

'West? Anything?' DCI Baker asks, without greeting.

'It's Sunday, guv.'

'And you're not working?' Baker hears the pause. 'As I thought. So, out with it.'

Freya glances at the file. 'Nothing suspicious, as far as I can tell. No evidence of suicide. Cause of death confirmed to be from the accident.'

'Had he been drinking?'

'Dr Harper's still waiting on results, but I can't find any evidence of it.'

Baker notices the reluctance in her voice. 'So why your hesitation?' he asks.

Freya's not sure. Maybe it's that her cop nature wants to see the crime in everything, so when there's nothing, she can't help looking for more.

'Why did you ask me to look into this? What information was the coroner sent?' she asks.

'Not much, to be honest,' Baker replies. 'An anonymous email from someone who knew him from AA. Who said that there was no way he'd been drinking, and even if he had, he wouldn't have drunk Jack Daniel's.'

'Not exactly concrete evidence,' Freya says, confused.

'No,' Baker agrees. 'But she threatened to go to the press, tell them what she knew.'

'It's hardly a front-page story.'

'And if the coroner wasn't such a cautious so-and-so, we wouldn't have bothered. But he was worried, so here we are. *Have* you found anything new?'

'Well, the wife agrees, says he wasn't drinking—'

'As she would.'

'Yes. And I can't trace the witnesses in the petrol station—'

'There were witnesses at a petrol station?'

'Stevens came in that night, bought fuel. He spoke to someone—'

'Who?'

'No idea.' Freya's never worked with Neal Baker before. He has a different style to Butler – more directive, questions firing at her before she has time to think.

'And no mechanical reason for the accident?'

'No. Just human error, no more than that.'

'Good,' Baker says, and Freya doesn't like to argue with the finality in his voice. 'Get your report to me by end of day tomorrow and get back to the Miller case. Between you and me, Butler's coming up a blank. I need someone else to help him finish his enquiries and put it to bed. Will that be a problem, West?'

'No, guv,' Freya agrees, and hangs up the phone.

She sits back on her sofa, the phone still in her hand, evidence twitching in her head. So Trevor Stevens was looking for salvation. Seeking to make amends. He reaches out to the husband, Liam Riley, has a nice chat. Not so much with Butler, but then that's not surprising. Freya doesn't take her boss for the forgive and forget sort. Stevens is going to AA meetings, speaking to his sponsor. There's no evidence he was drinking, bar the burnt JD bottle in the footwell, that Freya knows he didn't buy at the petrol station.

So where did it come from? Freya frowns. She could try and find out: track down every single place he shopped in the days before his death? It's possible, she thinks. She could pull his financials, contact every shop, assuming he paid by card. But it was two years ago, a tired voice says in her head. And what if he paid in cash? There'd be no trace.

And even if he had bought it, what then? It would wrap things up nicely, but wreck the wife's image of her dead husband. There are so many lives ruined already, why make it worse?

Freya gets up, goes to the fridge and cobbles together some lunch from the last pieces of cheese and bread. As she eats it, she sits in front of her laptop, running the CCTV footage again. The same couple, the man and the woman. The same faceless man, the same conversation. And no way of knowing who any of them are.

She gets up and makes herself a cup of tea. But when she sits back down, she realises the disc has still been running. Churning out the next file, black and white again, unrecognisable customers on the screen. And that's when she realises – it's a different camera. She didn't see the other one. It must have been hidden in the corner of the shop, quietly recording footage from the door.

Barely daring to think, she scrolls through the timestamp, the clock ticking round at the bottom of the screen. Daylight outside fades; the lights switch on in the petrol station.

More customers come in through the door, then go out of shot. They walk up the aisle, buy chocolate and sweets. Pay, chat, smile.

Then she stops. Trevor Stevens walks in, alive and well. He goes to the bank of fridges first, taking out a bottle of Coke, then he walks away, where Freya knows he pays at the till. Then he's back in shot, and here's the guy.

Freya lets her breath out in a rush. This angle's no better. The man's closer this time, but still turned away. There's nothing new here. No distinctive markings on his clothes that would identify him.

The two of them talk a while longer, and Freya sees Trevor laugh, then place his hand on the squaddie's arm. Then they turn. And Freya's body goes cold.

It's only a fragment of a second, but for that moment, the man faces the camera. And she sees him. With shaking hands, she rewinds the tape and watches again. She doesn't dare blink. It can't be him.

She watches it again, and again. And each time, her brain refuses to acknowledge what her eyes are saying is true.

Her brain just says, *oh god, it can't be. It can't be him.*

46

Monday

The instruction to see Baker comes early. Robin's barely reached his desk, coffee in hand, computer still booting up.

'What does he need to see me for?' Robin asks.

The woman shrugs. 'Didn't say, just told me to get you. Personally.'

'Personally?' Robin gets up and follows her. This can't be good news, and sure enough, Baker's face is grim when he walks into the office.

'Sit down, Robin,' he says.

Robin does as he's told. 'What's this about?'

'I've had a complaint.'

'What? Who from?' Robin can feel his face flushing, anger surging round his veins.

'Amy Miller.'

Shit. This is not going to be good, Robin thinks, but waits for Baker to speak.

Baker runs a hand across his shaved head, clearly exasperated. 'At least, we think that's what this is.' He points to the piece of paper on the desk. 'It's barely intelligible, making some accusation about you and her sister, someone called Olivia Cross. You know who that is?'

'She's a witness, yes.'

'Says you've slept with her.'

'That's bollocks,' Robin explodes.

'Says she's been to your house.'

'That's... Fuck.'

'So that part is true?' Baker asks, but doesn't wait for Robin to reply. He leans forward across the desk. 'Listen, Rob, and I say this to you as a friend, not your boss. Get your shit together. I have no choice but to pass this to Professional Standards, but to tell the truth, they'll have a hard time making sense of this collection of—' he glances down at the paper again '—ramblings. She sounds mental. So get your story straight. Fast. And for crying out loud, conclude all you can on her husband's supposed murder before PSD close it down. You hear me?'

Robin knows when he's beaten. 'Yes, guv.'

'Now piss off.'

Robin doesn't wait to be told twice. He walks quickly back to his desk, then picks up the phone, leaving a message for Greg to hurry up with the forensic checks on the car and the porn.

The complaint from Amy Miller still burns, but it confirms one thing to him – she's nervous. He must be on the right track. Something happened that day at the Premier Inn. And it wasn't a nasty accident with a belt.

He thinks about the data they have. The telematics from the car, geotagging on the phone. Maybe if they can compare the two, find some points that correspond – places both his car and his phone went so it would definitely be Jonathan Miller – it would lead them somewhere new.

He picks up the phone and calls Greg again.

'For fuck's sake, I got your message, Butler. I can't make them go any faster.'

'No, it's not that. Listen, if I send you two sets of Excel data, can you run one of your whizzy formulas? See if any of the GPS coordinates match?'

'Yeah, run a VLOOKUP, simple. As long as it's an identical sequence of information.'

'Can you do that for me, if I send you the spreadsheets?'

'Or maybe an Index Match...'

'Can you do it?'

'Yeah, sure.'

'Now?'

A sigh from Greg. 'You owe me, you dick. A proper introduction to the lovely Freya West, if nothing else.'

'Deal.'

Robin quickly emails them across, then sits back in his chair to wait. He taps his biro on the desk for a moment, then gets up and carries his mug to the kitchen to make a coffee. When he gets back, the email's waiting for him.

He opens it, his hand reaching for the mouse even before he's sat down.

Greg's merged the two spreadsheets into one. Hundreds of lines of data. GPS coordinates in columns, some highlighted in yellow.

'You genius, Greg,' Robin mutters as he opens Google Maps and starts typing them in.

It's slow work, and dull. Every location identified has to be checked against the list of known addresses for the people in Jonathan's life. His house, Kal's house, Waitrose, his office. Where's his DC when you need her to do the shit work? he thinks.

And where is West, anyway? Surely she should be done on her special assignment soon. How long does shitty admin work take? When he asked her about it, she was evasive; there was definitely something she wasn't telling him. He's not worked with Freya long, but from knowing her around the office her default position is articulating whatever's on her mind. There is no filter between her brain and her mouth. So if she is quiet, then...

Robin stops and sits back in his chair. He's assumed her unusual demeanour is a result of his influence. His less than cheery manner, driving the poor woman down. But maybe it isn't that. He's known DCs committed to an investigation, but this has been next level. She seems... emotionally invested.

He remembers her crying when they had to notify Amy Miller of Jonathan's death. Her protestations that she knew him, sure, but not well. The supposed sickness the next day. The detailed knowledge that Jonathan Miller had had a mole removed six months before. He didn't think much about it at the time. But now?

He leans forward, then types her address into Google, looking up the GPS coordinates. Then, testing his basic Excel skills to the limit, he tries a search. Nothing. He remembers Greg's words, *identical sequence of information*, shortens the number and tries again.

And then he sees it.

And everything makes sense.

47

Freya hears the ring of her doorbell and looks up in surprise. Since viewing the video the day before, she hasn't left the house. She barely slept, tossing and turning all night, debating what to do. Every now and again, going back to the laptop, rewinding, then starting from the beginning, hoping to see something different on the grainy black and white image. But she knows it's him.

The doorbell rings again, and this time she gets up and walks to it. She looks through the spyhole, then jumps back. She stops, her hand over her mouth.

'Freya! Open the door. I know you're home.'

Shit. But she has no choice. Slowly, she pulls the lock back and opens it.

'Sarge…' she begins, but Butler steams his way past her into her house. She closes the door, then turns to face him. He has a pile of paper in his hand, and he thrusts it towards her.

'It was you,' he says. His eyes are narrowed, his stance defensive. She's seen him this angry before, but never directed at her.

'What are you…' she starts, then looks at the paper in her hand. It's a spreadsheet, rows of numbers, and then a printed-out map. Showing her address.

'I compared the GPS coordinates logged from Jonathan's car to the ones on his phone. And your address comes up. Over and over again. It was you. Don't lie to me.' Her boss shakes his head, furiously. 'Not now.'

She walks past him into the kitchen and sits down at the table. He follows her.

'I need an explanation, Freya,' he says. 'I need to know why I shouldn't suspend you.'

'Sit down,' she says. He's still standing in the doorway, staring at her. 'Please, Sarge.'

He pauses for a second, then does as she asks.

'Was it you?' he asks. She nods, staring at the table. 'Were you the woman having an affair with Jonathan Miller?'

His tone is softer this time, and to her horror she finds tears blurring her vision.

'We were in love,' she manages. 'He was going to leave Amy.'

'But why?' Butler says. He gets up and fetches a piece of kitchen towel from the side and hands it to her, sitting back down, his concern battling against his anger. 'Why did you stay on the case? Hearing all those details? That must have been...' He shakes his head, resigned and tired. 'No one should see their loved one like that.'

Freya wipes her eyes and blows her nose. 'I knew if I told you, I'd be off the investigation. And I knew that there was no way Jon killed himself. Especially like that.'

He stops, staring at the floor. She can see he's thinking, no doubt trying to decide what to do with her. 'Why didn't you trust me to do my job?' he asks at last.

Freya looks at him. 'It's not that. I did. I just...' She dabs at her eyes again. 'When we left the house on that first day, you thought it was DV. You thought he'd been abusing her, and I knew it wasn't true. I didn't trust *her*. I thought she'd manipulate you, the same way she manipulated Jon.'

Freya stands up, then walks to the living room. She reaches under the sofa and pulls out the laptop.

Butler sees it and sighs, long and loud. 'Oh, Freya.' He takes it out of her hand and sets it on the table, looking at it. 'It's Jonathan's?' Freya nods, miserably. 'Where did you get it?'

'I nicked it. From his house. I didn't want you to find it and know about me.'

'But... oh shit.' He shakes his head. 'How are we going to explain this?' He looks at her, worry clear on his face. 'Baker will suspend you. He'll have to. Tampering with evidence. Interfering with a police investigation. *Burglary?*'

'I know.' Freya stares at the bit of kitchen roll clutched in her fingers. Then she looks up at her boss. She knows she has to tell him. 'But that's not the worst thing that's happened this week.'

She pulls her own laptop over and opens the lid. The video is still showing on the screen. She sees her boss glance at it, then back at her, confused.

'I found this,' she says.

48

Robin's anger has faded. Seeing the devastated look on Freya's face just confirmed what he already knew – that she had made a terrible mistake, but that she'd done it out of her love for this guy. And he knows what love can make you do.

But now this laptop's in front of him his anger has turned to confusion. He looks at the video on Freya's computer. It's paused, two grainy figures in what seems to be a shop.

'The special assignment that Baker gave me?' she starts. 'It was this.' She points at the screen. 'Looking into Trevor Stevens' death.'

'Trevor…' he begins, but a horrible feeling is starting to grow.

'The man that killed your sister and her twins, yes.'

'But, why?'

He knows why; Steph told him. But she also told him that she'd found nothing new. Everything had been burnt to a crisp in the fire. So, what has Freya been doing?

He listens to her waffle on. Talking about anonymous emails, someone from Trevor's AA group telling the coroner that Stevens couldn't possibly have been drinking. That the sort of alcohol was wrong, or some other such bollocks. Freya has been to see Stevens' wife, who said the same thing.

'So, what?' Robin interrupts. 'That's hardly reason to reopen the inquest.'

'No, but this is.'

Freya turns the laptop round to face him, then presses play. He feels her eyes watching him, as his fix on the screen. And that's when it dawns on him.

It's a petrol station, not a shop, and that's Trevor Stevens. And the other guy, the one in the black hood and jeans.

'That's you,' Freya says, softly.

He stares at the video. He can hardly breathe as he watches the man talk to Trevor Stevens. Laughing, joking.

'You follow Stevens out of the petrol station, Robin,' Freya continues. He notices her voice is shaking. 'What happened? What did you do?'

Robin can't bear to watch it any more. He reaches forward and slams the lid of the laptop shut. He looks at Freya. She's staring at him, her eyes wet, her face drawn.

'*Is* that you?' she asks quietly.

He knows she desperately wants him to say no. To come up with a reasonable explanation as to why that man looks so much like him. Or an alibi, anything, so she can breathe again. But there's no point in lying.

'Yes,' he says. 'That's me.'

He sees her body sag. Then he adds the words that he's kept quiet for so long. Words he thought he would take with him to the grave.

'I killed him. I killed the man who murdered my sister.'

Part 3

49

Oh, shit. Oh shit oh shit oh shit.

Freya feels the words loop in her head. Now he's said it, confessed to murder, she realises she didn't think through what she'd do next. This isn't just some criminal they've arrested on the streets; this is Butler. Her boss.

She slumps down in the chair opposite him. It's warm, too warm: she can feel damp patches under her arms, a faint sheen of sweat rising on her forehead. The room is quiet; the silence is deafening.

She knows he wants to talk. She can tell by the look on his face: his eyes constantly shifting focus, the internal monologue desperate for escape. Two hard lines appear between his eyebrows as he stares at the tabletop.

He's a detective, a sergeant in the Major Crimes Unit. She feels the anger growing. This isn't what they do. Killing? Murder? They arrest the criminals; they don't become one. But then these past few weeks have shown her just what she herself is capable of.

'What did you do?' she asks. 'Tell me.'

He looks up. She can see the conflict behind his eyes.

'Are you sure you want to know?' he replies, softly.

Does she? Maybe she should walk away now, leave the disc and the video with him and pretend none of it happened. But she's in too deep, with Jonathan, with everything she's done already. And her professional curiosity can't resist. She has to know what happened, on that fateful night in the rain.

'Yes,' she replies.

He nods slowly, then she watches in disbelief as his face collapses. His mouth turns down, his chin wobbles and he stares up at the ceiling, jaw clenching, trying hard not to cry.

'What did you do, Robin?' Freya asks again.

Butler meets her gaze for a second. His eyes are red-rimmed, his face tainted with grief.

Then he starts to talk.

And she thinks: I could never do that. Kill someone. Never.

But something in the back of her mind hesitates. She thinks about Jon. About his death, strung up in that hotel room, naked, all dignity destroyed. She thinks about Amy Miller. About the evidence they don't have, the truth they don't yet know.

And something whispers: *Are you sure?*

Are you sure?

50

Freya sits opposite him, quiet, her soft blue eyes fixed on his face. He expected anger, judgement, even fear. This sympathy is unnerving.

And now the confession is out of his mouth, he doesn't feel as he thought he would. He imagined that if someone else knew, he'd panic. That he'd run, or cry, or— Something other than the way he's feeling now.

All he feels is relief. A sense of calm. An inevitability that what will be, will be.

'What did you do, Robin?'

She uses his first name. It sounds strange coming out of her mouth, but correct, like a level of familiarity has been breached. He killed someone and she knows it. There will be no 'sarge' now. She's the one in charge.

'You got anything to drink?' he asks.

She nods and points towards the fridge. He opens it and looks at the bottle of white.

'You got anything stronger?' he asks, but she shakes her head. It'll do. Robin twists the bottle open then pours two large glasses, handing one to Freya. He takes a large gulp, then another, sitting back down at the table.

'He came to see me – Trevor Stevens.' Freya nods; she must have worked that bit out too. 'He talked about redemption, and forgiveness, and God, and I couldn't stand it. I refused to let him in the house. He shouted all of this through the door.' Robin takes another swig of wine. 'And then he said that he was rebuilding his life. That he was going to AA and making amends. And all I could think was, you can't bring Georgia or the boys back, can you?'

Robin reaches into his pocket and pulls out his wallet. He opens it and takes out a worn, folded photo, putting it in front of Freya. He noticed that the newspaper article he'd kept was gone. Taken, he assumes, by Olivia Cross. Stored as a reminder of what he'd done, that he must never go to those depths again. But this photo, thankfully, Liv left.

'That's them,' he says. She looks at it, then back at him. 'That's my sister Georgia, and Alex and James.' He points to each one in turn. 'They're dead, and he was alive, and happy.' He meets Freya's gaze. 'He was fucking happy, Freya, *happy*. I couldn't stand it. So that's when I started following him.'

'To do what?' Freya asks.

'I don't know.' He shakes his head, correcting himself. 'I did know. I wanted to catch him doing something illegal. Arrest him for breaching the terms of his parole. Get him sent back to prison.'

Freya's staring at the photo now, her finger tracing their faces.

'So I followed him,' he repeats. 'Not all the time, just when I could. He was dull. He went to the supermarket, to his AA meetings, nothing untoward. And then that Friday I watched him go into an off-licence and buy the Jack Daniel's. I shadowed him to an underground car park, and watched him drink the whole bloody thing.' He glances at Freya. Her eyes are locked on him, barely blinking. 'Then he started his engine. I couldn't believe he was driving drunk again, Freya. So I trailed him to that petrol station. I wanted – no – I *had* to confront him. I was furious. But then he didn't recognise me.'

'Weren't you at his court case, at the sentencing?'

'Yeah.' Robin nods and swallows more wine. It burns at the back of his throat. 'But it was clear he was pissed. He was holding it together well, but his eyes were all over the place.'

She frowns. 'There was no evidence of that in the path report…'

'I know, I read it. But he was, I swear. I watched him drink it. I could smell it on him. And the anger…'

Robin feels his hands ball into fists, remembering the feeling from that night. It was worse than the thought that Trevor Stevens was alive and happy – knowing that he was doing it again, that he would kill someone else.

'Why didn't you arrest him?' Freya says, the question he's asked himself so many times since.

'I… I don't know,' Robin replies. 'I told myself I should go with him, see what he'd do next. Potentially make it worse for him. But I think, in my heart, I just wanted him dead.' The stark truth. Out loud. 'I didn't want him back in prison, or to have his licence revoked. I wanted him dead.'

'What did you do?' Freya whispers.

Robin keeps on talking. He describes speaking to Stevens in the petrol station, laughing and joking, then mentioning he'd been in the army. He'd known Stevens had a history there, and that he wouldn't hesitate to give a lift to a fellow squaddie. He'd followed him out to the car, still unsure what was going to happen.

'And he was driving fast. Much, much too fast,' Robin says. He feels his chest tighten at the memory. Remembering kicking the Jack Daniel's bottle in the footwell by his feet, then the sudden exhilaration, knowing what he was going to do. 'So I reached over and grabbed the wheel.'

He remembers the rain, barely being able to see out of the windscreen as they careered down that road. He remembers Stevens with his foot hard to the floor, watching as the speedometer went past eighty. Feeling the car shake, the rumble of the wheels, then the loss of control as the tyres lost their grip.

Freya takes a sharp breath in. 'But you could have been killed,' she says, open-mouthed.

Robin clenches his jaw, then swallows, willing away the tightness in his throat. 'That was the plan, Freya.'

And then, to his dismay, he realises he's crying. He puts his hands over his face, trying to stop the flood of emotion, but it's too much. He can't help the great gulping sobs as he leans over the table. He feels a gentle arm round his shoulders, and slowly, slowly feels it abate. He knows Freya is still watching him, but he can't look at her: the shame, the feeling of worthlessness, of guilt, is too much. He feels that one look from him and she'd know it all.

'I woke up. In a huge amount of pain, but alive.'

The smell of petrol, damp leaves. The creak of crumpled metal sinking into new positions. And the sudden panic, knowing he needed to get out of there.

'I managed to kick the door open,' he continues, 'and pretty much fell out of the car. I made it about ten metres away before the whole thing caught fire.' The warmth of the flames on his body, the feeling of the hairs on his arms singeing in the heat.

'And Stevens?' Freya asks.

He sits up now, pulling his hands down his face, wiping the tears away from his eyes. Freya gets up and fetches a tissue and he smiles weakly at her.

'I think he was already dead. But I didn't wait to find out. I could barely see from the airbag. My body was in agony. I managed to get across the road, through the hedge, to the field. I think I passed out there, too, because when I woke I could hear the sirens from the fire engine.'

Freya clamps her hand to her mouth. 'I remember now,' she says. 'We weren't working together but the gossip from the station. You were off for two days, and when you came back you had a broken arm, broken ribs.'

'Broken collarbone, severe whiplash. I made it home, lay low until the morning and then went to the hospital.'

'You said you'd fallen down your stairs.'

'They believed me. Everyone believed me. What was the alternative? That I'd killed someone? Baker took me aside when I was back at work and said that Stevens had died, and that's when I knew.'

'They didn't think anyone else had been in the car,' she finishes for him.

Robin nods. He watches her. She sits silently, taking in everything he's told her. But he's left out the biggest secret. That before he dragged himself off to the field, he'd stood, watching. He'd seen Stevens start to move, shifting in the driver's seat, regaining consciousness and realising he was trapped. He'd watched as the man's movements got more frantic, as panic set in. And he'd done nothing as the car caught fire.

He'd stood, listening to his screams, watching the man burn.

He takes another swallow from the wine in front of him. A drop misses and falls on the table, and he puts a shaking finger into it, swirling it around in frenetic loops on the polished oak.

'Do you want me to go to the station and hand myself in?' Robin asks.

'No.' Freya says it quickly, and he looks at her in surprise. She shakes her head, her eyes shut for a moment. Then she opens them again, and reaches across, taking his hands in hers.

The contact feels strange. Too intimate between sergeant and subordinate, but Robin knows they've crossed that line tonight.

'No,' she says again. 'I want you to find Jonathan's killer.'

51

Robin's talking, but Freya can barely hear the words. Her superior officer. Her boss. This man who, like her, is a detective: something that stands for honesty, and upholding the law. And he's talking to her about how he killed someone.

She touches the photograph in front of her. The woman that looks so much like Robin. The kids that were so similar to him, they could have been his.

Then she puts it down and takes Robin's hands.

She knows that if he goes to prison, nobody is going to believe their theory about how Jonathan died. Nobody will care. He was a man with a liking for dodgy sex acts, and one day it got the better of him and he died. That's how he'll be remembered. And there's no way she can tell anyone else about how she knows none of this was true, because she knew, loved, Jonathan intimately. She'll lose her job, for sure.

'No,' she says. 'I want you to find Jonathan's killer.'

He stares at her.

'You can do that,' he says. 'Look at how well you ran this investigation—'

'No, no, I can't. You know I can't. Baker's not giving you much longer to work the case. This is the only way we get justice for Jon. We find out who did it.'

'But this…' Robin points at the CCTV footage on the screen. 'What will we do about this?'

Freya presses the eject button on the computer and the disc pops out. She takes it and puts it in the plastic box, shutting it firmly.

'We make this disappear, Robin. I'll hang onto it. Or you can. And I'll write a report for Baker saying that I haven't found anything new on the Stevens case. Steph's doing the same.' At the mention of Steph, Robin's face clouds for a second, but he stays quiet. 'I'll write this report,' she continues, 'then get back on the investigation tomorrow. We'll sort this.'

Robin's still silent.

'Please?'

He looks up at her, and then slowly nods. He takes the photo of his family from the table, carefully folds it again and replaces it in his wallet. Freya realises how tired he looks, hollows under his cheekbones, dark smudges under his eyes.

'Okay then.' Robin puts his hand on the disc on the table, looks at it for a moment, then pushes it across to her. 'You keep this. We'll find who killed Jonathan. And then you can decide what to do from there.'

They walk to her front door in silence, Jonathan's laptop under Robin's arm. Once they get there, Robin turns, as if to say something, then thinks better of it. She watches him walk away into the dark, rainy night.

She shuts the door behind him. She goes back to the kitchen and stops, looking at the computer, at the disc in its plastic case.

It isn't too late, she tells herself. She can call Baker, tell him everything.

But Jonathan's killer will go free. She picks up the disc and carries it up to her bedroom, hiding it in her underwear drawer.

The wheels are in motion. Robin knows everything about her, and she knows about him. There's no way either of them can turn back now.

52

Tuesday

There's nothing different about the incident room today, but Robin feels a disconnect from his colleagues. These are people – good people – who work hard, solve crimes. And he is one of them, but somehow, today, he recognises that he has more in common with the people they seek to put behind bars.

Since he killed Trevor Stevens, he's done his best to leave it in his past. To try and forget the events of that day which left him limping frantically across a field, arm, shoulder, chest in agony, to get away from the fire that was burning behind him.

He heard the second explosion as the petrol tank caught fire, and for a moment he turned, watching the fireball in the distance, stark against the black night. And he listened for the sirens, waiting, debating. Should he go back – accept the punishment for what he'd done, or keep walking?

And he strode away. He made it to the nearest main road, teeth gritted, then kept going until he got back to his car. Falling through his front door, he stripped off the clothes he'd worn in the accident, putting them in a bin bag to throw away the next day. He downed paracetamol and beer and tried to sleep. Twelve hours later he was in A and E, being patched up by a patronising nurse, who told him next time be more careful when you're going downstairs, pissed.

He nodded, accepted contritely, then spent the next few days in bed. His neck was so painful he was barely able to move. Then back to work. A bit of piss-taking from his colleagues, and it was done.

Nobody looked closcly at Trevor Stevens' death. Nobody thought it was any more than a tragic accident.

And he began to relax. Just a bit.

Freya arrives at her desk at half ten.

She clicks her computer on. 'I've submitted my report to Baker,' she says, without looking at him.

'Thank you,' he replies quietly. 'You okay?'

'Fine,' she mutters. 'What do you want me looking at today, Sarge?'

Back to the conventions of old. Slowly he runs through everything he knows about the case. About the unknown, taller man driving Jonathan's car. About the DNA and fingerprints in the car and on the porn. The lack of witnesses at the party, and the fish and chip shop on the Friday night.

'What *do* we know?' Freya asks. He sees her miserable expression and feels like he's let her down.

'We know from the CCTV that someone else was driving his car, and we know Amy Miller has an alibi.' He sees Freya about to protest. 'I'm sorry, but even if Olivia Cross is lying, we have the waiters from the restaurant who confirm her story. And the laptop's down with the techies,' he continues. 'I've asked them to get through the password protection but do nothing else.' She looks at him, but doesn't ask. 'Get on the backgrounds for all our main suspects,' he finishes.

'How far back?'

'As far as you can. Back to childhood, if there's something. I'll chase up forensics, have another look for CCTV.'

She nods and turns away from him. The techies didn't ask where the laptop had come from, now wiped down and placed in a new evidence bag; they just took it eagerly. A new code to break. But he knows people will ask questions about the continuity of exhibits, so first thing this morning he pulled up the report filed after the original search and carefully added it to the list of evidence seized. It isn't great, but it will have to be enough. And falsifying records isn't the worst thing Robin has done in his career.

An hour later, and constant phone calls to the council haven't brought up any new CCTV from the area around the Premier Inn. Robin's phone rings, and he hesitates, seeing the name on the screen. *Steph*.

He debates declining the call, but knows they need to talk.

'DS Butler, I have results back on the tox screen from your asphyxiation victim.' Steph's voice is hard and businesslike.

'Steph, please,' Robin begins, but she cuts him off.

'Robin, I don't have time today. I have two PMs to complete. I just need to give you these results.'

'Fine.' He imagines her face at the other end of the line, mouth tense, eyes cast down.

'Jonathan Miller had a blood alcohol level of 0.1 at the time of death—'

'So nothing significant.'

'No. And consistent with the alcohol found in his stomach contents. Plus trace of some sort of benzodiazepine, although I can't tell which at this stage, and a cyclopyrrolone.'

'Which means?'

'He was sedated, and by some amount. The quantities in his blood, and adding this to the fact that there was very little food in his stomach, means he would have been woozy, if not unconscious when he died.'

'Thanks. And Steph…' he begins, but she's hung up. 'Fuck,' he mutters under his breath.

Freya turns. 'That was Steph?'

'Yeah. Jonathan was sedated when he died.'

'So that proves murder?' she says, her voice rising.

'Not necessarily. Maybe he took something because he was nervous about what he was going to do. Maybe he got the dose wrong and it contributed to his death.' Freya scowls. 'I'm just saying,' Robin adds. 'We need to be sure.'

'He didn't take any sedatives,' Freya says. 'Here.'

He pushes his chair over to her screen, and watches as she pulls up his medical reports. 'See?'

They both read down the notes – and sure enough, Jonathan Miller wasn't prescribed with anything.

'What's that there?' Robin asks. He points to a line at the bottom of the page. An appointment, the Friday before he died. 'Why did he go to the doctor's?'

'I'll find out,' Freya says, but Robin stops her.

'I'll do it. You stick with the backgrounds.'

Robin picks up the phone. Even though their investigation, with Freya on it, is dodgy as hell, he wants to keep her as far away as he can. She loved Jonathan Miller, and her memory of him should be preserved as much as possible.

The phone's answered quickly, the voice at the other end bored and grumpy. He explains the purpose for his call, and the receptionist grunts in response.

'I'll send an update through to the email address from last time,' she confirms, then hangs up.

Robin sighs, then taps his finger on the desk while he waits. He picks up his mobile and stares at it, as if it'll somehow give him the solution to the problem with Steph. He feels like he needs to apologise, but for what? He was telling the truth, but the reality of why, and everything entwined with it is so multifaceted he doesn't know how to begin.

Yes, he is scared by the idea of having kids, but no, it isn't because he doesn't want children, or he doesn't want them with her. It's because of his sister, and the twins, and the man he killed…

Fuck.

Perhaps he should just leave Steph alone. Let her get on with her life and find a nice man with a steady job who hasn't committed murder.

His email pings, interrupting him from the black chain of thought. He opens it and reads the brief notes on the page. Then he reads them again. The medical terms talk about viscosity, density, motility, but he can get the gist of it.

Four days before he died, the man that was supposedly leaving his wife had a fertility test. And the results were normal.

He glances across to Freya. But why?

If he was in love with Freya, why have a baby with his wife?

53

Freya's too busy at first to notice Robin's abrupt change in demeanour. She's typing names into the databases – the Police National Computer, the Record Management System – eyes rapidly scanning the information presented to her on the screen.

For Amy Miller, there's nothing. No previous convictions, no warnings, nothing. For Jonathan, the same. Then, at the bottom, she notices one small note. No charges brought, but a brief comment.

24/3/18, PC Watts, domestic disturbance, DV?

She knows what the notes mean. That acronym again.

'Sarge? Look at this.'

She turns, but Butler is still staring at his screen. 'Robin?'

'Hmm?'

He looks at her at last, then reads over her shoulder.

She notices him hesitate. 'So there was some sort of domestic violence in that household,' he says at last. 'Did…'

She knows what he's asking. 'No, Jonathan was never violent with me.' She meets his gaze. 'Never,' she says firmly.

'What was he like?' he asks tentatively.

'Jon? He…' How to describe the man she loved? How to do him justice? 'For my last birthday, he bought me a kite.'

Robin looks confused and she laughs. 'I'd mentioned in passing that when I was little we used to fly kites on the beach, and that I'd loved it. The flutter of the ribbons, the bright colours against the blue sky.' Freya smiles. 'That was him all over. He'd listen and then months later remember stuff that even I'd forgotten. He made it one of my favourite days. Middle of December, we went down to the beach at Boscombe, freezing cold, wind like ice. Flew that kite for about five minutes, then went for fish and chips. It was perfect.'

He listens with a sympathetic wrinkling of the forehead. 'I'm sorry, Freya,' he says.

She nods slowly, not trusting herself to speak. She knows he understands.

'You want me to speak to Watts?' he adds.

'No, I'll do it.'

He turns away from her quickly, too quickly, and flicks his screen away from what he's been looking at, but not before she catches a glimpse of the heading.

'Why are you still looking at Jon's medical records?' Robin doesn't answer. 'Robin? Please. No secrets. Not now.'

He sighs, and flicks the screen back, letting her read the notes. She scans it once, then again. She can't take it in.

'So...' she begins. 'Jon had fertility tests done?'

She feels Robin scrutinising her face for a reaction. 'Did he ever mention it to you?'

'No.' Her face is getting hot; her body feels sweaty. 'All he ever said was they tried for a baby when they first got married, but it never came.'

'And you didn't discuss it?'

'Yes, briefly. He said he wanted them. Two. He never liked being an only child.'

She turns away from Robin, and he does the same, respecting the silence. She stares at her screen but she can't concentrate. The same question comes back into her head. Was Jon lying, all this time? Was he using her? How many times has she seen it? Women in the nick, being lied to by men. Their excuses, all the same. *He loves me, I love him. It's not like that. He'd never do that to me.*

She was no better than them. Deceived. But she can't believe it. She pictures his face, the last time she saw him. Smiling, happy, relieved that he was going to leave Amy. He couldn't have lied.

She needs to get to the bottom of this, once and for all.

Freya sends a quick message, trying to track down PC Watts, then moves on to looking at the Miller financials. They received permission to view their accounts when Jonathan was first murdered, although she knows Amy has rescinded that now. Still, they have a spreadsheet, downloaded in that first week, and Freya scans it, looking back over months of boring transactions for anything interesting.

Waitrose, Tesco, Co-op. Costa Coffee. A number of expensive clothes shops. Jonathan's pay going in – he earned more than Freya does, by miles – then Amy's. She didn't earn much, but enough to keep her going in the event of a divorce. Although, not if the money spent in all those clothes shops is anything to go by. Perhaps that was it. Perhaps he asked Amy for a divorce and she killed him. But how? *How?* Freya keeps on coming back to that.

The way he was found, in the Premier Inn. Just hanging. If someone had forced him there, there would have been signs of foul play. Defensive wounds to his hands. Even if he'd been sedated, surely he'd have fought back?

And the CCTV, showing one guy walking in. It makes no sense. Plus Amy has an alibi. Bloody Amy.

Her eyes keep scrolling down the list, and then she sees it. Mamas & Papas. Mothercare. JoJo Maman Bébé. Amy, or both of them, had been buying things from baby shops.

She clicks away, sending the report to Robin.

'You look, I can't see anything,' she says to him.

He stares at her, then nods.

She goes back to her background checks – Khalid Riaz next. But she still can't concentrate.

She hears Robin tapping. The constant beat of his middle finger on the desk, something that normally drives her mad, is, today, reassuring. He's concentrating, which is more than can be said for her.

'Frey—' he starts.

'I know, I know,' she interrupts. 'The baby shops.'

'Well, yeah,' he says. 'But look at this.'

She turns and focuses on the line on his screen. He's highlighted it with his cursor, turning it from white to grey.

Select Events, it reads. *£250.00*.

He points down – same thing a few lines below.

'Happens weekly,' Robin says. 'Then stops about a month before Jonathan's death.'

'Who are they?' Freya asks.

'Before you started with me, I was called out to a possible GBH,' Robin replies. 'Turns out it was a swingers' club.' Freya raises her eyebrows in surprise. He taps on the monitor. 'That was these guys.'

Freya frowns. She looks at the screen, then back to Robin.

'I hate to say it,' Robin says quietly. 'But it looks like Jonathan Miller might have been into weird sex stuff after all.'

54

Liv stands outside Amy's house and rings the doorbell again. She pulls her coat tighter round herself and shivers. The weather has grown cold, leaves now red and yellow, falling fast. The wind whips across the estate.

She looks around the cul-de-sac. It's modern, but dull. Liv can't understand why Amy would aspire to live somewhere like this. She dreams of a small cottage in the countryside. Thick oak beams, uneven floorboards, an open fire. Somewhere with character and life, not dead and empty like here.

But she still feels that flash of jealousy. She loves her own little house, and she's proud of it. But *how* she got the money to put down the deposit, not so much. Every pound, every penny hard-earned with her own flesh. Fucked, sucked and pounded out of her, piece by painful piece. What she wouldn't give to have had Amy's life over the past fifteen years.

The door opens at last and Amy stands in front of her. Liv blinks at her normally pristine sister. Her eyes are half-closed, her hair rumpled, a fluffy white robe wrapped around her.

'What do you want?' Amy slurs.

'Are you drunk?' Liv asks, confused. It's nearly lunchtime, early even for Amy.

'No, my pills...' Amy says slowly, 'not worn off yet.' She makes a vague gesture towards the inside of the house.

Liv takes it as an invitation inside and pushes past her. Amy shuts the door, then collects her post from the mat, shuffling into the kitchen and slumping at the table. She starts opening the envelopes, pushing the junk mail aside.

'Make me some coffee,' Amy mutters and Liv scowls, but turns on the expensive Nespresso machine, waiting for it to warm up. 'Guess what I did?' she adds.

Liv turns back sharply. She recognises that tone. The smug satisfaction, the joy that can only come from Amy doing something mean. 'What?'

'I wrote and complained. About that detective, coming to your house.'

'Amy! You didn't.'

'He can't do that. Bully you in that way. I won't have it.' Amy points back to the machine. 'Make my coffee,' she adds, her voice completely devoid of worry.

'He'll get fired! And more to the point, I'll get arrested!'

'It was two days ago. Have you?'

'No, but…' Liv turns back, clattering in the cupboard and taking out two mugs. She knows there's no arguing with Amy. There's no changing a woman so selfish, so convinced by her own actions. And now Robin Butler's been caught in her cross hairs. 'Just tell me next time, will you?' she adds, defeated, worried, placing the coffee down in front of her sister.

Amy looks up from the piece of paper she's been reading. She's a bit more awake now, a smile on her face. 'Hmm, what? Yeah, whatever, Liv. Why are you so bothered about him anyway? Since when have you been keen on cops?'

'I'm not, it's just…'

Amy laughs, no more than a cackle. 'You like him, don't you? Do you think he'll come and sweep you off your feet? You're no fucking Julia Roberts, Olivia! This isn't *Pretty Woman*!' Amy turns back to her post, still chuckling quietly under her breath.

Liv scowls, sitting down next to her. As much as Amy is right, it pisses her off that her sister finds it so amusing.

'How was work last night, anyway?' Amy asks, a bitchy emphasis on the word *work*.

Liv takes a sip of her coffee. A night at Frankie's, no escorting for a change, just straight prostitution. Standing in a line next to the other girls, in her underwear, as a man walked up and down assessing them. Sweating with anticipation; Liv smelt his eagerness and he disgusted her. But still, she smiled, pushed out her breasts.

He made his choice, handed over his money. Frankie, charming and accommodating next to him, outlined the rules. No incest role play, no water sports, the rest you can agree with the girl. Extra for anal, extra for fetish.

Liv knows every girl has her own boundaries. But the temptation of the money is sometimes too great – the bigger the risk, the more they pay. She knows from experience that common sense is ignored as you convince yourself the end justifies the means, as taste and security go out the window. As he brings along a friend, flashes the cash so you forgo the condoms.

But: 'Fine,' she replies to her sister, who rolls her eyes at her one-word answer.

And it was. The man last night was okay. Straight sex, thrusting naked on top of her, she made the appropriate noises, faking sexual enjoyment. And now, she wonders, as her thoughts turn back to Robin Butler, will she ever be able to separate work and play properly again? Has she forgotten what genuine intimacy feels like? Has she become so good at simulating it, she might feel nothing when it's real?

Next to her, Amy finishes her coffee and stands up from the table. 'I'm going for a shower,' she directs back, 'since you're in such a mood.'

Liv watches her go, feeling a burn of resentment. You're so fucking lucky, Liv thinks. And for a woman whose husband has just died, she seems to be taking far too much joy from the whole process. She was like that at the memorial: milking the sympathy.

Liv stands up, collecting the coffee cups. But in her annoyance, she knocks Amy's and it falls, coffee dregs cascading across the table.

'Shit,' she exclaims, as it soaks into the pile of post and junk mail, and races to get a cloth from the sink, dabbing at the mess.

Then she stops.

She looks at the document in her hand, corner now stained brown, and pulls it further out of the envelope. It's official-looking, addressed to Amy, the logo of a known bank across the top.

Liv nervously glances towards the stairs. Then, coast clear, she starts to read.

55

Mrs Franklin remembers Robin.

'DS Butler,' she says as she opens her front door. She looks normal this afternoon – no silk, no lace, just jeans and a tight-fitting jumper. Robin introduces Freya and they all shake hands.

'Bethany, please. You haven't reconsidered my offer?' she asks.

Robin shakes his head and Freya looks at him curiously.

'First time for free,' the woman laughs. 'We always need more men. And attractive women,' she says, turning her sights on Freya.

Robin grins as Freya turns red. 'That's okay, thank you,' Freya stutters politely, as the woman shows them in.

The house has been transformed back into a boring semi-detached. No low lighting today, no condoms in bowls on the table or vibrators on the mantelpiece. Just plumped-up cushions on the sofa and family photos next to the television.

'How is Emma doing?' Robin asks, of the woman who received the head injury before.

'She's fine, thank you,' Bethany replies. 'She told her husband. He was angry at first, but he's coming round. You never know, we might have a new member. Coffee, tea?'

'No, thank you. And your son?'

'On his best behaviour. At least, for now. He's allowed out with his mates again from tonight, so we'll see.'

They all sit down on the sofas. Robin can't help wondering what they'd see if he took a black light to the material. He pushes the thought quickly out of his mind.

'Now what did you want to talk about? You were very cryptic on the phone.'

'We're hoping you'll remember a few clients of yours.' Robin gets two photos out of his pocket and shows them to Bethany. 'Amy and Jonathan Miller.'

She takes them and looks closely. 'You know I can't break confidentiality,' she says, but Robin notices a flicker of interest.

'Jonathan Miller's dead. And we believe Amy Miller is involved. So any help you can offer would be much appreciated.'

'Dead, eh?' She stares at the photos again. Then she hands them back, thinking. 'How did he die?'

'Between us,' Robin starts, and Bethany nods. 'Suffocated. Auto-erotic asphyxiation gone wrong.'

'Jonathan?' Bethany pulls a face.

'What?' Freya asks, a little too abruptly. Robin gives her a quick look.

'Just, well. Didn't seem the type. If you'd said...' She stops again.

'Please. Anything you can tell us.'

Bethany looks at the photos in Robin's hand, then takes a deep breath. 'Between us,' she says, giving Robin a hard stare. 'Yes, they came here. But him—' She points at Jonathan's photo. 'Just the once.'

'What happened?' Freya asks.

'Couldn't get it up. Happens all the time. Too nervous, some of these blokes. But with him, it didn't seem like he wanted to. The wife—' She taps on Amy's photo. 'Was *very* into it,' she says with a knowing nod. 'But he hung back, didn't want to even look. Some guys like to watch, you know, and that's fine. You pay your money, and as long as everyone consents, you can do what you like. But he seemed... embarrassed. They left early, in the middle of an argument.'

'According to our records, they came here a number of times,' Robin says.

'Yeah, she did. She came back, alone. Got very involved,' Bethany replies, but her face clouds.

'In what way?' Freya prompts.

Bethany pauses. 'We're a relaxed club, we're used to the weird and wonderful. But we have one strict rule – condoms. Even on the vibrators. The last thing you need is someone spreading something nasty—' Robin can't help but grimace '—that's how clubs like mine go out of business.

'But she,' Bethany continues with a curl of the lip, 'actively encouraged the guys to go without. She said she was on the pill, said she was allergic to the spermicide, or something, which I know was utter rubbish. Besides, we have alternatives, if that's the case. And, you know, many of the guys didn't mind, liked it. But then some of the girls said they were being pressured into doing the same.'

Freya tuts, showing her disapproval. 'So what did you do?'

'I warned her. She said fine, but then I heard about her doing it again, and that was it, she was out.'

'Do you know if she went to any other clubs?'

Bethany shakes her head. 'We all know each other round here, look out for each other. I warned the other organisers, but I didn't hear of anything. Could ask around if you like?'

'Please,' Robin confirms.

Conversation over, the three of them get up and Bethany shows them to the door. 'Did you ask why?' Freya asks, as they stand in the hallway. 'Was she pregnant?' she adds quickly, and Robin knows she's thinking about the baby shops, the fertility tests. 'That would be a reason for not needing condoms.'

But Bethany frowns. 'I don't think so. It wasn't that she didn't need them, it was more that she didn't want them. And I didn't care,' she continues. 'I wasn't sad to see her go. She was one of the more attractive ones around here, but there was just something about her. She wasn't that popular.'

They open the door, and Bethany places her hand on Robin's arm. 'Any time you want to reconsider, handsome,' she says. 'You know where we are.'

Robin and Freya walk back and climb into the car.

'Why do you think she was doing it?' Freya asks, thoughtfully.

'The risk? Trying to please the men? I don't know,' Robin replies. He starts the engine. 'He didn't tell you about any of this?'

Freya shakes her head sadly, then glances back to the house. 'You'd never know, would you?' she says. 'From the outside.' Robin shrugs. 'Sure it's not your thing, Sarge?' she adds with a cheeky grin. 'Free, easy sex? Every man's dream.'

'Why does everyone keep on assuming I'm into this stuff?' Robin mutters.

'You've got that air about you.'

Robin screws up his face.

'A man with secrets,' Freya adds darkly. 'If only they knew.'

56

The case is getting weirder and weirder. So the person who liked the sex clubs is still alive, and the one who didn't is dead. Freya goes back to her background checks; Robin switches from screen to screen debating where to go next.

He stares at the whiteboard, at the timeline of the weekend before Jonathan Miller's death. The party, the quiet weekend with his wife, working from home on Monday. Robin wishes they had the laptop back from the techies, and picks up the phone.

'When?' he asks sharply when the voice at the other end – Robin doesn't care who – says they haven't got to it yet.

'I'll do it now,' the voice stutters in reply.

Next to him, Freya gets up and leaves, mentioning something about PC Watts. Robin watches her go. She seems okay, more focused if anything. But he can't help wondering what'll happen if they don't find a way forward for this investigation. What then?

She has the disc with the CCTV of him speaking to Trevor Stevens. When he offered to confess, he wasn't bluffing, but he doesn't like to think about what would become of a guy like him. Prison isn't kind to coppers, especially ex-Major Crimes detectives.

He turns to look again at the background information Freya has started on Khalid Riaz. Nothing of note in terms of convictions, but then something interesting on file just as he turned fifteen.

An arrest for GBH, charges dropped. Biological samples taken at the time were destroyed. Seems lenient, Robin thinks. He opens up the file and starts reading.

Pictures load. Photographs of an older man, his face a mass of blood and bruises. A list of medical afflictions: broken eye socket, broken nose, broken ribs. This man took a beating at the hands of Jonathan's best mate Kal. Then more photos, a woman this time.

She's older, like the man, and a large black bruise takes over most of her left eye. It's swollen shut, a cut running across her forehead. Robin frowns. So who's this?

He starts to read, and everything becomes clear. He picks up the phone.

'Greg?' he says, as a monosyllabic voice answers. 'The DNA in the car? Check for familial matches.'

57

Freya's desperate for something to do. She can't bear sitting at her desk any longer. She feels like Robin is always watching her, waiting for her to change her mind and turn him in. But nothing could be further from her thoughts.

She walks downstairs to the custody area. She knows PC Watts, now Sergeant Watts, is on duty but when she gets there, something is kicking off. There's a man struggling, uniformed PCs on either side, as the custody sergeant does his best to book him into the system. The man swears profusely, and Freya watches as they all remain calm.

She's always amazed by how smoothly the custody sergeants deal with the mess in front of them. She knows they're a certain breed – older, happy not to be out on patrol, dealing with one scumbag at a time from the safety of their desk. She looks at Watts now – what hair he has left is grey, his large bulk resting on the tall chair as he types on the computer with two fingers. She wonders how many years he has to go before retirement, maybe two or three at most. He's earned his peace and quiet down here, she thinks, although she'd go mad from the boredom.

The man stops shrieking and is taken away to his cell. Freya approaches the desk.

'DC Freya West,' she says. 'We spoke earlier?'

'Come round, come round,' Watts replies, diverting her into his inner sanctum behind the plastic screens. 'Sit down, you want tea?'

'I'm fine, thank you.'

'Biscuit?' He pulls a packet of chocolate Hobnobs from his desk drawer. 'I save the good ones for the visits from the pretty detectives.'

He's gently flirting, and Freya enjoys the banter. He's old-school police, from the days before #MeToo: a guy untouched by compulsory inclusivity and diversity training. Freya takes his comment in the way in which it's intended, and selects a biscuit with a smile.

'You wanted to talk to me about a call-out two years ago?' he says. 'I can't promise I'll remember much.'

Freya shows him the photos. 'Amy and Jonathan Miller. Domestic disturbance, possibly DV?'

He squints at their images through his thick glasses. 'Okay, yes, vaguely. I remember her, at least.'

'Who called you out?'

'The neighbours. Said it was a dreadful racket. And even when we got there, I could hear smashing from inside.'

Freya swallows. She can barely bring herself to ask. 'And what was he doing?'

Watts takes another biscuit from the pack. He shakes his head. 'Not him, her.'

Freya's surprised, and pauses, chocolate melting on her fingers. 'What do you mean?'

'That's why I remember it. We knocked, expecting the usual shitbag beating the crap out of his wife, but when the door opened it was him. Had a gash across his forehead. House was a mess, broken crockery and glass on the floor. And she was something else.'

He takes a bite and chews, thoughtfully. Freya waits. 'She was quite a wildcat. Still hurling plates as we walked into the room.'

'But you didn't arrest her?'

'No. He was apologetic, didn't want to press charges. We made sure he was okay, the cut had stopped bleeding, then left him to it.' He stops eating biscuits. 'Why do you want to know? Has she killed him?'

Freya stutters for a moment. 'Why d'you say that?'

'Because that's what normally happens, doesn't it, love?' he says, matter-of-fact. 'The abuser kills the victim. Men or women, doesn't matter,' he adds cynically. 'Did she push him out of a window?'

'No, we...' Freya stops. 'We don't know what happened yet.'

'But he's dead, yeah?' Watts says. And Freya nods. 'Always comes to that in the end,' he finishes.

–

Freya walks back to the incident room, her mind reeling. She met Jonathan a year after this happened, but she remembers the many times she saw marks on his body. Accident while playing squash, tripped over, he would say, and she didn't think anything of it. But had that been Amy?

The anger overtakes her, then the tears. She stops for a moment in the empty corridor, leaning against the wall, her hands over her face, trying to stop herself from crying. What must he have gone through, her kind, honest Jon? She feels her legs wobble and crumples, sliding down the wall.

'Hey, you okay?' A female PC she doesn't know stops and crouches next to her.

Freya takes a deep breath in. 'Yes, sorry.' She forces a smile. 'Just having one of those days.' She wipes her eyes with her fingers, sniffing back the tears.

The woman's eyes are sympathetic. 'Don't I know it,' she replies. 'Have a little sob, makes you feel better. That and a large G and T at the end of the day.'

Freya stands up again, feeling foolish for her public display of emotion. 'I'm fine. Thank you,' she says, and the woman smiles then continues on her way. 'Shit,' Freya mutters. She can't do that again. What if that had been Baker? She needs to hold it together. For Jon.

She starts walking again, and as she goes into the incident room, a bespectacled guy stops her.

'You're working with Butler, yeah?' he stutters nervously at the floor.

Freya nods and he thrusts an evidence bag in her hand, laptop inside. 'Greg told me to bring you this. Password on the front,' he mumbles, and scuttles off.

She carries it to Robin and plonks it on the desk.

'You've scared the techies so much they won't even talk to you now,' she says.

Robin looks at the laptop, then back to the door. 'Oh, for fuck's sake,' he grumbles. He starts pulling at the sticky top of the evidence bag, as she sits down. They set up the laptop in front of them.

'Was Watts helpful?' Robin asks, clicking and logging on using the password hastily scrawled in biro on the plastic.

'Yes, but not what we thought. DV, but her abusing him.'

Robin looks up, surprised. 'She was beating him up?' he asks. 'Did he ever tell you?'

She shakes her head.

'That's not unusual,' Robin says, softly. 'Many victims don't report the abuse.'

She knows he's trying to let her off the hook, and she appreciates his efforts. But she still feels shit. 'I'm police, we're trained to recognise this stuff.'

'But we expect to see men abusing women. When it's the other way round it's not so easy to spot. Was there anything in his medical records?'

She turns and looks, scrolling down, eyes flicking through the many lines of text. 'Broken ribs in 2015, fractured wrist in 2019.' She looks up. 'I remember that one. He said he'd slipped on ice in his driveway. You think that was her?'

Robin lets out a long breath of air. 'We'll never know.' He frowns apologetically, then goes back to the computer. 'Oh, see, this is odd,' he says, pointing at the screen.

Freya looks. It's Jonathan's inbox, rows and rows of emails. Robin scrolls down, until the line of bold abruptly stops.

'That's where the read emails end, and here are the new ones,' he says, cursor hovering over the subject headers. They all say things like *Risk Assessment* and *Contract 4896.4*, all boring stuff Freya assumes is related to his work. She looks at the dates.

'So he hadn't read any emails since Friday at four,' she says. 'That's when he met me.'

'And nothing Monday, when apparently he was working from home,' Robin adds.

They carry on looking at the computer in silence. Freya watches as Robin loads up Jonathan's work diary. No meetings on that Monday, so no one would have noticed his absence. Nothing in sent messages.

'What does his car telemetry say he was doing?' Robin asks.

Freya scoots across to her computer and opens the file. 'Nothing,' she confirms, 'until the driver's door opens at 16:47, then closes again.'

Robin looks over her shoulder. 'Seat position five,' he reads. 'What does that mean?'

'The car records every change from the sensors. So that includes the electronic seats moving.'

'Freaky-arsed cars,' he replies. 'So position five is…?'

He watches as Freya does a quick search and pulls up a Mazda owner's manual. She reads for a second. 'Furthest away from the wheel,' she replies at last.

'So consistent with the man driving being taller,' Robin replies, then mentally curses himself for not matching it up sooner when Greg told him about the man in the CCTV. 'Satnav?'

Freya goes back to her reports. 'Satnav wasn't used, but the telemetry shows the car going from the house to the Premier Inn. Then the driver's door opens and shuts.'

'So all consistent with him working from home on Monday, as Amy said.' He looks back at the laptop and the emails. 'Except he wasn't working. Oh, here's something.' Freya watches as he clicks on a folder, simply called *video*. 'Our hidden cameras?' he asks, clicking on the first icon.

They're .mov files, multiple recordings, seemingly one per day, the first a fisheye view of his office. Freya checks the date – it's from Friday morning, and they watch as Jonathan goes into his study, picks up his laptop and bag, then walks out again.

Her breath catches in her throat. The air suddenly feels hot and thick. He's wearing a suit and tie, and Freya remembers it from him arriving at her house later. He's walking in his usual loping stroll, and Freya misses him so, so much. She's been so absorbed in the case, she hasn't stopped to think. About not seeing him again. About how this, this grainy shit black and white video, shows the last traces of his life.

'You okay?' Robin asks softly. She nods, sniffing back the tears.

'He was just so…' She pauses. 'He was so much more than this.' She taps the screen angrily. 'This video. He was funny, and smart, and…' She angrily wipes the tears away with the back of her hand, glancing around the incident room, relieved that none of their colleagues have noticed. 'I can't believe he's gone.'

'I know,' Robin says, almost in a whisper. 'And it'll come back to you at the weirdest possible times. You'll see traces of them in someone else's smile. Or you'll watch a TV programme and it'll make you laugh because of something they said.'

Freya looks at him. She hasn't stopped to appreciate just what Robin has been going through these past few years. She's lost Jonathan, but he's lost his entire family. Suddenly she understands him just that bit better. And how strong he must be to have kept going.

And in a flash, she understands why Robin killed Trevor Stevens. That anger, that rage. It's what she's feeling now, bubbling below the surface.

While she's been thinking, Robin's been scrolling through the other videos. She's barely noticed as he's moved through hours of nothing but the empty Miller study, and has now progressed on to the living room. There's video as Jonathan Miller passes through, bag in hand, out to work on Friday morning. Then Amy Miller comes into shot.

They watch as she stands at the window, looking out at their driveway.

'Waiting for Jonathan to leave?' she asks Robin, but he doesn't reply, his hand covering his mouth, his gaze locked on the screen.

She looks at it too, then freezes. Because what's showing on the video is so strange, so bizarre, she can't articulate it in words.

Freya opens and closes her mouth. She looks at the video then back to her boss.

'What... the... fuck...?' Robin whispers.

58

Wednesday

Kal lies motionless in the darkened room. It must be seven o'clock, maybe eight in the morning, he's not sure. He's been here for days, at home, doing nothing more than wander around his house. He called in sick to work on Monday. He can't concentrate. He just thinks about him. About Jonathan.

He can't sleep. He can't eat. He can just about manage to drink, whatever he can get his hands on, to take the thoughts away. He knows he needed to shower, but what is the point any more?

He thinks about calling the police. But even when the phone is in his hand, he can't bring himself to do it. So when he hears the doorbell ring and pulls aside the curtain to see the blue and yellow of the patrol car, he feels a swell of relief. It's out of his hands now. He knew they would come.

He walks slowly to the front door and opens it: two detectives wait – the man and woman who interviewed him in London that day. He doesn't say anything, just moves out of the way of the door and gestures for them to come in.

The man's wearing the same shit suit from days before. Even through his addled haze Kal still recognises cheap off-the-peg when he sees it. But then, who is he to judge? He knows he hasn't cleaned his teeth; he can sense the smell of his own sour sweat.

The male detective is holding handcuffs.

'Khalid Riaz,' the woman begins, and he turns to look at her. 'We are arresting you on suspicion of the murder of Jonathan

Miller. You do not have to say anything, but it may harm your defence if you do not mention when questioned something which you later rely on in court.'

He feels his wrists being pulled behind him, the cuffs fastened in place.

'Anything that you do say may be given in evidence. Do you understand?' the woman finishes.

'I didn't kill him,' Kal says. It's the first time he's spoken in days, and the words feel rough on his throat. 'I didn't kill him.'

59

Freya's ready. Robin can feel her fidget beside him as the two of them sit opposite Khalid Riaz in the interview room. He's wearing a police-issue grey tracksuit, the blue blanket draped over his slumped shoulders.

Robin was shocked when they turned up at his door this morning. He'd been expecting Kal to lawyer up immediately, to confront them with arrogance and cries of discrimination and unfair treatment. But the man they arrested was broken.

He was wearing dirty boxer shorts and a T-shirt. With some persuasion they managed to get him dressed, shoes on his feet, and a coat round his bony shoulders. He looked like he hadn't eaten in days.

Apart from his first words when they arrested him, he was silent the whole way in. He gave the bare minimum as he was booked into custody. The transformation to this husk of a man is so absolute that Robin asked him to be checked over by a doctor before they interviewed him.

But the doctor came and went, and Kal was given a sandwich and a bottle of water. So here they are.

Robin was reluctant to allow Freya into the interview room, but she insisted, on the proviso she stays quiet. They have a bulky file in front of them, packed out with spare paper from the photocopier to make it look like they have more on him than they do.

'Kal,' Robin begins, gently. The video is rolling, the warnings have been issued. 'Do you know why you're here?'

Kal stays staring at the table. He nods slowly.

'We know why you did it, Kal,' Robin says.

Kal looks up quickly. He meets Robin's gaze for a moment, then drops it back to the table.

'We know what your father used to do to your mum.'

This time Kal's head lifts, and he stares at Robin as he pulls photos out from the beige file in front of him. First, the photo of the woman. Face bloodied, nose broken.

'We understand, Kal,' Robin says.

A look crosses Kal's face. 'You understand?' he says angrily.

Robin waits.

'Your dad used to hit your mum, did he?' Kal hisses. 'You used to watch as your father beat your mother senseless, as he dragged her round by her hair, as he threw her down the stairs?' The man's features contort with anger. 'You don't know shit.'

'I know you stood up for your mum,' Robin says. 'I know you got your father convicted for what he'd done.' He takes the second photo from the file – this time of the older man. His eyes are blackened, and Robin knows that his jaw is broken, his ribs shattered. Kal glances down at the photo then glares again. 'That takes bravery, Kal.'

Kal shakes his head. 'Not soon enough.'

'Is that why you killed Jonathan Miller?'

Kal stares back at the table. Robin can see his hands are shaking as he picks up the plastic cup of water and takes a sip.

He carries on. 'You thought Jonathan was beating Amy up, and you had to do something about it.'

'Cowards,' Kal says quietly. 'That's all they are.' He looks up at Robin. 'Bullies.'

'And you had to stop Jonathan?'

Kal shakes his head again. 'I didn't kill Jonathan,' he whispers.

'Tell us what happened, Kal,' Robin says. 'We understand. You couldn't stand by again. You couldn't let someone beat up their wife and do nothing. You should be commended, Kal,' Robin says, and he feels Freya tense next to him. 'Any jury in the land will go easy on you, after what you've been through with your mum. Just tell us what happened.'

Kal looks up. He meets Robin's gaze.

'I didn't kill him,' he says again.

Robin sees Freya look at him and nod. He knows what she's saying: put everything on the table, show him what we have. But Robin's reluctant. They know there's domestic violence in Khalid Riaz's background, but everything here is backwards. Amy wasn't being beaten up, Jonathan was. And he's the one that's dead.

But they have one chance to find out what happened. Robin opens the file.

'Kal. Here's what we know. A man of your height was seen getting out of Jonathan's car on the night of his murder. You're what, six foot three? We know the seat of Jonathan's car was pulled right back, to a position that someone of your height would need to drive it. We're still waiting for your DNA results, but we've already used your father's DNA from the file, and it comes back as a familial match to the sample we found on the steering wheel of the car.' He pauses, then takes a photo out. He notices Kal's gaze flick to the picture.

'Do you recognise this magazine, Kal?' Robin asks. 'Porn, found in the room along with Jonathan's body. And it has your fingerprints all over it.'

'I gave it to him,' he says, but his protest is weak.

Robin continues. 'We got back in touch with Lisa, your now ex-girlfriend, I believe? And once we explained that making a false statement to the police can come with a prison sentence, she was keen to put us straight. You weren't with her Monday night, Kal. You left work at three, and then where did you go?'

No response.

Robin glances at Freya, and she opens the lid of the laptop. 'We know you would have seen the bruises on Amy's face on the night of your party,' Robin says. 'But what you don't know is how she got them.'

Kal's head snaps up. Robin knows he has his attention. Freya turns the laptop to face him, and now Robin presses play on the video, winding it forward to the part of the tape he needs.

At first, Kal seems confused. He glances at Robin. 'What is this?' he asks.

'For the benefit of the video, exhibit Five B. This is a video camera, placed by Jonathan Miller in the living room of his own house. We believe it was put there so that Jonathan could record Amy attacking him.'

'Amy attacking Jonathan?' Kal says. His forehead creases.

'Yes. We know they'd had run-ins in the past. Police had been called, Kal. Amy had been beating Jonathan.'

'No, no, you've got it the wrong way round. I've seen the marks on Amy's face. He was beating her.'

'No, he wasn't,' Robin says. 'Watch the tape.'

They all stare at the video as Robin presses play. Robin knows what must be going through Kal's head, the same as Robin and Freya thought when they first saw it. The video is bonkers, almost unbelievable if it wasn't there in black and white.

Kal watches as Amy stands in the middle of her living room. She's still, thinking. Then she walks to the open door, between the living room and the hallway. She stands with her feet either side of the door, her hands gripping the handles on each side. And then rams her head hard against the edge.

Kal gasps. The force of the impact makes Amy reel slightly, step backwards from the door. Then she steps forward and does it again. This time her hands go up and she tentatively prods with a finger at her forehead, then walks to the mirror on the other side of the room and looks at it, poking gently.

Kal looks at the video, then back at Robin.

'She did it to herself?' he asks, disbelievingly.

'It seems that way,' Robin says.

'But why?'

'We're hoping you'll be able to tell us that.'

Kal reaches forward, winds the video back, then presses play. They all watch the bizarre display again.

'But she said…' he mutters. He shakes his head. 'This can't be right.'

'You believed Jonathan was beating her, Kal,' Robin says slowly. 'But she was lying to you the whole time.'

Kal shakes his head again, his mouth open. 'I thought… oh god…' His hands fly to his mouth.

'What happened on that Monday when Jonathan died?' Robin asks. He watches as Kal shuts his eyes tight. 'How did you kill him?'

'I didn't kill him,' Kal repeats. He starts to cry, shaking his head. 'I didn't.'

'Then what happened?' Robin asks quietly.

'I didn't,' Kal says. 'He was already dead.'

60

Kal can't think. He leans forward over the table, pushing his fingers into his eyes so hard he sees colours. He needs to make it stop. The constant thoughts, the guilt, the fear. And now... So Amy had been...?

Kal feels like he might vomit. The sandwich he ate earlier sits in his stomach, hard as rock. He takes a sip from the cup of water; saliva fills his mouth. But he can't be sick, not here, not now.

'I didn't,' he repeats. 'He was already dead.'

Kal remembers the frantic call from Amy that Monday. 'He's dead,' she was screaming. 'He's dead. You have to help me.'

Kal tried to persuade her to come and see him, but she wouldn't. She just said, 'You have to help me. We have to make it look like an accident.'

'But how?' he replied. And she explained.

He drove to the Miller house, picked up Jonathan's car, keys left in the ignition, and took it to the hotel. He used the key card left in the glovebox to let himself in, then went to the room. Room 302.

And there he was. Jonathan was lying on the bed. Just laid out, in his shirt and suit. Not a mark on him except for the bruises circling his neck. And the belt, still looped tightly round.

Amy was clear with her instructions.

'Check into the room next door,' she said, '303. I've reserved it in Jonathan's name. Wear gloves. Move the body.'

Kal stripped him naked, left his clothes on the chair. Then put the belt back into the bruises, the ridges round his neck, and pulled up. Jonathan wasn't light, the angle difficult. But eventually the belt held, and Jonathan stayed. Hung from the door. Like a piece of meat.

All the time he told himself: he's not your best friend. He's not the guy you thought you knew. He's a wife beater. A coward. Amy was only defending herself. She would be dead, if she hadn't killed him.

But part of him couldn't comprehend what was going on. What he was doing.

He pressed Jonathan's hand against the page, then left the porn open on the side. He pulled the door shut. And he left, running out of the hotel, leaving Jonathan's car behind.

Since then all he can see is Jonathan's face. All he can feel on his hands is Jonathan's skin: cold and dry. When he sleeps he feels the belt on his own neck, pulling, tightening. Jonathan getting his revenge.

He's constantly questioned what he's done. If Amy killing Jonny was an accident, why the belt round his neck? Why was he at the hotel? Why stage his death in such a horrific way? Why didn't Amy call the police? Why didn't he? *Why didn't he?*

And now everything he believed about Jonathan was wrong.

He tells all this, in fits and spurts, to the detectives. He knows he shouldn't. That he needs to get a lawyer, that someone needs to stop him, but he can't help it. He feels like that guilty kid again. That fifteen-year-old that stopped his father. Except this time he was wrong.

Oh god, so wrong. What has he done?

'How did Jonathan die?' the detective asks.

'I don't know, I don't know,' Kal says. He can feel his heart beating, faster and faster. 'He was dead when I got there.'

'In the hotel?'

The detective doesn't believe him. Oh god. His hands are clammy; he feels a bead of sweat run down his spine. He's going to go to prison for murder. For his best friend's murder.

'Yes, in the hotel.'

'And how did his body get there?'

'I don't know.'

'Who killed Jonathan, Kal?'

'I don't know.'

'Was it Amy?'

'I don't know.'

Oh god oh god oh god. What has he done?

Kal looks up. 'I want a lawyer,' he stutters. 'I need a lawyer.'

61

Freya and Robin sit in Baker's office. The look on their DCI's face is grim.

'So the CPS will charge Riaz for preventing the lawful burial of a body and perverting the course of justice, but not murder or conspiracy,' Baker tells them.

'We have no evidence he was involved in his death,' Robin confirms.

'And he says he just found him dead in a hotel room?'

'Yes.'

'The hotel room next door? And you didn't notice this in your investigation?'

Freya glances at Butler. It's not going well. 'It was booked in a fake name,' Robin explains. 'Although Jonathan Miller's credit card was used to pay.' He holds his hands up apologetically. 'We missed it, guv. Buried in all that data.'

Freya feels the blame for that one. She should have spotted it. But she was so overwrought in the days just after Jon's death, detail wasn't exactly her forte.

'Forensics are working the room now,' Robin continues. 'But we don't hold out much hope. Someone's been staying in there since. It's been cleaned many times.'

'Bloody hell.' Baker frowns at them both. 'So what do you have?'

Robin takes a long breath in. 'We have video of Amy Miller beating herself up—'

'Which is strange, but not a crime.'

'We can put Riaz at the hotel and in the car because of the CCTV and the telematics. And we know Jonathan Miller wasn't at work on Monday.'

'But Amy Miller was.' Freya can see Baker losing his temper, his eyes narrowing, his body tensing.

'Yes, guv. She has an alibi.'

'Christ, Butler!' Baker shouts. 'What are you arresting her for? You can't even prove when Miller was killed!'

Robin looks at the floor. Freya knows he's right. But they're so close. Khalid's confession was incomplete before he lawyered up, but they know Amy is implicated, there is no doubt. She feels the frustration. An unbearable tension of knowing that they are so close to the truth. It makes her muscles ache and her stomach contract in knots. They're on the brink of getting an arrest for this. Getting justice for her Jon. And that means more to her than anything else.

'Guv,' she begins, her voice shaking slightly. 'Let us arrest her.' She can feel herself gabbling, but this is their last desperate chance to convince him. 'Riaz's testimony is enough, you know that. Jonathan Miller was drugged. And the video proves something strange is going on with that woman.' Baker blinks at her tone, but stays quiet. 'Then we can search her house properly. See what else we can find.'

Baker sits back in his seat. Robin looks at her, the faint hint of a smile on his face, then over at the DCI.

'Fine.'

'Sorry, guv?'

'Fine,' he says again to Freya. 'Arrest her. But if she puts another complaint in about your skipper,' he says, gesturing to Robin, 'I can't protect you. And I hope to god you find something that proves she killed him.'

62

Thursday

Fuck you.

Amy sits ramrod straight in the interview room, staring directly at Detective Sergeant Robin fucking Butler. *I will not be intimidated by you*, she thinks, over and over in her head. *Fuck you.*

She looks closely at the man accusing her of her husband's murder. His hair could do with a cut, he's obviously made the effort to shave this morning, but his skin is sallow, he looks tired. Worse than her, she thinks. She's been here overnight, in that stinking, putrid cell, but she knows her hair is still clean, make-up in place.

She didn't know they were going to arrive the evening before, but like every day, she'd made the effort. Prepared for anything life might throw at her, and today is turning out to be no exception.

Her solicitor sits next to her, primed and on the alert, iPad in his hand. She was ready.

'Tell us again about the events of that weekend, beginning with the party on Friday the eleventh of September,' Butler says. His voice is measured and calm.

She sighs. 'No comment.'

'What is your relationship to Khalid Riaz?'

'No comment.'

'Did you phone him on Monday the fourteenth of September?'

Interesting, Amy thinks. 'No comment.'

'Because we have a warrant for your phone records, Amy,' Butler adds. 'We can find out.'

'No comment.'

He raises an eyebrow and looks down at his notepad.

She knows they're searching her house again. But she also knows they'll find nothing.

Butler pulls a photo out of the file and puts it in front of her. She looks at it. It's a small black box with a few wires trailing, a ruler next to it to show size.

'Do you know what this is?' he asks.

'Should I?' Amy says, and receives a look from her solicitor. 'No comment,' she adds.

'It's a wireless camera, sending video feed from your house to a remote laptop.'

The solicitor sits up straight in his chair. 'You had no authority to place video cameras in my client's home.'

'We didn't put it there,' Robin says. Amy sees a smug smile appear on his face. 'Jonathan Miller did.'

Amy feels her muscles tighten. Jonathan was filming her? What the hell? But she forces herself to stay calm. They don't have anything. They don't.

'When did you recover this item?' her solicitor asks.

'Last time we did the search. With your client's permission,' he adds pointedly. 'And it shows some interesting footage, Amy.'

She stays silent, waiting as Butler puts a laptop in front of her and turns on the video. She watches. It's from her living room, and she can't help but stare as it shows her hitting herself on the edge of the door. The solicitor watches it, then turns to stare at her. But he doesn't say anything to Amy.

The solicitor clears his throat. 'What's your point, Detective?' he asks, regaining his composure.

'Why are you doing this, Amy?' he asks.

'No comment,' she replies. And she smiles. So this is all they have? It's okay. She's right, they have nothing.

Butler closes the lid of the laptop.

'We've arrested Khalid Riaz,' he says. Amy waits. 'And he's told us on record how you phoned him and told him to move the body of your husband and stage his death to make it look like an accident.'

Has he now? Amy always knew Kal was going to be the weak link. She was wrong there, on many levels. Not the man she thought he was.

'Is that a question?' Amy says.

Robin stares at her. 'Did you?'

'No comment.'

She can see her calm is starting to get to him.

'Did you ask Kal to stage the death of your husband?'

'No comment.'

'Did you deceive Khalid Riaz, tell him that Jonathan was beating you up?'

'No comment.'

'Did you tell him to strip your husband's body naked?' Butler's eyes flare; his jaw tightens. 'Hang him with a belt? Suspend him, undignified, cold, rotting, in that shitty hotel room?'

She sees her solicitor cringe. 'No comment,' she says.

'Did you kill your husband, Amy?' he asks, his voice raised.

'My client has no more to say on this matter, Detective.'

'Yeah, no fucking comment,' she hears Butler mutter. Then, louder for the tape: 'Interview concluded, 12:46 p.m.'

He stands up, his chair making a bang as it hits the wall behind, and walks out of the interview room. 'Take her back to her cell,' she hears him snap at the uniform outside.

Amy stands up, her solicitor following her. They pause in the corridor, the uniform waiting. Amy watches Butler walk away, then stop at the end.

'They have nothing concrete on you, Mrs Miller,' her solicitor whispers. 'Just hold tight and we'll get you out of here.'

But Amy's not listening. Butler's talking to a woman at the end of the corridor – Amy recognises her from the funeral: the other detective, the blonde one. She's clearly angry, glancing back at where Amy is standing.

And then, as Amy watches, she notices the woman's manner change, her body tensing, emotion taking over. Amy frowns. Is it anger? Then it comes to her slowly. It's grief. She should know. Butler puts his hand on the woman's arm, his head bowed towards hers.

Amy stares. She can barely believe what she's seeing.

In a flash, she remembers the woman's face from the funeral. The sadness, a level of anguish you wouldn't normally see on a detective. Especially not one so used to investigating murders.

And that's when she knows. The blonde hair, the blue eyes – Jonathan's type to a tee. This is the woman who was having an affair with her husband. And she's working the case.

She feels the churn in the pit of her stomach. Her solicitor is still talking, but she's not listening. She wants to get away. She needs to make sense of what she's seen.

'Take me back to my cell,' she demands. Amy knows that all she needs to do is think. Think – and there'll be a way she can use this to her advantage. 'I want to be alone,' she says again, fragments of a plan forming in her head. 'Take me back now.'

63

'What do you mean, he's gone?'

Robin stares at his boss, as the three of them stand in the incident room. He's aware he's getting looks from his colleagues, and that shouting at his chief inspector in the middle of the office might not be a good idea, but he can't help himself.

Bloody Amy Miller, with her *no comments* and infuriating calm. Bloody Freya, looking at him with her wide blue eyes like he'd personally let her down by not locking Amy up there and then. And now this.

DCI Baker glares back. 'Gone. To Midfield Psychiatric down the road. To be assessed. Apparently, your little barrage of questions yesterday, plus a stay overnight in our finest custody suite have tipped him over the edge.'

'Riaz's faking it. He knows he's in trouble and he's pulling the diminished responsibility card.'

'Well, whatever the reason, we can't touch him. And Miller's solicitor is claiming his testimony was given under duress.'

'Shit!' Robin turns, his hands on his head. He stares at the board in front of him. The timeline, the reports from the PM, from the car, from the PCs – it's all come to nothing. 'How long do we have?'

Baker glances up at the clock. 'You've got five hours left. You've got SOCO at the house, right?' Robin nods. 'So give it your all. And then we'll have to pull them out and let her go.'

'Unless we find something.'

Baker gives him an incredulous look. 'Unless *you* find something.'

Robin watches Baker leave. Freya has been standing, mute, next to them this whole time, and now she slumps in the chair, her head in her hands. He watches her.

'You okay? Should you be here?' he asks, placing a hand gently on her shoulder.

She looks up at him with bloodshot eyes. 'Where else am I going to go, Robin?' Then she sits up straight. 'Tell me what to do.'

Robin sighs. He looks at the board again, then rubs his eyes. He went back over the camera footage following Miller's death. Multiple files, selecting the one for last Wednesday, watching Freya breaking into the house. Her shifty expression as she walked through the lounge, searching the study, then leaving via the window with the laptop. His finger hovered over the delete key for a second before he pressed it. And the file was gone.

Such a fucking mess. He can't stand her looking at him any more.

'Get me a coffee,' he mutters.

She gets up and leaves without a word.

'Shit,' he growls under his breath. The case is falling apart. What do they have? They're waiting for Amy Miller's phone records to come in, but all that will confirm is that she called Kal, not what they discussed. They've checked the rest of the camera footage from the house, and apart from the weird display of self-harm, there's nothing exceptional. They have no evidence in Miller's car linking it to Amy, nothing on his phone. He's sent a message to Steph asking for her to look at the PM results again, but she hasn't replied, and it's a shot in the bloody dark as it is.

He sits down at the desk and makes a call to the woman in charge of the SOCOs at the Miller house.

She answers immediately. 'It's too early,' she says, without waiting for Robin to ask, her voice slightly muffled. Robin's worked with Jess for years – an experienced crime scene manager – and now imagines her standing in the house, dressed in the full white suit, her mask over her face, hood over her ears.

'But any suggestion of anything?' Robin pleads.

Jess sighs. 'This place is spotless. There's nothing back from the initial run-through with luminol—' so no obvious traces of blood, he thinks '—and the whole house stinks of bleach. My guess is she's been over it, top to bottom, and if there was anything it's gone.'

'Any sign of the life insurance paperwork?'

'Not yet, no.'

'And you'll look for prescription drugs?'

'Yes, Robin.' Her tone is slightly patronising now; he knows she's barely humouring him.

'And what about the freezer in the garage?'

'We've impounded it, but nothing stands out, no. There's not even any rubbish in the wheelie bins.'

'Shit!' Robin leans back in his chair. 'The rubbish! We took that last time we were there.'

'You did?' Jess says. 'Well, have a look through that. It'll give you something to do instead of bothering me. I'll call you if we find anything.'

Robin hangs up the phone, and gratefully takes the coffee from Freya as she comes back.

'Nothing?' she asks.

'No.' He stands up. 'But come with me. We have work to do.'

64

Freya stands in the doorway of the evidence storeroom.

'You're having a laugh,' she says.

In front of them are six large balls of rubbish, bundled up again into huge see-through evidence bags. Even through the plastic, Freya can detect the smell, and it's making her feel faintly nauseous.

Robin's frowning. She knows he likes it as much as she does.

'Do we even know what we're looking for?' she asks.

He sighs, blowing his cheeks out, then takes a long swig from the coffee. 'Not a clue,' he says. 'Anything that looks suspicious.'

He glances at her and notices the slightly green look on her face. 'You do the recycling. That lot will be clean, at least.'

'And what? You're going to wade through a week's worth of rubbish?'

'I guess so, yes,' he says.

–

They fetch massive sheets of brown paper and white protective suits, commandeer two rooms and get to work. They set up video recorders and cameras. They fetch two of the admin staff to stand, watch and take notes.

'Video everything,' Robin says. 'Every item documented, photographed, then exhibited in its own bag. I don't want them accusing us of any shit.'

And they start. Freya slowly opens out the bags of recycling, one at a time, recording everything coming out of the plastic and spreading it across the floor. Even though it's supposedly clean, it doesn't smell great, and Freya is glad of the protective mask covering her face, however hot and breathless it makes her. The admin woman makes notes as they go through it, itemising, detailing Freya's thoughts.

And three hours later, Freya couldn't feel more discouraged. This look into Jonathan's life is both dehumanising and strange. An insight into the habits of him and his wife, trying to decipher what might have once been her lover, and what was Amy.

- *Plastic milk bottles – from Waitrose, both semi-skimmed and skimmed.* (Freya knows Jonathan had semi-skimmed on his breakfast.)

- *An empty cardboard box of Special K.* (Amy? With her, Jonathan always ate Weetabix.)

- *Aerosol can of shaving gel.* (Jonathan.)

- *Two cardboard pizza boxes, one Hawaiian* (Amy?), *one Meat Feast* (Jonathan).

Endless domestic rubbish that could have been either of them:

- *Empty plastic bottles: lemon washing-up liquid, Tresemmé shampoo.*

- *Tin cans: chopped tomatoes, baked beans, pineapple.*

- *Two empty cardboard cartons and inner cardboard rolls of cling film.*

- *Three empty cans of Diet Coke.*

- *Envelopes, flier for Domino's Pizza, the local newspaper.*

And so, so much more. Freya stands up and looks at it all, her back aching. So what? she thinks. How can any of this help?

She feels a sudden gnawing hunger. She didn't eat much for lunch, and she wonders how Robin's getting on. The admin woman looks at her hopefully.

'Shall we call it a night?' Freya says, and the woman pulls off her white suit and scuttles out of the room before Freya has a chance to thank her.

Freya picks up the laptop, saves the notes, then takes off her own suit, leaving it in the room to pick up again tomorrow.

She closes the door and locks it, then goes next door to where Robin is working. She pushes the door open, and instantly realises how kind her boss has been to her.

The smell fills her nose, immediately making her gag. Like her room, brown paper is laid out on the floor. But unlike hers the items strewn across it are stained, wet, stinking, liquid.

And in the middle of it stands Robin. His white suit is stained with brown and red and yellow. He turns and looks, then points a finger in her direction. She knows he wants to say something, but he just points, his eyes narrow.

Despite everything that's going on, or maybe because of it, Freya feels a bubble of laughter erupting from inside her. And then, before she can help it, she's doubled over in hysterics.

'Fuck you,' she hears Robin growl, but it only makes her laugh more. He walks out of the mess, carefully manoeuvring round the disgusting, indescribable items. And up close, he stinks.

She bites her lip, trying to quell the giggles.

'I'm so sorry, Robin,' she manages at last. 'Let me buy you dinner.'

He shakes his head; she knows he's scowling behind the mask. Then he gestures to a large reddish-yellow mark on his leg.

'Just not curry,' he replies. 'Please.'

65

Robin's changed his clothes, had a shower, but the stink of the Miller rubbish still clings to his skin. He's convinced it's in his hair, under his nails, even though he was wearing a full suit and gloves. Double layer tomorrow, he resolves.

They've agreed on a takeaway rather than dinner out, and he hears Freya open his front door to the delivery driver as he's finishing getting dressed. He pulls a hoodie over his head and smooths his hair down with his fingers, looking in the mirror as he does so.

He needs a haircut. He needs a shave. And when did he get so grey? In the past he's been able to convince himself that it's only here and there, but now he can see great tufts of it on the top, patches in his stubble. He looks old. And he feels it. Every one of his forty-one years. Or? He does the maths in his head. Christ, he's forty-two, how did that happen?

He goes downstairs into the kitchen, where Freya has managed to find knives and forks and plates and laid the Chinese takeaway out on the table.

He sits down and takes a prawn cracker, enjoying the polystyrene-like texture as it dissolves on his tongue. She passes him the rice and he tips it out on his plate, then adds chilli crispy beef, sweet and sour pork, lemon chicken.

'I think I over-ordered,' Freya says, through a mouthful of something.

'No such thing,' he replies.

They eat in silence for a while, both of them starving.

'How are you feeling?' he asks tentatively.

'About what? Jon, or…' She doesn't finish. She knows he's referring to Trevor Stevens' murder.

'Both, I guess.'

Freya offers him the last prawn cracker and he shakes his head. 'About Jon, okay, generally,' she says. 'He wasn't a part of my day-to-day life, because of the way we were. So when I'm at work and distracted, I can almost forget. But then it'll catch me unawares. I'll pick up my phone without thinking, to check if he's messaged. And that will be it.' She laughs, awkwardly. 'Waterworks.'

He nods. He's not sure what to say. He remembers those early days, just after Georgia and the twins died, but their lives had been so completely intertwined that everything he did came with a paralysing tiredness. Yet he carried on, in the same way that she is.

He watches as she puts a forkful of rice in her mouth and chews. 'Are we going to get her, Robin?' she asks quietly.

He doesn't reply. He trails his fork in his leftover food, then puts it down, his appetite lost. 'I don't know, Freya, I really don't. We need something.'

They're still waiting for any results to come back from the search of Amy Miller's house, but he doesn't hold out much hope. They found Amy's prescription medication, diazepam and zopiclone, which could tie to the sedatives found in Jonathan's system, but there is no way to prove that she gave them to him. As he said to Freya before, he could have easily taken them himself.

Freya considers his words, nodding slowly. 'Why do you think she did it?' she asks.

'I don't know. Why does anyone kill?' he says, before he realises that he can include himself in this group. Why did he? 'Revenge? Love? Money?' he asks.

'Revenge for what?'

'Did she know about you?'

'He might have told her that weekend. But otherwise I don't think so. And I don't think it's money. We haven't found anything in their financials that would show any sort of motive.'

He knows what Freya means. Not too much, or too little. He thinks about the video of her beating herself up. 'Perhaps there's something not quite right there,' he says. 'I mean, why make out your husband's abusing you? What did she have to gain from that?'

Freya frowns. 'Sympathy? Attention?'

'From who? Kal?' Robin suggests.

'Maybe. Was she in love with him? There were certainly a lot of phone calls between them.'

The phone logs had come in while Freya and Robin were sifting through the rubbish and Robin gave them a quick look, searching for Kal's number. Sure enough, Amy Miller had called him on Monday afternoon, and looking back, their conversations hadn't started there. They'd regularly messaged and spoken on the phone.

'But there's nothing in their texts to show any sort of romance,' Freya replies. 'Can you get anything else from Olivia Cross?'

Robin screws his face up. He has no desire to speak to her again, risk adding fuel to the complaint. But he agrees, 'Worth a try. You finished?' he asks, pointing to the near-empty takeaway trays.

Freya nods, and Robin stands up, clearing away the plates. He picks up a half-full portion of rice and adds it the leftover lemon chicken.

'Breakfast?' Freya asks.

'Maybe.' Robin smiles, and takes out the cling film, covering it and putting it in the fridge. He turns and Freya's looking at him strangely. 'I'm kidding,' he adds. 'Even for me that's disgusting.'

'No, it's not that.' She points at the tube in his hand. 'How many rolls would you say you get through?'

'Er…' He looks at it, confused. 'One a month, at most.'

'Right.' Freya gets up and collects her laptop from her bag. She opens it and pulls up a document on the screen. 'See, here. Two empty rolls and boxes of cling film.' She looks up at him. 'In the Miller recycling. That strike you as weird?'

'Yeah, but why? What would you use it for?'

They both stare at each other for a second, neither daring to articulate what's in their heads.

Then Freya says, 'You don't think…'

Robin nods. 'That's exactly what I'm thinking. To wrap up a body.'

66

Robin doesn't know what to say. It's a theory, but how do they prove it?

He can make an intelligent guess at why Amy Miller would wrap her husband's body in cling film: some sort of forensic countermeasure. A way of stopping skin and hair from the body spreading elsewhere. She's not daft, he has to give her that.

Freya leaves, and Robin carries on clearing up the kitchen. If what they're assuming is right, then... He can hardly bear the thought.

And when? Robin's head is starting to hurt. There's still so much of this case that doesn't make sense.

He remembers Freya's suggestion, about speaking to Liv, and picks up his phone and dials. It rings, then goes to voicemail, and he tries again. Then again. Eventually he gives up, carries a beer into the living room and slumps on the sofa. He switches the television on but he doesn't watch it; he just rolls the case round in his head.

Freya's convinced Amy Miller killed Jonathan, and even he has to agree, something isn't right about the woman. But how? She has an alibi, and there's no getting round that. If it was just one person's word for it, then maybe, but CCTV has her working at her hotel all day, the restaurant confirming the night.

His phone rings and he jumps, then answers it.

'Stop calling me,' Liv snaps.

'I need to speak to you. It's about Amy.'

'I'm not going to tell you any more about my sister.'

'You know something's up with her, Liv. Let me help her.'

'Oh, piss off,' she says. Robin expects her to hang up on him, but he can still hear the background noise. A thud, thud of bass, the chatter of people shouting over music.

'Are you working?' he asks.

'I'm busy, Robin,' he hears, and this time the phone disconnects.

He sits for a moment longer. Then he puts down his beer, pulls on his shoes and coat and walks out of the door.

—

The neon sign of For Your Eyes Only lights up the grubby street. Two large bouncers in white shirts and black trousers stand by the entrance, and for a moment Robin sits in his car and watches. It's late, just past midnight. A busy time for strip clubs as pubs close and drunk, horny men need somewhere to go.

He gets out of the car and walks to the door. He waits behind two younger guys, their skinheads pink and glossy in the street lights, arms bare and tattooed, then pays his money and goes inside.

The music is loud, pounding out beat after beat in time with the throbbing in Robin's head. The club smells of old beer, of sweat and cheap aftershave. His feet stick to the carpet as he goes to the bar, buys an overpriced bottle of beer and waits, looking around for Liv. He doesn't know what she does here. He takes in the sparsely dressed waitresses and the women in less, barely underwear, rotating around the tables, smiling, no doubt trawling for private dances. He's been to a few of these places in his time, but never this sober, and never this uninterested.

Two women dance on the stage, thrusting at a pole, nearly naked, throwing their hair around to the catcalls of the men watching. He wonders about Liv, about how she got into this. But then, which is better? Dancing and stripping on a garish stage, or shagging men privately, earning money while lying on your back?

Then he sees her, emerging from a door to the right of the stage. She's wearing a low balconette bra, a thong and a pair of skyscraper heels. Her hair is large, her make-up overdone. He watches as she walks slowly round the tables, knocking a straying hand back, bending down with a grin to a punter, only to get a shake of the head in return.

But then she catches his eye, and her face instantly clouds. She walks quickly towards him.

'You can't be here,' she snarls, a forced smile on her face. 'I'm working.'

'Talk to me and I'll go.'

She glances to the side, clocks someone watching her.

'Okay, but you'll need to pay.'

'What?'

'You'll need to pay for a private dance.'

He digs in his pocket for the cash, and then follows her into a small room on one side of the club. There's no door, just a few low chairs, and Liv pushes Robin down onto one.

'I don't want the fucking dance, Liv,' he replies.

'They're watching, now take your coat off and look like you're enjoying yourself.' He pauses. 'Do you want me to get fired?' she hisses.

'Fine.' He does as he's told, and she slowly twirls in front of him. He doesn't feel turned on, just awkward, not sure where to direct his eyes.

'What do you want to know?' she says.

'Did she kill Jonathan?' he asks.

She moves closer to him, her bum hovering over his legs as she gyrates. 'If she did, she hasn't told me.' She glances over her shoulder, catches his disbelieving expression. 'I don't know, honestly I don't. But is she capable of it? Probably, yes.'

Liv turns to face him, then sits on his lap, straddling him. She's very close. He can feel the warmth of her body, smell her perfume. 'When we were teenagers, there was this guy. She wanted him to take her to some party, but he had a girl-friend, and turned her down flat.' She's still swaying on his lap, and Robin's finding it hard to concentrate, his face near her breasts. 'And then the day before, the girlfriend gets sick. Proper vomiting. Had to be taken to hospital. She was okay in the end but turns out she was poisoned.'

'And it was Amy?'

'She didn't admit it, but I thought so, yes. I was just in college, so she must have been about fifteen. And if she could do something like that then...'

She leaves the words unsaid; Robin knows what she's implying.

'Then help us, Liv, please. Help us find something so we can charge her.'

He can see her thinking. Then she says: 'The life insurance. It's a lot. I saw the paperwork for it in her kitchen. If it's a motive you want, you've got it.'

'We looked. We couldn't find it.'

'Try her wardrobe, it's probably got a false bottom. Mum used to do the same.'

But Robin knows they're short of time. The SOCOs will be out of the house by now; Amy Miller will have been released.

'Get it for us,' he begs.

'No, Robin.' She shakes her head, then glances through the doorway. She moves again, in a slow sway, her hair falling over his face. He meets her eyes, noticing the curve of her breast, the feeling of her sitting on his lap, moving closer.

'Please,' he whispers.

'She's my sister,' Liv says. Her face is almost next to his, barely centimetres away. 'She may be nuts, but she's all I have.'

And then she leans down and kisses him.

'Oi!' Loud words are shouted from the doorway, and Robin feels hard hands on his arms. Liv jumps away as a large, meaty bouncer hauls him off the chair. 'No touching the girls,' the bouncer shouts.

Robin glances back. Liv's standing in the room, hands on hips, smiling. It was deliberate, the kiss; she knew he'd get dragged away.

'Okay, okay,' he says, his hands raised above his head in surrender.

The bouncer propels him towards a side door. 'Out!' he hollers, and Robin goes without protest, the bouncer following close behind. Then he hears a yell from behind them.

'And he didn't pay,' Robin hears Liv shout. He opens his mouth to protest, but the bouncer is on him again, pushing him out into the silent alleyway behind the club, then back against a wall.

The bouncer's huge. Bulging biceps, white T-shirt stretched across defined abs. He glares at Robin with a roid-raged stare.

'Hand it over,' he growls, but then pulls at Robin's jacket, prodding at his inside pockets. He takes the wad of cash that Robin withdrew from the cashpoint only an hour previously, but then he digs again, pulling out Robin's warrant card.

The bouncer opens it and looks at the shiny badge, then the ID.

'You're a fucking copper,' he growls.

'Off duty,' Robin says.

'Still a fucking cop, whether you're in uniform or out.' And before Robin can speak he sees a blur in front of him, then a shock of pain as the bouncer's fist connects with his eye. It pushes his head back, bouncing hard against the brick wall behind.

He stands for a second, leaning against the wall. His vision's blurry, black leaching in from the edges, the bouncer still in front of him.

'Are you the one that sold her the roofies?' Robin mutters.

He's not sure why he says it, except that something feels fitting as the pulse of agony grows across his face. A second blow connects to his stomach, then a third in his side. The punch folds him in two, winded, and his legs crumple, throwing him down to the concrete floor of the alleyway. His eyes are streaming; he's unable to breathe. Pain everywhere. He tastes blood in his mouth; he must have bitten his tongue.

'Don't come back, fucking cop.'

He hears footsteps, then the slam of the metal door closing. Robin stays there for a moment, in a crumpled ball, next to the smell of the bins, the drip of leaking guttering. He listens to men on the street outside and takes a slow, juddering breath in.

'Shit,' he manages, at last, with little more than a groan.

He tries to open his eyes, but his left one is refusing to comply. He tentatively raises a hand to touch it, before pulling away as it stings bitterly in response.

Using the rough wall, he raises himself to his feet, then staggers out of the alleyway, back to his car. He passes people walking on the pavement, but nobody even gives him a second glance at this time of night. Just another man, in another fight. Getting what he deserved.

He climbs into his car and starts the engine. Every time he takes a breath he feels a sharp ache in his ribs. He can feel something warm running down his cheek, and pulls down the visor, looking in the tiny mirror at his face. Sure enough, there's a cut just below his eyebrow. His eye is a mass of purple and red. He finds an old tissue and holds it there for a second, wincing at the fresh sting.

Then he puts the car into gear and drives to the police station.

67

Friday

At two in the morning, the police station runs on a skeleton staff, close to deserted. But it's a good thing, Robin thinks, as he staggers through the empty corridors, blood running down his face. He walks into the empty incident room and takes the first aid kit from the wall, then carries it into the men's toilets.

The overhead light is hard and bleaching, but he knows even without it he looks a state. His jeans are muddy from the alleyway, his hands dirty and grazed, black under his fingernails. He washes them, the water turning grey and pink from the blood, then he leans forward and peers at the mess the bouncer has made of his face.

He knows he should register it as a crime, get the guy formally charged. But there's a whole load of questions he doesn't want to answer if he does. He can only imagine the look on Baker's face when he starts to explain why he was in a strip club in the early hours of the morning interviewing the sister of a key murder suspect, while having a lap dance. Oh, and she's the one that he got the complaint about, the one he'd got drunk with before and she'd stayed the night at his place? And has he mentioned that she's a hooker, too?

Hell, no. He's going to stay quiet about this one.

He takes a large handful of toilet paper, soaks it in water, then dabs at his eyebrow. He cleans up the worst of the blood, noting with grim satisfaction that it'll probably scar. But it's stopped bleeding, and he doesn't think it'll need stitches. He should get some ice for his eye though, the swelling already causing him a problem, and settles for a wad of cold, wet toilet paper. Then he goes along to the rooms where all the rubbish from the Miller house is being kept.

The sooner he gets this lot sorted, the better.

—

'Robin, what the hell?'

Even before he opens his eyes and looks at Freya, he knows the expression on her face. Disbelief, mixed with pure horror at what she's seeing.

At five a.m., he decided to have a little pause, and took the hood down from his white crime scene suit and settled in a corner of the stinking, rubbish-strewn room. But the short break obviously turned into a nap, and now here she is.

He sits up, wincing as his stomach protests from the bruising last night.

'What time is it?' he mutters. He tries to open his eyes but only one is functioning.

'What on earth happened to your face?' Freya crouches next to him and tries to touch it. He winces and pulls away.

'It's a long story.'

'So tell me.'

He sighs, then sees the coffee cup in her hand. 'Is that for me?' he asks. She passes it to him, then pulls a chair over to his side, waiting.

He slowly tells her the story of the strip club, and Liv. Her tale about teenage Amy and the life insurance. And then the bouncer.

'So you got a beating for your efforts, but didn't move the case any further forward,' she says, and he nods, slowly. 'Christ.' She sits back on the chair. She looks nice – she's had a shower, a good night's sleep, put on clean clothes. Unlike him. He hates to think what he must smell like, but knows it's probably masked by the lingering stink of this room.

'And have you found anything in here?' she asks.

He shakes his head and finishes his coffee. 'You done next door?' he says.

'Yeah. I've bagged up the cling film tubes and boxes as evidence, sent it down to forensics in the hope of fingerprints.' He looks at her, but she holds her hand up before he can speak. 'And yeah, I know. If they're hers then they'll just say so what, it's her house. But at least we can show that she put it there.' She glances round at the rubbish piles. 'Shall I come and help you with this?'

'Sure?' he says.

'Yeah. But first, let's get you tidied up.'

Freya ushers Robin up and out of the evidence room, then to the men's shower room upstairs. She forces him in to get cleaned up, muttering, 'I'll find you something to wear,' as she leaves.

The shower room is empty, its usual occupants – keen commuter cyclists and gym goers – having finished and left hours ago. Luckily there's some shower gel someone's left behind, along with a semi-wet towel hanging over a radiator. Robin gets undressed, putting his clothes in a grubby pile, then gets into the shower. He washes his hair, wincing as the shower gel hits the cut on his eye, something also stinging at the back of his head. He gets out, wraps the towel round his middle, then stands in front of the steamed-up mirror, looking with fascination at the red and purple bruise across his stomach. He's never been a man to get into fights, so this physical damage is new to him. Mentally, the battered, bruised, broken feeling is familiar, but this pain, and the tangible reason for it, makes a nice change.

He leans forward towards the mirror to look at his face, then hears a knock.

'Can I come in? Are you decent?'

Robin glances down at the towel. 'Sort of.'

A hand comes round the door holding something grey in a plastic bag. He takes it and rips open the covering, realising she's collected a standard-issue police tracksuit, normally intended for those in custody.

He puts it on quickly, not wanting to think how appropriate this outfit actually is. One statement from her and he could be in one of these for real.

'Dressed?' Freya asks.

'Done,' he replies, socks and trainers back on his feet.

She pokes her head round the door, tentatively checking, then comes into the room. She passes him a small parcel wrapped up in a blue and white tea towel.

'Persuaded the canteen to give me this. For your face.'

'I think that ship has sailed,' he says, but he holds the ice pack to his eye anyway. 'Can you look at the back of my head? I think there's something there too.'

'Sit down.' She gestures to a chair, and he does as she asks, bending forward. He feels gentle fingers exploring his scalp, working their way through his wet hair. It's a pleasant feeling and he closes his eyes for a second, feeling another swell of tiredness.

'There's a bump, and yeah, a scab here too,' Freya says at last.

Robin opens his eyes, then clamps the tea towel to his eye socket, standing back up. 'Banged it against the wall when he hit me,' he says with a wry smile. 'You should see the other guy.'

Freya snorts. 'I very much doubt it.' She steps away from him. 'I think you'll live.'

'Thank you, Freya.'

'I didn't do anything.'

'No, I mean...' He pauses. 'For everything. You know.'

He doesn't need to say any more. She knows what he's referring to. She just nods, then, to his surprise, steps forward and wraps her arms round him.

He stands there awkwardly for a moment, then does the same, resting his cheek on the top of her head as she stays buried in his chest. Then she pulls away and walks quickly out.

He waits for a second, looking at the closed door. Then he takes a long breath in and follows her out of the room.

68

She's out of that stinking cell, out of the police station, and home. Last night the only thing Amy had the energy to do was go straight to bed, handful of pills from her emergency supply down her gullet. But this morning she runs a full bubble bath, pours a large glass of wine and slowly lowers herself into the hot water, the scent of lavender filling the steam-filled bathroom.

Her solicitor is right: they have nothing on her. He said Kal had been taken away to the local funny farm, so any testimony he'd given would be subject to doubt. But still, she's pissed off with herself for relying on a man.

Her whole life she's known she can only count on one person: herself. Even her own sister showed to be unreliable and useless by the time she was sixteen. Always drunk, always shoving something up her nose or into her arm. No: Amy knows she is alone in this world.

Once, she thought that Jonathan was the exception to that rule. When they first met, she saw something in him. His potential. He was a clever man, with a good job. They would buy a house, a nice new home, and have kids and be a family. But fuck, he never did what he was told.

And then he had the affair. With *her*. That cop, of all people.

The water's growing cold, so Amy pulls herself out, wrapping a large fluffy towelling robe around her. She lets the water go, then carries her wine glass down the stairs to the kitchen, pouring another.

Amy got her first job at the age of fifteen. Pot washer in the local pub, but she worked hard and soon she was a waitress, then behind the bar the moment she turned eighteen. She showed some aptitude in the kitchen, and the chef took her under his wing, showing her the basics. More pubs, more restaurants followed; she yearned for the respect, for the kudos of working for the best places in town. She put in the hours, did the graft, but it wasn't just that: she was prepared to go above and beyond. She would do *anything* to get the job she wanted. She made that perfectly clear.

And for every restaurant manager, every chef she opened her legs to in a storeroom, there was a wife or girlfriend who couldn't find out. Favours worked both ways, as Amy would remind the men involved.

But she wasn't like Liv or her mother. She wasn't. She didn't do it for money; she had enough of that. Sex can get you where you want; that's something neither of them ever understood. Amy thinks of her mother, dying alone on the sticky lino floor of that council flat. Lying there for days, until the smell alerted the neighbour. That will never be her, Amy tells herself, looking round her pristine kitchen.

The crime scene officers have gone now, and Amy resolves to spend the day doing another deep clean. They didn't leave too much of a mess, but Amy can still sense them in her house. Touching her things, looking for *evidence*. How ridiculous. As if they would find anything.

They've taken her pills, though. That is a pain. She'll need to go out today, refill the prescription. There is no way she can do without those for long.

Amy stands up and pulls one of the cookbooks from the shelf, turning to the middle page. She takes out the newspaper clipping that she stored there, the one Liv had stolen from that detective. The complaint doesn't seem to have put him off, but everyone has their weaknesses, and she wonders about his.

She picks up her phone and does a quick search. *Trevor Stevens car accident*. Multiple results fill the screen and she reads a few of them, topping up her wine as she goes. Liv was right;

Stevens was made out to be a virtual saint. A picture of redemption and newly renewed zest for life. She snorts. No such thing.

One of the news reports mentions a sighting at the local petrol station before the crash, and a request for witnesses to come forward. She pulls up the site of the accident on the map.

There's a petrol station less than a mile away. Amy wonders what the articles aren't saying, and what more they could tell her. She dials the number.

An old man picks up, his voice full of age and tremor. She says hello, mentions the accident, but before she can go any further, he interrupts.

'Are you a colleague of DC West's? I meant to call you.'

So that detective, the blonde one, has been speaking to him. How interesting.

'I work with Detective West, yes,' Amy says without missing a beat. 'Have you found anything new?'

'Yes, actually. My grandson, well, he managed to track down those witnesses on the CCTV. The ones that were in that day? All digital, you know, nothing I understand.'

'He did?'

'Yeah, the couple? I can send a photo of their credit card information across—'

'Actually, I'll come to you,' Amy says quickly. 'Detective West doesn't trust email, she says anyone can get access to it.'

The man chuckles. 'Couldn't agree more.'

'And if I could have another copy of that tape, while I'm there,' Amy adds, with a smile. But her hopes quickly fade.

'I'm sorry, love. DC West took the only copy when she was here. Haven't you got it?'

'Yes, yes,' Amy says quickly. 'Just that she's away, and I wanted to have another look. No problem, I'm sure these witnesses will be more than helpful.'

Amy hangs up, and puts her phone down slowly. Why is the blonde looking into a car accident from two years before? One linked to her own boss?

It doesn't make sense to Amy, but one thing's certain: she has one hell of an incentive to find out.

69

Freya walks quickly away from the men's shower room, her heart thumping in her chest. That was stupid. She shouldn't have bloody hugged him. But he looked so helpless, so pathetic, standing there, his face a mess, his hair wet, actually smelling nice for a change, that she couldn't resist him.

But, Christ, that's the last thing she needs. Fancying her boss? And one as screwed up as Robin? Hell, no. But there is no doubting some sort of attraction there, a connection that seems to be reciprocated.

Her phone rings, and she looks at the name on the screen, *Steph*, then feels an irrational flash of guilt.

'Freya?' Steph says, as she answers it. 'I have the tox results for you. The ones from Trevor Stevens.'

Freya listens, grim-faced, then hangs up and pockets her phone. She debates what to do with the information. Tell him? But she doesn't want anything to distract Robin right now.

She walks quickly to the rubbish room and pulls on a white suit. The smell is just as bad as it was yesterday, but she feels ready. She slept well last night, her belly full of terrible Chinese food, her body knackered from the long day at work. Her resolve is as strong as ever. She knows – yes, *knows* – that there's something odd about Amy Miller. And this room holds the key. It has to.

Robin joins her, and pulls on his own white suit. They work quietly without speaking, a video camera running, wanting to avoid inflicting the stink on the admin staff this time. The rubbish is as disgusting as she knew it would be. Old coffee grounds mix in with everything, a gritty, wet black coating. Leftover food, things she can't even imagine in their original form. They take photos but it's impossible to separate the crap into individual lots of evidence, scooping it together into one big mess in the corner of the room.

She stands up, stretching out her aching back. Not for the first time, she doubts whether they're going to get anything useful out of this fetid pile. She thinks about the results from Steph, and how Trevor Stevens demolished Robin's life in the same way that Amy has ruined hers.

Robin sees her stop and pauses.

'You okay?' he asks.

'Yeah, just… Who was that guy?' she asks him, after a moment. 'The one that came to see you in the police station last week?'

He pulls the mask down from his mouth for a moment and pauses, one foot scuffing in the mess on the floor. 'Liam,' he says at last. 'My brother-in-law. It was the anniversary of their death last Thursday.'

'And you've fallen out?'

'Yes.'

'How come?'

He frowns, and Freya wonders if she's overstepped the mark. Then he speaks, his voice quiet, barely more than a whisper: 'I don't understand why he's not more angry than he is.'

Freya remembers the callous words from the PCs, back when they found the hidden cameras. *Like shut down… he wasn't the same.* She wonders if it could happen to her. Maybe it has already. Would she be the same person if she fell in love again, now she has lost Jon?

'Perhaps he is angry,' Freya says. 'Just expresses it differently.'

'Or perhaps he changed, and I didn't.'

'In what way?'

He sighs and shakes his head solemnly. 'Maybe I was always this much of a miserable bastard, but I was too busy to notice.'

It's a strange place for them to have a heart-to-heart. Both standing in white crime scene suits, a heap of stinking rubbish between them. She desperately wants to comfort him, but has no idea how.

'You're not—' she begins, but he interrupts her.

'Come on,' he says, putting the mask back over his mouth. 'Let's get this done.'

Freya takes the hint, conversation over, and bends down again to the last bin liner. She assumes the bags Robin opened first were the oldest, because when they get to this last one, it somehow doesn't smell as bad as the others.

Robin helps her lay out a new sheet of brown paper, and they open up the black bag fully, pushing everything out. Robin moves the rubbish around while she photographs the contents. There's the coffee again, but there's something else permeating the detritus. It's a smoky, charred smell, like old barbecues.

She wrinkles her nose.

'Anything?' Robin asks. She can only make out a small portion of his face above the mask, the black and red swelling still growing above his left eye.

'No, nothing.' She crouches down and pokes in the waste. Potato peelings, the plastic box from something, maybe a punnet of strawberries. More indescribable mess. Internally she hopes nobody ever digs around in her rubbish; god knows what they'd find.

'Freya.'

She turns. Robin's kneeling down with his back to her on his side of the room. She stands up and joins him.

He's staring at something on the ground. It's black, shrivelled; she can't make out any form or shape.

'What is it?' she asks.

'I think it's plastic. Or it was.'

Robin picks it up between two fingers of his gloved hand and holds it up to the light. She grabs the camera and takes a few photos, then looks more closely.

It's clearly the source of the smell of burning, the plastic contracted into a small black ball. There are a few edges where the fire didn't catch, clear plastic, perhaps some sort of bag. And at one end is a clump of something grey. Tape.

Robin looks at her. His eyes stare, wide and wild.

'I know what happened,' he says slowly. 'I know what happened to Jonathan.'

70

Slowly, carefully, they bag the evidence. Freya writes a note and gives it all to one of the DCs to take down to the lab.

'Put a rush on it. Please,' Freya begs.

But before they can do anything else, Robin's mobile rings. She waits as he answers it, watching his face change from interest to barely concealed boredom.

'Yes, fine. Will do,' he says. 'Send me the details.'

He hangs up and she looks at him quizzically.

He sighs. 'There's been another break-in. Last night. That's the sixth now, and Baker's getting twitchy. He wants us to go down there.'

'And do what?'

'Interview the neighbours. Personally. See if anyone heard anything.'

'He said that?'

'No, some lackey. But the message was the same.'

His phone beeps, and he looks at the address. His mouth drops open and he turns the screen round to face her.

'You're kidding me...' she starts.

The address: ten Ashcroft Drive. Amy Miller's next-door neighbour.

–

They walk out of the police station, ready to drive to the house. Freya feels strange, like every event is conspiring to take them closer to Amy Miller. But before they go, Freya stops him.

'You can't go like that,' she says, pointing to his tracksuit. 'You need proper clothes.'

They drive to Robin's house and he gets out.

'Do you want to come in and wait?' he asks. She pauses, then follows him inside.

He closes his front door and turns to look at her. His eyes are dark, his face solemn. Things feel odd between them. Slightly charged, like the atmosphere before a thunderstorm, an excess of energy in the air. She feels him hesitating, doubting himself.

Then, without thinking, she steps forward and kisses him.

The first thing she thinks is, *he's not like Jonathan*. Then the second: *I don't care*. He's clumsy, slightly rough, and they stagger, half fall into the living room and then onto the sofa, her on top of him. She hears him make a gasp of pain, and goes to pull away, but he kisses her again, one hand in her hair, the other under her shirt. She does the same to him, the crappy police tracksuit top coming over his head easily. Shoes are kicked off, her shirt over her head. She feels sober, so very aware of what she's doing, but almost powerless to stop it. Just wanting to be next to someone, wanting to be with him.

Wanting to be with Jonathan.

And then suddenly she's crying.

She feels the sob reach up from her chest, grab her insides and pull. The gulf overwhelms her. The emptiness, the black hole knowing that she'll never, ever hold him again. She notices Robin move away, realising something is wrong, then pulling her close, wrapping his arms around her.

It's not about sex any more. She squeezes her eyes shut, her hands ball into fists and she cries, her face pushed hard into his chest. They're both half-naked, and she's conscious of the inappropriateness, the awkwardness of all this, but she can't stop herself, caught in the flood of loss and sadness. She misses him. She misses him so fucking much.

Robin isn't Jonathan. And nobody will be Jonathan, ever again.

71

Robin holds Freya tightly, feeling both completely devastated for her and overwhelmingly uncomfortable at the same time. After a while, she sits up, mumbling apologies, then grabs her shirt and runs off. He hears the slam of the bathroom door.

He pulls himself up slowly, wincing as his ribs protest. He leaves the wretched grey tracksuit top on the floor and goes to his bedroom. He gets dressed in his own clothes, jeans and a shirt, all the while listening out for signs of Freya emerging from the bathroom.

He feels shit. For taking advantage, for kissing her back, for— Oh, fuck, all of it. She is his DC, his subordinate. He should not be coming on to people who work for him, let alone newly bereaved, vulnerable ones. Although, given there's so much wrong with their situation at the moment, perhaps one more mistake wouldn't have made much difference.

He finishes getting dressed then goes into the kitchen, flicking the kettle on. He listens to it boil, taking two mugs from the cupboard, putting in teabags and milk. He'd prefer coffee, but a mug of warm reassuring sugary tea seems more suitable. He turns as he hears footsteps behind him.

Freya stands in the middle of the kitchen, once again fully dressed, her face puffy, her eyes bloodshot.

'I'm sorry,' she says.

'No, I'm sorry. It was all me,' Robin replies.

She attempts a smile, then her gaze shifts to the mugs.

'You making one for me?'

'You want one?'

'Please.'

Tea made, they sit at Robin's kitchen table in an awkward silence. He sweeps what seem to be prawn cracker crumbs onto the floor. What would Georgia think, looking at the state of him now? He knows what would be going through her mind. She'd look at him, eyebrows raised, mouth pursed. Then she'd say, *Pull yourself together, Rob, you're embarrassing yourself.*

He also knows what she'd say about him ignoring Liam. Georgia always was a better person than him. More patient, more forgiving. But for killing the twins? Never. He takes a sip of his tea. She would have died for those boys, a hundred times over. As would he, he realises.

But he also knows that deep down, a small part of the anger he feels towards Liam is fury at himself. The part he played in Trevor Stevens' death pulls at him; it creates a constant state of conflict in his head. He is a police officer, through and through, and has been one for nearly twenty years. Yet look what he did.

Liam is no more than a convenient conduit for his rage.

He looks at Freya.

'You up to this?' he asks. 'Going back to that house?'

She pushes her tea away. She knows what he's talking about. She stands up, pulls her shoulders back, then looks at him.

'Absolutely,' she says.

–

The day is getting late. Rush hour traffic has abated, and they drive in silence through rain-drenched streets. They pull up outside ten Ashcroft Drive. The lights are switched off, the front window barricaded with cheap plywood where the vandals had got inside. Robin's been informed that the owners have been and gone, inspecting the damage. They won't be able to rent that place out again any time soon. Robin mentally schedules a visit out to their main residence tomorrow. It's no doubt some posh place in the sticks, Robin and Freya playing the part of the all-important detectives who will reassure and pacify them.

Meanwhile they have their orders from Baker: have a look around. Interview the neighbours. For fuck's sake, do *something*, he exclaimed, in contrary to the scarce investigation that had come before.

Robin glances at the house next door, thinking about Amy Miller inside, then looks over at Freya.

'You know we can't arrest her this time,' Robin says. 'We're still waiting on forensics. Nothing to justify a warrant until we hear back.'

'We'll just ask her about the break-in,' Freya replies. 'And then leave.'

They stare at the Miller house. They can see lights on; there's a good chance she's there. Robin turns and looks across to the empty field on the other side, to the dark silhouettes of sleeping bulldozers.

They both get out of the car and walk slowly towards the house.

At the door, Robin turns to Freya. 'You sure you want to do this?' he asks.

'Yes,' she replies, and reaches for the doorbell.

As it rings, he feels a flutter of worry ball in his stomach. They wait, hear footsteps, then the door opens.

Amy Miller stands in front of them.

She's wearing jeans and a casual T-shirt, but it looks expensive, ironed and crisp. Her hair is perfectly in place, her make-up precise and natural.

She glares at them.

'What do you want?'

'We need to talk to you,' Robin starts.

'This is police harassment. I've done all the talking I wanted to yesterday. You know you can't ask me anything now, not without my lawyer present.'

'We know. This is about the break-in next door.'

'I didn't hear anything. I was asleep.'

'Not even the front window smashing?'

'No.' She pauses. 'I took sleeping pills last night. I thought I'd need them, after my traumatising day in the hands of the police.'

They all stare at each other. Then a look of disgust crosses Amy's face and she goes to close the door.

'You missed something, Amy,' Freya says. Amy stops. 'You thought you were careful, but not enough. We found it.'

Robin takes a sharp breath in. He glances across to Freya – the anger is clear on her face and he can tell all previous good intentions have disappeared.

'Don't be ridiculous,' Amy snaps. Robin knows he should pull Freya away, but he can see her words are getting to Amy. She's curious. Her arrogance won't let her believe her plan hasn't worked.

'Let us in and we'll tell you about it.'

'You're bluffing.'

Freya shrugs. 'Fine. We'll see you and your solicitor at the station tomorrow. And tomorrow, we'll make sure you're charged with murder.'

Robin watches Amy hesitate. Then she opens the door wide, turning and walking through to the living room. They follow her, and as they go Robin looks into the kitchen. It's spotless, as it always has been. Draining board empty and gleaming, counters clear, except for a small white package sitting on the side. Robin recognises it as a bag from a pharmacy, no doubt replacing the prescribed drugs they seized. He gets a small flare of satisfaction knowing they've inconvenienced her, even by a tiny amount.

He follows Freya into the living room. Amy waits, perching on the edge of the sofa, watching them, poised. He slowly sits down opposite her, next to Freya.

'So? What amazing proof do you have? I know you have nothing else from that camera, because you would have used it already.'

Robin hesitates. He tells himself that this is okay. That they'll put the evidence to her and she'll agree to come in for a

voluntary interview. But he knows there's bugger all chance
Amy Miller will comply. This is a woman who *no comment*-ed
her whole way through her formal police interview – what are
the chances she'll nod meekly and come with them again? Slim
to nothing. But Robin senses Freya's impatience, and he feels
it too.

'We know you killed him,' Robin says.

Amy's eyes narrow. She's thinking, and glances across to
Freya.

'You're close, you two?'

'We're colleagues,' Robin replies, blankly.

'You're more than that. Have you slept with her?' Amy
directs to Robin.

Freya fidgets beside him but stays silent. 'No,' he says firmly.

'But you know about her and my husband, right?' Amy says,
and Robin thinks, fuck. If Amy tells her lawyer about Freya and
Jonathan's affair, their whole investigation won't be worth shit.
Freya won't withstand the scrutiny. Nor Robin.

Everything about this is wrong. They're police. They should
leave now, return to the station, wait for forensics, get the arrest
warrant and interview Amy properly. In a video-equipped
interview room, with her solicitor present. Then they'll call the
CPS, charge her with murder, and she'll never leave.

But Robin has experience of taking justice into his own
hands. He knows sometimes there are situations where there's
no going back. And this is one of those.

'Tell us how you killed him, Amy,' he repeats.

She meets his stare, and a smug smile appears on her lips.

'Let's say I did,' she says quietly. 'Hypothetically. How might
it have happened?'

Robin feels a jolt of anticipation. He slowly breathes in,
trying to hide his nerves. He thinks about what they found,
in the rubbish. The melted plastic bag. The screwed-up tape.

'You drugged him. And then you suffocated him.'

He feels Freya tense next to him. Keep quiet, he wills her.
Keep quiet.

315

Amy Miller gives a slow nod. 'Okay, then. Where? When?'

'In this house. Upstairs.' There were cameras in the rest of the ground floor, except in the kitchen, Robin knows. 'And not on Monday. Way before that.' He watches Amy's expression, sees a flicker of something cross her face. Amusement? Satisfaction? He's not sure, but he knows he's on the right track. 'Friday night.'

'Friday night we were at a party with Kal. Everyone saw us, everyone confirmed.'

'No, Amy,' Robin says slowly. 'Everyone saw *you*. And they were all so drunk by that point, they assumed Jonathan was there too, but he was already dead.'

'Your pathologist can prove that, can she?' Amy asks. She leans back in her chair, crossing one skinny leg over the other. 'No, I didn't think so. And answer me this. Why didn't he struggle? Why didn't they find evidence of defensive injuries in the post-mortem? I've seen the report, DS Butler. My solicitor has it. He has all of your so-called evidence. The only findings in that post-mortem were consistent with how he was found – asphyxiated in that hotel room. Sex play gone wrong.'

'Jonathan was never into that shit, and you know it,' Freya snaps.

'But you can't prove it, can you?' Amy says again.

'We have the plastic bag. We have the tape that you wrapped round his neck. And the ends of the tape will perfectly match up with the roll we seized from your garage,' Freya says, clear, confident.

'So fucking what?' Amy replies. She's still calm, although two matching red spots have appeared on her cheeks. 'How did he get to the hotel? What about his movements on social media? Why is there no evidence of Jonathan anywhere except in that hotel room?'

But Robin knows. 'You wrapped his body in cling film, and then at some point over the weekend you drove it to the hotel.'

'How precisely did I do that?' Amy scoffs. 'Given I'm assuming you have CCTV? And you've found nothing in my car.'

She was right. They checked the CCTV for the whole weekend and neither Jonathan's car nor her Audi were seen.

'Your work van,' Freya says, and both Robin and Amy turn to her. 'You transported the body in your work's van. Nobody would think anything strange of a catering van from a hotel turning up at the trade entrance. And then you shipped the body in on a catering trolley.'

Amy raises her eyebrows. 'Not just a pretty face, are you, sweetheart? But the question remains, can you prove it?'

Robin watches as Freya's whole body tenses. No, they can't, he knows. There is no CCTV at the trade entrance, no cameras in the corridors. And a dead body wrapped in cling film leaves nothing behind.

Amy stares at Freya, her eyes amused.

'Do you know how long a strangled man takes to die?' she says. 'No more than a few minutes—' a glance to Robin, a small smile '—hypothetically. But fuck, it feels like longer.'

Next to him, Robin hears Freya start to cry, but he doesn't dare look away from Amy. He doesn't want to break her concentration.

'Holding a belt up high enough, it takes effort. Listening to him gasp and choke, the bag going in and out...'

'You're a monster,' Freya whispers.

'He promised!' Amy shouts suddenly. 'He promised me everything! A perfect life. Kids. Love. And – what? Nothing!' Her composure has gone, her cheeks are bright red now, leaning forward into Freya's face. 'You know he couldn't even get it up some days. Wouldn't even try.'

Robin looks across at Freya. She's sobbing now, tears rolling down her face, dripping from her chin. 'So why didn't you divorce him?' she cries, her voice stuttering and wet. 'If he was so useless?'

'What? So you could have him?' A look of pure disgust crosses her face. 'Did you honestly think you and Jonathan would be together?' Amy continues. 'Living in domestic bliss? *Happy?*' she mocks. 'Fuck that. Fuck you. Anyway, he was worth plenty dead.'

'His fertility results came back, Amy,' Robin says. 'There was nothing wrong with him.' Her head whips round. 'It was all normal.'

She shakes her head. 'No. We couldn't have children. It was his fault.'

'No, Amy. It wasn't.'

And that's when Robin realises. The unprotected sex at the swingers' club. It was to get pregnant. He feels sick. The lengths this woman had gone to, to try and create some sort of perfect life for herself. Sleeping with random men. Deceiving Jonathan's best friend. And then killing her husband.

'Why did you make him get tested?' Freya says. 'When you didn't even care about the results?'

'For you two, for the police,' Amy snarls. 'To show you what a devoted couple we were. How we were trying for kids. And he went along with it, although I knew he didn't want to. He'd have done anything. Anything to avoid pissing me off. But what did it matter, in the end?'

Then Amy leans forward, facing them both. Her demeanour has changed. The anger has faded, the arrogance returned.

'Can you prove I committed murder, DS Butler?' she says quietly. Calmly. Too calmly. 'Because I can prove you did, Detective. I can prove you killed Trevor Stevens.'

And Robin's blood runs cold.

72

Amy sees Butler turn white, his mouth open in surprise. And the woman, too. So, she knows? That's interesting.

They think they're so smart, Amy thinks. Look at the state of them. Butler looks worse today, if that can be possible. He has a painful-looking black eye on his left side, and his face is grey and drained. West looks the same – bloated, red eyes. This is the woman Jonathan wanted? She's a fucking mess.

West stands up suddenly. 'I need a drink,' she mutters.

'On duty?' Amy mocks.

'I don't give a shit, where's your alcohol?'

'Make yourself at home,' Amy scoffs sarcastically, gesturing back to the kitchen. 'Wine in the fridge, spirits in the cupboard.'

West leaves in the direction Amy has pointed. Amy watches her go, then turns her attention back to Butler.

She's surprised, Amy will give them that. They've got most of it right.

She remembers that Friday night. Jonathan was late back, and she knew where he'd been. Quiet, secretive, barely meeting her gaze. He'd been with *her*. And then he turned and said, 'Amy, this weekend, we need to talk. Properly talk. About us.'

And she knew.

The way he'd been asking about their weekend plans. He was going to leave her. Her! Jonathan, with his defective sperm and his inability to give her a baby. Except that wasn't true, was it? Everything functioning normally, how ironic. Still, all the more reason to kill him.

She went downstairs and carefully dissolved her ground-up pills in his whisky. Diazepam and zopiclone, perfect for knocking someone out. She waited as he downed his drink. Watched, as his body grew wobbly and weak, and he collapsed on their bedroom floor. She made sympathetic noises as he slurred and complained about not feeling well. She stood in front of him, prepared. Ready.

She put plastic gloves on, the ones she used for preparing food at work, then picked up their oven gloves, gently placing them over his hands.

He looked at them, confused, his eyes unfocused.

'What are you doing?' he said, his voice almost incoherent.

She took the tape and wrapped it quickly round both gloves, securing them together.

That was the touch she was particularly proud of. His hands were bound, and as he struggled pathetically, she knew there would be no marks found later. Nothing the pathologist would notice.

And then she took the plastic bag and put it over his head.

At that point, Jonathan realised what was going on. That he was in trouble. He wriggled, his legs kicking out against the carpet, but his movements were sluggish. Everything was in slow mode, information not feeding properly to his brain. She quickly did up the zip tie – one of her industrial-sized freezer bags, easy to close – then secured it round his neck with another length of tape. He lifted his bound hands to his face, redundantly trying to pull at the bag as it went in and out with each breath. She watched his eyes widen. His mouth gaped; the inside of the bag misted with condensation. His breathing came faster and faster as he panicked.

It was starting to stick to his face now. The plastic sealed tight against his cheeks and forehead as the air inside was depleted of oxygen. Jonathan sucked harder. Amy could see his chest rising and falling, as he tried to take heavier and heavier breaths.

For a moment she just watched, fascinated.

It wasn't as she had expected. She'd thought she would feel something towards her dying husband, but the only emotion she felt was pity. That his life would come to this. Suffocating, painfully, on his own bedroom floor.

But it wasn't over yet. She took the belt – his belt – in her gloved hands, pulled the end through the buckle then stood in front of him and looped it over his head. She pulled it tight as his hands came up again, desperate and useless. She took a big step onto the bed, and tugged up.

He was heavy. Heavier than she'd thought he would be, but she didn't need to do much now. She didn't need to kill him this way – the bag would do that for her – but she needed the marks on his neck. She needed it to look like a hanging. He was weakening. His eyes still open, his mouth barely moving, his hands collapsed in his lap.

The plastic bag moved inwards, one last time, and his body gave an involuntary twitch. And then he stopped.

Amy stared at him. She tried to find a pulse on his neck, but there was nothing. Just to be sure, she left him lying there while she continued with her preparations.

She pulled at his body so he was lying stretched out on his back, his hands still bound in front of him. Then she fetched the cling film from the drawer.

She had debated how many rolls she would need. Seventy-five metres was a lot, surely? She took the roll out of the box, peeled back the end, then, starting at the bottom, started to wrap. She covered his socked feet, then up his trousers. She took his keys and wallet out of his pocket as she went, double-layering, just to be sure. And as she got to his hands, she snipped away the tape and took off the oven gloves. She looked at his wrists. Nothing. No marks at all – and she gave a satisfied smile. She carried on wrapping, rolling his body first one way and then the other. No more than a large hunk of meat, getting ready for storage.

To do his torso and his head, she pushed him up to a sitting position, finishing at his shoulders. She got a new roll, then looked at him, his head still encased in the plastic. She took the scissors again, and gently cut away the bag.

His eyes were wide open, but now glassy and empty. His skin was red, slightly wet from the condensation in the plastic. The marks around his neck were clear and pronounced; she left the belt there, pulled tight.

And then it was done. She stood back and surveyed her handiwork. A clear plastic mummy on her bedroom floor. No trace would escape. Her husband, hermetically sealed.

She picked up Jonathan's phone and unlocked it using the code she had seen him use so many times before. She sent a message to Kal: *On our way, mate.*

Then she tidied herself up, checked her reflection in the mirror, and left her house to go to the party. Fashionably late, when she knew everyone would be pissed out of their minds. Nobody would miss her husband. Everyone would believe her when she said he was over there, in the smoking area, talking to so-and-so. Self-absorbed pricks.

She went to the party, and she left her husband dead on the bedroom floor.

Late Friday night, in the early hours of the morning, she carefully transferred his body onto a hand trolley. It was one they used at work for moving the large sacks of food around, and slowly she manoeuvred it down the stairs and out into the garage. The freezer was standing by. Empty. Not too cold, to avoid the telltale signs of freezing, but chilly enough to slow down his decomposition. Panting with exertion, she lugged him inside and closed the lid.

The rest was easy in comparison. The posts on social media. Driving Jonathan's car around – documenting his weekend trips. To the dump. Off for a walk. Then, Sunday morning, she moved him to one of the trolleys in the back of her van, ready for transport via the loading bay to the Premier Inn that Sunday night. She'd already checked into the room under a fake name, booking it out until Tuesday. Plenty of time.

And she knew Kal would do what she asked. She knew about his childhood, had listened to him tell the stories when he was drunk, growing maudlin and weepy. She just needed to push the right buttons, make it look like Jonathan was an abuser. And he helped her, as she knew he would.

The chest freezer was turned up and loaded with food. Back to normal.

It was perfect. Until these two started digging.

But she knows about them. She knows about Freya's little secret – the affair with the victim, how she shouldn't be working on this case.

And DS Butler? He acts like he is superior, but he is the same. He is a cold-blooded murderer, just like her.

DC West comes back into the room, three glasses of dark brown whisky balanced in her hands. She hands one to Amy.

'I never was one for hard spirits, but I'll make an exception for you two,' Amy comments, taking a sip of the brown liquid.

'I spoke to the old guy in the petrol station,' Amy says to them both. 'I pretended to be your colleague. He didn't even ask for ID, silly old fool. He told me about the CCTV.' Amy looks at Freya, takes another gulp of the whisky. This is nice, she thinks, why hasn't she tried it before? 'Where is that now, DC West? Do you have it?'

Freya just lowers her head to the floor. Beaten.

'He gave me the details for the other people that were there that night. And, do you know, I went to see them and they remembered that day. The accident had cemented it in their minds. And they remembered you.'

She points a shaking finger at Butler. 'I showed them your photo, and they said you were there. You spoke to the dead guy.' The detective shakes his head slowly. 'And Liv told me how Stevens had given up drinking. How he never drank Jack Daniel's. And I put two and two together.'

'So what?' Butler growls. 'That doesn't prove shit.'

Amy sips her drink slowly, enjoying holding the detectives in her power. 'Oh, I'm sorry,' she says sweetly. 'Did you assume there was only one copy of the CCTV?'

She sees their faces change in surprise and laughs. 'I said you'd lost it. And did they have a spare?' Her vision feels hazy and she blinks, trying to focus her eyes. 'The old man said no, but I got the impression his grandkid knew differently. I went back later.' She winks at Freya. 'Amazing how resourceful a nineteen-year-old can be with the prospect of a blow job.'

She sees the repulsion on West's face; she hates these detectives. She'll enjoy destroying their careers, watching Butler go to prison.

She feels herself sway slightly and leans back on the sofa, finishing the last of the whisky. She lets the glass drop to the carpet. 'I'll raise a complaint, another complaint,' she continues. She smiles, but her mouth feels dopey; it's hard to get the words out. '...to the police commission,' she manages, 'give them the CCTV, and they'll investigate. They'll pull your medical records, they'll follow up. And your life will be over, DS Butler.'

Amy raises a hand to point at them, but her limbs won't obey. Her brain feels muddled. All she wants to do is sleep, her eyelids heavy.

She looks down to the whisky glass, then slowly back to Freya.

'What have you done?' she slurs. 'What did you do to me?'

'No more than you deserve,' West says.

Then her eyes close and everything goes dark.

LOCAL WIDOW FOUND DEAD AT HOME

Local resident Amy Jane Miller, 37, a chef at the Hotel Continental, was found unresponsive on Friday night in her home in Ashcroft Drive, Winchester. Miller is the widow of Jonathan Miller, 39, who died earlier this month following a tragic accident in the Premier Inn in Winnall.

Amy Miller was pronounced dead at the scene. The coroner has opened an inquest, but initial reports speculate cause of death as a subdural haemorrhage, sustained from a blow to the head from a fall. The large amounts of prescription medication found in her blood are believed to be a contributory factor in the accident.

Olivia Cross, her sister, said she was depressed following the heartbreaking death of her husband and would frequently resort to prescribed medication to help her cope. Cross added, 'Amy and Jonathan were a devoted couple. Amy was struggling to live her life without Jonathan by her side.'

Ms Cross last saw her sister alive at her house, on the afternoon of Friday 2 October. Later that night, Ms Cross entered Mrs Miller's house again, this time using a spare key, and found her dead on her kitchen floor.

DS Robin Butler, Investigating Officer on the Jonathan Miller case, stated, 'We were saddened to hear of the untimely loss of Amy Miller on Friday night. We ask that if anyone knows anything about the death of either Jonathan or Amy Miller to come forward and assist us in our enquiries. All information will be treated with the strictest confidentiality.'

Investigations are ongoing.

73

Monday

'Jesus Christ.' Baker looks at them both across the desk. 'What a mess.'

Freya glances at Robin. She doesn't dare speak.

'Our accidental death turns out to be a murder,' Baker continues, 'and then the main suspect has a tragic accident the moment we let her out of custody. And you didn't notice anything suspicious when you were there Friday night?'

'No, guv. As my report says, we rang the doorbell, but she didn't answer. It's unfortunate,' Robin mumbles.

'Damn right it's unfortunate. I want to see the video from her interview, all the recordings from her time in custody. The IOPC are going to be all over this, and I don't want anyone accusing us of anything dodgy.'

Freya nods.

'And where are we on the evidence relating to the Miller murder? Jonathan Miller,' Baker adds for clarification.

Freya looks to Robin.

'Forensics have come back on the burnt plastic bag we found in the Miller rubbish,' he says. 'The tape edges match up perfectly to the roll we found in their garage, and the inside of the bag contains saliva and DNA from Jonathan Miller.'

'And we think she suffocated him?'

'Yes, guv. We think she killed him on the Friday night, then staged the rest of the evidence to look like he was still alive.'

'Clever,' Baker mutters, then looks up quickly. 'Do we have anything else to back this up?'

'Khalid Riaz has confirmed that the photo on Twitter was an old one from months ago, and he's willing to plead guilty to a count of preventing unlawful burial of a body if we take assisting an offender off the table.'

Freya knows Kal was released from the psychiatric unit this morning and attended an interview with another DS and his solicitor. He was a mess, full of remorse for hiding the murder of his best friend.

'Do we know why she did it?' Baker asks.

They found pregnancy tests and ovulation kits in the bathroom cabinet. And Riaz confirmed again how he'd slept with Amy, drunk, unprotected, same as she had at the swingers' parties. Robin relays this to their DCI.

'All this because she wanted to get pregnant?' Baker replies, incredulously.

'We think it was more than that, guv,' Robin says. 'We've learnt that her childhood was a mess, unpredictable, and we believe Amy was desperately trying to create a perfect life to compensate for that.' Freya remembers the obsessively clean and tidy house, the diazepam Amy took for anxiety, the zopiclone to help her sleep. 'So when Jonathan Miller couldn't get her pregnant, it tipped her over the edge.'

'Well, let's leave the amateur psychology here, shall we,' Baker replies. 'We know for sure Jonathan Miller had a healthy life insurance policy. Money is a motive I can properly get behind. A cool million, right?'

Robin nods.

'Good. Plus you've wrapped up the criminal damage cases, too?'

Freya listens as Robin outlines the evidence returned from the beer cans at the vandalised houses. At last, they had a hit on the system – to prints taken from the note thrown through the broken window at fifty-six Wellington Crescent. They were expected to belong to David Franklin, son of Bethany Franklin, organiser of the swingers' club. A fifteen-year-old kid, in with the wrong crowd, now terrified and confessing to what him and his mates have been up to, sitting in an interview room a few floors down, his mother by his side.

She feels sorry for the boy, and knows Robin blames himself. Maybe if he'd arrested him at the time of the original smashed window incident he wouldn't be in the trouble he is today. But Freya can't worry about that. She has bigger things to think about.

Robin finishes talking, and Baker looks happy.

'Now,' Baker asks, leaning back, clearly satisfied their conversation is nearly over, 'is there anything else I should know?'

Freya doesn't move. She feels her boss's gaze on her face, and she remembers what happened Friday night.

–

Freya looks frantically from the sleeping Amy to Robin. She didn't think it would actually work. She didn't think it would happen this quickly. Robin's staring at her.

'What did you do?' he hisses.

'There were some pills on the side. Diazepam. Something else. I thought… I didn't think. I ground them up with the back of a spoon and put some in her whisky.'

'How much?' Robin asks, his eyes wide.

Freya looks at the unconscious Amy. 'A lot.' Freya feels defiant. Justified. 'It's no more than she did to Jonathan.'

'Fuck…' he says. He stands up and starts pacing the living room, his hands on his head. 'FUCK!' he shouts, furiously, and Freya jumps. He turns back towards her. 'And what do you think we're going to do with her now?'

'I don't know!' Freya reaches forward and touches Amy, then leaps back. 'But she knows about you. She knows about Trevor Stevens.'

She watches Robin. He's stopped pacing, silent now, looking down, thinking. She can see him chewing the inside of his lip. His gaze shifts to Amy Miller, slumped to one side on the couch.

'Since we're here,' he says quietly, and she knows what he's going to say. He continues: 'We can't leave any trace. Go to my car, get whatever PPE you can find out of the boot.'

Freya rushes out the front door. She returns with gloves, and shoe covers, and full white crime scene suits. They put them on in the living room, standing in front of the unconscious Amy, Freya still not convinced she's not going to wake up any second.

And they start their search.

They begin in the bedroom. Robin remembers Liv's instructions, and they pull away the baseboard of the wardrobe, quickly locating the life insurance documents. There are a few other items in there: a bundle of cash, some spare prescription medication and a small bottle with *syrup of ipecac* written on the side. Freya recalls Jon's weight loss, his statement that he'd had a nasty bout of food poisoning, and feels the burn of anger towards Amy deep in her bones.

They put it all in evidence bags. Freya knows the continuity of exhibits will need to be falsified in some way, additional paperwork here, a forged signature there. But there's no DVD. Nothing that might hold the CCTV footage from the garage.

'Do you think she was bluffing?' Freya asks Robin, and he shakes his head.

'Even if she was, I can't risk it.'

They start looking again. Freya's only too aware they don't know how long the drugs will hold. But she tries to keep her panic at bay, carefully checking and replacing belongings where they find them.

She leaves Robin upstairs, and goes back down to the living room. Amy hasn't moved, still slumped on the sofa. Freya stands in front of her, looking at her slack features, her mouth open. Unguarded. Defenceless. She feels her heart start to beat faster. A wave of anger, adrenaline spiking. She's never felt energy like it, fuelled by rage and hatred.

'You don't want to do it.'

She doesn't turn. She knows Robin's standing behind her. She knows what he's implying.

'If I'd asked you that two years ago, in that petrol station, what would you have said?' she whispers back. Now she turns, looking at her boss. Deep lines appear on his forehead as his eyebrows draw together. His shoulders slump. 'He was drunk, Robin. Steph confirmed it. He was out drink-driving that day.'

He stops. He blinks, once, twice. She knows there would have been no hesitation in his mind.

'Freya, listen to me.' Robin stares right at her. 'You may think this will be okay. That Amy Miller deserves it. That she killed Jonathan, and it's right you get this revenge. But however strongly you feel it, nothing can prepare you for the reality of taking someone's life.' He stops, pressing his knuckles against his downturned mouth. She sees his jaw clench, holding back the emotion. 'It takes a part of you, too. That guilt, it eats away at you, until there's nothing left.'

Freya turns back to Amy Miller. 'She can't get away with this,' she whispers. 'She can't.'

She feels gentle hands on her shoulders. 'We'll get her,' Robin says. 'We will.'

Freya notices him step away, his reassuring contact missed when it's gone. And along with it, her intention to do harm to Amy Miller. She turns away from Amy's prostrate body, and watches Robin. He's facing the bookcase now, staring at the same spot where they did that first search all those weeks ago. Robin reaches forward and takes Jon's economics textbook from the bookcase. He glances to Freya, then opens it.

In the hollowed-out centre, where the camera was concealed before, is a small black memory stick. He takes it between two gloved fingers.

'She has a sense of humour, if nothing else,' Robin says.

—

Amy's cleanliness works in their favour: they start from the kitchen, with bleach and cloths and antibacterial spray, erasing every shoe mark and fingerprint. Any sign they were in the house. Freya wipes down the boxes of pills, the whisky bottle, the cupboards, making sure everything shines. Exactly how Amy would have wanted it.

They plump up the cushions in the living room, carry their whisky glasses into the kitchen and wash them up. Robin collects a bin liner from a drawer.

The two of them walk towards the front door, wiping down handles, light switches, door frames. In the hallway, they pull off their white crime scene suits, putting them in the bin liner with the used cloths and their gloves and masks. They pull the front door shut and walk quietly out to the car. Nobody sees them leave. The neighbours are away. The road is empty.

They leave Amy Miller unconscious on the sofa.

All traces of them have gone.

Robin throws the bin liner in the boot and gets into the driver's seat. He starts the engine, but Freya stops him, digs around in her bag, then jumps out. She wipes the key, the spare key, free of fingerprints and replaces it in the fake rock in the flower bed.

Then she gets back in the car and, wordlessly, they drive away. As they go, she risks a glance at her boss. His eyes are narrowed, hard ridges between his eyebrows as he stares at the road.

'Robin...' she begins. 'What happens when she wakes up?'

His hands grip the steering wheel so tightly his knuckles have turned white. 'It'll be her word against ours. We went there, we asked her about the break-in, we left. Right?'

'Right.'

'We didn't talk about Jonathan. We didn't even walk in the door. We certainly didn't drug her.'

Freya notices how he says 'we', although she's only too clear it was her that put the pills in her drink.

'We stick to that, we'll be fine,' he finishes, but Freya's not sure who he's trying to convince – him or her.

At last they stop at Freya's house.

'Robin,' she says, and he looks at her. 'Thank you.'

He doesn't move. Then slowly he nods.

'Dispose of the clothes you're wearing,' he says. 'Just as a precaution. Burn them, preferably. I'll do the same, as well as the bag in the boot.'

'I will.'

'And Freya?'

'Yes?'

'We will never speak about this again. You hear me? Never.'

But they do.

The next day is Saturday, and she spends it distracted. She wakes late, leaves the house only briefly in a taxi to retrieve her car from the police station, then watches mindless television, eats junk food. Until Robin calls.

'Log on to the RMS,' he says, without greeting. 'She's dead.'

'What do you mean, she's dead?' Freya replies, her voice no more than a squeak. But it's true.

Amy Miller has died. Her body discovered by her sister, later that night. Initial reports put it down to a tragic accident – she must have been walking round, prescription meds rampant in her system, when she fell, hitting her head on the corner of the kitchen worktop. Massive subdural haemorrhage. Would have taken her a while to die, but with no one there to help her, she had no hope.

'That's it, Freya,' Robin says, his voice low and final. 'It's over.'

She hangs up. He's right, she knows he is, but she doesn't feel the relief she expects. It's justice, of sorts, but all Freya can feel is the guilt. She did it. She didn't intend to kill, but because of her Amy Miller is dead.

She stands, numb, in the middle of her living room. And then her legs can't hold her any more.

She sinks to the floor, her knees up to her chest, her arms over her head. And she cries. She sobs until her body is cold and shaking, all her emotion spent.

–

She turns now to DCI Baker. He's looking at her expectantly.

'Is there anything else I should know, DC West?' he asks again.

'No, guv,' she replies. 'Nothing at all.'

74

After Amy Miller's house, after Robin drops Freya home, he only has one thing on his mind.

He drives a well-trodden route, away from the city centre, out of town to where the nicer houses are. Where people go for the better schools, with parks and green spaces where children can play. Where Georgia lived with Alex and James. And Liam.

He stands outside the familiar door. Lights are on; he hears a distant sound of a television coming from inside. He rings the bell.

The hallway light comes on, and the door opens. At first his brother-in-law's expression is one of confusion, turning to disbelief when he gets a better look at Robin.

'Rob, what...?' He opens the door wide and ushers Robin inside.

'I'm sorry to drop by unannounced, it's just...' Robin doesn't know how to finish the sentence. He needs to see family. He needs unconditional acceptance, and Liam is the only person he has now.

'It's fine, it's fine. What happened to you?'

Robin knows he must look a state. He's tired and sweaty, a black bin liner clutched in his hand. His head thrums with pain, his eye and stomach still ache from where he was punched. And he's just left someone drugged and unconscious in their living room.

'Let's just say it's been a long week,' Robin mutters. 'Listen, I need a favour.'

'Anything,' Liam replies.

'I need to burn something in your firepit, no questions asked.'

Liam's mouth opens and closes again. Then he points towards his back garden.

Robin takes the bin liner and carries it outside, through Liam's garden to the back. They used to have bonfires out here, years ago. Letting off fireworks, watching them arc in the night sky, the boys' mouths gaping, laughing in joy as the bright colours exploded above them.

Now it's just Robin. He glances back and he can see Liam watching him out of the kitchen window. He places the bin liner in the big metal firepit, then goes into the shed for the lighter fluid and matches.

The fire erupts with a whoomph, flames leaping towards the sky. The crime scene clothes catch light quickly, the smell of burning plastic in the air. Robin pulls his shirt and jeans off, adding them to the pile, then his socks and his trainers. Robin knows he must look crazy, standing there in the light of the flames in only his boxer shorts, but he doesn't care. He stares into the fire, feeling mud under his bare feet, listening to the crackle, and at last he feels like everything has been put to rest.

Then the final thing.

Before he drove off, Freya came back out of her house. She held out the disc of the CCTV from the petrol station, containing the footage of him meeting Trevor Stevens on that fateful day. She handed it to him without a word. And now he tosses it on the fire, along with the memory stick taken from Amy Miller's house.

It melts slowly, bending and charring into nothing.

And he knows it's over.

Once the fire has burnt down to cinders, he returns to the house. Almost naked, stinking of bonfires, shivering and pale. Liam looks at him, still speechless.

'Can I have a shower?' Robin says. 'And some clothes?' Liam nods.

Liam cooks him a pizza while he showers, and Robin eats it ravenously. He's sitting on the sofa, wearing his brother-in-law's clothes, washing it down with two bottles of beer. Nothing has ever tasted so good. He feels like he hasn't eaten or slept for a week.

'Listen, mate,' Liam starts hesitantly, breaking the silence. 'Do I need to call someone?'

Robin knows what he's asking. And he doesn't blame him. But he doesn't need the doctors from the Priory. He doesn't need their drugs, their injections, their therapy.

'I don't know much about what you've been doing lately,' Liam continues. 'But one thing I do know is that Georgia would never forgive me if I let anything happen to you. You were her little brother. She loved you.' He pauses. 'I love you,' he adds awkwardly.

Robin nods, feeling tears threaten, wiping his hands free of greasy cheese on a napkin.

'I'm sorry, Liam,' he says at last. 'I shouldn't have been such a dick.'

Liam accepts his apology with a slow nod. 'You were hurting.'

'You lost your entire family. It was up to you whether you forgave Trevor Stevens or not.'

But Liam shakes his head. 'I never forgave him, not for a moment. But I needed to do something, to move forward, and that small step helped a fraction. But when I heard Stevens had died...' His brother-in-law looks at Robin, his face hard. 'I felt the universe had put something right. Just for a second.' He gives a long sigh. 'And you're here now.' Liam smiles across at him. 'Want another beer?'

'Please.'

Liam gets up and Robin watches him as he goes to the fridge. His brother-in-law looks skinnier than he ever has, but in considerably better shape than Robin. And the house is tidy, at least reasonably so.

'You seem to be doing okay,' Robin says as Liam comes back, handing him a beer and taking a swig from one himself. 'I mean, that's a good thing.'

'One day at a time,' Liam says. 'You want to watch the football?'

And, conversation over, they do. But even before half time, Robin is fast asleep on his brother-in-law's sofa. Like so many days from the past.

–

Now, sitting in Baker's office, he knows things could have been considerably worse. Freya's holding it together; Baker seems to know nothing. Everything forensics have found supports their theory that they were right to try to nail Amy Miller for the murder. And Baker seems happy.

'Right, then,' their DCI says, putting both hands on the desk and leaning towards them. 'CPS are happy to leave all this as is. Amy Miller is never going to be tried for her husband's murder, but justice is served as far as they're concerned. Now, if we could all go back to work, and you could apply some of that dedication to the unsolved cases you have piling up on your desk, Robin, everyone will be happy.

'So, DS Butler, is this over? Will you leave this alone now?'

Robin looks to Freya, and she gives a slight nod.

He looks back at his boss. 'Yes, guv. Absolutely.'

–

Robin walks with Freya back to the incident room. He stops her in the doorway, his hand on her arm. Since discovering Amy Miller's death Saturday morning, he's been over it a million times in his head. They have no proof she killed her husband. A charred plastic bag and some tape won't convict someone for murder. No CCTV, no traffic cams, no evidence of a body transported in the back of a van. Just eyewitness reports confirming Jonathan Miller at a party, and the testimony of a man racked with guilt, with a past of heavy drug use and now a stint in a mental institution. Amy Miller would have walked free, exactly as Trevor Stevens did, that day. Both murderers, both having killed people they loved. And both likely to do it again.

They didn't kill Amy Miller on Friday night, but it isn't a bad thing she has died.

He doesn't say any of this to Freya. He says nothing, except, 'You okay?'

She looks awful, heavy black smudges under her eyes, hair pulled back untidily from her face.

'Didn't sleep,' she says.

'It wasn't our fault.' Freya doesn't reply. 'It wasn't,' Robin continues. 'We weren't to know she'd have an accident. She'd probably wandered round that house drugged up to her eyeballs a thousand times.'

'Yes, but—'

'No. It wasn't our fault.'

She nods slowly.

'Are you sure you don't want to take any time off?' he finishes.

'Positive.'

'Okay, then.'

They walk to their desks, switch their computers on. Robin tries to focus on the many emails he's received since the Miller case began. The monotony of the basic admin is soothing. Warnings about not refilling pool cars with petrol. Notices about menu changes in the canteen. Life goes on.

He picks up his phone, and sends a text to Steph.

Can I see you? I need to apologise. Properly xx

He knows there are things that he will never tell her. But there is much he should, if they have any hope of being together. He needs to tell her about Georgia, and how she died.

His phone beeps. *No. Please, Robin. I need some space.*

He reads it, knowing she's right. He's a mess. Starting a new relationship now is not a good idea. But one day, perhaps. He holds out that hope. Maybe Steph, maybe not. But maybe someone.

The phone rings on his desk and he answers it.

'DS Butler? I was told you were on call.' It's Control, with a potential new deployment.

'Absolutely, what do you have?'

Robin takes the details, then looks at Freya. She's already got her coat on, waiting.

'Business as usual, Sarge?' she asks. The old formalities are back, but he knows everything has changed between them. Secrets mean they are no longer colleagues, him and West. Something more. Something undefined.

But for now, there's a dead body that needs their attention.

He smiles, then plucks the car keys out of her hand. 'Business as usual,' he confirms. 'I'm driving.'

Epilogue

Olivia Cross sits at her make-up table, thinking. Around her women bustle: strippers in various states of undress. Chatter, perfume and the bassline from the club outside fill the air. But Liv doesn't notice any of it.

She's sitting, half-dressed, in a bra and ridiculous lace panties, ready to go on stage. She knows it's busy out there tonight; the potential to earn extra tips has the girls excited, and she should be too. She should be making the most of it, but she can't concentrate. She can't stop thinking about him.

She knows Robin won't come back and see her again, not after what Tommy did to him last time he was here. She watched him punch Robin, watched him fall, and part of her felt the satisfaction. She felt the power of the pain she could inflict. And she enjoyed the lap dance: being close to him, seeing his breath quicken, his face flush. Knowing she had got to him, that he wanted her.

But she ruined it. Amy ruined it.

She isn't sad her sister is dead. Far from it. Amy was nuts. Her sister always had the air of respectability – the good job, the nice husband, the big house – while she was the black sheep. She was the alcoholic, the stripper, the hooker. But even now Amy is dead, the insanity still haunts her.

Liv holds the black memory stick in her hand. Amy had given it to her the day she died. 'For safekeeping,' Amy had said.

But that night Liv fired up her laptop and plugged the memory stick in the side.

There was one file. A grainy black and white video – looked like a shop. A petrol station, she realised after a moment. Two people on the far side, talking to each other. Liv instantly recognised the older man, Trevor Stevens, from her AA group, and then…

Robin.

Liv didn't know what it meant. Not fully. She read the newspaper articles about Trevor's death, looking for something that would say for definite what Amy had found. But she knew that Robin being there couldn't be good.

'Livvy?' One of the strippers calls to her from the doorway. 'You're up.'

Things need to change, she thinks. She looks down at her bare stomach, and gently runs her hand across her smooth skin. Toned, flat, perfect. But not for long. She knows that soon the baby will grow and people will notice. There'll be no way she'll be able to do this job when that happens.

It was unplanned, of course, but not unwelcome. Already Liv feels the attachment to the tiny person inside. She'll do anything to protect it, anything to keep it safe. And she knows that keeping Amy away was part of that.

She went back to Amy's house that night. She rang the doorbell and received no answer, but the lights were on – she knew her sister was inside. And they needed to talk about this video. What did it mean? What was Amy planning on doing with it?

She let herself into the house with the spare key, calling her sister's name as she shut the front door behind her. The house seemed normal. Clean, stinking of bleach, perfect Amy to the last. Then, in the doorway to the kitchen, Olivia stopped. Her sister was lying on the tiled kitchen floor, her body collapsed into an unnatural position, a halo of blood growing around her head.

Liv's first thought was to call 999, and she even took her phone out of her bag. But then she paused. She looked at her sister's face, and all she could feel was disgust. This was the solution. She would be free of her sister, and not only that, but everything Amy owned would go to her. Her next of kin.

She could start a new life with her baby. One with security, and space to carve out a new career. Why should Amy have the perfect life? After everything Olivia had been through, why should her sister have everything?

So she stopped. And waited. Her sister half opened her eyes. Amy blinked, trying to focus on Olivia, but her pupils were wide. She opened her mouth, but only a soft groan came out. Liv could see the head wound, a large gash to the left side of her head, still bleeding, staining her blonde hair dark red. And she watched. Until she was dead.

Then she picked up her mobile and called 999.

The coroner ruled accidental death. Case closed.

Liv looks at the memory stick in her hand, then stands up, carrying it across to her locker. She buries the black USB in among her clothing, in her spare jeans, her old costumes, unseen in the feathers and sequins.

And she goes out to do her show. To gyrate around the pole, to take her clothes off for the jeering men. To allow them to see her body, her tits, her arse, all in exchange for a few quid.

She'll keep the memory stick. Not for now, but for some day.

Because who knows when it might come in useful.

Who knows when she might want to see Detective Sergeant Robin Butler again.

Acknowledgements

The first thank you must always go to Ed Wilson for making all this possible – and for tolerating the endless nagging and impatience that comes with it. Thank you also to Hélène Butler and everyone else at Johnson & Alcock.

I am incredibly grateful to Louise Cullen at Canelo, for providing the perfect home for Butler and West. I have loved discussing Robin and Freya with you, and working on the vision to bring the both of them to life. Thank you also to Siân Heap, and the rest of the team who worked on this book, including Jenny Page for her eagle-eyed copy edits and Becca Allen for the proof read.

I am forever surprised by how much people will tolerate my bizarre questions, and help me write these books. No more so than Dr Matt Evans, who spends an incredible amount of time correcting my dire attempts at medical terminology. One day, Matt, you will actually read one of my books and the spell will be broken, but until then, thank you.

As always, thank you to PC Dan Roberts and Charlie Roberts, who keep me sane on the school runs and answer my every conceivable ridiculous question about police procedure and being a copper. It's about time I dedicated a book to you both. Thank you to Sergeant Jon Bates for his incredible insights, and Steph Fox, my favourite real-life CSI. To Laura Stevenson, Susan Scarr, AR (you know who you are) – thank you. All mistakes, deliberate or otherwise, are mine.

Thank you to my brother-in-law, Jonathan Scarr, for letting me use his name, despite how poor old Jonathan Miller ended up.

And finally, to my family. To Chris and Ben, to my mum and dad, to Tom and Mel. I love you, and I couldn't do this without you.

● CANELOCRIME

Do you love crime fiction and are always on the lookout for brilliant authors?

Canelo Crime is home to some of the most exciting novels around. Thousands of readers are already enjoying our compulsive stories. Are you ready to find your new favourite writer?

Find out more and sign up to our newsletter at canelocrime.com